All That
Life

By

Leah Toole

All That Life

Also by Leah Toole

<u>The Tudor Heirs Series</u>

I – The Saddest Princess

. . .

II – The Haunted Queen

. . .

III – The Puppet King

. . .

IV – The Forgotten Prince

. . .

V – The Hopeful Duke

~

The Rose and the Pomegranate

~

1500

Prologue

Wolfgang

<u>Germany</u>

The first person I ever saw die was staring right at me. One moment she was alive with fear, and the next instant the light in her eyes went out.

There was no other way to describe it, and I had heard of such a thing happening, 'the light in their eyes burned out.'

But I'd never *seen* it. And I wish every day since that I hadn't.

"We weren't meant to *kill* anyone," I rasped at Erich in complete shock, bile turning in my stomach.

He shrugged and stepped over the lifeless body, his hammer – with which he had struck the woman in the head – gripped so tightly, his knuckles were bone white.

I looked down at her, crumpled on the ground. The growing puddle of blood glowed an eerie silver in the moonlight.

The air was filled with smoke and the bloodcurdling screams of both adults and children. The sound of shattering glass was like a backdrop of hate among the destruction.

We were wild, lost in the fever of a mob mentality.

Even I, who had not been able to destroy a single shop window as we'd been instructed to – nevermind hurt anyone – had run about with a shovel in my hand, my face and neck flushed, and my clothes damp against my skin with sweat.

But then, I stood planted to the spot where the woman lay bleeding out in front of me, and I observed the horror of our making.

SA stormtroopers were kicking in the doors of innocents' homes and dragging them out. Most were in their pyjamas or nightgowns, shaking with cold and terror.

Shop windows were being broken and their interiors destroyed, glass crunching underneath hundreds of hurried boots.

A man screamed as he was kicked to the ground and made to strip naked. Boys I knew from training were laughing at him, smacking him with their shovels and telling him to hurry. He was holding a child in his arms, who cried into his neck, trembling so much I could sense her fear from where I stood. The man set the little girl down and told her to stay behind him, then he began to take off his clothes. One by one, he peeled them off, then stood naked and shivering before them.

I looked away, I didn't want to see any more. But the laughter and the crying mixed together into a sickening song, one which would haunt me for many months to come, a ghostly whisper in the shell of my ear. The first of many that would follow.

I was twenty, and I knew, even then, what that night was all about.

It was a message. To let the Jews know that they were at our mercy. Us, the 'pure' Germans.

It had all been in retribution of course – as if that made it any better – punishment for the assassination of Ernst Eduard vom Rath, in Paris. He had been a German official, and it was a Polish Jew who had killed him.

Hitler had warned that 'retaliation from the German people for this attack on us would not be stopped.' We'd been given free rein. Our actions were justifiable, a knee-jerk response.

And it was the first of many occasions where I could do nothing but blend in.

Chapter 1

Germany

Josef, her lemele, *comes running down the stairs just as she knew he would, and she smiles at the sound.*

"Mamaleh! Mamaleh!" *he calls excitedly, his little boy voice still high and sweet, his grin flashing tiny milk teeth. She turns from the window where she'd been observing the very thing which causes his delight.*

"It is snowing!" *he calls as he plummets into her, wrapping his little arms around his mother's legs. She strokes his head, ruffling his wavy brown hair, then kneels down to his eye level.*

"It is, lemele," *the mother says, referring to him as she always has – her little lamb – for he was just that.*

Ever since that cold winter's night of his birth, she – an alone and frightened girl – had known that she could never again be the weak one. With the cutting of his umbilical cord, the young girl she had been, would be no more. And in her stead, a mother had been born.

It had been just the two of them for as long as she cared to remember, Josef's father continuing but a shadowy face within her memory. Though he had been little more than that on the night of Josef's conception.

He was not worth remembering, and so she does not. And instead, she hauls her sweet child into her arms, noting with sadness that his limbs have grown gangly.

It is becoming more awkward for her to carry him. Though, he is skinnier than he ought to be – their rations having been scarce now for some time.

"Can I go make a snowman?" he asks his mother, taking her cheeks in his hands and pressing his face into hers.

She laughs and pulls out of his grasp, "Let's get you wrapped up."

Moments later, Josef is wearing three pairs of socks and his only pair of boots, which are a whole size too big for him. They are, as yet, free of holes, however, so she counts her blessings for that at least. She dresses him as warmly as she can with the little that they have, including an orange scarf she'd knitted – badly – last year. She wraps it around his little neck three, four times, only his brown eyes peeking out over the wool.

She looks out the window as she buttons his jacket, "The snow has stopped falling. Good," she says, "There will be just enough of it to work with."

She takes his hand and leads him outside.

The look on his face when he steps onto the white ground – his boot disappearing within the deep snow, is priceless – and her eyes sting with emotion. He has seen snow before of course, but at four years old he is finally old enough to enjoy it.

She stays with him for a while, mainly watching as he runs about discovering the new texture, sound, and even taste. But after a while her fingers grow numb, and she yearningly looks back to their little hut.

"Let's go back inside, Josef," she says, envisioning the glowing fire she'd made earlier.

"I haven't built my snowman!" he calls back, then kneels down in the powdery snow and starts rolling a little ball before him.

Slowly, it grows larger, and as she watches, her toes begin to throb.

"I'm going inside, lemele,*" she says, "Don't stray too far from the house and stay out of the woods!"*

He nods at his mother absentmindedly and she heads back inside, casting one last quick glance over her shoulder.

Once inside, she blows into her cupped hands and stomps her feet, then hurries to the fire and adds another log on top. She puts water on to boil and tells herself that she will call Josef inside when it is bubbling. That should give him enough time to finish his snowman.

She begins peeling two potatoes – their daily ration since the boycott of her father's business – and quickly remembers they cannot afford to waste the skins. She leaves them on, taking extra care when washing them, and before she knows it, she hears the water simmering. It has been almost fifteen minutes, long enough for him to have created a masterpiece.

Wiping her hands on her apron, she heads for the door, catching a glimpse of his creation through the small kitchen window.

With a ready smile, she steps outside, "Come on back in, lemele!"

She looks left to right.

"Josef!" she calls, frowning as she scans her surroundings.

She trudges around the corner of the hut, the snow crunching underfoot.

"Lemele!" she yells, anger entering her voice to think he is trying to frighten her.

No reply.

"Josef?" she shouts again, his name cracking in her throat as she continues unable to find him.

Out of the corner of her eye, she spots something orange – his scarf – and turns towards it only to be faced with the snowman he had built.

It is a bit of a lumpy mess, though she didn't expect much better from her young son. Instead of a round body and a round head, his snowman is but one solid, waist-high mound. Josef's scarf is wrapped around it, and she notices two pebbles on top, which she imagines was Josef's attempt at giving his creation eyes. They are lopsided, she notes vaguely, and her chest tightens to think he has gone into the woods to search for more pebbles to give the snowman a mouth.

She runs towards the edge of the wood and screams her son's name into the darkness, but only a flock of birds burst from a spruce tree nearby. There is no sight or sound of her boy, her sweet little lamb, and with a panic she has never felt before, she picks up her skirts and begins running down the road to the village, in the hopes of finding someone who will care enough to help her find her baby.

Abel

<u>Germany</u>

"We have to leave," I hear my father tell my mother when they think I am asleep.

"What's happened?" I hear my mother ask, her voice hitching with dread. She's had that same tone ever since I got expelled from school last month.

Until that day, I'd had no idea that I was different from the boys I played with every day. But when I was told to exit the school premises for the simple fact that I am Jewish, I realised that life was more complicated than I ever imagined. I may have been born in Germany, lived in Germany all my life, have two German-born parents. But according to some, that was no longer good enough.

My father clears his throat now, and I hear their soft footsteps padding across the room, a creak as one or both take a seat on our old sofa. I could open my eyes and watch – my bed being tucked in the corner of the living room in our small house – but I cannot afford to be caught eavesdropping.

"The shop was looted today," I hear my father say, though he is trying to whisper.

A gasp escapes my mother, and I envision her hand shooting up to cover her mouth.

"But we are all German, all born and bred –"

"It does not matter," my father interrupts, "We are Jews. And the new regime has turned people against us. I am accosted daily in the streets. Abel has been expelled from school. And now this. Tensions are rising, *Schatz*."

A silence befalls our small house, and I wonder if I have fallen asleep. But then I hear father speak again.

"That is not all," he says, his voice strained, "There has been an attack."

"An attack?" Mother echoes.

I imagine my father nodding, "Esther Rosenberg? On the hill?"

"The young mother?"

"Yes."

"What of her? What has happened?"

My father clears his throat, a habit of his that I have learned means he is unsettled, "Her little boy has gone missing."

"Little Josef? But what –"

"People are whispering that they were targeted for being Jewish. They say he is likely dead."

"*Oh, mein Gott,*" Mother gasps, and then all I can hear is soft crying and my father's gentle *shhh* as I imagine him rubbing my mother's back.

"Poland?" I ask the next morning, when our parents inform us – me and my sister Mia – that we are to leave, following the attack on our family's shoe shop.

"Yes, to Lodz," Mother says now as she wraps a loaf of bread in cloth, and I can tell the smile on her face is forced. Mia, who is four years older than me, stands staring wide-eyed, and I wonder how she is taking this news. I'm not particularly thrilled to just up and leave all my friends behind. Except, I'd already lost them the moment we'd been branded as too different to go to the same school. Mia, at least, is still being allowed to attend her school, although she must be facing dismissal any day now, too.

"Aunt Ayla will take us in until we find our own place," our father says as he hands me a leather suitcase, "Be good now and pack only what you will *need,*" he instructs us, squeezing my shoulder with his big hand, "We're starting a new life, and we don't want our old possessions to drag us down."

Alma

<u>France, Le Chambon-sur-Lignon</u>

"*Maman!*" I call as I open the front door and walk inside.
The smell that welcomes me is mouthwatering, and I quickly strip off my jacket and throw it over the back of a chair.

"That smells delicious," I tell my mother as I enter the kitchen, where I knew she would be – her favourite room in the house.
I peck her on the cheek, and she smiles but keeps stirring the stew.

"Where's *Papa?*" I ask, plucking a cherry tomato from the counter and taking a bite, immediately regretting it as its contents spill down my chin.
Maman hands me a tea towel without so much as a glance in my direction. I smile. She knows me too well.

"Your father is working late," she tells me as I wipe my chin, "All this business with Germany is giving him an ulcer."

"It will be over soon, I'm sure," I say absentmindedly.
Maman turns to me and I hand her the tea towel, which she slaps over her shoulder, "You're sure?" she says rhetorically, "How can you be so sure? You young people don't seem to quite understand."
I frown, but it's true. I don't fully understand. But I know that Germany wants Czechoslovakia – or maybe just part of it? And in order to obtain it, France – as well as other European countries – have had to put pressure on Czechoslovakia to submit. If they do not submit, Germany has threatened war on the country. So surely, to avoid it, Czechoslovakia will yield?

I do not say all this to my mother, however, for she will find a flaw in something, and a discussion will ensue. And I am not in the mood for a heated debate. Not least one that my dear *maman* will surely win.

"How is Azriel?" my mother asks now as I slide into a chair at the kitchen table.

The mention of the man I have been seeing makes my stomach turn with guilt, "He's…Azriel," I say noncommittally.

He, too, is French-Jewish, which my parents appreciate.

"If you don't feel romance for him, you should be honest."

"I know," I sigh, "He's so nice, though. I fear I am letting a good man go for something that may not exist."

A soft chuckle escapes my mother, and she turns back to the stew, bringing the wooden spoon to her lips to taste it.

"Oh, it exists," she says.

"*Maman*," I grin, "You and *Papa* are a rarity. If I find a love even half as wonderful as yours, I shall be happy."

"You are young yet, Alma. At eighteen, you do not need to rush into marriage."

The door opens then, and my father enters, "*Bonjour!*" he calls, taking off his hat, "How is my lovely family?"

I get up, offering him a smile and an embrace, "We were just talking about you, *Papa*."

"Oh?" he says, his brown eyebrows shooting up, "Am I in trouble?"

I laugh and return to my seat at the table.

"Quite the contrary," *Maman* says as she comes out of the kitchen, beaming. They kiss, a quick but firm peck, clearly merry to be reunited after a long day apart.

And my stomach roils with hope.

If my Russian-born, Jewish mother can find her true love in a French man from this small village of Le Chambon-sur-Lignon, then surely so can I.

Annika

<u>The Netherlands, Giethoorn</u>

"Helga," I hiss into the darkness, knowing that my sister, too, will have felt the wobble of our barge.

"Go back to sleep, Ani," she tells me, rolling over so her back is to me, "It is but the new family Mother and Father are hiding."

Helga is only a year older than me, and I take comfort in her higher wisdom, but I cannot go back to sleep until I know more.

"Don't you think we should go meet them?" I ask.

"No," Helga says sleepily, "It is best we do not rock the boat."

I giggle at the metaphor, since we quite literally live on a flatboat.

My sister, mother, father, and I live in Giethoorn, a small village in the province of Overijssel, in the Netherlands. I was born here, as was my sister. And ever since I could remember, we have lived on this barge, which is small and cramped for even just the four of us.

But over the past few months, our parents have been allowing other people to live here with us. Usually, one or two at a time, sometimes an entire family of four – but families only ever stay for a few days because of the lack of space.

Mother says we have to help these people, and I agree! Even at just thirteen years old I can understand that what is happening is horrifying, made more horrifying still when those we shelter share what they have witnessed with their own eyes.

Last month, we took in a woman and her daughter, who stayed with us for over a week. The daughter was about my age, though the fear in her eyes had catapulted her into adulthood. She stayed in mine and Helga's bedroom a couple of the nights, and though the intention had been for us to distract her with card games and funny stories, it appeared she did not wish to – or couldn't – forget the horrors she had seen.

"The world needs to know what is happening," she told us in a shaky whisper as the moon shone through our small window, illuminating her face, "They took them. Those who we trusted. Policemen, our neighbours. They rounded up Jews and marched them into the forest. I don't know how, but Mother knew well enough to flee when they began taking people from our street. We escaped out the back of our house and ran across the field under cover of darkness. By some miracle we were not seen."

"What did they do to the people in the forest?"
The girl had looked me dead in the eyes, "I can still hear the crying and the gunshots sometimes, when I'm drifting off to sleep at night. We could hear them for miles as we ran."
The girl and her mother left not long after that night, and I was quietly glad for it.
Though I am proud to be helping people escape the countries that have turned on them, it is frightening to hear their stories. And after that night, I made sure not to ask any others for details of what they were fleeing from. The nightmares that came from it were too vivid.

My parents separate soon after that, and Helga and I move into an apartment with our mother.
Perhaps the hiding of strangers in our boat has caused tension between them. Perhaps the brewing war has caused fear to fester inside them.
I don't know. I can only guess that they no longer love each other enough to stay together, and so they are going their separate ways.

Except, my sister and I miss our father living with us. It is strange not to see him every day.

Despite that, I quite enjoy living in an apartment, though I sometimes struggle to fall asleep at night without the gentle lulling of the barge.

Helga and I still sleep in the same room together, our apartment not being much bigger than the boat had been. But I don't mind, and neither does Helga.

We do everything together. Always have, always will.

◀▶◀▶

<u>Germany</u>

He watches from the gloom of the woods as the mother's frantic face searches the area.
At one point, he is sure that she looks right at him and he almost gasps with dread.
Did she see him?
If she confronted him, tears streaming and blubbering, would he admit to what he did?
But then her brown eyes dart away, none the wiser that her precious boy – and the man who made him disappear – are so close by.
"Lemele!" she calls, "Josef!"
Her cries make the birds in the spruce he is hiding behind burst into flight, and he looks up at them involuntarily, disappointed in himself for having flinched at the sound.
He is the predator here. He should not be the one to jolt.
The man sighs deeply to steady his nerves.
He must not be found. Not this early on in his plan, when he's only just begun.
He tries to shake off the amounting guilt by telling himself that the mother was partly to blame. She had made it too easy for him by leaving her small child unattended outside. It was a tragic mistake on her part. But one that led him to his first kill, and what would lead him to his signature method of disposal.
He peers around the trunk of the tree now just in time to see the mother pick up her skirts and hurry down the road, leaving her son behind though he remains in plain sight.
He presses the back of his head against the trunk and curses under his breath.
It had been simpler than he'd imagined. But it wasn't perfect. The boy had struggled and even whimpered in pain before the end. The man would have to remedy that.

19

Which means he will have to kill again. And soon.
The snow is his ally in this fight against the rats.

Chapter 2

Wolfgang

<u>Germany, Bamberg</u>

As a boy, I'd always wanted to become a professor, but instead I joined the SS.

It was my father's wish, he himself having fought in the Great War, and he had wanted for his only son to follow in his footsteps. My mother had been less pleased about my decision, but it felt only right to do as I was bid by my old man. Especially when he made me swear on his deathbed that I would.

"You don't have to do as he asked," my *Mutti* had argued when I'd announced my decision, "He will never know!"

But I didn't think I could've lived the life I had wanted with that kind of shame weighing me down. And back then, I'd still been naïve enough to think that there was no greater weight on the soul than a son's guilt.

As it turned out, there were much worse things out there than my need to please my already-deceased father.

It was fairly easy to enrol into the SS. All I'd needed to do was walk into the recruiting office, and join up.

The physical requirements, however, were a bit rigorous. One had to be at least 5ft 7" for the regular division. Which, for me at 6ft 2", had been a non-issue. Next, they enquired about my ancestry, tracing back as far as they could – and preferably back to 1800 – to make sure I had no Jewish lineage whatsoever. Eye tests, body fat checks – *mustn't be above 20%* – dental checks, and more questions about my family later, I was admitted.

It was as simple as that.

Soon thereafter, I was sent off to a training camp, where I and hundreds of other young men were taught military traditions and learned close combat.
And as my mother had predicted, I had hated every minute of it.

Now, a year has passed since my enrolment, a year in which I had seen things I wish I could erase from my mind; and done things I never would've imagined myself capable of.
With my training complete, I was appointed to Avegoor in the Netherlands. But before being shipped out, I was given two weeks leave, and I wanted only to return to the safe haven that was my home.
Back in my city of Bamberg, I feel myself relax, the tension that had accumulated over the last few months leaving my shoulders.
"*Mutti?*" I call as I swing open the door, my mouth watering as the scent of her signature dish – *Rouladen* – greets me.
My beloved mother comes from around the corner, wiping her hands on her apron. She exclaims with joy and flings her arms around me, and I instantly notice how my body has changed. Where once she had managed to enfold me in her arms completely, her hands no longer meet on my back. I have grown broader, carrying myself like a soldier, and I imagine she feels saddened to note the difference.
But she does not say anything, her face showing only delight at my return.
"*Hast du Hunger?*" – Are you hungry? – she asks.
I nod eagerly, and we head towards the kitchen.
No sooner than I have flung my backpack in the corner and taken a seat, she is presenting me with a steaming plate of her delicious beef dish. We eat mostly in silence, *Mutti* probably unsure of what to ask me, figuring she would not like what I might say.

She settles for ambiguity.

"Are they treating you well?"

I meet her gaze and offer her a reassuring smile, "*Ja,* they are."

And that will have to be enough, because what I won't tell her is that I had been made to do things I wish I could scrub from my brain: The dozens of doors I had kicked in to seize people's radios and valuables, anything to aid the war effort; the synagogues that were blown up with dynamite or set on fire before my very eyes, sometimes with people still inside them; the rabbi I had been ordered to beat for praying past curfew.

She – like most of the German population – did not know of all the horrors we were responsible for, nor did she need to. What good would it do to share the horrifying load?

"Have you made any friends?" she asks.

At that, I breathe a laugh, covering my mouth with my fist as I continue to chew my forkful.

"It isn't like school, you know?" I say gently, "I don't need to make friends."

Worry contorts her face, and I feel terrible.

"Don't worry about me, *Mutti,*" I say, reaching across the table to take her hand, "I swear to you, I am fine."

A lump forms in my throat at the lie.

I look down at our hands, noticing how frail hers feels in mine, when it had once felt like the very thing that tethered me to Earth. And I'm not sure if it suddenly feels so small and brittle because I have grown up, or if her worry for me, her only child, has chiselled away at her.

Abel

<u>Poland, Lodz</u>

We move in with my Aunt Ayla in Lodz, Poland, just as my parents had explained. And though we miss our old lives back in Germany, for a time, we are happy, despite the growing unease.

That is, until September 1939…

It is the strange sound of vibrating that wakes me, and I sit up to find my windows are rattling.

"*Papa!*" I hear Mia call out from the darkness, and then a plane flies overhead, followed by a *BOOM* so loud, I fear it has rendered me deaf.

I fall from my bed, my hands over my ringing ears and my face twisted in panic. My father appears before me, scooping me up suddenly as if I am still a child, and hurries to the kitchen where the rest of my family huddle. He puts me down, and I stand, hunched together with the rest of them. I cannot hear anything past the plane engines overhead, but I see Mia's tearstained face as our father shouts instructions at the women. They nod and scurry outside, my father waving them out one by one, before steering me out in front of him.

I watch in horror as bursts of orange and red illuminate the black sky, mushrooms of fire bursting in the distance as the German *Luftwaffe* drop their bombs over us.

"They are aiming for the airport," my father shouts as he runs behind me, his voice sounding as if underwater.

But then another drops, much closer this time, and we all flinch and cry out.

At the bottom of Aunt Ayla's garden, Mother bends down and pulls open a wooden latch in the ground with shaking hands, the terror in her eyes hurrying us inside.

It is dark in the cellar, but Aunt Ayla quickly lights an oil lamp and holds it before her. I look around myself once I reach the bottom. It is a small space, with no comfort and little supplies, but it is big enough for all of us to fit, and that is all that matters.

"What is happening?" Mia whimpers as she holds our mother tightly.

I know. At least, I think I do. Because I have heard the adults whispering when they think I cannot hear: The Germans have invaded Poland.

Father confirms my thoughts when he says as much, and Mia's chin wobbles in terror.

"What are we to do?" my mother asks, her eyes trying hard to remain dry for her children's sakes, but I can see the clear shine of angst.

Father exhales out his mouth and gets down on the dirty ground, his long legs tucked up against him to give the rest of us room to do the same, "We settle in. It will be a long night."

Mother gets down beside him, pulling Mia with her and wrapping an arm around her teenaged daughter's shoulders.

"I did not mean only tonight," she whispers.

And at that, Father shakes his head, "We are Jews. It does not matter that we are German. Hitler has made his ideology perfectly clear."

That night, as bombs rain over us, each sounding nearer than the last, I feel a depth of torment that I have never known possible.

As every explosion sounds, I re-live my own death again and again in my mind, my thoughts circling from relief for having survived another onslaught, to the tension of awaiting the next blast; certain, each time, that this one would be the one to blow us to pieces.

But it doesn't come, and after hours of hiding and shaking underground with nothing but my father's arm around me to keep me warm, the cellar fills with the rancid smell of our acidic fear.

And my determination to *live* has never burned so brightly.

Months go by and life returns somewhat to normal, though Lodz is now under German occupation and to be known as Litzmannstadt.

Each morning, our father heads out to work and comes home in the afternoon with a glum face and bad news after bad news.

He works at the post office – *I can spare a job in the back room, where no one will see you*, his employer had said upon our arrival in Lodz, and he'd accepted the position gratefully, ignoring the man's disdain. But though he is out of sight, he often overhears the latest gossip: that ghettos are being built all over Poland; that Jews, Roma, Sinti, are being rounded up and made to leave their homes. The first ghetto to open was in Piotrków, the second in Radomsko, and now there was another being built, this time in Lodz. Terrifying tales of illness and starvation have begun to circulate, of people dying of typhus by the hundreds in Piotrków and Radomsko. And that, if the disease does not kill them off, cold or hunger surely will.

"It is all part of their dehumanisation of us," my sister Mia and I overhear now as we eavesdrop on Aunt Ayla whispering with our parents.

It is 1940, just a few months after the Nazis had taken Poland by force, and already it feels like a completely different world.

"They're keeping Jewish people by the *thousands*," Aunt Ayla is saying, "in confined quarters with little to no food and disgraceful living conditions – of course disease will spread! But to the outside world it appears as though we are unclean. Soon we will no longer be human in their eyes."

"The Nuremberg Race Laws have already stripped us of our humanity," Father adds, taking a slurp of his coffee, "To be a Jew is no longer simply a religion, but a race. It does not matter to Hitler if someone is born and bred Polish, Russian, even German. If they practice the Jewish religion, they are inferior. I hear even those who have converted are still regarded as Jews if their parents are. Hitler's head of propaganda, Goebbels, has seen to it that the people see us as no more than vermin with their antisemitic art, posters and books. That mysterious killer in Germany that targeted Jewish children in '38 is proof of that! I am just glad we left Germany before *Kristallnacht*."

I have seen the posters my father speaks of: horrible depictions of Jews as rats or even snakes, blaming us for the war. They call us vermin and fault us for the typhus outbreak. It is hurtful to see these posters, of course, but surely everyone knows they are lies…

A whimper erupts from our mother as she tries to stifle a cry. I swallow hard and look to Mia, who puts a finger to her lips. We are hiding in the corridor so we can listen to this information, but if my parents could help it, we would remain none the wiser.

"We need to save the children," Aunt Ayla says in a dull murmur then, interrupting our mother's sobbing.

No one speaks, and I imagine father nodding his head pensively as he holds mother's hand.

"We need to save the children," he finally repeats in agreement, and fear takes a hold of my heart.

Alma

<u>France, Le Chambon-sur-Lignon</u>

I am stunned when France declares war on Germany. My mother, less so.

"Germany's interest in Czechoslovakia was tactical. It was never going to be simple. It was all part of something bigger," *Maman* says, like a wise woman three times her age, "There are antisemitic outbursts throughout Paris already. Their slogans and actions are being met with favourable responses among some of the public. The propaganda against us is working. People are being brainwashed."

"But *Papa* is French," I say.
Maman nods, "As are you. Born and bred a Frenchwoman. But even 'half-Jews' will be looked down upon," she scoffs then, "'Half-Jews'. Listen to me talking like them. But that is how they will label you for being my daughter. Having a Jewish parent makes you 'half-Jewish' in their eyes, regardless of your own religious beliefs or where you were born."

"I thought Hitler wished to fight the communists," I contend, hearing the naivety in my argument, "Why would they care about us?"
My mother shakes her head again, "We must be prepared, that is all I am saying," she says, squeezing my hand, "We are but engaged due to France's obligation to defend Poland, which Germany aroused by invading. It is unlikely that a full-scale war will find us in France, much less in our sleepy village of Le Chambon. But it is important to be aware of the hatred that is being spread. As the daughter of a Jew, whether you practice or not, our family could be targeted by those who believe the vile lies."

Nothing really happened for a few months, and people began to refer to this state of unease as the Phoney War, since there was minimal to no fighting in Western Europe. Life went on in our little village. And I went on one more date with Azriel.

"How was your chicken?" Azriel asks me now as he walks me home after our third – and what will be our final – date.

"Very nice," I reply, "And yours?"

"Very nice," he copies, to which I smile at him.
We are walking slowly through Le Chambon, my arm in the crook of his elbow more for warmth than romance, and a knot tightens in my stomach as we approach my home.
I still do not know if I am making a huge mistake, but I have made up my mind, and Azriel deserves to find someone who will find his lukewarm conversational skills endearing.
At my front door, Azriel leans in to peck me on the cheek – just as he has done at the end of every date we've had – but I pull away gently.

"Azriel –" I begin, my head hanging down and my hand on his chest, "Thank you for dinner. It was wonderful."
He beams at me and nods.

"It's just…" *I can't do it I can't do it,* "You and I…I do not think we are right for each other."
He visibly recoils, "Oh," he says, "I'm sorry."
He's sorry?

"No, *I* am sorry, Azriel," I protest immediately, "You are an incredibly nice man. You've been nothing but gentlemanly. But…"

"You don't think we're right for each other," he says, repeating my words back at me again.

"Right," I say, feeling awful.

He nods down at the ground for a moment before looking up with a smile.

"I understand," he says.

"You do?" I ask, relieved.

He nods again, and I think he looks like a friendly dog.

"If you don't feel the spark, then who am I to force it?" Then he takes my hand, kisses my cold knuckles and walks away.

He took it well, I think as I watch him go for a moment before heading indoors, and I begin to second guess myself.

He is a good man, handsome, too. Have I made a huge mistake by letting him slip through my fingers?

He would have no doubt made for a good husband and a decent father to any children we might've had. We'd have shared some common interests and had mutual respect for one another.

But no, I long for passion to be present in a relationship. Like the one my parents clearly feel for one another even after twenty years of marriage. I believe I will find the love I am looking for.

Inside, I peel off my coat and hang it up, then kick off my boots.

Letting him go was the right thing to do. I wouldn't settle. I would only end up resenting him if I did.

Throughout the months that followed, Azriel would sometimes crop up in my mind, my continued single life mocking me over Christmas and New Year, and again for my birthday in May.

But the topic of romance was quickly dashed from my thoughts in mid-1940, when the Phoney War we had learned to live with was suddenly no more.

Germany had launched its invasion of France.

Annika

<u>The Netherlands, Giethoorn</u>

Planes roared overhead on the 10th of May 1940, and we knew the Nazis had invaded our country.

I was fifteen years old.

The Dutch troops tried to fight back, blowing up bridges to slow down the German army. But it did little to stop them, and the *Wehrmacht* soldiers fooled our troops by dressing up in Dutch uniform and overpowering them.

The Netherlands surrendered just four days later, and our queen, Queen Wilhemina, fled to England. Many civilians were also forced to leave their homes, tens of thousands of people evacuating the city of Breda on foot, many getting killed due to the aerial combat in the area as they fled.

We learned all of this from radio broadcasts that mother listened to for most of the day, every day.

"We will not just lay down and take this," my mother muttered under her breath one day as she chewed her thumbnail and paced up and down in front of the metal box spouting the news.

Helga and I exchanged a look. Knowing our mother, who was strong-willed like a man, she meant it.

"But what can we do, *Mama?*" I asked, my voice hitching with a terror I hadn't felt before. Because until then – in my mind at least – this war was happening far away; but suddenly it was on our doorstep.

Our mother took my face in her rough hands, and pressed her face to mine, "You must quash that fearful blubbering right now! Weakness will get you killed!"

I tried to nod but she was holding me too tightly. My eyes stung, but I willed them not to produce tears.

"Yes, *Mama,*" I croaked.

She let go and wrapped me in a hug, "I'm sorry, *mijn liefste.* But we need to be strong now."

That night, I learned something incredible about my mother.

I was awoken by her hand gently stroking my cheek as she held a candle aloft, and I knew immediately that it was the dead of night.

"Get up, my child," she said to me, "You and your sister are old enough to know."

I rose from the mattress on the floor where Helga and I slept and slipped my feet into a pair of socks against the cold. Helga, I noticed, was already up.

We made our way to the kitchen, following the light of the candle, the only sign of life in the gloom of our apartment.

"What is all this, *Mama?*" I asked when we found her sitting at the table, surrounded by strange papers.

"This, my daughters," she said, and I sensed a strange shift in the air, "Is how we will fight back."

The resistance, our mother explained, was an organisation she'd secretly been a part of for some time. It was why and how we had been sheltering refugees on our barge for so long – she and our father having been part of a clandestine establishment that was quietly fighting to take down the Nazis.

Helga did not appear surprised by our mother's confession, but my mouth hung open in disbelief.

"Your father no longer believed it safe to continue hiding people," our mother told us after she'd explained that the papers before her on the kitchen table were anti-Nazi pamphlets, which we would be distributing, "It is why we chose to go our separate ways. I *needed* to continue helping. No matter what it cost me."

It finally made sense then. Father had allowed his fear to control him. And Mother would not let the weakness of her husband dictate what she would be permitted to do.

Pride for my *mama* filled my chest, and I reached across the table and held her hand.

My mother, I thought, *the bravest woman on Earth.*

"You knew?" I ask Helga now, as we walk to school the next morning, the pamphlet I'd hidden in my bag feeling like it weighs a ton.

"I heard things," she says with a shrug.

I look down at the ground as we walk, "Did you hear *Mama* and *Papa* fighting?"

At that, Helga looks away and squints as though she's thinking, "They didn't agree on things anymore, Annika. Let's just leave it at that."

Helga has lost all interest in our father after he failed to visit us since our parents' separation. And this, learning of his weakness, has solidified her disdain for him.

She looks about herself then before reaching into her bag and kneeling to push her pamphlet under a door.

"*Stop!*" I hiss, reaching for her, "We already did that house yesterday."

She looks up at it.

"We did?"

I nod, "I've been keeping count of them. We want the next one."

Helga nods and steps away from the house without second-guessing me, and a swell of delight bubbles in my chest to be trusted with such an important matter.

"You're right," she says as she reaches the next house and repeats the safety precautions before pushing the flyer under the door.

"Let's go," she says hurriedly, looping her arm in mine and taking the next right down an alleyway just as we hear the front door of the house opening and someone stepping out to search for whoever had pushed the dangerous paper into their home.

A giggle escapes me, and I press my hand over my mouth.

"Number 12 is the next house up on the street ahead," I say, slipping my hand in my bag and feeling the edge of the pamphlet against my fingertips.

"You're quite clever, aren't you?" Helga says, squeezing my plump cheek playfully and grinning in that carefree way of hers.

I slap her hand away and stick out my tongue, and we skip to the next street, feeling like we could take on anything, as long as we're together.

Chapter 3

◐◑

<u>Germany</u>

The mother wakes up, rubs her eyes free of sleep, and stretches.

She swings her legs off the bed, immediately shivering against the cold as the pads of her bare feet touch the stone floor. She reaches over to the chair beside her bed and pulls her holey gown around herself, securing the tie around her middle.

Only then does she look over her shoulder to the other side of the double bed, where the small figure of her child should be.

But, to her horror, the bed is empty.

"Mila?" the mother calls, her voice croaky from sleep. She looks around the room, the holes in the rag over the window allowing for some lazy sunlight to peek through. She heads towards it and rips it aside, illuminating the bedroom further.

And yet, still there is no sign of her child.

"Mila?!" the mother calls again, newspaper articles flashing in her mind. The town gossip ringing in her ears. The mother pulls open the bedroom door and races into the kitchen, praying she will see her three-year-old daughter rummaging through their sparse cupboards for a scrap of food. But there is no sign of her.

Panic flutters in her chest, as though a frightened pigeon were trapped within, and out of the corner of her eyes, she sees it.

A snowman.

With a hand pressed to the base of her throat, she turns her full attention out the kitchen window and stares the man of ice in the face.

The symbol. The killer's sign that their house has been targeted.

Complete with twig arms and a smiling stone grin, the snowman stares back ominously.

Without wasting time on footwear, the mother rushes outside and runs frantically towards the creation, caring little for the tears and snot that run down her cheeks and chin. She rips its arms clean out and pushes its round head off its body before clawing at the rest of it. She scratches and scrapes at it like a woman possessed, all the while looking about the white blanket of snow, calling her baby daughter's name over and over again.

"Mila! Mila!"

When her energy is spent, the mother looks down at the mess she has made, breathing raggedly like a wild animal, satisfied she has destroyed the monster's work.

But is she too late?

"Mama?"

The mother whips around at the sound – the most beautiful sound she has ever heard – and comes face to face with her child.

The one she thought to be dead.

The man watches from behind the stone wall as the crazed mother envelops her daughter and carries her swiftly back indoors where the cold isn't quite as biting.

He exhales slowly and turns, pressing his back against the wall.

It appears his reputation precedes him. But it doesn't bring him any joy.

Who would have thought that the neighbour's snowman, built last night by the boys next door, would have had such an impact on the young Jewish mother.

The woman's daughter had indeed been the man's next chosen victim, and he had been prepared to stay hidden within the small cottage's confines for as long as it would take for the child to come outside unattended.

But now the man is certain that the mother will not allow her precious cub outside for one moment. Not after the scare she's just had.

And he doesn't even blame her. He wouldn't either.

The man rubs his cold hand over his face in exasperation. He'd worked himself up to do this today. But now he'll have to come back tomorrow, or maybe the next day. Give the woman some time to calm down and regain her false sense of security.

And then, when her guard is lowered once more, the man will return and build his own snowman. One whose destruction won't bring with it even a shred of relief.

And he feels physically sick at the prospect.

Abel

<u>Poland, Lodz</u>

Our parents and our aunt have decided we cannot simply wait for the Nazis to burst down our door and drag us all to the ghetto. So, we pack our bags and flee.
Except, not all of us can go.

"We cannot leave you here!" my sister protests, her brown eyes wild with worry when our parents and Aunt Ayla tell us that they will be staying behind.

"What will happen to you if you stay?" my sister cries. Our mother hugs her tightly, "You get on that train, Mia," she says, ignoring her daughter's question, "You get on and take good care of Abel for us. And when this war is over, you'll come back, and we'll be waiting for you."
A lump forms in my throat to hear the lie, sugar-coated and sickly sweet, so that it may be easier to swallow.

"But I don't want to leave you," Mia blubbers, though she is nineteen years old, "I don't wanna go away!"
Suddenly I can no longer hold back my own tears, and they spill out onto my cheeks as I look up at Father.
He chucks me gently under the chin and smiles, "None of that, *zun*. You're a man now."
But I am only fifteen…
He leans down and wraps his long arms around me, "Look after Mia for us."
I can but nod against his shoulder. No words seem able to get past the barricade in my throat.

"Remember who you are, Abel," my father says, so I stand up straighter and nod, "Don't ever forget it."
The train behind us screeches, warning people to get on or miss their chance.
Mia exclaims and grips our mother tighter, digging her fingers into her dress.

Aunt Ayla tries to coax her to let go, but she will not.

I watch through my blurry, teary vision as Father pries my sister's clawed hands off our mother and bundles her on the train, then my mother takes my face in her hands and kisses my forehead.

"Go," she whispers as she looks into my eyes and I into hers. I try to commit their colour and shape to my memory.

"Go now, *meyn kind*, and live!" she orders, before Father's strong hands reach under my armpits and he hoists me onto the train. I reach my hand out to my mother, but I grasp only air.

And then, Mia and I are severed from our family as the doors are banged shut and the train shrieks again.

I press my palm flat against the windowpane as Mia bangs on it and yells.

My heart physically hurts to see them grow smaller as the train pulls away, and before long, their faces are no longer distinguishable.

I see my mother double over, and my father kneeling down to hold her as she shakes, my aunt standing as stiff as a statue behind them.

And I wonder, as Mia raises a shaky hand to her mouth and mumbles incoherently under her breath, if we will ever see them again.

We weren't told much about where we were going, and what little we did know has momentarily slipped our minds.

My mother's words echo in my ears as Mia and I sit side-by-side in one of the compartments, the train swaying us gently like a mother's arms, as if it could feel our pain.

Go, my child, and live.

We have our faces turned towards the window, and yet I would wager that Mia is taking in about as much of the scenery as I am: none of it.

All I can see is Mother's bent body as she watched us go, all I can feel is my father's hand on my shoulder as he told me to remember who I am.

I squeeze my eyes shut, lift my feet onto the seat and hide my face against my knees. Like I used to when I was small.

"We will see them again," Mia whispers to me suddenly. It is the first time either of us has spoken in what feels like hours.

I turn my face towards her and press my lips into a tight smile, but I'm not sure I believe her.

We change trains once, though I don't know at which station; and quickly, we are off again.

Mia and I settle into our seats in a relatively quiet cabin and resume our sombre positions, staring out the window as people around us chatter quietly.

Night falls and we no longer see anything but darkness outside, our own morbid expressions reflected back at us in the glass. Silence descends over the cabin, and eventually, despite our reeling minds and troubled souls, we fall asleep.

I wake with a stiff neck and feel like I have only just nodded off, but the sky outside has that peachy, lilac hue of dawn.

Mia is snoring lightly beside me, so I leave her to sleep and check our bags are still under our seats.

I pull out a paper bag containing a sandwich and bite into it, chewing slowly. It tastes like home, and I can hardly contain the hurt in my chest.

On the seat beside us, a man stands up and exits the train at one of the stops, leaving his newspaper behind. I reach over and begin to read it to pass the time.

Killer Hunts Jewish Children

The title captures my attention and sends a shiver down my spine, the hairs on my arms standing to attention as I read on about how Jewish children have gone missing in Germany, in the very town I had grown up in.

Little Josef, I remember my parents saying that night two years ago, when they decided to leave for Poland.

He must've been the killer's first victim, and according to this article he'd gone on to kill three more that same year and then mysteriously stopped.

I shudder to think that I could have been one of those unfortunate kids if we hadn't left Germany when we did.

I read on, the article describing how the unknown person had tormented their targets' families by leaving behind a snowman as some type of sick, ritualistic symbol. 'The Yeti' they called him.

The way the article is worded, I'm not certain if it is condemning him, or celebrating him.

I don't know what to make of it. The world really is on a downward spiral…

The train whistles and Mia stirs beside me, and I fold the paper in half, glad for the interruption.

She stretches, "Where are we?"

"The whistle just blew for Berlin, I think," I say, to which she gasps, and wipes the sleep from her eyes.

"Mother said to get off here."

I have about enough time to toss the newspaper aside before she hauls me to my feet and grabs our leather cases. I take one and nod at her that I am ready, our parents' instructions from two nights ago coming back to me. I confess I hadn't been paying much attention at the time, since I'd still believed them to be coming with us. I wish now I had listened more carefully, and am only glad that Mia clearly did.

"Come," she says, taking my free hand in hers and leading me off the train.

Normally, I would have protested at being led like a child, but right now I am thankful for it. I have never felt so vulnerable and lost in all my life.

We climb off the train and hang our heads, knowing not to draw attention to ourselves.

"We are to meet the man by the archways. He'll be wearing a brown hat and gloves."

I nod and follow her, trying to avoid the dozens of men, women and children bustling all around us. I notice, as we walk, that most men are wearing hats and gloves against the early morning cold, and I pray we will identify the right person.

We slink past the many commuters, trying desperately not to bump into anyone and cause a fuss.

I spot the occasional group of armed men, but they appear relaxed. I guess they aren't actively searching for any wayward Jews in the middle of Berlin.

Suddenly Mia stops and I nearly crash into her, "The archways," she breaths, and we both start searching the crowd.

Alma

<u>France, Le Chambon-sur-Lignon</u>

France was unable to withstand the German invasion for long, and after just over a month of pushbacks, by the end of June 1940, France signed an armistice with Germany.

"The German forces have raised the Swastika flag over the Eiffel Tower," my French father says, shaking his head defeatedly, "Paris is overrun."
I reach over and place my hand over his.

"But we are safe here, *non*?" I whisper, as though the Nazis might hear me and prove me wrong, "Our little village is remote. Perhaps they will not come here."
My parents share a look, but they say nothing. And I wonder if their silence means they agree with me, or if they're choosing to keep me in the dark.

Each morning since the German occupation of our country, I make my way to work taking much more care than ever, though Le Chambon continues safe.
Tension rounds my shoulders as I walk through the village to the primary school where I am a teacher, and I grip my jacket closed tightly against my chest despite the sunshine.
The weather is wonderful, but with my early morning starts to the day, I find a light jacket is handy to have, especially when, like today, there's a chilly gust in the air.

"Lovely morning!" someone calls across the road from me as a whirl of wind blows my hair into my face, chestnut whisps obstructing my sight. I brush them aside and look up to find Pastor André Trocmé waving at me.
I smile at him, "It will be once I'm out of this wind."
He jogs over the road towards me, "How are the children?" he asks as he falls into step with me.

I have known Pastor Trocmé for as long as I can remember. He has been the village pastor since I was a baby, and he is a well-liked and respected member of our community.

"Most seem unaware, which is how I hope they'll remain," I admit.

The pastor nods, "They are young. And until this war reaches us here, there is no reason to upset them."

I make a sound of agreement.

"And you?" he asks then, "Your mother tells me there is not to be a wedding after all."

He chuckles but my cheeks burn. My mother always was too chatty about my romantic life. But then again, even without *Maman's* chattering, everyone knows everyone in our village, and word spreads rapidly.

"No," I confirm, "Azriel and I –"

"Ah, there is no need for details," the pastor interrupts, "It is private and none of my business. As long as you are well, that is all that matters."

We have reached the school and are both standing facing each other. I don't know what to tell him, because truthfully, I am *not* well. This business with Germany has created a knot in my stomach that seems to be tightening every day.

"I am frightened, Pastor," I confess in a quiet voice, "We may be a small village but there are many of us here who are of the Jewish faith."

The old man nods, but as a spiritual leader of the Protestant congregation, I am not sure if he can fully understand my fears.

But then he grabs my upper arms and squeezes them gently, "We will look out for one another, *oui?*" he says.

I feel tears pricking my eyes, "*Oui,*" I croak, and he smiles at me before raising my chin with his knuckle.

"Keep your spirits up, Alma," he tells me as he turns to walk away, "No harm will come to you or your mother if I can help it."

Abel

<u>Germany</u>

Mia and I wait by the arches for what feels like hours, but judging by the clocks all around us it has only been eight minutes.

"Abel and Mia?"

The voice behind us sends a shiver down my spine and I swivel around to find a man, dressed in a brown coat, hat and gloves. His coat collars are pulled up, to conceal his face, I think, but if anything, it makes him look more conspicuous.

"Yes," I say, lifting my chin and remembering what my father had told me: I am a man now.

The stranger, who has a leathery face and a moustache, looks us up and down, then jerks his head over his shoulder.

"Come," and he turns.

Mia and I glance at each other but do not question him.

We follow the man through the streets of Berlin, zigzagging across busy roads and down questionable alleyways until I feel out of breath.

"Wait!" I call when I can't take it any longer, a stitch stabbing me in my side, "Where are we going?"

Without slowing down or warning, the man turns around and walks towards me, all the while searching the crowd over his shoulder. Then he leans down to my eye level.

"The less you know, the better."

I frown, and he straightens up and turns back around.

"What?" I burst out, "No! Who even are you?"

"Abel," Mia warns me, grabbing my hand and urging me to control myself.

A couple of people have slowed their pace to watch us, and I can't help but think I've messed up.

I lower my voice as we catch up to him, "We don't even know your name," I argue, "Give us your name so we may feel more at ease."
At that, the man smirks from underneath his moustache, and I can practically feel Mia shrinking beside me.

"The less you know," he says again, slow and deliberate, "the better."

As it turns out, we really didn't need to know the stranger's name, because just ten minutes later he bundles us into the back of a car with another stranger in the driver's seat, this time a woman. And she, too, does not give us her name.
We aren't the only ones in the car; a frightened looking child sits in the front passenger seat, and I have a feeling she isn't the woman's daughter.

"Where are we going?" I ask, having gathered all my bravery to ensure I do not sound scared, though I am. I am absolutely terrified.

"*Le Chambon sur Lignon*," the woman says, and I frown at Mia beside me, who shrugs.

"We were told we'd be going to France," Mia pipes up. The woman sniggers, "It is in France."
An hour later – during which there was no sound except for the child's occasional snivelling – the woman pulls over and I look frantically out the window.

"Come," she says to us in the back, then climbs out and walks around the car to open the passenger door and lift the kid out into her arms.

"What now?" I whisper to Mia, searching her face for a shred of reassurance, but she, too, is wide-eyed with uncertainty.

"Mother said something about a horse and cart," she shakes her head, willing herself to remember, "But I don't know if that is the next step or the one after."

"But the man, the woman, the car. You remember it from their instructions?"

She nods vaguely and I nod back in confirmation, though I don't really know. A knot of guilt twists my stomach. I should have paid more attention.

We step tentatively out of the car and spot the woman handing the child to another woman, who briskly turns around and shows the little girl the horse she is standing beside.

"A horse and cart," I breathe, taking Mia's hand in mine and squeezing. She squeezes back, and I draw strength from it.

"We are almost there," she assures, then takes a step towards our next mode of transportation.

Alma

France, Le Chambon-sur-Lignon

In contrast to other labyrinth-like French villages, Le Chambon has an orderly quality with tile-roofed stone houses dotted along its main road. It has a restful, private atmosphere due to its seclusion, and glimpses of forest are visible in almost every direction.

It is very likely then, I tell myself each morning, that the Germans do not even know of its existence. And it certainly feels that way as more and more news reaches us that French towns and cities are either being taken over by the Nazis, or being ruled by a puppet government known as the Vichy regime, while we continue pretty much unaffected by the goings on around us.

And yet, updates on the developments of the war are unavoidable.

"All Jews over the age of six are now made to wear a yellow star on their clothing," Azriel tells me as we walk leisurely to the square for the Saturday market.

We'd decided to remain friends despite my lack of romantic interest, which I am very glad about. Because though I do not wish for Azriel as my partner, I have to admit, he is good company.

"The decree was signed by Reinhard Heydrich," Azriel continues, "it is an offense to fail to comply."

"Will *we* have to?" I ask, "We are yet to be disturbed."

Azriel looks down at the ground while we walk.

It is a fine summer morning, and were it not for the gloom of our conversation, I could almost imagine that our country is not, in fact, at war.

"We won't remain hidden forever," he replies, effectively bursting my bubble of hope that the war would go on and end without us ever experiencing it.

"I feared you would say that," I admit.

He smiles at me sadly, and I am again reminded of how easy life could be if only I could force myself to feel something beyond friendship for him.

"When it does reach us –"

"Let's not speak of it," I interrupt, picking up my pace and heading towards a stall selling peaches and apples. The saleswoman, who I have known since kindergarten, tells me the price. I take three peaches.

"I would want you to be prepared," Azriel says now, as if I hadn't interrupted him and walked off. I turn to him, raising a hand to shield my eyes from the sun.

"How can anyone be prepared for invasion?" I demand. He arches one dark eyebrow, "As the daughter of a Frenchman, born in France, you may not be targeted. Same as me. We are only 'half-Jewish'."

"But my mother? Your father?" I counter, "They do not have that advantage."

"And for that reason, I do not accept simply 'waiting and seeing' what happens."

I exhale in frustration and anxiety, "What can we even do? We cannot run. This is precisely the kind of place I would seek to run *to!*"

"No," Azriel replies, "We should not run. But…just be prepared. Wear the star. We never know when the Nazis might come knocking."

It is just nine days later that a frantic pounding at our door wakes us from our sleep.

"*Machen Sie auf!*" someone shouts from outside in a language I don't understand, banging repeatedly against the wood.

My *maman* emerges from the bedroom, holding her gown closed tightly at her throat, as if to ward off evil. *Papa* holds a gas lamp aloft, his face orange in its glow, his anxiety quite visible. He heads towards the door despite his uncertainty, while *Maman* pads towards me and takes me in her arms. I hold onto her like I did when I was a small child.

The banging continues.

"*Öffnen Sie die Tür!*"

Bang bang bang.

"*Bitte…*"

I look confusedly at my father then, who turns around to frown at us. This person's tone is pleading…

Our defences are lowered immediately, and I peel away from my mother.

Papa and I exchange a look as the shouting outside subsides into whimpering, and hesitantly, he unlatches the door.

To our utter surprise, it is not the Nazis at our doorstep in the middle of the night as we'd expected, but a young and frightened-looking woman.

"*Oh, mon Dieu,*" I hear my father breathe as he sets down the lamp and reaches down to help her up.

We bundle the girl inside and *Maman* throws a blanket over her shoulders before pulling my father aside by the elbow and whispering to him in the corner.

I glance at them briefly, curious what they are discussing, but my attention returns to the young woman.

"Who are you? Are you hurt?" I ask in French, trying to remain calm, though my heart is racing.

The girl does not reply, continuing only to stare wide-eyed at the floor and breathing heavily.

My parents return to us then and my mother takes the girl's hands in hers while *Papa* steers me away.

"Go fetch the pastor, Alma," he instructs me.

I frown, "Pastor Trocmé? What will he –"

My father interrupts me, "Just do as I say and tell him we have a girl here. He will know what to do."

I do not protest further. The entire situation has thrown me for a loop, and I understand that this is an important task.

And so, I quickly pull on my coat and boots and head out into the dead of night, while my parents fuss over the mysterious stranger.

Annika

<u>The Netherlands, Giethoorn</u>

The Nazis, as well as the Dutch police, are searching for us after we'd successfully distributed over three-hundred anti-Nazi pamphlets all around our village without being apprehended.

Well, not searching for 'us' specifically, but for whoever could possibly be responsible for such insubordination. It being two little girls never crossing their minds.

On one occasion, Helga was quite literally caught red-handed with a pamphlet in her bag after a group of soldiers had stopped and searched us on our way to school, and somehow, they'd still let us go.

"Where did you find this?!" the soldier had barked, holding up the pamphlet he'd found in her bag.

Helga, to her credit, had not faltered. She'd looked up at them, all doe-eyed, and pointed down the street.

"I found it on the ground over there," she'd said.

And the men had marched in the direction she had given, knocking angrily on the doors of the houses.

Helga and I had skipped away arm in arm and melted into the crowd of school children, laughing at the Germans' stupidity.

"It is your youth that keeps you safe," our mother had told us later, "They look at you and see just two young, giggling fools."

And in response to that, Helga and I had indeed giggled, because if being a young fool granted us invisibility, we would make good use of our superpower.

Not long after that, my sister and I are repeating our ritualistic checks over our shoulders and up into windows, before slipping a flyer underneath a house's door. By now, we carry five pamphlets each, having grown bolder with our continued inconspicuousness. We hurry along the road and do it again, Helga checking our left and I checking our right, when I suddenly spot a man watching us.

I clear my throat just as Helga is about to pull a flyer out of her bag, and she stuffs it back in upon hearing my signal. Then, without looking back, we take each other's hand and skip steadily away.

We turn left down a quiet road and duck underneath a broken fence, then emerge out onto the marketplace. There is much noise as the shopkeepers haggle, and people gossip. We skirt around the fishmonger, and I casually slip one of my pamphlets into a young mother's basket of groceries while she's busy fussing over her baby. I smile to myself and look back over my shoulder to see if she has noticed, when I see the man has followed us. My stomach drops with dread.

"Helga," I warn, and she picks up her pace, her hand tightening around mine.

We hunch our shoulders, hurry out of the marketplace and down towards the river, skidding on the dirt path. We huddle behind a pile of crates, hidden from view but positioned in a way that we can see if he follows us down the path.

We sit still and try to breathe quietly, Helga keeping a look out through the cracks in the crates. My heart is hammering in my chest, and not just from the running. This is the first time I have felt actively frightened.

I observe Helga as she watches the trail, and for a moment I think we are safe, when suddenly, I notice her tense.

She raises her hand, palm towards me, to show I should remain still. And so, I do, though my armpits begin to sweat and my fingers begin to tingle, my flight instinct kicking in.

I cover my mouth with my hands and hold my breath, my eyes growing wider as hers do, too.

I can hear my heart beating in my ears and am about to stand up and run when I see her shoulders relax.

It is a long moment before she speaks, but when she does, relief washes over me when I spy the hint of her carefree grin pulling at her lips.

"He's gone."

I turn around and peer over the crates, "Who was he?"

Helga shakes her head, "I don't know," she says, serious again, "But I can tell you this much: if he'd caught us distributing these pamphlets, you, me and *Mama* would be thrown in prison. Or worse."

Wolfgang

<u>Germany, Bamberg</u>

When I was a child, I used to wonder what kind of horror could possess a man to beat his beloved wife.

Most nights, I would wake to the sound of something crashing to the ground, a yell in anger, or a muffled cry of pain. In the morning, my parents would act like nothing had happened, and I was expected to play along. But it was visible in *Mutti's* cut lip when she smiled, or the tremble in her hands when she made my breakfast. More apparent even than that, was my father's gushing over her: telling her how beautiful she was, leaning in and nuzzling her neck, whispering how sorry he was, how reckless he was, how it would never happen again.

It lessened the older I got. Not because my father tried to be a better man, but because he could no longer muster enough energy for a fight – not that it was ever much of a fight to begin with. His body was betraying him, he called it.

Me? I saw it as him getting exactly what he deserved. Maybe it was God intervening. Maybe it was just the illness that had taken hold of him after years of alcoholism. Who knows? But bit by bit he lost control of his body.

He changed in those final years, though. And in him I finally saw the man he might've been had he not ever gone to war. *Mutti* cared for him after he lost his ability to walk, hold his own fork, wipe his own arse. And in her I saw the kindest, most generous person on Earth. She must've either loved him beyond comprehension, or forgiven him for his failures.

Either way, though he had been the one to fight in the Great War, in my eyes, *she* was the real hero in their story.

Before he passed away, expressing – for the hundredth time – how he wished to have seen me in uniform, I took a leaf out of my mother's book. And instead of hating him for what he had become, I chose to honour him for what he had done for his country, thinking that maybe then, I would grow to understand him a little better.

Now though…now I wish I had heeded my *Mutti's* words: that I didn't have to fulfil my promise to him and join the SS.

God knows I wish every day since that I hadn't.

How then, after ignoring her warning, could I confess to my mother of all the things I had seen?

How I had witnessed a young Jewish man – a teenager really – press his forehead to the muzzle of my colleague's gun, as if goading him to pull the trigger. His compliance to die had been more unsettling than if he had cried and screamed. To accept it so eagerly was unnatural, which – to me at least – only emphasised the unnaturalness of what *we* were doing. His blood had spurted from the back of his skull a moment later, and I had watched it pool at my feet. And all I could think was, despite his supposed uncleanliness, as the Reich would have us believe, this Jewish boy still bled red like the rest of us.

I couldn't tell my mother these things. That I sometimes imagined I could feel the weight of their lives piling onto my shoulders. That I drank to keep the visions of what I'd done at bay. How could I tell her that I'd get so drunk, that the following mornings I'd believe I was dying. And that sometimes, I wished I was.

At first, it had felt strange to have been told to cause destruction. I remember feeling like a lost child when my supervisor had pressed a shovel into my hands that night – which later became known as *Kristallnacht* – and ordered us all to cause mayhem. I had been brought up to be a good German boy, my mother instilling in me good behaviour and my father reprimanding me when I stepped out of line.

But the terrifying reality that I quickly grew to learn with each dreadful thing that I did, was that when something is repeated often enough, anything can become natural.

Even, it turned out, causing harm.

I heard some of the officers went crazy.

Those who had – unlike me – shown great promise during training by *enjoying* violence, had been sent to Poland and Northern Ukraine. There they were ordered to round up all those who were 'racially inferior', march them to fields, and kill them. These round-ups included men, women, and children.

I heard the stories. Heard, too, how some officers could not live with what they had done, that they had gotten up in the middle of the night and shot themselves in the head. Or hung themselves. Anything to put an end to the cries echoing in their ears, anything to wipe away the memories from their minds.

Whatever their way out, the reason for it was always the same: we were not meant to inflict such horrors onto our fellow man.

The Netherlands, Ellecom

Following my time back at home, where I realised I have outgrown my former life – both in the physical and psychological manner – I am deployed to the Netherlands. There, I am sent to Avegoor, an educational institution for the Dutch SS near the village of Ellecom, some 12 miles northeast of the city of Arnhem.

"Your task here at the Avegoor estate is to supervise the military training of the new volunteers for the Dutch SS," my commander, German SS-officer Alphons Brendel, says upon my arrival.

I nod, ever the obedient soldier, and follow the other officers to our quarters.

I am fairly certain I have been sent here as some kind of punishment, a penalty for being a below average soldier. Perhaps they hope I will grow to accept Hitler's ideology more easily if I am here, re-learning it through osmosis. Perhaps they simply wish to keep me out of the way.

Regardless of their reason, I am secretly glad to be here, knowing through lived experience that there are much worse places to be.

The training I am to supervise will be very much the same as my own had been: combat training, weapons training, classes in tactics, terrain and map reading. The volunteers will go to the shooting range, and learn how to survive in the wild. They will be groomed into soldiers, just as I had been. And those who'll perform well will be praised and honoured.

I can already see my future: six months here, implementing Nazi ideology I do not believe in and enforcing policies I do not agree with, surrounded by people I have nothing in common with.

But I will play the part of a loyal comrade nonetheless, all the while hating every step I take in unison with them. Because I know I cannot beat this fucked up regime on my own, and that leaving will do nothing to change its trajectory.

But to remain hidden within the belly of the beast, *that* will surely present me with some opportunities to try to make a difference.

Annika

<u>The Netherlands, Giethoorn</u>

Helga and I make our way home, taking a detour to ensure we aren't being followed after the frightening pursuit of the mysterious man.
That was our first taste of danger. Never before have we been seen distributing our anti-Nazi pamphlets. It has shaken me, I can't deny that. And by the way Helga holds my hand tightly while we walk home, I would wager she is shaken too. Though she will likely never admit to it.
We will have to be more cautious. Perhaps I could wear my hair in two braids. *Mama* always says it makes me look younger than my fifteen years –
"Girls," my mother's voice says in greeting suddenly as we step into our home, "Come in, come in," and she ushers us inside, wringing her hands together nervously.
I frown at my sister, who returns the same expression.
"*Mama?*" Helga asks tentatively, "What's wrong?"
She smiles at us over her shoulder, pats her jaw-length blond bob, "Wrong?" she parrots, "Nothing is wrong."
And she leads us into the lounge, where the man who had chased us, casually sits.

I exclaim – I cannot help it – and Helga takes a step in front of me, shielding me.
"*Mama…*" she says cautiously, glancing at her quickly.
"Don't fret, girls," she says, waving her hand at the man, who continues to sit on our small two-seater sofa, raising a cup of coffee to his lips.
I look from the man to our mother to Helga, my heart racing as I consider bolting out the door.
"Sit down, Helga. Annika," *Mama* commands gently.

"This man was chasing us today!" Helga hisses in explanation then.

The man observes us now, looking us slowly up and down. He is younger than I'd initially thought – perhaps early twenties – with piercing green eyes that unnerve me, and I shrink further behind Helga.

To our utter surprise, *Mama* laughs. And it is a trilling sound I have never heard her make, not even when she and our father had been happy.

"Yes, I know all about it," she says, taking a seat *right next* to our pursuer.

"Girls, sit down," she orders again. And this time, our curiosity is stronger than our uncertainty.

"Who are you?" I ask, stunned by my own bravery to speak up.

Mother places a hand on the man's arm, "Forgive my daughters," she says, "I may have kept them a little too well in the dark."

The man, finally, opens his mouth to speak, "My name is Jakob Meyer, and I would like to recruit you both to formally join the Dutch Resistance."

Helga looks at me.

So, this man was part of the resistance. No wonder *Mama* was not concerned when we said he'd chased us. Had it been some kind of sick test?

"We are already distributing your pamphlets," Helga answers the man defensively, no doubt wondering the same things as I, "What more can we possibly do? We are teenagers."

The man – Meyer – leans forward in his seat, a lupine grin pulling at his lips, "You are invisible. No one suspects you."

A moment of silence befalls us, during which time the man and our mother stare at us as though expecting an answer.

But we are dumbfounded.

What exactly can two teenage girls possibly do to help fight the Nazis, besides what we are already doing?

Chapter 4

<u>Germany</u>

It has been three years since the man began his mission, and yet he still thinks about it often – his first kill.
He had returned to the scene of that first crime a couple of weeks after it had happened. But as part of the search party arranged to help find the boy's body, nobody suspected him. He was shrouded in a cloak of concern.
Three others had followed that same winter. But none of the other kills stuck with him like the first.
Little Josef.
He had been the only one to truly suffer, and it still weighs heavily on the man's conscience.
He had etched the boy's name into his headboard on the day of the act, the other three a mere numerical epitaph.
It was the least he could do to remember them.
And yet, it didn't assuage any of his guilt; in fact, it only inflames it every time he looks upon it. But it is the burden he will bear for what has done to perfect his craft.

Josef
III

That is how his headboard now looks, and a shiver runs through him as he sits on his bed, recalling the day of the boy's discovery. The way the snow had glittered in the morning sunlight. How the mother's cries had rung through the air.
And still, three years later, he has not yet been able to do what he'd set out to do all along.

He is no longer even certain that he can do it! He shakes his head and drops it into his hands with a groan.

He will have to act quickly, or all of it, all his practice, will have been for nothing, will have meant nothing. Because with each passing month, she grows older, and his time is running out.

Abel

<u>France, Le Chambon-sur-Lignon</u>

It's been a year since Mia and I crossed the borders of France, hidden under tarps and hay, in the cart drawn by a horse.

A year in which we have been living in the quiet village of Le Chambon-sur-Lignon, where no Nazis have yet stepped foot due to its seclusion – a forest encompassing it almost from all sides.

Upon our arrival, we were immediately placed in the care of an elderly couple who would pass for our parents. Their names are Marie and Pierre, and they are incredibly kind and patient people. And having been unable to have any children of their own, they gladly accepted us into their lives.

They began to teach us French the same day we moved into their little home, to help us integrate. But until we understood each other, there had been a lot of hand gestures and universally understood grunts and head bobs or shakes.

The little girl we travelled with – who we learned was three years old at the time – is called Olga. She has been placed to live with a young couple who already have a daughter, the two girls both sporting black curly hair making her fit in perfectly as their child.

Olga is four now, and already she speaks better French than Mia or I.

"The younger you are, the easier it is to pick up a new language," Mia tells me now as we watch Olga chasing her new 'sister' down the road towards the village centre, calling after her in near-perfect French.

I nod, "She looks happy," I say, a hint of jealousy in my tone, since she is clearly not haunted by those she has left behind.

Mia offers me a sad smile and takes my hand as we walk, "Olga has the gift of youth. She may not be able to recall the family she came from as well as we do ours. But is that a blessing or a curse?"

I frown, "A blessing, of course."

My sister sighs, "I know you feel guilty, but they wanted us to flee. They did what they did to save us."

"And where are they now while we walk merrily to market?"

My tone is monotonous, but it is cutting.

Mia searches my face, "We do not know that they are in the ghetto," she says.

I look at her sideways. Everybody knows that the deadline to enter the ghettos was March 1941. We know they are in the ghetto. Because they are. Unless they're already dead. She must have come to the same conclusion, because she quickly adds, "They, too, could have escaped."

I scoff, "You cannot possibly believe that?"

We both turn at the sound of sweet laughter, as Olga and her sister run back this way holding a kite aloft.

"I'd give anything to be so blissfully unaware," I say.

"Olga may be blissfully unaware. But when this war is over, she will not know where she belongs. If her real family survives and she is reunited with them, she loses *this* family that she has grown to love. If her true family is dead, then she will grow up never knowing where she came from. If anything, it begs the question as to which scenario is better, ours or hers?"

"Hers," I say without a moment's hesitation, "To have but a wisp of a memory of someone you *think* you may have loved at some point, is surely kinder on the heart than remembering every single wretched detail of your separation from them."

Mia is nodding sombrely beside me, saddened by how morose I have become, "Perhaps you are right," she says. And we continue our walk towards the bustling stalls, my youthful rage burning inside me like a flame.

   We quickly realised we were not the first nor the last new inhabitants of this secluded village, Le Chambon having become known through word of mouth for its courageous efforts to hide refugees.

Many made their way on foot to the village, having come from Germany, Poland, some even from Lithuania, and made their way through occupied France to reach Chambon. Sometimes people would arrive in the dead of night, banging on the door of the first house they came across. Locals would then run to fetch the leader of their resistance effort, a protestant pastor called André Trocmé, who Mia and I have gotten to know very well since our arrival.

He and his wife Magda, we later learned, embarked on their campaign of peaceful civil disobedience against the authorities by rallying locals and their congregation in a bold plan to hide Jewish refugees in attics, barns and cellars across the village. Those who could be integrated and hidden in plain sight as members of another household's family – like us and Olga – would be placed in locals' homes.

The entire village committed to maintain their secret, and they were all breaking the law to save us, since foreign refugees were to be surrendered to the enemy. And for that, we would be eternally grateful.

In the months that followed our arrival, Pastor Trocmé approached many humanitarian organisations who had put plans in motion to smuggle children to safety but who needed a transitional hiding place, and he volunteered Le Chambon as an asylum.

"We will need to establish children's homes," Pastor Trocmé had informed the villagers during one of the regular meetings, of which we were part of, "It is no longer possible to hide everyone in our attics and barns. Our numbers have increased into the hundreds, and an orphanage is the safest course of action to maintain a plausible hiding facility for Jewish children."
The locals had agreed and swiftly began their joint efforts to complete the task, and, of course, I offered my services. And it was during the building process of the orphanage that I met the beautiful Alma.

Alma

<u>France, Le Chambon-sur-Lignon</u>

The young girl who came knocking on our door at night the previous year was the first to have found sanctuary at Le Chambon.
Since then, we have taken in dozens of Jews, as well as some Roma and Sinti, and even full-blooded Germans whose only 'crime' was to have been born homosexual.
Our small village's furtive reputation is growing, and while it warms my heart to know we are a safe haven for those in need, I cannot help but worry that our secret will not remain as such for long if the wrong person were to catch wind of our efforts.

"What escape is there for us if the Nazis find out about what we are doing?" I ask my father now as he walks with me to the orphanage's official opening.
The whole village helped to build it, every able-bodied adult putting in many hours to erect it as quickly as possible. And after just a few months, it is now ready to receive its young inhabitants.

"Do we have any means of moving them if the enemy comes?"
Father nods, "I hear the pastor is negotiating for parties to take small groups of Jews over the mountains to Switzerland."

"Switzerland? On foot?"

"*Oui,*" he says, "It will be a long trek, but it is the only way to get them safely out of France. Le Chambon cannot house however many more people come our way. Our small village does not have the means. It will be but a pitstop for most here on out I hear."
I nod at the new information, pleased that there is a plan other than keeping people here like sitting ducks.

Father rounds on me then and takes my hands in his, "When the time comes for people to flee," he says, "I want you to go with one of the groups to Switzerland."

I frown, "You mean you want me to lead a group over the mountains? *Papa*, I cannot –"

But he shakes his head, "No, *ma fille*, I mean your mother and I have discussed it. She and you are not safe here."

I recoil from him as I understand his meaning, "*Maman* and I would never leave you!"

My father laughs humourlessly, "Oh yes, you will. Your *maman* has already agreed. But don't fret. It shan't happen for some time."

I swallow my response, choosing to allow him to believe that his plan would ensure our safety. But I could never imagine myself without my *papa*. Even at twenty years old, I am not ready to be parted from either of them.

We have reached the new orphanage now, a sea of people already having gathered, all of them beaming with pride for their part in its creation.

We greet a few who turn to welcome us, then slot into the crowd as Pastor Trocmé continues his speech, thanking all who helped. I smile and offer him a nod as his gaze falls briefly to me.

It had been backbreaking work, but I'd enjoyed being a part of this incredible thing we were doing.

"Young Abel is looking at you," my father says under his breath now, followed by a chuckle, "The boy is mad for you."

I search the crowd and, sure enough, catch the retreating glimpse of the young man.

"Let him look," I say, "There is nothing in it. He is much too young for me, in any case."

My father nods sagely, "He is indeed too young for you," he says, though I hear the hint of laughter in his voice.

Annika

<u>The Netherlands, Giethoorn</u>

As it turned out, there was *a lot* two young teenagers could do to help the Dutch Resistance beyond distributing pamphlets and defacing Nazi propaganda.

In the five months that followed our official joining of the resistance, Helga and I were taught how to use our ability to go unnoticed by the enemy more boldly.

At sixteen and seventeen, we were just two young girls; no threat, no importance.

It was why they had dismissed us so easily when Helga had been found with one of the anti-Nazi flyers in her bag. It was why I had so effortlessly been able to slip a pamphlet into that young mother's basket in broad daylight.

The Germans were busy looking for suspicious men and women, not frolicking young girls. We were but mere specks of dust to them. And as *Mama* had previously said, it was *that* which would grant us our safety.

Today, however, we would be stepping out of our training and committing our first official assignment; and I would be lying if I said I wasn't nervous.

"Ani, you ready?" my sister calls, banging against the bathroom door where I am applying the finishing touches.

"*Ja!*" I call back, brushing invisible lint from my floral dress, which was becoming a bit too short, coming up to my knees. The side of my mouth twitches, there was nothing I could do about that now. I didn't exactly have many other options.

I step out of the bathroom and head to the front door to put on my sandals. My mother and sister are already there.

"The braids," Helga grins, nodding in approval, "Nice touch."

"You look just like when you were a little girl," our mother says, and I frown slightly to think that really, I still am.
But I play along, bending my knee just so and kicking my heel up, the very image of an innocent little child.

"Let's go," Helga says, pressing the item into my hands, "I steer, you –"

"Yes, yes," I say, as if we've done this a thousand times. Outside, *Mama* kisses us both on the cheek and waves us goodbye, giving the illusion that this is an ordinary day, and we are on an ordinary errand.
When in actual fact, we have been sent out to shoot Nazis.

Helga is pedalling the pushbike while I sit on the back. It is uncomfortable, the metal rack digging into my buttocks and thighs, but that is not what is causing my unease.

"Just breathe, Ani," Helga comforts me quietly, sensing my nervousness. I can hear the easy grin in her voice, and I wish, not for the first time, that I could be as laid-back as my sister.

"We are but two little girls, remember?" she soothes.
I swallow hard and pretend to laugh as we cycle past a group of German soldiers loitering outside a bakery.
The ration line is short today, I note, and I wonder if that means the shopkeepers are running low on provisions or if the Nazis have spooked people from waiting.
My stomach growls at the idea of a soft, warm bun, fresh out of the oven. A luxury we are no longer allowed.
We turn the corner, and Helga pedals up a little hill, where we know there will be a denser crowd of Nazis during this time of day.

"We're nearly at the café," she says, "Meyer said to expect a group of them sitting outside eating like kings."
My stomach rumbles again.

Is it not enough that they have invaded our country, driven out our queen and bombed our people? Now they have to confiscate the only pleasures we have left by claiming cafés and restaurants as their watering holes and leaving us to starve on pitiful daily rations.

Hidden under my dress, I stroke my thumb over the revolver's wooden handle, "I am ready," I tell my sister.

"Good," she replies, "Because our target is in sight."

Wolfgang

<u>The Netherlands, Giethoorn</u>

My time at Avegoor had come to an end the previous week, and I'd been moved to Giethoorn, just two hours north of Ellecom.

Apparently, there has been some resistance activities going on in this picturesque village, and with only around two-thousand inhabitants, my superiors thought more SS presence in the area alone would be enough of a deterrent to spook them into submission.

So far – I was told upon my arrival – there have only been minor occurrences in this village: distribution of pamphlets, defacing Nazi property and posters, and the like.

In the week that I have been here, the other soldiers and I have done little else but casually patrol the streets at night, and inundate the eateries during the day. My colleagues appear completely at ease here, fearing no uprising no matter the warnings. They gorge themselves on the cafés' pastries and coffees – of which there are fewer and fewer, with the country's struggles and our overeating – and when their bellies are full, they sit sprawled out on the tables and chairs outside, lazing in the gentle sunlight. Not even our *Obersturmbannführer*, who is with us today, seems to mind their laziness. He, too, appears to think no active resistance is occurring here.

But I have seen some things in the few days I've been here, things I had not, and would not, share with the others.

Like a woman slipping something underneath someone's door and hurrying away, and a man whispering with another in a dark alleyway.

And even…these two young girls riding their bike around the square, casting sidelong glances at us when they think no one is looking…

Annika

The Netherlands, Giethoorn

We pedal past a group of maybe twelve guffawing Germans in uniform.
He will be wearing more medals than any other.
That was all we were told, and all we needed to know, according to our instructions. I'd been fearful at first, for how would we know from a distance which of those chumps had *more* medals than his dimwit friends?
But as soon as we approach the group, sitting outside on the terrace, enjoying the warm summer morning, laughing like they have not a care in the world, we see him.
In fact, it is hard to miss him. And if the sun twinkling against his many medals isn't enough to identify him, his arrogance surely is.
"First lap," Helga states quietly.
"Identified," I reply, just as we were taught.
She takes a left turn and then another as we make our way around the building.
"No civilians nearby," I say, looking about, giving her the all-clear and confirming that the plan is to go ahead.
Helga nods and I grip the revolver tightly under my dress. As we turn the final corner to come round the front of the café again, I spot that the target has stood up and is facing his comrades. His back is to us as he calls their attention, and he reaches into his pocket, retrieving a cigarette and a lighter. He lights the cigarette and takes a long drag, then continues to speak. Helga and I are too far to know what he is saying, keeping our hundred-feet distance as ordered.
Blood pumps audibly in my ears, and my stomach roils not with hunger this time, but with anxiety.

The other officers are paying close attention to him, as if awaiting the punchline of a joke. And just as Helga and I ride past them on the opposite side of the square at casual speed, I whip the gun out from underneath my dress and fire one single shot, aiming at his torso in the hope of hitting a vital organ.

The *splatter* that sounds as the bullet makes impact is unlike anything I had expected. The dummies we'd practiced on had sounded nothing like it.

But it is the spray of blood on the others' stunned faces as the target's top right side of his head comes away that makes me gag. And yet, despite my horror, a bubble of joy burst from my lips just as Helga turns the corner of the building, and the Nazis spring to action, none the wiser what has just happened or where the bullet has come from.

Wolfgang

<u>The Netherlands, Giethoorn</u>

I feel the warm spray of blood on my forehead, but it is a whole two seconds before I register what has happened. One moment, the *Obersturmbannführer* stands in front of us, his mouth open, his joke unfinished, and the next he falls face first into the table and chairs, half his skull missing.

I hear an echo of laughter disperse into the wind just before chaos ensues, and then my fellow officers draw their weapons, shouting at one another to take cover.

"There's a shooter!"

"At the window! There! I see him!"

"No, on the roof!"

They cower behind overturned tables for protection as they try to make sense of what has just occurred.

Hidden behind a couple of chairs, I raise my hand and wipe the blood from my face. It's in my hair and on my lips, and my stomach turns at the scent of iron in the air. Not because I am not used to it. But because it allows for disturbing memories to infiltrate my troubled mind.

The shouting and mayhem continues for a few minutes before we stand. Our brave SS-officers, everybody!

It is all I can do not to slow clap at my comrades. But I'm not about to give my true feelings away.

Gingerly, I stand. I am not ashamed to say my knees are shaking underneath my SS uniform.

"They must've fled," I say, to which some of the others nod.

And then, we all look down at the corpse of our *Obersturmbannführer*, his brains spilling out of his destroyed skull.

We'd been informed of a resistance group in the area. Been briefed on their minor actions.

But this? This is a clear message that the Dutch people are fighting back. There is no denying it any further.

And I wonder, in the safety of my own mind, how I might be able to help them.

Abel

<u>France, Le Chambon-sur-Lignon</u>

Objectively, Alma is no great beauty.
Her eyes are two onyx orbs, like that of a snake, or an owl, so dark I could swear she has no pupils at all. Her right front tooth faintly overlaps the other, and her mouth hangs slightly downwards when she is relaxed, as though saddened by the world simply by being in it. And yet, she has an aura about her that draws me in. A kindness and a warmth that I can't help but admire. And, to me, she is the most beautiful woman I have ever seen, though I know I am but a mere boy to her.

"Alma," I say, bringing my wonderment to my adoptive father, who has no doubt known her since birth, "Would she accept an invitation to walk with me if I asked her?"
Pierre smiles at me and my broken French, his bristly grey cheeks rising with the seldom achieved motion.
I subconsciously run a finger along the dark hairs that have sprouted as if overnight above my lip. Pierre has offered to show me how to shave, but I feel too guilty to acquiesce. My father should be the one to teach me.

"Alma may be only a little older than you," Pierre says, speaking slowly so that I might follow, "but she is ready for marriage and children. She was born in…" he looks to his wife who is sitting on the worn sofa, stitching a hole in one of my shirts, "1922, was it not, Marie? She is twenty?"
My new 'mother' nods, "A spring child," she adds, not looking up from her needlework.
I straighten my back, "So you do not think she would entertain even one meeting with a *schmuck* like me?"
At that, Pierre *tuts* as he returns his attention to feeding the fire, "Who said anything about you being a *schmuck*?

It is not your character we speak of, but your age. She is ready to settle down. You have only recently turned seventeen years old. Live a little."

I sigh, admitting defeat before even heading into battle.

"Live a little," I repeat with a gentle scoff, "In this day and age, how can I?"

Marie and Pierre share a look then, "My boy," Pierre says, to which I flinch slightly, still feeling guilty for the way I feel – accepted and safe – when I hear it, "It is precisely in times such as these that we *should* be seeking out the simple joys in life."

'Seeking out the simple joys in life' is exactly what I did in the weeks that followed that conversation.

My sister Mia has started seeing a man, Azriel I think is his name, and she is mostly out and about with him lately; meaning that if I'm not needed to help maintain the household by chopping wood or mending the house with Pierre, I am pretty much left to my own devices. And in my solitude, I take the family bike and ride around the village's perimeter, appreciating the peace and quiet of nature.

Mostly, I ride into the woods, discarding the bike on its edge and continuing on foot, where I climb a tree and simply perch on a thick branch, observing the animals as they go about their business, unaware of my presence.

Sometimes I make up songs, humming into the wind; and for the most part, my songs lead me back home, memories of my mother, father and aunt cropping up in the lyrics.

The chestnut brown of Mother's hair, the splash of amber in Aunt Ayla's eyes, the hairy mole on my father's ear. Sometimes, the tunes take a quirky turn, and I allow myself a little chuckle.

But guilt quickly follows, because with thoughts of my previous life comes the unavoidable reality that they are undoubtedly *not* at the place I call home, readying dinner or reading together by the fire as my songs suggest. It is far more likely that they are starving in a ghetto, working their fingers to the bone and hope they avoid typhus.

Or worse…

There has been talk of fouler places than the ghettos. Whispers of 'worker camps' have reached us here at Le Chambon, the most recent refugees bringing with them terrifying stories of trains that take thousands away at a time, never to be seen again, worked to death. I cannot imagine it, so I shake my head free of the unknown. Because, sometimes, not knowing is scarier than having the full truth. The mind can imagine terrible things…

Whenever the darkness threatens to overcome me, I force myself to think of alternative outcomes: that my family escaped Lodz somehow, that they have heard of the kindness of Le Chambon and are on their way here this very moment.

But today, no tunes come to mind, only silence encircling me as I lie in the grass at the edge of the woods, watching the blue sky.

Birds fly up ahead, a handful of swallows, two, three at a time, chirping sweetly. A crow caws once, then takes flight from a treetop. I squint, hoping it doesn't defecate when it flies over me.

The warm sun and the sounds of nature are lulling me to sleep, my eyelids becoming heavy, and I allow drowsiness to take me. I can feel myself slipping away from this world and into slumber when, all of a sudden, a shadow covers me.

I open one eye, but the shape hovering above me is unidentifiable, the sun behind them hiding their face in shadow.

"What are you doing here?" the voice asks, and immediately, my stomach clenches with dread.

Alma

<u>France, Le Chambon-sur-Lignon</u>

The boy who has a crush on me is lying on his back in the grass as though he has not a care in the world.
And for a moment, I sort of envy him.
"What are you doing here?" I ask, and he instantly scrambles up and brushes down his trousers.
Giggling bubbles up from behind me and I turn a smiling face to my young pupils.
"It's alright," I call, "He was just sleeping."
The boy, who, if I remember correctly is called Abel, cocks his head to one side, "What did you think I was doing?"
"Me? Well, sleeping," she says with a shrug, "But the kids – they thought you were rather dead."
I chuckle, and he peers around me and frowns at the children.
"Morbid," he mutters, then returns his gaze to me.
"Yes, well," I say, a ghost of a smile still on my lips, "They wanted me to make sure."
A moment of silence.
"What *are* you doing here, anyway?" I say then, curious.
He makes a face, "I could ask you the same question," he counters.
I wave my hand at my students, "We're on a field trip."
"Yeah, we're looking for 'nature's treasures'!" one of the kids pipes up.
"'Nature's treasures'?" Abel parrots.
I nod, "Hence our way into the woods."
He steps aside, "You'll find plenty of treasures in there," Abel calls to the children, and I nod for my class of twelve six-year-olds to follow me.

"Come along, children," I say, heading into the shade of the dense trees, "The first to find a pinecone the size of a fist will win a special prize!"

I hear Abel chuckle softly under his breath and I turn to find him walking away. I watch as he picks up a rusty bike, and swings himself onto it, before riding off towards home.

And I'm surprised to find I am disappointed that he does not turn around.

Chapter 5

Annika

<u>The Netherlands, Giethoorn</u>

"I need to work on my aim," I tell Helga as we make our way home from our successful hit.
The spray of the German soldier's blood all over his colleagues' faces threatens to flash in my mind, and I swallow hard to keep myself from retching.
Helga frowns at me, amused, "You hit him right in the head, Ani! That was perfect."
"I was aiming for his torso, though," I confide in her.
A slow smirk creeps over her face, "Oh," she giggles, wrinkling her freckled nose, "Well, he's dead. That's the main thing. We accomplished our first mission and Meyer will have more jobs for us to come. It was a success!"
I nod hesitantly, "Yes, it was a success."

Our 'success' haunts me at night and sometimes during the day, the sound of the man's brains being blown to bits resounding in my mind like karmic justice. I am being punished for my sin, of that, I am sure.
And yet, I cannot stop.
"Ready?" Helga asks me a week after the event, which had caused the Nazis to crack down even harder on our small village.
We've had to lay low for a while since, Helga and *Mama* only leaving the house this past week to stand in line for our daily rations, and I only to attend school.
Helga has already completed her education, and I, at sixteen, have only a few more weeks left.

But as ever, the Germans were not looking for two teenage girls, and our sense of security returned quickly. My innocence, however, *that* will most likely never return.

"Ani?" my sister says, bringing me back to the present, "You ready?"

I nod, running my fingers over my two long mousy blond plaits. But I am not ready.

How will I ever be ready for this?

We make our way down to the river and past several barges as they bob lazily up and down. I tense slightly at the sight of the one where we once lived with our father, and wonder if, this time, he will see us walking past.

Helga must sense my unease because she tells me a joke I've already heard a dozen times. I laugh at the punchline anyway, not out of obligation but out of gratitude for her lightening the mood.

There is no sign of our father. There is not much sign of any life on that barge at all in fact, and I wonder if he has left our village entirely. It would explain his lack of contact and the fact we haven't seen him for as long as I could remember.

Just a few minutes later, we arrive at our destination: an abandoned flatboat stranded on the bank of the river.

It looks like the kind of place you could catch some type of illness. Certainly, any sane person would not want to dwell in there. Which made it the perfect meeting place if you wished not to be disturbed.

We rap three times on the flimsy door, the secret knock we'd been taught, and it opens to reveal a short, black-haired woman.

"Come, come," she says, waving us inside and peering out along the path behind us to check we haven't been followed.

"Any problems getting here?" the woman asks, before plonking down on a ratty chair and lighting a cigarette.

We have seen her at meetings before, of course, but we haven't yet learned her name. From what I understand, it is safer for all of us if we know as little as possible about one another.

I try not to linger onto *why*.

Helga smirks, "None."

The woman nods her head slowly, observing us through slitted eyes from behind the swirling smoke of her cigarette.

"I hear only good things about you two," she says as we await Meyer, "Only good things."

A tight-lipped smile from me, even less from Helga.

We do not know this woman well, and there is something… intimidating about her.

Suddenly, there's a knock at the door, same as our secret knock, only firmer.

Meyer enters the barge once the woman opens the door for him, his tall frame stooping in the shadows. His black hair almost touches the ceiling, and his expression is troubled, hard.

"The Velvet Glove approach has ended," he says to the woman without so much as a hello.

I look at Helga, clueless about what the 'Velvet Glove approach' means.

"The Nazis are clamping down here now too, even more so. They might have begun their invasion of our neutral country with the aim of annexation, but our resistance and others' have made it clear to them we are not in agreement with their terror."

The woman shrugs and returns to her seat, picks up her cigarette from the tray and taps the ash off the end.

"It was only a matter of time," she says, "We knew this."

Meyer nods, his eyebrows furrowed together, "It's taken longer to happen here but it's happening, nonetheless. Jews are to wear the star, just like in the rest of occupied

Europe. They will be forbidden from attending school and from marrying non-Jews..."

"And the rest," the woman adds, waving her hand before her and blowing smoke out of her mouth.

Meyer nods down at the floor, his arms crossed over his chest as a silence befalls us.

Helga and I have been listening, though we haven't understood a thing. And a hunger to know braves me to interrupt their thoughts.

"What do you mean with 'and the rest'?" I ask, first looking at the woman and then at Meyer.

They exchange a glance, then the woman shrugs her slender shoulders. They must've decided that if we are old enough to shoot a man in the head, we are old enough to know of what they speak, because Meyer clears his throat and explains.

"Throughout occupied Europe," Meyer says, his eyes meeting mine, "the Nazis have been putting people on trains by the thousands. They do not take them simply to ghettos anymore. They have progressed to much viler strategies."

I shift in my seat, wondering if I really want to hear this.

But I do. I need to know. If I am to conquer my amounting guilt for killing a man, I have to know of the extent of the enemy's depravity. Maybe then I will finally be able to sleep again at night, knowing that I may be doing bad things, but they were bad things done for a good cause.

"Where are they taking them?" I hear myself ask, though my ears are ringing.

"Worker camps they are calling them," he says, glancing swiftly at the woman, "But we have received reports of the goings on in there. It is worse than the ghettos. Far worse."

Helga looks at me, then back at them, "How can it be any worse than being left to starve and die of disease?"

The woman scoffs, then leans forward to stub out her cigarette, "You two are too young to imagine how much worse it can be."

"Careful," Meyer grumbles, a warning.

"No, Meyer," she replies, "They want to know so let them know," then she turns back to us and looks us square in the eyes, "Mass extermination. That's what is going on at those camps. Mass. Murder. Not only of Jews but of anyone they do not classify as 'Aryan': Gypsies, homosexuals…"

She shakes her head and inhales deeply while Helga and I stare wide-eyed.

"And the Allies?" Helga asks then, turning her head to address Meyer directly.

He shrugs, runs a hand through his black hair in exasperation, leaving it tousled.

"The allied nations have signed the Declaration by United Nations. They are coming together to defeat Hitler. The bombing of Germany has begun. But we need to keep laying our groundwork. The Nazis will be feeling the pressure now from all sides. It will be dangerous going forward. More dangerous than before."

Helga nods her head. I can sense she is steeling herself for whatever our next task is, however dangerous it might be. And I? I will go wherever Helga goes.

"Now," the woman sighs, clapping her hands together and bringing our attention back to her, "Let's put our heads together. The sooner we take out even one more of those bastards, the better."

Wolfgang

<u>The Netherlands, Giethoorn</u>

I guess when you think like an ally, you notice things that others might miss: fresh footprints in the mud near an abandoned flatboat, a young woman looking over her shoulder before entering a building.

I choose to focus on the flatboat, hoping to make my case to whoever appears there, rather than approach them in public. For what I want to achieve needs to be discussed in private, lest risk it all.

For three nights, I hide in among a copse of alder trees on the opposite side of the river facing the abandoned barge. By the end of the third night, someone approaches it, and I am both relieved and disappointed by how easily I have found them.

Perhaps they need me as much as I need them.

A woman with short, black hair, a slim build, and sharp cheekbones. The same woman I'd spied looking sheepish before entering a building I later found out she was not registered at.

It cannot be a coincidence.

I watch her from the shadows as she lets herself into the decrepit boat, and then there is complete silence once more.

For a moment, I stay still, unsure of what to do next. A rook caws overhead, a fish jumps in the river.

What exactly had I expected to do? Surely these people are armed, same as I? Surely, they won't hesitate to shoot me if I make my presence known.

I look down at my uniform. I should have come in civilian clothing.

I exhale sharply through my nose in irritation. And then I hear voices. I crouch back down quickly and observe as two young women – *girls*, really – walk side by side to the flatboat. They are the same two I had spotted riding their bike around the square the day of my superior's assassination. Could those two teenagers really be heading to a resistance meeting?

I watch in astonishment as one of them knocks on the door, my mouth hanging slightly open to think girls this young are opposing the Reich. The black-haired woman opens the door and ushers them in, and already I can spy another figure approaching in the distance.

A lanky but sinewy man with black hair and a deep frown stalks towards the boat. I'd wager it was his large footprints I had seen in the mud the other day. He is young. Younger than I would've thought. Probably no older than twenty-two.

I do not wait around, slowly retreating into the trees. I cannot make my case like this, not when I am so greatly outnumbered.

I will have to approach one of these people another way. And because I'm not completely naïve, I know I have to find a way of speaking to the person in charge of their party one-on-one.

I follow the man home one night to a building where he ascends to the second floor.

I am wearing my civilian clothes, which I had changed into in an alleyway not far from here.

Making sure to keep my footsteps firm but calm, so that he is not surprised at my approach on the staircase but also not alarmed, I make my ascent a few steps behind him.

He stops at a door and pulls out a key, and I intend to walk past him before making my introduction, so that he does not feel like I am blocking the exit. But before I have a chance to go beyond him, he suddenly spins around and grabs me by the collar. I yelp, purely out of surprise, but then the blood rushes from my face when I feel the metal banister of the staircase pressing against my back, and he pushes my top half over the side. I have a hold of his forearms, but if he plans to push me over the railing, I am done for.

"Who are you?!" he snarls, his eyes boring furiously into me.

I am suddenly grateful for my time at Avegoor, where I learned some rudimentary Dutch from the new recruits.

"A friend," I gasp, hoping it is enough for him to let me go, because I cannot think to have this conversation right here, like this.

He looks me up and down, assessing me, his lip curled up, his teeth bared. I get the distinct impression of a wolf.

"What do you want?" he asks, slightly less aggressively, "I don't know you."

I shake my head and swallow, looking over my shoulder at the great height I am hovering above. I feel dizzy. Heights have never been my forte.

"I want – I want to help," I admit quietly, fighting the urge to push him off me.

I could. If I wanted to. My body has undergone years of physical exercise and training, while he has been living off scraps for who knows how long. Just looking down at our arms, mine are bulky, while his are wiry. If he ever did defeat me, it would be purely on adrenaline.

He must sense this, too, perhaps taking it as a sign that I mean what I say, because he lets go of me.

"Can we talk inside?" I ask, aware of how forward I am being. But I will not speak out here. At a time like this, even the walls have ears. And the ceilings, and floors.

He watches me curiously, but nods once and waves me in. It's sparse inside his tiny apartment, but I didn't exactly expect much.

I take a seat when he offers me one at the kitchen table.

"So," he says in a gruff voice, "Who are you?"

I clear my throat, "I am sure you have gathered already that I am not from here," I say, referring to my accent and poor grasp of the language. He nods, "And I think you knew before you decided to let me in that I am an SS-officer."

He shifts in his seat and pushes his hand in his back pocket.

I freeze, certain he's about to draw a gun on me. But he extracts a packet of cigarettes, and my shoulders relax. He puts one between his teeth and grabs a box of matches from the table. He doesn't offer me one, and I don't blame him. A cigarette is likely all he will get past his lips today besides water, food being a luxury in this country these days.

His silence is confirmation that I was right.

"My name is Wolfgang Herrman. *Hauptscharführer*. Though I see a demotion in my future."

At that, his dark brows twitch, "How come?"

I shrug, "Let's just say, I am not like my fellow soldiers."

"An arsehole?"

"That," I admit with a small smile, "But also, brainwashed."

He nods at me slowly from behind the curling smoke of his cigarette.

"Why are you here?" he asks, "My guess it's not to exchange pleasantries and get to know one another."

"No, not really," I chuckle, and I realise I am more at ease than I thought I would be. I hope he is too.

I lean forward, placing my elbows on the table and lacing my fingers together.

"I do not want your name, nor that of the women you met on the abandoned flatboat –"

He squints menacingly at me, misinterpreting my words.

I raise my hands, showing my earnestness, "Sincerely, this is not a threat. I do not want anyone's names. It is safer that I don't. All I want, is to help."

He stubs out his cigarette on the sole of his boot.

"Well, that much is clear, or else you wouldn't be here," he says, puffing out a stream of smoke into the air, "But what is it you think you can help us *with?* We're pretty well informed as it is."

He is playing hard ball, perhaps hoping to maintain the upper hand. What he doesn't understand is that I don't care to be in charge here. Whatever I have to offer is entirely his to take or leave.

"I have a list of names that might interest you," I say, showing him my hand and hoping he'll accept it, "And I know exactly when they'll be at their most vulnerable."

Abel

<u>France, Le Chambon-sur-Lignon</u>

Mia and Azriel are in love, it is so plain to see.
The mere mention of his name evokes a bright blush to Mia's cheeks. His knock at the door has her rushing to answer it with a ready smile. She floats around the house as though her bliss defies the laws of gravity, and no chore is too challenging to alter her mood.
From what I can tell, he is a good man. A little dull perhaps, but he makes Mia happy in a way I have never seen before, and Pierre, Marie and I are sure that soon, there will be a proposal.
It comes as no surprise then, when Mia returns from their outing one day, that she presents us with a beaming face and a beautiful ruby ring.
"It was his grandmother's," she tells us, practically hopping up and down with glee.
"Mia!" Marie squeals excitedly, embracing her tightly, "I am so happy for you."
A lump forms in my throat to see our adoptive mother hold Mia's face in her hands, beaming with emotion in a way our real mother ought to be.
I shake my head. Force myself to concentrate on the joy.
"I'm so happy for you, sister," I tell her, taking her hand and examining the ring, "It's lovely."
"Isn't it?" she says, turning to hug Pierre, "We're hoping to marry soon," and she looks directly at me as if to convey a secret.
A quick frown twitches between my brows, but before I can enquire further, she takes Marie's hands and jumps up and down like a lovestruck schoolgirl.

Later that night, after Pierre and Marie have gone to bed, Mia comes out of her tiny bedroom and pads across the living room to sit on my bed in the corner.

When we'd moved in, Pierre and Marie's house had not been big enough for us all to have separate bedrooms, and their spare room being so terribly small, I'd offered for Mia to have it for herself. I didn't mind. I'd grown up sleeping in the corner of the living room when we lived in our small house in Germany. This wasn't any different to that.

"Are you asleep?" she whispers into the darkness.

I shift into a sitting position, "What is it?" I say, referring to the look she had given me earlier.

"Nothing bad," she says, and I can hear the grin in her voice, "I just wanted you to be the first to know."

She clears her throat and takes my hand, "I don't want you to think that Azriel and I are getting married *because* of this. God knows he didn't even know until after he proposed," she breathes a laugh to herself, "But, well, you're going to be an uncle, Abel. I'm pregnant."

Immediately, my face lights up and I lean in to hug her tightly, "Mia!" I exclaim, tears pricking my eyes, "Congratulations!"

She laughs, "Can you believe it? I'm going to be a *Mama* and you an *Onkel*."

She crawls under the blanket with me, like we are still little kids, and we talk until way past midnight. About our lives before the war, about the family we have left behind and how happy they would be about this wonderful news. But mainly, we talk about the life her child might grow up to have, whether it will be a boy or a girl, and how it doesn't matter. She tells me she wants to name it after our father if it is a boy, after our mother if it is a girl, and that, so far, it has been an easy pregnancy. She giggles to retell the story of how I had made our mother nauseous for weeks when she was pregnant with me, and I smile fondly at the tale, pushing the sadness down into my gut when it threatens to invade this beautiful moment.

A month after Mia's two wonderful announcements, the influx of refugees seeking shelter at Le Chambon increased drastically, and the parties that would lead small groups of people across the mountains into Switzerland were carefully selected.

To my great disappointment, I was not to be one of them.

"You are too young, Abel," Mia argues when I complain about it, repeating Pastor Trocmé's reasoning, subconsciously holding a hand over her small bump.

I look down at it, wondering briefly how we didn't notice it before. I don't know much about babies and pregnancy. But given the size of her belly, she must already be over four months along.

"Yes, I have heard it all before," I say coldly, "Meanwhile he allows women to take groups of children. How does that make any sense?"

Mia *tuts,* "You know it makes perfect sense. Don't be so stubborn. A woman leading a group of young children is much less likely to be stopped than a man."

I don't reply, ignoring her logic and heading for the door instead.

"Your time will come, *Bruder!*" Mia calls after me as I head into the night and grab the pushbike.

But all I can think of is how everyone's lives seem to be progressing, while I remain still and stagnant; useless. I should be doing more. More for the family I have left behind. More for those here who need protecting. More to assuage some of my amounting guilt. More – just *more!*

Alma

<u>France, Le Chambon-sur-Lignon</u>

"I want you and your mother to go with the next group." My father says this, again, over dinner, same as he has done every evening since Pastor Trocmé had assigned those who would lead the refugees over the mountains.
In the two months that groups have been shepherded to Switzerland by our brave volunteers, Le Chambon has saved over two hundred lives – as well as the roughly two thousand that have found refuge in the village since 1941. But I refuse to be one of those to flee. Because this is not just a pit stop for me, a respite before salvation. This village, and its people, is my home.

"I will go when *Maman* goes," I say now, knowing that though she had previously promised to go when the topic was broached last year, my mother would never leave the love of her life behind.
At my remark, my father looks at his wife, and she averts her gaze to her soup.
An exasperated sigh, "I cannot keep you two safe here," he says.

"But we *are* safe," my mother argues, reaching a hand across the table to squeeze my father's arm, "There is no point in them coming here. If they haven't cared to reach us yet, whyever would they do so now?"
Truthfully, her reasoning is not accurate, because the Nazis need only catch wind of our disobedience, and they would waste no time in storming our village. But I do not dare to correct her, because, essentially, we are both in agreement that the only way that we will leave Le Chambon is if we were physically forced to.

Annika

<u>The Netherlands, Giethoorn</u>

Following our kill of one of the Nazi leaders in broad daylight at the square, they become more vigilant.

They no longer allow themselves to be carefree out in the open, though they still enjoy monopolizing our restaurants and cafés, allowing civilians no access.

As the war intensifies throughout Europe, the Germans demand higher contributions from occupied territories, like our country. And this has led to a vast and swift decline of living standards.

Farmers in the surrounding areas are called upon to support the war effort, ordered to hand over all their produce to the Germans in exchange for food rations. These food rations are pitiful compared to the supply they are handing over, barely seven-hundred calories per person, per day. And we soon hear stories of farmers being shot for keeping 'contraband' food from their own farm to feed their starving families.

Understandably, this affects rations within the towns and villages, and they are now at an all-time low. Food shortages have become a real issue in our small village, and *Mama* spends most of her day standing in queues at the bakery or the butcher's only to come back with a packet of flour or a lump of lard.

"We will be fine," *Mama* tells us when we all return from queueing for hours only to present meagre findings. Thankfully, at least, neither Helga nor I attend school any longer, meaning there are three of us queueing for food now instead of just two. And yet, it still never seems like we receive enough.

The gnawing pain in our stomachs and fatigue aside, it all becomes increasingly apparent how quickly we were wasting away when our clothes begin to feel loose and baggy around our shrinking frames.

"How will I be able to lure one of them out with a body like this?" Helga complains to me now as she stands before the mirror holding her small breasts in her hands, "Look at me, Ani! If I didn't know any better, I'd say I was thirteen. I certainly have the breasts of a thirteen-year-old."
I snicker as I watch her from the mattress on the floor.

"You're beautiful, Helga," I tell her, "That's all they'll care about."
She doesn't respond, continuing instead to examine her bony features, and I try not to stare at her protruding collarbones.
She isn't wrong, of course. All of us have lost a frightening amount of weight, even with *Mama's* little garden on the patio providing us with the odd potatoes and carrots.

"Tomorrow, I will get up at five in the morning to be the first in all the queues," I promise her as I roll off my stomach and onto my back, dreaming of food we will likely never see, "I'll get the finest cuts of meat and the softest loaves of bread."
Helga turns from the mirror and chuckles humourlessly as she sits down on the corner of my mattress.

"Tomorrow, my dear sister," she reminds me, "We shall all be laying low if tonight goes to plan."
I nod, forced back to reality.

"If tonight goes to plan," I repeat.
And suddenly, weirdly, I have lost my appetite.

"How do I look?" Helga asks me for the seventh time as we stand outside the back entrance of the inn. She's wearing her cheery grin, but I can tell it's strained.

"Pretty," I tell her again, adjusting her frilly collar and touching up her red lipstick, the splash of colour making her appear at least her actual age of seventeen.

She nods at me and exhales sharply, "Give me an hour," she says.

"Helga…Meyer said no more than thirty minutes."

"Give me an hour," she repeats, pleading, "I may need to practice on someone before I approach him."

By 'practice' she means flirt. I chew the inside of my cheek as I ponder this.

Then I nod briskly, "I will run to tell them and then I'll be right back."

"*Goed*," – Good – she says, then turns on her heel – literally, she is wearing a pair of our mother's old kitten heels – and heads into the inn through the back entrance.

A burst of laughter and music leaks out into the night as she pushes the door open, then diminishes as it closes behind her, and I am left alone in the dark alley.

I don't waste any time. It will take me five minutes to run to our agreed meeting point by the woods – where Helga is to lure our next target – and five minutes to return. Even at top speed I will make it back to the inn in plenty of time to tail Helga and our prey when she guides him out for a midnight stroll. But still, I want to hurry.

Just in case something doesn't go to plan.

"She asks for an hour," I hiss into the darkness of the small wood near the river, knowing that they will hear.

I do not see them, but I hear the woman *tut* angrily.

Footsteps crunching on leaves signifies someone's approach.

"If you do not make it back here within the hour," Meyer's gruff voice whispers from within the gloom, "we abort, and you or your sister will have to fulfil what that officer is expecting."

Sex, I think. And I swallow hard at the vile notion.

Meyer says it not as a threat or punishment, but rather as a warning, and I nod my head in gratitude, knowing he will see my response as I stand in the moonlight. Then I turn and hurry back, hoping Helga does not take too long to entice the German officer.

I make myself comfortable behind a dumpster overlooking the front of the inn, where Helga will exit from with her 'date' if she is successful.
We don't know where Meyer got his information from, but shortly after the incident at the square, he had come up with a new plan to target these monsters in a more discreet way. The woman had protested a little, arguing that we were too young and inexperienced to be trusted with this role.
I chose to believe she meant it from a place of concern for us. But I doubt it. And really, I completely agreed with her internally, though I would never admit to being scared. And I knew that Helga wouldn't either.
A couple emerges from the inn, but it is not Helga and her officer. Laughter echoes down the road and the couple kiss passionately before hurrying away into the night.
I exhale, shifting slightly to keep my legs from going numb. Two more people exit the inn, this time from the back entrance that spills into the alleyway, the same one where Helga and I had stood just half an hour ago. But it is not a man and a woman this time. I squint and observe as the two uniformed men take a quick look around themselves, then almost gasp when they crush into each other, lips locked and one of them fumbling with the other's belt. I stare in both horror and awe, unable to look away as one of the Nazis kneels down before the other and suddenly takes him into his mouth, a groan escaping him. I have never seen such an intimate act before in all my – almost – seventeen years, and certainly not between two men. My cheeks flush as I continue to watch, surprised to

find that I am craning my neck to see better, a tingling curiosity humming beneath my skin. Though, I am also suddenly grateful that it is Helga who is tasked with flirting with a Nazi soldier and not I.

As the two men continue their clandestine tryst, I begin to worry that they will notice me spying and have me killed for knowing too much – homosexuality being considered by the Nazis as a crime.

But quickly enough, the one on his knees stands up and kisses the other on the lips before going their separate ways, one of them looking over his shoulder as the other hurries away, whistling.

I am still stunned moments later when Helga breezes out of the inn, giggling like a schoolgirl. I shake my head clear and focus on the task ahead.

"Oh, Hans," Helga titters, pressing a hand to his chest as she plants a kiss on his cheek.

The man – Hans – seems responsive to this, and takes her firmly by the hand, pulling her towards the alleyway his colleagues had just vacated.

I jolt slightly where I sit, worried he would think to take her up on her offer right there like those two men had done.

But Helga turns the other way, "Not down there," she pouts, "I had somewhere much nicer in mind."

Hans grins stupidly at her but does not argue, and instead follows her like a love-struck puppy.

She giggles again as they walk arm in arm down the deserted street, and I carefully lift myself up off the ground.

I maintain a good distance, just as we had practiced, and to my credit, even Helga fails to spot me when she looks over her shoulder one time to check her surroundings.

They have reached the edge of the village now and Helga has turned to face Hans as she continues to pull him seductively by the arm towards the woods. The smile on her face and the look in her eyes is easy enough to read, even for someone like me, who has never even kissed a boy before.

Hans begins to peel off his jacket, I assume to lay down on the ground for their better comfort, and for a split second I feel sorry for him. Underneath the murdering and terror, he still cares enough about a girl he has just met to consider a scrap of luxury for her during their midnight coupling.

A scoff nearly escapes me as my train of thought takes me down such a ridiculous path. He doesn't care. None of them do. They are all monsters.

Aren't they?

Helga kneels down on his jacket and smiles up at him as he begins to unbutton his trousers. And for a moment I fear that we have taken too long, that Meyer and the woman have fled and left us to our own devices.

But then, just as I notice a twitch of doubt on Helga's face, a figure comes marching out from behind a tree, a handgun raised in front of them as they approach. The Nazi notices it too and looks up, freezing for a moment. His mouth opens to protest but before even a gasp escapes him, Meyer stuffs the muzzle of his gun into the Nazi's open mouth and pulls the trigger.

Chapter 6

Where does he keep the bodies?

How does he make them disappear?

The man stares down at the headlines from four years ago, when those had been the questions on everyone's lips.
Back then, he never thought that his method of disposal would become front page news.
On the day of the discovery of Josef's body, the man had trudged out of the woods behind the other searchers. He'd lingered on the outskirts, however, as the others had gathered all around the manic mother, who was kneeling in the snow and screeching like a lunatic. They'd exchanged worried glances at one another. Glances that questioned the woman's sanity.
But the man had just waited. They would all soon understand why she was clawing savagely at the mound of half thawed ice that had once been a messy snowman.
She must have seen a tuft of hair, or maybe a toe poking out. Something had clearly triggered her knowledge as to where her child had been all along.
He'd been right under her nose, right in front of her whenever she had looked out the window.
She'd thought her son had built it, the snowman the boy had wished to create that fateful morning. She had

regarded it longingly whenever she'd walked past it during her search for her lost child, unaware that he had been within it the entire time.

For weeks, the public had believed the snowmen to be symbols. That their homes had been marked, and that Death would soon come to collect, or – worse – that it already had.

Oh, the terror they must've felt to finally learn the snowmen were not symbols at all, but the man's method of making his victims disappear, of hiding them in plain sight. The other three children were found quickly thereafter, all of them curled up like babies in the womb, preserved within icy bellies.

He sighs deeply at that memory now, and throws the old newspapers in the bin. They, and the memories, continue to constrict his heart, because four years on, he has not yet achieved his goal. Those articles – and the etchings on his headboard – only goad him now. They twist the knife of guilt in his gut.

But every kill had been for a good cause, he tells himself again. All in preparation for what he had truly set out to do. And with each kill he had felt more and more able to go through with it.

But ultimately, he'd been too weak, is still too weak. He cannot do it. He can't. He can't!

Those four practice runs had been for one thing: preparation.

But they were acts of mercy. He'd spared them a much worse fate.

But this is different, this is harder.

Because what kind of a monster would he be if he killed his own child?

Annika

<u>The Netherlands, Giethoorn</u>

I cover my face but it's too late, I have already seen enough, and a squeal escapes me to see the German soldier's head fling back, the sound of the gunshot ringing in my ears.

"Annika," Meyer's deep voice comes from above me a moment later, and I peek through a small gap in my fingers, breathing raggedly.

He's standing in front of me, a hand outstretched and his face – though partially hidden in shadow – offering reassurance. I take his hand and notice I am shaking. He pulls me up and gives me a nod. Whether in approval of my ability to stand or in satisfaction that I am okay, I do not know.

"Helga?" I call then, remembering she was much closer to the scene than I.

She is frozen in shock, still kneeling on the Nazi's jacket on the ground, staring at the dead body as the woman stands behind her, squeezing her shoulder. I rush over and throw myself in front of my sister, wrapping her in my skinny arms.

"We need to move," Meyer says behind me, "We are out of the way but if someone heard the shot, they might come and investigate. Marta, help her up."

I look up at the woman briefly, finally able to put a name to her face.

Marta hauls my sister upright, her hands underneath Helga's armpits like she is a ragdoll. But Helga's eyes remain fixed on the dead body before her.

I cup her face, forcing her to meet my gaze.

"We need to go, Helga," I tell her, shaking her gently.

She meets my stare and blinks, as though waking from a trance. She licks her dry lips, "Yes, let's go."

Helga changed after that night.
No longer did she exude her natural light-heartedness. That always-present carefree aura she conveyed, was gone.
Days would go by without her even cracking a small smile, nevermind holding much of a conversation.
After the assassination of the German officer, Helga and I laid low, as planned. Just to be safe. And every night, she would cry out in her sleep, her pillow soaked with tears and sweat. Sometimes, her screams were so loud, *Mama* and I worried the whole street would hear her.
But, as always, the enemy was not looking in our direction. They were not searching for two young girls.
And yet, nearly two weeks later, Helga still did not return to her usual self, and I began to really worry about her.

"*Mama*, I think Helga needs to stop," I state to our mother early one morning while Helga is asleep.
It is still dark out, but the gnawing pain in my stomach had woken me, and by the looks of it, so had *Mama's*.
She is doing laundry, folding the few items of clothing we each have.

"She cannot stop," she says without hesitation, "The resistance needs you both."
I bite my lip, "But she is affected," I whisper, "She is not herself."
Mama looks away and continues folding the laundry. I sense a hint of guilt in her, at least, so I know she is as worried as I am.

"Give her some more time," *Mama* offers, "Maybe I can ask Meyer to assign you pamphlet distribution again –"

"What are you talking about?"

I spin around to see Helga standing in the doorway, a frown etched between her light eyebrows, the dark circles under her eyes highlighting my point.

"I'm not going back to doing the pamphlets," she says, crossing her arms over her chest, "Ani?"
I can't help but hear the accusation in the way she says my name.

"We are worried about you," I admit, "You have hardly spoken since…" I trail off.
At that, Helga raises her chin, almost like she is trying to prove to us – or herself – that she is resilient.

"We have the meeting at the barge today," she says, "We don't have time for this kind of talk and frankly, Ani, I am a little offended you would think me so weak."
I bite my tongue and swallow my reply. Nothing I say will make a difference anyway.

When we arrive at the secret location, the door of the abandoned flatboat is flung open, and we are pulled inside by a flustered-looking Marta.

"They have him," she tells us in a rash whisper as she wrings her hands together before her, "The SS have Meyer."
A fearful gasp escapes me, and a knot of dread tightens in my chest. Will they come for us next?

"What happened?" Helga asks incredulously.
Marta is pacing up and down the small barge, chewing frantically on her thumb nail. Her short black hair is a mess, and I wonder if she has slept at all since we parted ways nearly two weeks ago.

"He didn't meet me as arranged, so I went to his building," Marta explains, then looks up at us, "One of them was there."

"The enemy?" I choke.
But Marta shakes her head, "He appeared as one. Has trained as one. But he and Meyer had been

communicating, he said. He told me there had been a raid, and that Meyer had been taken."

"Oh God," Helga breathes, pressing the heels of her hands into her temples, "How do we know if we can trust this man? He might be outside right now! To arrest us all!"

"He's an ally," Marta replies calmly, "He told me he would look out for Meyer however he could. He was sincere. I believe him."

I don't know why, but I suddenly wonder if Meyer and Marta are an item, and am alarmed by the pit of jealousy in my stomach. Then I wonder who this man is, and why he is in the SS if he doesn't share their beliefs.

"What are we to do?" I ask, when no one has spoken for a moment.

Marta exhales and rubs her forehead, like she's trying to coax out a genie to grant us three wishes, "Another resistance member is to meet us here instead of Meyer, to discuss our new assignment."

I nod, and yet I cannot bring myself to correct her. Because I wasn't asking about the assignment. I was asking about what we are going to do to get Meyer out.

If, in fact, there is anything we *can* do.

Wolfgang

<u>The Netherlands, Giethoorn</u>

Luckily, he was captured with no damning evidence on his person. I saw to that by seizing his pistol off the side and looping it through my belt to pass as mine as soon as I'd barged in with my party of soldiers. By some miracle, none of them – besides him – had noticed.

I'd stepped forward to give him a beating when we apprehended him, knowing that at my hand he would suffer far less than at the hands of my colleagues.

As he was hauled upright, handcuffed and bleeding from his lip, I'd curtly voiced that I thought he couldn't possibly be the resistance leader, throwing him a disparaging look and mocking his frail body.

It was all I could do for him. To have done more at this point would've risked my own cover, and my intention to use my position in this war for the greater good.

He will be taken to a police detention centre for interrogation, most likely in Westerbork, since it's closest. From there, depending on his answers, he will either be released or sent to another facility, perhaps a prisoner camp or a concentration camp.

The recent chaos has caused a reshuffling, and a week later, I am replaced with soldiers who the Reich has more faith in to find the members of the Dutch resistance in Giethoorn.

As I travel to my next post, I can only assume that it means he has not given them any concrete information as to his colleagues' whereabouts, and I cringe to think how much torture he must have endured by now. If he isn't already dead.

I don't know where I am to be sent next, or what my new assignment will be. But, as ever, I keep my head down and do as I am told.

Abel

<u>France, Le Chambon-sur-Lignon</u>

Three months.

That's all it took for one of the parties trekking over the mountains to Switzerland to be caught with false papers and to be arrested and interrogated.

Whatever happened to the people who they were smuggling over is anybody's guess.

Tensions arose in the quiet village once news came that we had been compromised, and for the days that followed, there was a palpable buzz of unease in the air.

A sharp screech and the barking of dogs wakes me from my sleep in the middle of the night, and I know it is bad news.

"Aufmachen!"

BANG BANG BANG

"Raus!"

BANG BANG BANG

Out the window, I see SS officers banging and kicking on every door as they make their way past and towards the village centre, where the Protestant Church stands proudly.

"Quick!" I hiss at Marie and Pierre as they hurry to me, "Go out the back door and hide in the woods. They will not search for you there."

Pierre begins to protest, but I shake my head.

"Where is Mia?"

Marie blinks in quick succession and stutters her reply, "Sh – she stayed over. She stayed over at Azriel's."

My stomach drops with dread. But I push my fears aside when another hard knock at our door makes my adoptive parents jump.

I hurry them out the back, grabbing a blanket off the sofa and shoving it at Pierre, "Go!" I command them, our roles suddenly reversed, "Only come back when they have gone!"

When I am satisfied they have taken my advice and are almost out of sight, I close the door quietly behind me and pull on my jacket. Then I rip off the yellow star band from around my arm and hurry to find my papers.

Whistles are blown sharply outside, and I can hear people crying out and the police shouting in German.

Thankfully, having grown up in Germany, I know exactly what they're saying.

They want the pastor, they shout. But the people of Le Chambon only whimper and cry in response, unable to understand.

Quickly, I sneak out the back door again and kneel down in the dirt where I dig a shallow hole with my bare hands. I stuff my yellow star inside, as well as my papers identifying me as a Jew, then I cover it up and pat it down before heading back inside.

"*Aufmachen!*" a German barks, and I reach for the latch and swing open the door.

With my hands raised, palms facing forwards in surrender, I step outside and allow the officer to grab me by the collar.

"*Raus mit dir! Bewegung!*"

He throws me down onto the ground in the middle of the street and I huddle together with the other villagers, some of them children. Over the SS's shouting I hear nothing but crying and begging as the enemy points guns at us and continues searching the houses.

They barge into people's homes, dragging them out by their hair as they scream. I realise that they are separating us into two groups: the ones wearing yellow stars in one clutch, those without in another.

Remaining crouched and with my hands behind my head, I search the crowd of those wearing their stars. I see little Olga whimpering on her new mother's lap. Her new sister cowering in the father's arms. I feel nauseous at the sight but am slightly relieved when I fail to spot Azriel and Mia among them. I pray only that they are smart and do as they are told. Hiding will not serve them well, and unfortunately, Azriel's home is too far from the woods to attempt an escape like Pierre and Marie.

As the chaos continues all around me, gunshots are fired into the air, causing us all to flinch and cry out in fear. And when I gather enough strength to look up, I notice Alma is staring at me from within the crowd wearing their stars. She is looking at me with confusion and regret, as though she wishes she hadn't worn her badge identifying her as a Jew.

The SS call to each other that they have caught the pastor, to which one of them *whoops* and begins to fire shots at the group of Jews before him.

I scream. A bloodcurdling, throaty scream. I cannot stop myself. I am in such utter shock.

With my eyes open wide and my mouth wider still, I stare at the carnage, several people lying face down in a puddle of their own blood as the few lucky survivors cower and cry into the dirt.

I notice Alma on the edge, unhurt, and relief flickers in me for a brief moment.

But it is quickly dashed, when I see Olga and her family, shot down, the father gasping for air as he chokes on his own blood, his wife and the two little girls sprawled dead on top of him.

And then I see them: the man and woman beside Olga's dead family.

Their arms are locked around each other in their moment of despair, as though their love could've shielded the other from this evil.

"Mia…?" I whisper, my voice cracking when I notice the bullet hole in her throat, and the blood gushing from it where she lies, glassy eyed. One of her hands is grasping her belly, her grip slackening as her soul leaves her body, a last-ditch attempt to protect the child within.

"Mia?!"

I scramble up but one of the officers kicks me in the stomach, and I double over in pain, winded.

My sister is dead. The man she'd hoped to marry is dead.

Their child, my niece or nephew – dead.

Just for being Jewish.

I clasp a hand over my mouth as my insides threaten to spill out, but I cannot keep from retching at the madness that surrounds me.

Alma

<u>France, Le Chambon-sur-Lignon</u>

I cower in the dirt with my shaking hands over my head as if they would be able to prevent a bullet from piercing my skull, and I hear one of the Germans hissing angrily.
I look up just as the one who fired at us smashes the butt of his rifle into another's stomach and snarls something at him. Then he calls to the others and waves his arm in a circle, disregarding the one he'd just hit as he is bent over double, recovering himself.
Those of us who are not dead are hauled upright and forced forward.

"Abel –" I call as I am marched past him. He is a retching mess on the ground, but he, along with the others without stars, are not being taken away.

"*Schnauze, Jude!*" one of the officers shouts at me, and I drop my head and keep walking.
Someone takes my arm in the crowd, "Alma!" and I turn to find the pastor's cousin, Daniel Trocmé, who is a fellow teacher at the primary school.

"Daniel," I mumble, a cold dread running through me, "Where are they taking us?"
He does not reply, but by the bob of his Adam's apple as he swallows hard, I know it is nowhere good.
There are maybe twenty of us being bundled into the back of trucks, trucks I had failed to even spot in this terrible darkness until they were right in front of me.
I am pushed forward and nearly fall, only for someone to take hold of my elbow and help me upright.
I instinctively think it is Daniel and am about to thank him when I look upon the face of one of the Nazis. I gasp in terror and recoil.

"Steady," Daniel whispers as he catches me from behind and helps me up into the truck bed.

All around me, people are crying silently as they squeeze first onto the wooden benches of the cargo hold, then on the floor. I climb up behind them, searching each face as people continue to board.

"*Maman!*" I call when I see my mother in the gathering. Relief and dismay overcome me when she meets my gaze, and tears start to fall freely. I'd been certain for a moment that she'd been shot along with the others.

"Where's your father?" she asks me as she bundles me against her chest like when I was a child.

I can but shake my head.

"He wasn't with me in the crowd," she cries, her voice cracking and her eyes pleading, "He must have been put in the other group…"

"Then he is safe –" I tell her, but she is looking around herself frantically, breathing heavily, "Hey, *Maman*," I say, trying to reassure her as best I can, though I, too, am sobbing, "that group will not be taken. They had no star." She nods her head vaguely, "We should have gone when your father said…"

I press my lips together, regret overwhelming me, "I know, *Maman*, I know."

A loud *bang* sounds then as the tailgate of the truck is slammed shut and the Nazi that helped me up moments ago pulls himself inside and stands sentry at the end.

"*Zwölf!*" he shouts at the driver after doing a quick head count of us. As though we were nothing but cattle.

I glare at him, hoping that my hatred will bore a hole right through his skull.

He must feel me scowling at him, because as the truck pulls forward, his eyes meet mine and I realise he is the same Nazi who had hissed angrily at the shooter, the one who had received a sharp thump in the gut for – what? – disagreeing with the random gunfire?

I look away quickly, but not before noticing something in his expression I did not expect. And without really knowing why, I begin counting those around me.

One.

Two.

Three.

Four.

Five.

Six.

Seven.

Eight.

Nine.

Ten.

Eleven.

Twelve.

And me – thirteen.

There are *thirteen* of us on the back of this truck.

And yet I know enough from my Jewish mother – Yiddish and German being similar – that he'd told the others there are twelve.

Abel

To my great surprise and horror, one group of SS officers stayed behind when the others drove away anyone still alive wearing a star. And I can only pray that Marie and Pierre stay in the woods long enough to remain safe. I am standing in a queue now as the sky begins to show signs of dawn, the pale sun slicing into the darkness above, peering over the horizon as if nothing untoward had happened last night. As if the world hadn't been turned upside down.

"*Name?*" the German before me says now as I reach the front of the queue.

I've had hours to think of this moment, and I wasn't about to stutter.

"Walter Schmidt," I tell him, giving the name of one of my old friends from childhood. Back when I was still allowed to have German friends and attend a German school. A good, strong German name, for my brand-new identity as an ethnic German.

"*Alter?*" – Age?

"Seventeen," I tell him, to which he asks me about my parents.

"*Tot,*" – Dead – I tell him.

He looks at me queerly, then scribbles 'orphan' on his list beside my name.

"*Papiere?*" he says then, thrusting his outstretched hand at me.

I give him my best apologetic look, "I lost them."

To my utter astonishment, he believes me, "That way," he points over his shoulder, and I hesitantly walk towards two young teenagers, both looking as confused as I feel.

Chapter 7

Alma

<u>France, somewhere</u>

The dawn comes in soft wisps of lilac and powder blue but two hours after we'd been herded onto these trucks like animals.

There are three trucks in total, though I know there had been four when we'd left. I wonder what the other one had stayed behind for.

Though it is summer, the thirteen of us huddle together as best we can to stay warm in the jerking truck, as well as to offer some semblance of comfort to one another. I look around at their scared faces. My mother, Daniel, several people I have known all my life, and two little girls, a set of eight-year-old twins who I know from sight for being Daniel's students at the primary school. Their father sits beside them, a protective arm wrapped around each of them as they stare eerily ahead, their faces stained with dirt and streaked with tears.

Dust spurts on either side of us as we travel along the road, the truck jolting up and down due to pits in the rural track. My back feels bruised from the constant bumping and banging against the metal side, and yet I know that is the least of my problems if the stories we have heard of the worker camps are true.

If that is even where they are taking us…

As time goes on, I notice the Nazi officer standing guard over us is acting more and more edgy, often looking over his shoulder at the truck behind ours.

I wonder, as I dare to stare up at him defiantly, what he could possibly be so afraid of, when he is the one holding a rifle and we are the ones at his mercy.

A honk of the horn sounds, making us all flinch and the children cry out.

"*Stop! Anhalten!*" someone calls from the truck behind us, and we roll to a stop.

Suddenly, those of us who had been asleep – as asleep as anyone could be in these circumstances – are wide awake, and all our necks are craned like a flock of chickens in a coop, eager to know what is happening.

The truck behind us drives past and parks up beside the one in front. I can just about see the driver of the one truck leaning his elbow out the window as he talks to the driver of the other, a couple of hand gestures, then faint laughter. I sit back, my face contorted with hatred for these men, our captors, who have the gall to laugh and banter while we worry for our lives.

"What is happening?" one of the children whispers, her little voice hitched with terror.

"*Shh,*" hisses our Nazi guard immediately, causing the little girl to duck her head in fright, and I throw a look at him that could have curdled milk.

His eyes briefly dart to mine, but then quickly zeroes in on my mother, who sits nearest to him. I follow his gaze. Is he trying to threaten me?

"*Weiter!*" someone calls, and the truck that overtook us speeds ahead, spluttering dust and stones out behind it. Our truck, I realise, is now the last in line.

Suddenly, once all vehicles have resumed their steady pace over the dust roads, the Nazi clears his throat, and we all turn our heads towards him.

"*Keine Bewegung,*" he mutters, without looking down at any of us.

I glimpse around at the frightened people in the truck, searching for understanding in their eyes. But they, too, are as bewildered as me. Yiddish and German might be similar, but it isn't the same.

The Nazi nudges my mother with his boot, *"Du,"* he mutters, then jerks his chin slightly.

I feel rage boiling inside me to see him kick my mother when she is down, but I know better than to cause a scene. After all, he is the one in control here.

When none of us move, he looks down at my *maman* and jerks his head meaningfully. She turns to me with pure terror in her eyes. I shake my head ever so slightly, trying to communicate that she should not antagonize him, though none of us know what he even wants.

The Nazi's jaw clenches, and then he kneels down to tie his boot lace.

We all flinch, some of us gasp, and I can see his shoulders tense.

He looks up and past us to the driver of our vehicle. I follow his gaze to the back of the other Nazi's head, unconcernedly staring ahead as he drives. And I suddenly realise what he is trying to do.

Zwölf! He had called to his comrades. Twelve. Though we are thirteen in this truck.

Had he meant to save one of us all along?

"Raus," he hisses at my mother now, and again she looks entirely confused and scared.

I search his expression. He is practically pleading. This is her chance.

I grasp my *maman's* face in my hands and make her look at me, "Go, *Maman*," I mouth.

She shakes her head, a soft squeak in her throat escaping, *I won't leave you,* written all over her face.

But I smile tearfully back at her, *Yes, you will.*

In her eyes flashes my entire life: the first moment she held me, the endless, sleepless nights, my first birthday and all the ones that followed, my first day of school, the tantrums, the falls, the tears, the laughter. I can tell it physically pains her heart to be cleaved from me like this. I kiss her cheek and try to smile reassuringly at her.

And just as the German soldier stands back up from tying his boot lace, my mother, my wonderful *maman*, heaves herself over the tailgate and out of the moving vehicle, to safety.

Wolfgang

<u>France, somewhere</u>

She is the first person I have truly, *truly* saved, and it is exhilarating!

Adrenaline rushes through me with each second that passes since she hauled herself off the truck. And when I am sure that my colleagues haven't noticed, I look over my shoulder and search the road.

She is nowhere to be seen, and unless we double back for whatever reason, that woman will be spared.

I had selected her out of the thirteen present not only for her proximity to the edge, but because she appeared resilient. Though, more than anything, I would've wanted to save the children, or at least one of them. But I hadn't been sure if they'd survive the fall off the moving truck, let alone find their way back home. But now I am glad I chose that woman. She has succeeded in getting away – hopefully – unharmed.

I look down at the twelve remaining faces before me, fighting hard not to smile with joy at my achievement. But that delight is quickly dashed when I look upon their terrified faces, some streaked with dust, others with blood on their clothes or caked in their hair. And my achievement is put back into perspective. Compared to the many, saving but one is not a triumph.

It is pathetic.

Especially, since I know exactly where these poor souls are being taken.

Abel

<u>France, Le Chambon</u>

It is just hours after the raid at Le Chambon, though it feels like it has been days.

I and two other 'orphans' – who had displayed falsified German papers – are bundled into the last remaining truck and driven away without so much as a moment to say goodbye to our loved ones. I imagine – the officers believing us to be orphans – that they think we don't have anyone left to say goodbye *to*.

Which is why, as the truck picks up speed along the dirt road out of the village, I do not dare shed a tear over my sister's murder. Though the image of Mia's dead body, wrapped in Azriel's lifeless embrace, and her limp hand hovering over her baby bump, pounds in my mind's eye. It is why I do not dare to even glimpse towards the woods behind Marie and Pierre's home – *my* home.

I don't know where they are taking us, and for the longest time, I don't care.

The three of us – I, a boy, and girl who appear no older than thirteen – are silent on our long journey, occasionally smiling thinly at one another, or look away entirely.

In the hours that go by, two Nazi officers sit inside the truck, while one stays with us, guarding us in the cargo bed.

I could ask where we are headed, I suppose, being able to communicate with them in their mother tongue. But I cannot bring myself to.

Everyone I have ever cared about has been taken from me. And I will likely never know if either my real family back in Lodz, or those I have grown to love in Le Chambon, are alive.

So then, what is the point of anything anymore?

I wonder where they took Alma and the others. Will they go to one of those worker camps we'd heard so much about? Her expression of pure regret as she saw me in the group without my star haunts me still, her onyx eyes flashing with a thought I had no business knowing. I wonder if I will ever see her again. If I will ever see anyone I care for again.

A sharp stinging seizes my throat, and I know the threat of tears is close. I wonder if these Nazis will even notice if I cry. If they'll even care.

But in the effort of maintaining my disassociation with Le Chambon, in the effort of staying alive, I force the tears away.

I am Walter Schmidt now, and Walter Schmidt has no affiliation with that French village.

I continue to tell myself that lie again and again as the truck rumbles on underneath me. Because in order to do what my dear mother had told me when we first left Lodz – *Go, and live* – I will have to accept this lie. I will have to shape a new self from this falsehood.

Because the truth, *my* truth, wants to kill me.

Germany, Plön

We arrive back in the country of my birth and travel to the town of Plön in the district of Schleswig-Holstein, just two hour's drive from where I had grown up.

I'd never been here before, and yet I feel a hint of nostalgia simply for being back in Germany in general. I hadn't realised how much I'd missed it. And I only wish the circumstances of my return were entirely different.

"Plön Castle," the Nazi guarding us in the back of the truck says, jerking the butt of his rifle ahead.

We follow his gaze just as we turn a corner, and a great big, old building comes into view.

Situated on a hill overlooking the Lake Plön, the castle is a striking, tall white structure surrounded by a green garden. And despite myself, I gawk at its height and architectural style.

We drive through the gate, and I am surprised to see several young men walking about in uniforms, laughing and talking.

"Where are we?" I say, speaking for the first time since being, essentially, kidnapped, "Why did you bring us here?"

The Nazi scoffs, "You three are too young to join the army," he juts his chin at the castle, "You'll stay here at the boarding school for Hitler Youth."

At that, my eyes widen in terror, but I am able to quickly disguise it as fascination.

"There are only boys," the girl beside me whispers in French, noticing the lack of her gender.

The soldier hops off the truck when it comes to a halt, "*Komm*," he says to me and the other boy, "*Raus jetzt*."

The girl whimpers, "What about me?" she asks me, her voice breaking.

I turn to the Nazi and translate.

He shakes his head, "She will be taken to an all-girl's Hitler Youth. The Band of German Maidens," he says, "Tell her to stay there."

I tell the scared young girl what our enemy said, then sidle past her, offering a reassuring smile. I want to convey to her to simply keep up the pretence, that she at least does not have any way of being caught out as being Jewish unless she outright tells someone – unlike the boy and I, who are circumcised.

"Stay strong," I tell her quietly in French, "Remember who you are, but keep it secret."

She nods at me and wipes her tears, then sniffs loudly. I can practically feel her steeling herself for whatever lies ahead, and I squeeze her arm companionably, "Stay safe,"

I mumble, and then I walk away towards my new, new, new life.

Chapter 8

Alma

<u>Somewhere</u>

I think only of my *maman* as the trucks continue on, none the wiser that one of their captive Jews has escaped. Regardless that we'd been travelling slowly due to the rough terrain when she dove out, I think of how much pain she must be in as she stumbles back home following such a fall.

We'd been driving for at least two hours by that point, which means she would have to walk for a fair few hours before she made it back to Le Chambon, if she even knew the way.

But despite all the worrying, I tell myself that she is safe. Safer than she would be had she remained on this truck, at least.

The Nazi who aided her escape hasn't looked at any of us since it happened, and even when I cast quick glances at him, he remains stiff-backed and staring straight ahead. And I wonder why he helped her, while, at the same time, continuing to hold the rest of us hostage.

<u>Poland</u>

I know we have arrived because the smell of death is growing stronger.

"Where are we?" I whisper to Daniel, who has moved to sit near me.

He shakes his head, and we all stare wide-eyed at the electrified, barbed-wire fence and gate ahead.

It is one of the worker camps we have heard so much about. That much, at least, we know.

ARBEIT MACHT FREI

The German words hang like a warning over the gate as we enter, and I wish I knew what it meant and where we are.

I look at the children in the truck with us, and my face crumples up with worry for them. We've heard horrifying stories of what goes on in these camps. People being shot for sitting down to take a break. People dying of starvation or disease. A heaviness takes root in my chest to think that we cannot even save ourselves, nevermind the little ones who count on us grown-ups to keep them from harm.

Through the gate, I am met with a world I could never have imagined, not even in my darkest nightmares.

"Oh my God," I breathe.

There are ghost-like figures, corpses really. Some watching us, most ignoring us, and all of them with shaved heads and great big protruding eyes.

The truck rumbles past them and comes to a stop, and then the officer who saved my mother jumps off and opens the tailgate.

"*Raus,*" he orders – dare I say, somewhat gently? – and we hop out one by one.

Daniel offers me a hand to climb down, then I turn to help one of the twins. I hold her in my arms as though she were a much younger child.

Suddenly there are dogs barking angrily at us. I flinch and the girl in my arms squeals with fear. Laughter erupts from the officers standing around, and then someone cracks a whip, and instructions are shouted at us.

We understand that men are to go one way, and women another, and the girl in my arms turns a terrified face to her father.

She wriggles out of my grasp and throws her arms around him.

"No, *Papa*, don't leave us," the twins say in unison.
He comforts them with kisses and strokes their hair, but I do not hear what he says to get them to comply, because I am being dragged forward to join the line.

"Alma!" Daniel calls then, and I search the crowd of uniformed corpses to find him being hauled away.

"Hey!" I shout, waving my hand in the air to get the officers' attention. Where are they taking him?!
I am about to go after him when the officer that had saved my mother grabs me roughly by the arm and forces me to stay in line with the women.

"Let go!" I dare to grunt, ripping my arm free.
He only stares me down, but not before I see in his eyes a hint of something besides what I had expected. Instead of pure anger and hatred, I notice a warning. Like he's pleading with me to keep quiet.
These are not the eyes of a murderer, but that of a human being.
I am stunned by my thought, and watch him closely as he steps back, heading away from me and into the crowd.
The group of women I have travelled here with are led away.
I think I hear a child screaming and I look over my shoulder to see the twins being ripped from their father, the three of them crying loudly. Snot and tears stain their faces, and before I know it I, too, am a wreck.
I try not to stumble and fall in this muddy terrain, but I cannot stop crying. Because though I have never been here before, somewhere deep in my soul, I know that those little girls likely won't survive the day.

Abel

<u>Germany, Plön</u>

In the days that follow my arrival at Plön Castle, I quickly learn that the curriculum we are being taught is vastly reduced from that of the mainstream school system I remember. Every morning, we are woken by a trumpet call – which, at first, had made me jolt upright out of bed, scared for my life – and expected to line up for a healthy breakfast.

Health and hygiene are of great importance in the Hitler Youth, and where grammar and mathematics had once been a core element of education, physical exercise and learning how to fire a gun are deemed of much greater value here.

I learn to shave, German military regulations emphasising a clean-shaven face to ensure a proper seal for gas masks. Though I have only fine black tufts above my lip and chin, I cut myself the first time, and it takes me back to the time Pierre had offered to teach me this life lesson. I wish I hadn't been so stubborn. At least then I would've learned from someone who cares for me.

Showering is tricky. The shower blocks are not private, and the boys from my dormitories all bundle in together at the end of each day. Being Jewish, however, I know I will immediately be found out if someone notices that I am circumcised, and so I refrain from showering with the other students whenever possible. Sometimes there is no avoiding it, and I stand facing the wall, or even shower while wearing underwear, claiming timidity. Better that, than being caught out and imprisoned...

We hike, and sing, and do workouts. We learn how to march in military formation. By the end of each day, I must admit, I am glad to lie down in bed. And I am asleep within mere moments.

There are swastika flags *everywhere*, as well as photographs of Adolf Hitler – as if we could ever forget why we are here.

On Fridays, there was a type of assembly, where the *Schulleiter* would begin by patrolling up and down the auditorium.

"If the *Führer* asks you to die for Germany, what do you do?"

Die! we all roar in unison.

"What do you fear?"

Nothing!

The boy I had arrived with and I, have gone our separate ways, silently agreeing that to stick together would only increase our chances of being discovered. I sometimes spot him in the dining hall or at track. But otherwise, we are strangers.

It is on the third day of my arrival that I meet Otto.

"*Na, komm, du bist dran,*" – Hey, come on, it's your turn – he says, waking me from my open-eyed sleep.

I look about myself, a warmth of embarrassment creeping up my neck, "Oh, sorry," I say, before pressing the butt of the rifle against my shoulder and taking aim.

I fire, the rifle knocking back against my tender flesh, and I grimace. I'm not yet used to shooting.

"Next time," the boy says. And we both look at the target, where my shot is completely off.

I breathe an embarrassed laugh, and we move aside to allow the line to continue.

"I'm Walter," I tell him, the lie tasting bitter on my tongue, "Sorry about before. I think I was sleeping with my eyes open."

He laughs easily, "I have those days. They work us to death."

I grin at his joke and accept his offer to sit with him at lunch. All the while thinking about the stories I've heard of the worker camps. And I doubt very much that it is anything like this.

Otto is the same age as me and has a mop of curly blond hair, an infectious laugh and a loud, confident voice, which I quickly realise has earned him respect among the others.

"What do you think of Professor Weis?" he asks me and the small group of boys we are sitting with as we take our lunch break.

I look up from the sandwich I am eating but do not offer an opinion, since I am yet to meet said professor.

One other boy shrugs, "His classes are fascinating."

"Boring is the word I'd use," says another.

A couple of the boys chuckle.

Otto takes a swig of his water, "I'd agree that they are fascinating," he says, and the few who deemed the man boring a moment ago are now looking awkwardly at one another.

"Yes, fascinating," one of them says, changing his mind as to Otto's opinion.

I smile as I take another bite of my food, entertained to see how Otto has a way of making people dance to his tune. I have no doubt he'll climb the ranks effortlessly in the years to come.

"What does he teach?" I ask Otto, wiping my mouth with a napkin.

"Eugenics," Otto replies, "Race studies and the inferiority of Jews."

I raise my eyebrows and nod vaguely at the information. And I already know that I'm going to hate the man.

As we enter the classroom, which is decorated with a huge swastika flag on the rear wall, we take our seats and face the front, where a short but stocky man stands holding a skull.

The famous Professor Weis, I think, assessing him.

He has a smoothly shaved face and dirty blonde, almost brown, straight hair, which he wears at a side parting. As the class settles down, he watches us from behind round-rimmed spectacles, which he pushes up his nose with his pinkie finger.

"How do you recognize a Jew?" he says as way of introduction to the lesson. And I almost fall off my chair.

"Well, it's quite simple!" he continues, not waiting for an answer and turning his back on us to put the skull on his desk.

I look at Otto, who sits beside me, and cock my head to one side as if to say, *seriously?*

He nods and grins back at me enthusiastically.

"Jews," Professor Weis says, elongating the word so that the 's' carries on like the slither of a serpent, "Have a completely different skull composition to ours."

He turns around to face us again, this time holding up an image, a rather unflattering picture of a Jewish man.

"As you can see," he says, pointing at the image, "Jews have a high forehead, a hooked nose, and the back of their skull," he whips round and grabs the skull on his desk with one clawed hand, "is flat."

I notice I am subconsciously running a finger along my nose, checking for a hook that might've appeared overnight. I quickly cross my arms over my chest before someone sees.

"In contrast to the Jewish man," the professor continues, "the Aryan man has no such imperfections. And if you are able to understand and spot these racial differences, no Jew will ever be able to deceive you."

I hold back a scoff. I was right in thinking I would hate the man.

Just then, the professor stretches his arm and points straight at me, and I swear I almost lose control of my bladder.

"You, young man," he says, "Come forward."

Oh, no.

This is it. The moment I'm discovered.

Did he notice me fidgeting?

Did he spot me the moment I'd entered the classroom?

Did my 'misshapen' skull give me away?

I glance at Otto as though he could save me, but he is staring excitedly at me. He would give anything to be called on by the professor.

How surprised he will be to learn he has been becoming pally with a Jew.

I swallow hard, but I stand up and walk to the front.

"This specimen right here…" the professor says, as he pulls a chair in front of him and pushes me down onto it. I am now sitting facing the class of twenty something young men. If I weren't terrified of being discovered, this moment would be nerve-wracking enough already.

The professor, standing behind me, clamps my head with his hand and moves it side to side. He proceeds to measure my forehead and nose, and the circumference of my head. At one point I am sure I hear him mutter something under his breath, but I do not enquire as to what he thinks he has found.

"This specimen…is perfect."

What?

I have misheard. Surely…

I let out a puff of air and blink in quick succession, relief flooding my veins.

"Aryan traits!" Professor Weis announces.

He waves me away and continues to talk, though I hear nothing besides the blood pumping in my ears as I walk back to my seat, my feet as heavy as two blocks of lead.

Annika

<u>The Netherlands, Giethoorn</u>

Following Meyer's arrest some months ago, we were instructed to keep a low profile.

A short, round-bellied man with a goatee had come to the barge that day in Meyer's stead, and introduced himself as Pieters. Marta appeared already to know him, which relaxed us a little.

Following feedback from other resistance groups in the surrounding area, Pieters had advised we lay low until we heard more about Meyer.

That meant nothing from distributing pamphlets, to luring Nazis to their deaths, and anything else in between.

"It will do him no good if we continue to aggravate the enemy while they have him," Pieters had said, stroking his goatee.

We agreed, of course. Marta more reluctantly than Helga and I. Though she nodded her consent eventually.

But one month turned into two. And then three.

And before we knew it, ten months had gone by where we'd done nothing but wait around. I couldn't help but think that Meyer would not have wanted us to waste so much time for his sake. For all we knew, he was already dead…

That thought would crop up in my mind from time to time, and a strange sadness would form in my throat. But I pushed it away. If he was dead, surely, we would know.

One silver lining from this was that Helga seemed to no longer suffer from her nightmares – not that I knew of, at least – and our nights returned to normal.

And yet, I for one, was getting tetchy.

Helga and I spent our days tending to our pathetic little garden with *Mama* – carrots, onions, and potatoes growing in whatever pots we could spare – or queuing up at shopkeepers in the hope of even the smallest morsel of nourishment.

Food shortages continued throughout the country, and things that had previously come in abundance were now luxuries we thought we might never see again.

Today – like most days – I wake up at four in the morning with a pain in my stomach so intense that I know sleep will not find me again until I have something to eat. With a look out the bedroom window into the dark early morning, I decide to get dressed. If I am the first in line today at the butcher's or the bakery, maybe we will get something that will actually fill our stomachs for once.

All the way there I begin to salivate at the thought of the juicy cut of meat, or the soft, warm bread we would surely be able to feast on today.

My stomach grumbles so loudly all of a sudden that I am sure I have woken up half the street.

But when I arrive at the butcher's – my skinny arms wrapped around myself against the night chill, our basket dangling from the crook of my elbow – my excitement is snuffed out.

I am not the only one to have this bright idea, at least twenty people having gathered outside the butcher's already. The bakery around the corner has even more hopefuls standing in line.

"Here, take this," the butcher's wife says to me almost four hours later, pressing something wrapped in cloth into my hand.

I look down. I hadn't expected anything else when her husband gave me a lump of lard and two chicken feet – which was already enough to make my mouth water again.

"What's this?" I ask as I start to unwrap it.

"*Nee, nee,*" – no, no – she says, pressing her hands over mine and looking around, "When you are home," she mumbles, "Keep it hidden under your other items."
I look down into my empty basket and she follows my gaze. Her eyes shine with pity, but I smile at her in thanks and nod my goodbyes, trying not to think of how gaunt I must look to have warranted such a gift.
Next, I head to the bakery around the corner, where I stand for three hours before reaching the front. By then, I am not only feeling exhausted but also hopeless.
"Ani," the baker greets me.
I nod and offer him a small smile, "Please," I mumble, same as I'm sure everyone does.
But he shakes his head, "I only have two crusts of rye bread left. I can spare one for you."
I nod enthusiastically. It was more than I had expected, and I almost cry with gratitude as I stumble out of the queue.

"*Mama!*" I call as I burst through the door to find my mother and sister hunched over the pots of our pitiful garden, picking at weeds.
They stand up, wide-eyed and fearful until they see my beaming face.
"I got us lard and a crust of bread and chicken feet," I announce, as if it were a feast fit for a king.
Helga sighs contentedly and puts the watering can down while *Mama* comes over to me and takes the basket off my arm.
"What's this?" she asks, and I remember the butcher's wife's secret bundle.
"Oh, I don't know," I say, Helga and I gathering around *Mama* to see what is wrapped in the cloth.
And the three of us almost faint in amazement to see three beautiful, fat, juicy sausages rolling out into my mother's palm.

Meyer is released thirteen months after he was taken, the Nazis having been unable to source any connection between him and the Dutch resistance.

According to Marta, who met with him briefly following his return home, he had remained steadfast to his innocence, never once letting on that he even knew the Netherlands was fighting back against the Germans.

After all, the Dutch Resistance was such a small minority, it could well be that the average citizen didn't know about its existence.

"He pretended to be deaf," Marta informs us with a chuckle at our first meeting in over a year. She shakes her head, "Didn't stop them from torturing him, though."

My chest pinches to think of what he's had to endure to survive. But truth be told, I couldn't even imagine it.

"Is it safe for us to begin our missions again?" I ask, "So soon after Meyer's release?"

Marta pulls a face, "It's not ideal. But we cannot hold back any longer. Too long have we waited for his safe return. People are dying every day."

I nod slowly.

If Meyer is clever, he will simply remove himself from the resistance. In order to survive, he needs to stay away.

And for some reason, that thought makes me as sad as when I'd thought he was dead.

Chapter 9

Alma

<u>Poland, Auschwitz</u>

They shave us.

Not just our heads, but all of us. Even our pubic hair. What they want with it, I do not know.

Afterwards we're given drab grey dresses – the women's uniform – and sent on our way to stand in another line outside.

I squint at the midday sun, feeling suddenly like a creature instead of a human being. Without my hair and my own clothes, I no longer feel like myself. I look around at the women walking with me: we all look the same. Even the terror in our eyes is a commonality.

I don't dare to speak, not even to ask if anyone knows where the two twins from my village have been taken to. I don't think anyone could tell me, anyhow. And honestly, I'm not sure I want the answer. Which in and of itself means I already know what has happened to them. My stomach clenches, and I am sure I'm about to throw up when suddenly a cry bursts out near me, and three men in striped uniforms and caps throw themselves on the floor.

I jump back and notice some people stepping away and some others inching closer. I don't know what is happening.

"Probably a blade of grass," a woman's voice beside me says in French, and I realise I must have spoken aloud.

"What?" I ask, dumbfounded and simultaneously filled with relief to have someone understand me. I look back at the three men as one of them elbows another right in the nose, but he does not stop fighting.

"A blade of grass," the woman repeats, "If you see such a rarity, here in this shithole, you eat it."
She says it so nonchalantly, as if it is obvious, and yet I could never imagine being so hungry. Nor could I imagine anything growing here, where the ground is a trampled, grey mass of mud. A wasteland.

"Esther Rosenberg," she says, standing beside me as I inch forward in the line.

"Alma," I reply, "Alma Basson."
I search her face. Brown eyes, a small nose, thin lips. Her hair is short but not shaved to the scalp like mine.

"Did they not take your hair?" I ask.
She reaches a hand to her head, "Oh this? You think this is my doing?" a humourless chuckle, "No, they took mine too. Everyone has their hair shaved off. First thing they do. This is my regrowth."
I look at it again, "What's the next thing?"

"Hmm?"

"You said the shaving was the first. What comes after that?"
Esther nudges her chin along the line, "If you're lucky, and get placed in this line, you get your number."
I look up see a row of tables where men in striped uniforms sit holding something. Men in white coats stand behind them.

"My number?" I ask, my voice shaking.
Esther pulls her sleeve up and flashes me her forearm. On it, I see a row of five numbers tattooed onto her skin.

"What did you mean 'if you're lucky?" I whisper, "What happens if you don't get put in this line?"
She looks over her shoulder and I follow her gaze to a big, low building in the distance with two tall chimneys.

"They put you in the shower," she says simply, and I cannot imagine why that would be so bad.
But before I can say anything further, I feel someone push me forward and force me down onto a chair. I look over

my shoulder in search of Esther, but she has gone, and the man in front of me grabs my arm and pulls up my sleeve.

"What is the number?" I hear myself ask, though I hadn't meant to voice my confusion.

I look up at the man's expressionless face. He is wearing a striped uniform and is as thin as a skeleton, a prisoner, just like me. But he doesn't reply, and focuses only on my arm as he brings the needle down. A croaked yelp escapes me as he pricks the inked needle repeatedly into my skin, and my vision blurs.

I watch, powerlessly, as I am marked.

289102

Afterwards, I stare down at it, the numbers oozing a mixture of ink and blood, a black sap seeping from my skin as though evil itself had just been poured into me. Tears continue to haze my vision as I stand and walk away, holding my arm. But they are not tears of pain or sadness. They are tears of hot white fury. A rage that burns from deep down inside me, to realise that I am no more to them but a number. One among hundreds of thousands. I clench my teeth together tightly to keep in the scream that threatens to thunder out of me. For not only have they managed to take my family, my home, my *hair*…they have just succeeded in taking my entire identity.

Wolfgang

<u>Poland, Auschwitz</u>

Following my confrontation with my superior officer during the raid at Le Chambon, where he had struck me hard in the gut with his rifle, I was deemed 'unreliable' and 'insubordinate'.

True, I had acted spontaneously, disturbed by his random firing into the crowd, leaving dozens dead. But I did not, and do not, regret my reaction, regardless of my punishment. I had reacted on impulse, my horror overshadowing my need to keep up my façade of a loyal Nazi soldier.

My defiance has landed me here in Auschwitz, demoted for my 'unruliness'. And frankly, it could not have been a better outcome, because now I was well and truly where I needed to be.

There was nothing I could've done for the children that had been brought here with me. From the moment they had been herded onto the truck, their fates had been sealed, too young to work and deemed useless to the Reich.

I squeeze my eyes shut to clear my thoughts of their frightened faces as they flash in my mind. To show any emotion for the prisoners in front of the other officers would only lead to further demotion. And then what good would I be?

By now, the twins will already have gone to the gas chamber – if they were lucky! – or to Dr. Mengele to be experimented on – if they weren't. My skin crawls to think of it. But I cannot linger on their fate for too long, however much they deserve to be remembered.

After all, I am only one man, swimming against a tidal wave of reckless hatred. There is only so much I can do.

But I will try. God help me, I will try.

Abel

<u>Germany, Plön</u>

Each day consists of studying history and Eugenics, of marching with my fellow students and firing guns. Physical exercise is of main priority. Boxing is compulsory.

And despite the fact I know exactly why I am here, despite the fact I am a lamb in the lion's den, I am slowly beginning to understand just *how* the Nazis are getting these young men to believe in their own superiority.

When Professor Weis puts up a caricature of a Jew on the board for us to see, pointing at the traits that are supposedly associated with inferior species, the young men trust his word. He is not only our elder, but also our teacher, a learned man, a man of science. Surely, he knows best.

And paired with constant praise, daily celebration of their superiority and Germany's power, it only makes sense that these young minds would be shaped to believe themselves as such. After all, what child does not want their country to be the best in the world?

I make sure to excel at Eugenics in order to maintain my exterior persona of a pure Aryan, ensuring I extensively study the Nazis' ridiculous criteria for spotting a Jew. Though it pains me to read about some of the vile things the subject teaches. Professor Weis often praises me in class, and I take comfort in the knowledge that I am firmly hidden in plain sight.

I have embraced Walter Schmidt. He and I are one and the same. Though we are – according to the Nazis – complete opposites.

Otto and I have become fast friends, doing almost everything together when our schedules permit it. We sit beside one another in Eugenics and fall in line during marches. We eat lunch with a handful of other boys, and take target practice together, my aim having improved greatly since those early days.

I am beginning to feel a sense of pride for what we, as young people, are achieving here. The sense of community is exhilarating.

And yet sometimes, the guilt sneaks in and shames me for how I am surviving. A little voice whispers in my ear at night that I am betraying my family, my religion, myself. It is true. I know it. But in order to survive, I have to detach myself from Abel Freidman and carry on pretending to be Walter Schmidt. If I do not, if I give in to my shame and admit I am an imposter, it would be suicide. And so, I learn to live with the amounting remorse that eats away at me, and I try to bury it, instead, with the growing delight I feel for being part of something bigger than myself.

"Squeeze in closer there on the end!" the photographer calls, waving his hand at me and the other boys on the edge. We are posing for a photograph of Professor Weis' class, twenty-eight of us in matching uniforms standing tall behind the professor in his white coat. He looks more like a doctor than a lecturer in that garb.

We scootch closer to our fellow youths and grin at the camera. The flash goes off and the photographer stands up straight.

"*Wunderbar!*" he confirms, and we all relax.

"Mr Schmidt!" I hear my name – my alter ego's name – being called and I turn towards the voice.

The professor – who I continue to dislike despite my growing acceptance of my surroundings – stands before me now. He pushes his glasses up the bridge of his nose and grins at me. I notice, for the first time, his exceptionally straight teeth.

"Excellent work in class, Schmidt," he says with a nod. Otto, who stands beside me, elbows me in congratulations. I smile in thanks.

"*Danke*, Professor Weis," I say, though a knot of shame squeezes my insides to know I am doing well in his class.

"I would like to invite you to dinner at my home," he says now, and I am completely taken aback, "As my most exceptional student. It is somewhat of a tradition I began a couple of years ago when I became a professor here."
I suddenly feel a chilling tingling all over. I look at Otto, hoping for clarification. Is it true that it's a tradition of his? Judging by my friend's excited – yet, jealous – expression, I gather this is a much sought-after occurrence.

"Dinner?" I ask, stalling for time to think. Do I really want to go to this Nazi's home? Will it really be as innocent as a simple dinner? Will it even be safe? "Dinner, ju – just you and I, Professor?"
At that, the stocky man laughs.

"No, no," he says, "My daughter will also be present. She is the one who cooks, actually. I cannot boil an egg."
I nod slowly in understanding, unsure if the presence of this supposed daughter brings me any comfort or not.
The professor and Otto are both staring at me, awaiting an answer, and I can no longer avoid it.

"It would be my pleasure," I say, forcing myself to grin enthusiastically.
Otto slaps me companionably on the shoulder, and Professor Weis shakes my hand, then walks away.
And I am left regretting every single decision that has led me to this moment.

Later that day, as I arrive at Professor Weis' house just beyond the perimeter of the boarding school, I wipe my sweaty hands on my trousers and inhale deeply to calm my nerves before knocking on his door.

I hear footsteps approaching and just a moment later, the door is swung open.

Before me stands a young woman with long blond hair hanging over her shoulder in a plait. She is wearing a blue floral dress underneath a white apron, and a soft smile.

"Walter, is it?" she asks, though she doesn't wait for an answer before stepping aside and waving me in, "*Papa* is in his study."

She closes the door behind me.

I stand there feeling both extremely exposed in the Nazi professor's house, as well as slightly awkward to be singled out for this dinner.

The daughter offers me another smile and walks ahead, but when I do not follow, she looks over her shoulder and jerks her head for me to follow.

I hurry after her and immediately feel my cheeks burning when her eyes crinkle with amusement.

"In there," she says, showing me to a room just around the corner, then turning to leave.

For a brief moment, I watch her. She is heading towards a room with an open glass door I assume is the kitchen, humming lightly as she goes.

"Come in! Come in!" the professor's voice calls then, and I step into the room.

Weis' study is warmly decorated with portraits on the walls and a Persian rug on the floor. There's a brown leather sofa with a coffee table beside it on one side of the room, a wooden desk on the other. The professor sits at the desk, holding a glass of amber liquid in his hand as he examines a map under the light of a Kaiser Idell desk lamp.

"Schmidt," he says in greeting, turning around and knocking the drink back in one gulp. He stands up to shake my hand, "Good to see you."

I nod, "*Vielen Dank*, again, for the invitation," I say, though I wish I were anywhere else but here.

Weis waves my thanks away, "It is tradition! My best student should receive special treatment. That is my belief, anyway."
I smile tightly.
"I see you have already met my daughter, Frida?" he says, looking over my shoulder.
I turn to find the daughter bringing in a tray with cups and a teapot.
"Uh, yes, briefly," I say, unsure what I am meant to say. The daughter – Frida – places the tray down on the coffee table by the sofa and looks at her father.
"Dinner will be ready in fifteen minutes," and she turns and leaves us alone again.
Weis glances at the wall clock above his desk, "Perfectly on time," he says, then offers me a seat on the sofa.
I feel…anxious. That is how I would describe the buzzing of my skin and the tightness of my chest, like I am ready to sprint out of here at any given opportunity. I feel especially aware of my tongue all of a sudden, as I watch the professor pour two cups of the tea.
I shouldn't have come here.
I should have made some excuse. Feigned sickness or even a broken leg, and then gone on to *actually* break my leg as a cover story. Anything to get out of it.
"Here you go," the professor says, smiling at me from behind his glasses as he hands me one of the cups. I notice he has dark eyes, black almost. I never realised before.
Not very 'Aryan', I think sardonically.
I take the cup and try to hide that my hands are shaking. To avoid him noticing, I place it down on the table after taking a small sip.
Then I sit there awkwardly for what feels like a hundred years as Weis leans back in his leather chair and makes himself comfortable. It squeaks, as leather sometimes does with the slightest friction. He rests the ankle of one leg on the knee of the other, appearing perfectly at ease.

Quite the opposite to how I'm feeling, and how I know I must look.

I open my mouth to speak. The weather is always a safe topic of conversation, I think.

But Weis cuts me off before I can even get a word out.

"So, tell me," he says quite casually, as if this wasn't the tensest moment of my entire life, "How does a Jew end up in a Hitler Youth boarding school?"

Annika

<u>The Netherlands, Giethoorn</u>

In the three months following Meyer's release, Helga and I went on to lure four Nazi soldiers out from inns or hotel bars around town under the pretence of sordid open-air sex. Four times they had followed us through the darkness like randy dogs only to be met with a pistol pressed to their temple.

Marta carried out the shootings every time. Helga or I were the bait.

After that first time, where Helga had been left out of sorts and shaken up to witness a man's head being blown off right in front of her, I had taken the next assignment.

At eighteen, I was yet to kiss a man, but there I was, being sent to tempt Nazis out with the promise of sex. I'd have laughed if it wasn't so awful. I was frightened that first time, I won't lie. My hands were shaking throughout the entire time I was flirting with the unwitting soldier. But actually, looking back on that night, I'm pretty sure he *enjoyed* that I appeared nervous. Perhaps he found it endearing. Perhaps he liked to think he held all the power. No matter. I didn't need to do much except bat my eyelashes at him and laugh at his stupid jokes. And yet, he was the one who ended up flat on his back – with a hole in his head no less. And I grew stronger from my very own success.

Helga took the next assignment, and I the one thereafter, and so on, each time leading the soldiers to a different part of the outskirts of town, and each time they were completely unaware what was about to happen. It was almost like they paid no heed to the rumours of the Dutch Resistance's reawakening. Or – and I thought this was more likely – when a young, pretty and willing girl was showing interest in them, they were simply thinking with their peckers.

"You look nice," Helga says to me now as I apply the finishing touches to my makeup – a light dab of rouge to my cheeks and a smudge of mascara to my lashes, both borrowed from mother's ancient supply that she no longer bothered with.

"*Dank,*" I mumble, then take a step back and assess my ensemble in the mirror.

I look at myself, now a young woman, skinny as a rake and with limp blond hair I'd tried to curl, but to no avail. In the end, I pinned it up instead. The makeup has brightened my face a little, making my blue eyes pop and my cheeks come alive. By some stroke of luck, my breasts had developed despite the lack of nutrition – much to Helga's envy – and they filled out my dress nicely. It will have to do.

"Do we have a sighting?" I ask Helga now, as she sits on the edge of her mattress on the floor. I sit down on mine. *Mama* had found a relatively good mattress near our home not long ago and dragged it back for us so that we didn't have to share anymore. It is lumpy and has a questionable stain on one end, but covered with a tablecloth (we don't have a spare sheet after mine had been made into a new dress) it is suitable enough.

She nods, "Target has arrived at the hotel. He is scheduled to eat with some comrades first. You've got time."

I nod, then smooth down my dress – the one *Mama* had made from my old bedsheet. The food shortage aside, our country has barely any fabrics or other materials, and we have to make do with what we've got.

Given the fact this was once something else entirely, it is not a bad looking frock. And I'm thankful to *Mama* for making it for me. The other two I had, had become significantly too short.

Upon arriving at the hotel, I sneak in, same as usual, avoiding the main entrance and scurrying in through the back like a little mouse. Helga stays across the street, hidden in shadows to keep watch and follow us when the time comes.

I spot my target easily enough by searching for the one wearing a monocle.

Remember, Marta had warned me the day before, *This is not your average soldier. He is a high-ranking military officer. You need to be on your A-game.*

Seeing him alone across the room, I straighten my back and raise my chin before making my way through the crowd.

"Do you have a lighter?" I ask him, placing a cigarette between my lips and looking up at him helplessly, as though I am in desperate need of rescuing.

Rescue by Zippo, I think wryly.

To my internal amusement, the German military officer does indeed whip out a Zippo lighter from his breast pocket and proceeds to light my cigarette for me. I look up at him suggestively as the flame burns the end and I take a puff, thinking back on that time I saw the two men in the alley behind that inn. By taking a drag of my cigarette while maintaining eye contact I will no doubt make him think of me between his legs.

He grins down at me, and I raise my eyebrow just so. A slight but seductive tick.

We proceed to dance around the topic of sex by talking about anything but, and yet constantly making subtle – and not so subtle – innuendos. His hand is on my lower back within ten minutes of flirtation, and I can feel it hedging lower still.

"I have a room upstairs," he says to me now as he pulls me in close, and immediately my blood runs cold in my veins.

"You do?" I ask sweetly, running a finger down his uniform jacket, trying to think how I could get him to ditch the hotel room in favour of the great outdoors.
I look over his shoulder then and get the waiter's attention from behind the bar where we are standing.
"Two Jevener," I tell him, and he nods his head and hurries to get our drinks.
"Dutch courage?" he says, then laughs at his own joke. I smile to gratify him.
When our drinks arrive – Dutch gin, neat, in a tulip glass – I offer him his and clink mine to it. Then I raise the glass and knock the spirit back.
It burns my throat. I'm quite sure I have never tasted anything quite so foul. But I contain the disgust from my face and lick my lips.
"Let's not be so dull as to go upstairs," I tell him, pressing myself up against his chest. He takes a generous swill of the Jevener.
"Dull?" he echoes, his eyebrows twitching as he looks down at my cleavage.
"Yes," I drawl, "I had something more," I look around myself as if I was about to share a secret, "*wild* in mind."
At that, he smirks down at me, "Oh," he says, readjusting his monocle.
"What, exactly, were you thinking?"

I lead him outside by the hand, then, as I sense him hesitating slightly, I turn around and push him roughly against the wall outside the hotel. He grunts but exhales a laugh like he likes it.
With my hands clasping his arms, I reach up on my tiptoes and plant a kiss on his thin lips.
My first kiss.
And it's with a Nazi.
I try to suppress my disgust. I have never had to engage in any intimacy with targets before beyond flirtation, but

his slight hesitation worried me. Enough at least to resort to this kind of drastic step.

I can feel him responding to my kiss, his mouth opening hungrily and his wet slug of a tongue pushing against my lips.

Truth be told, I did not expect this. Is *this* how people kiss? Is it not simply puckering up and pressing against the other's mouth?

I want to pull away, but I know I must not. Nor do I think I could at this point, while his arms are wrapped around my waist and crushing me to him.

I slowly open my mouth instead and allow his tongue free access to meet mine. I try to think of something else. Anything else to get through this most awful experience.

Meyer pops into my head. And surprisingly, I feel myself relax slightly.

I pull away then, to regain my breath but also my control. I do not want this man to get carried away here.

I notice the Nazi's monocle has fallen down and is now dangling from a gold chain. He takes my hand in his and begins to lead me down the road.

I hop into step beside him, then urge him down the track to where Marta will be waiting, "This way," I whisper excitedly to him, and he follows me like a bumbling idiot. We reach the meeting point, down by the river on the opposite end of where we hold our resistance rendezvous in the abandoned barge.

The moonglade shines an ethereal silver path on the water. An owl hoots in the distance. If circumstances were different, it would be quite the romantic setting.

I turn to him and announce our arrival, presenting him with a soft patch of grass.

He begins to peel off his jacket, just as the others had all done before him, and lays it on the ground.

So sweet, I think sarcastically.

I kneel down onto it, looking up at him as he lowers himself in front of me.

This is usually the moment when Marta comes out from behind a tree, or a boulder, or the shadows, and surprises the Nazi with the cold kiss of her gun against his temple.

But, to my horror, she does not spring out, even as he begins to fumble with his belt and runs his hands over my breasts.

He grabs my face now, and again, his disgusting tongue tries to enter my mouth. And this time, I cannot help but flinch.

"*Was ist?*" he asks, pulling away and frowning, "You cannot go cold on me now."

I breathe a laugh, trying to look around me, "No, no, of course not –"

Suddenly – thank *God!* – Marta emerges from one of the barges docked on the river and raises the gun at him.

But my hesitation must have alerted him because in a flash, I see his face contort into fury, and he knocks me out of the way, turning just in time to seize Marta's wrist. He punches her in the face and she cries out, topples back with the blow, and falls onto the ground. Blood splutters from her nose in a spray over her chin and the gun goes flying out her hand and into the mud behind her. The Nazi grunts as he tussles himself on top of her.

And I?

I am frozen in shock as the scene unfolds before me.

I look up at the sound of someone running towards us then and see Helga racing down the track, having followed me and the Nazi from the hotel.

"The gun!" she calls to me, and I begin to frantically search my surroundings as the sound of choking and gurgling comes from Marta.

I cannot find it, and the terrifying image in front of me holds my attention. He has her pinned, his knee pressing down onto her stomach as both his hands are wrapped around her throat.

"*No!*" I shriek, finally coming to my senses, and I throw myself on him. I do what I can, slapping, kicking, biting for him to let go of Marta.

He pushes me off and I fall, but at least I managed to get him to let go long enough for Marta to gasp for breath. By now, Helga has reached us, and she skids to grab the gun just on the edge of the river.

I step away from the struggle, certain we are saved now that we have the upper hand once again.

"Let go of her!" I scream, my face stained with tears and my throat raw with emotion.

But he ignores me, and with his hands around her neck, he bashes Marta's head into the ground. I can see her eyes rolling back in her head.

"LET GO!" Helga shouts, the gun raised and aimed at him.

"*Helga!*" I scream, willing her to take the shot.

She wavers, and I can see it then: she is not better. Her nightmares may have stopped haunting her, but in her eyes, I can see that she cannot do this, no matter the hard façade she puts on.

I pick up my skirts and rush towards her, ready to take the gun from her and kill this monster myself, when suddenly a tall figure emerges out from the shadows, grabs the gun out from Helga's unsure grasp and fires a single, perfect shot into the man's skull.

My ears ring. But other than that, silence befalls us as we stand frozen in shock.

And when I look up and focus upon the face of the man who has saved us, my heart skips a beat at the sight of Jakob Meyer.

Chapter 10

Alma

<u>Poland, Auschwitz</u>

I try to search the faces of those around me, hoping to find someone I recognise from my home. But there are too many of us, too many prisoners. Instead, I find the young woman – Esther, was it? – waiting around a corner for me after I received my tattoo, my number.
She grabs me and we walk together behind the barracks.

"What happens to them?" I ask, going back to what she was telling me earlier, "Those who get sent to the showers."

"Dead," she states simply, her head down as she walks, scanning to-and-fro, "It isn't water that comes out of those shower heads…"
And a *pang* of realisation hits me right in the gut. I feel sick… I look around myself. This is no 'work camp' as we'd been hearing about for years. This is Hell.
I was given a bowl shortly after receiving my tattoo, and Esther points to it now.

"Guard it with your life," she says, "It will quite literally depend on that bowl."
That night, we are herded inside the low wooden barracks, and I am again stunned. Inside the barracks are ceiling-high bunkbeds, but as I look around, it is clear to see that there are more bodies than beds.

"Get in," Esther says when I continue to simply stare, dumbfounded. I watch as she awkwardly lies down on a thin straw mattress beside four other women.
I do as I'm told, because what else am I supposed to do?

She introduces me to two of the women in the bunk. Gita, who is too weak even to wave, and Trudi, who nods at me before turning around and going to sleep.

I'm about to peel off my shoes – wooden clogs I'd been given along with my grey dress – when Esther hisses at me to stop.

"*Never* take them off," she says, a warning, "You sleep with them on. And even then, it's not guaranteed you'll wake up with them on your feet. People will steal anything to aid their own survival. You lose your shoes, you're dead."

I flinch, tears pricking my eyes for the hundredth time today. How could I be here? How could *any* of us be?

She proceeds to tell me to sleep with my bowl tucked under my dress, so that it, too, won't get stolen. Again, for the same reason.

"You lose your bowl, you're dead."

I lie awake, stiff as a board, for hours, Esther's warnings whirling in my head, and the indescribable smell of unwashed and slowly rotting bodies clinging in my nostrils.

I wake to the harsh blow of a whistle and before I know it, everyone around me scrambles up and heads outside.

I hear one woman wailing, and I look towards the sound to see a skeleton with skin pulled tightly over her cheekbones searching her bunk. I notice her feet are bare, and I turn to Esther beside me, who raises her eyebrows as if to say, *See?*

I wonder what will happen to the woman. I think I already know.

I follow the crowd and stay close to Esther, realising suddenly that I am trusting this complete stranger with my life. Thousands of bodies make their way to the large central square of the camp, situated between the gates and the barracks.

"What is happening?" I whisper to Esther.

Someone *shushes* me immediately and I shrink away when one of the German soldiers shouts angrily into the crowd.

"*Schnauze, Mistjuden!*"

Once we've reached the square, I do what everyone else is doing, which is standing completely still and facing forward.

Noise blares over speakers then, and one by one, numbers are called out and I realise it's a roll call.

What I don't realise is how long it will take.

For hours, we stand there with the sun beating down on us as the soldiers call out numbers. Any time a person does not make their presence known according to the number called, other prisoners are sent to search for them. They then return, dragging the person out by their arms and dumping them on the ground, dead.

I gasp aloud the first time it happens, but Esther squeezes my hand in warning, and after that, I try not to look.

Turns out, dying in the night of starvation or illness is common around here. Just another thing to get used to.

Soldiers march slowly up and down the length of the rows as we await the end of the roll call, peering at us with downturned mouths and checking us for weakness. I notice my whole row straightening up and staring down at the ground when a soldier makes his way down our line, so I do the same.

I later learn that anyone deemed too weak at roll call to work is 'selected' and sent to block 25.

What is block 25?

It's where you wait. It's the waiting room for the gas. Once it's full, everyone inside is sent to the gas chamber.

After roll call, everyone disperses, and I grab hold of Esther's sleeve.

"Where are you going? Take me with you."

She shakes her head, "Don't make a scene. Keep your head down, do as you're told, and you might live to see another day."

She hurries away.

I don't stand about for long, because suddenly, I and half a dozen others are rounded up and told to follow one of the guards.

I go where they send us, my dread mounting as we get closer and closer to the building with the chimneys.

A lump forms in my throat and I look around at the bald men and women around me, do they know what is to become of us?

The German takes us around the back of the building, whistling as he goes as though it was nothing but a glorious day.

He leads us inside, and I begin to sweat. The blood rushes to my feet and my knees turning to jelly. I'm surprised I don't collapse with each step further into this pit.

He stops in front of a pile of naked dead bodies and proceeds to bark German at us. Most of us do not understand the words, but it is clear enough that he means for us to bring more dead bodies here.

A few dozen prisoners appear from along the long room, all of them with their heads bowed as though they have seen things that will haunt them forever, which, given our surroundings, I'm sure they have.

"*Sonderkommando*," the Nazi says by way of introduction, and I watch as the men begin piling dead bodies on stretchers and bringing them to one side of the room. It takes two prisoners to carry one stretcher, and I cry out when I see one stretcher holds the dead bodies of a woman and a baby. Someone next to me elbows me in the ribs and I swallow my sobs.

I watch. I just watch. As the prisoners open metal latches on the wall, dozens of them, and one by one, heave the bodies inside the fiery mouths within. The limp corpses flop inside without much ado. As if they are no more than ragdolls.

This is a crematorium, I realise, and these men are in charge of burning Auschwitz's deceased.

"*Ihr seid Leichenkommando*," the guard says, supposing we would just understand because he wants us to.

He points at the pile of bodies, then waves his hand to suggest *out there*, and I realise what we have been tasked with.

To bring any new deceased here, so that they too, may be turned to ash.

Leichenkommando, Corpse Squad.

"I moved away from Germany in '38," Esther tells me dreamily, when we are squished closely together in our bunk after the worst day of my life.

For hours, I had gone up and down the camp, heaving dead bodies I found in corners, or in their beds, or bleeding out on the ground, onto a wooden cart. Two men were tasked with pulling the cart to and from the crematorium, but more often than not I helped them push it along from behind, the two men being too weak to do it alone. And all day, I had wondered just how long I would last before I, too, was just another cadaver, lying glassy-eyed and lifeless on that cart.

Esther's tone suggests a shared understanding, but when I continue silent, she goes on.

"That winter of 1938…it wasn't safe for Jewish children in that area."

I frown. I don't know what she is talking about. Was it safe *anywhere* for Jewish children? Ever since Hitler had come into power in 1933, his hateful ideology had caused a division, a rift. How was the place she was from in Germany worse off than anywhere else?

"Have you heard of The Yeti?" she asks me then, turning her face to me.

I shake my head in the darkness, but over Esther's shoulder we both hear a gasp.

Trudi is watching us, listening to Esther's story. I note pity in her eyes, and I gather she knows of what Esther speaks.

"*Der Schneemensch*," Trudi whispers in German, and Esther nods sadly.

She turns back to me, her mouth twitching slightly, "Ah, why would you know? His actions hardly made the newspapers in Germany. You won't have heard of him, all the way in secluded Le Chambon."

"Tell me," I encourage her, suddenly curious to know. Anything to take my mind off the gnawing pain in my stomach and the horrifying things I have seen.

She inhales a ragged breath, "He was this sick, Jew-hating, monster," she says, "No one knows, even now, who he was. Who he *is*, I should say. He's probably still free. Murdering Jews isn't exactly frowned upon right now."

We look around ourselves, at the human beings squashed together like sardines, lying in our own filth, sharing beds with not only other people but lice and mice, too. A heavy sense of foreboding hangs in the air.

"I, well, my son…he was his first target," she continues, her voice cracking, "Left a snowman outside our home to taunt me with his disappearance."

"Taunt you? By building a snowman?"

Esther looks away for a moment, blinking the pain away, "That was his signature, we later learned. He'd build the snowman, such a simple thing. But it turned out to mean so much more…Josef. That was my son's name. My *lemele*. He was four. He just disappeared one morning. For weeks the community helped me search for my boy. But the snow made it hard…"

A beat of silence, one in which I can clearly hear a mother's unspoken desperation.

"I found him eventually," she says woefully, staring up at the bunk above us, "When the frost began to melt…He'd been strangled, then laid down in a foetal position, like he was sleeping. And the snowman was built on top of him. He was already dead before I'd even realised he was gone. And all that time I thought – I thought it had been my son's snowman."

She wipes her cheeks, sniffs, "I used to look at it and think of him. Think of the excitement he'd felt while building it…Only to then find out he'd been dead within it all along, the damned thing having been built by the man who'd killed him…I moved away after that, to live with family in France."

I nod, "That's how you speak French," I whisper, more to myself than anyone else, stunned by her story.

The silence that follows is heavy and ugly.

The Yeti. I've never heard of him. And yet he's murdered children – Jewish children – in Germany. I wonder if he ever stopped, if he was ever caught. I wonder if I've ever met him, if he is, maybe, right here, where he could continue to inflict pain on us, kill us, without reproach.

"Do you know what he looks like?" I ask, my voice breaking.

She scoffs a bitter laugh, "No. And I'll probably never know. But I search for him in every one of them. As if, maybe, I might have some motherly instinct as to who killed my baby."

She shakes her head in exasperation, "But who am I kidding? I didn't even know my poor boy was lying dead right outside my house for weeks. I couldn't *feel* him. The truth is, even if I ever came face to face with my son's killer, I would probably never know."

My whole body feels heavy with grief, and it is not even my own. And when her face crumples and she turns away,

I scooch and press my body against her back, rubbing her arm companionably and holding her hand when her shoulders stop shaking.

It isn't much. In fact, it's absolutely nothing at all. But it's all I have to give to this poor woman, who has lost her entire world. And who, even if she makes it out of here alive, will never regain it.

Abel

<u>Germany, Plön</u>

"So, tell me. How does a Jew end up in a Hitler Youth boarding school?"
He sips his tea casually, while I sit frozen in place, my mouth hanging slightly open, the ringing in my ears growing louder by the second.
I blink, I think I'm going to pass out. Did he really say what I think he said?
The clock on the wall *ticks, ticks, ticks*. His daughter Frida dishes up dinner in the kitchen.
Each minute feels like an hour, and still he simply looks at me with quiet expectation. As if my survival doesn't hang entirely in the balance.
Finally, I come to my senses and manage to breathe a shaky laugh.

"Professor Weis," I begin, shaking my head. I clear my throat, "What – what makes you say that? How? How does a Jew –? I'm quite sure I don't understand."
Weis shrugs and leans forward to put his empty teacup down on the coffee table.

"*Doch*," he nods wisely, "You, 'Walter Schmidt'," he makes quotation marks with his fingers, "Are a Jew."
I swallow hard, then stand up in a flash. My vision blurs. Head rush. I blink to fight off the darkness that confiscates my sight, reach out a hand to steady myself against the wall.

"Woah," the professor says beside me all of a sudden, "Relax."
Relax?!

"Please," I beg, my vision returning after a moment, "Please, don't tell anyone."

Professor Weis scoffs, then resumes his seat on the leather seat.

I look to his office door, which is still wide open. Could I make a run for it?

"Don't run," he says, as though he's read my mind, "Come. Sit back down."

He has retrieved a cigar from his breast pocket now and cuts off the end before lighting it. He puffs at it one, two, three times, then looks at me through the smoke.

"Sit," he says again, though it sounds more like an order this time.

My palms are sweaty, my throat is dry, my legs are weak. I don't even think I *could* escape if I tried.

I do as he says and sit down gingerly at the edge of the sofa. And then, to my shame, a floodgate inside me bursts.

"Please, Professor," I beg, tears streaming down my face as it crumples, and I am reminded of my own youth, the life I have yet to live. At eighteen, I am too young to die.

I'm sure I look a mess, and yet all I care about is that he takes pity on me, "What will happen to me? Will you kill me yourself? Will you hand me in? Oh, please –"

He raises his hand, the cigar clamped between two stumpy fingers, "Stop the whining," he says, and I try to contain my sobs.

"Dinner is ready," comes Frida's melodic voice from behind me, so pure and unfaltering that I wonder for a moment if she is crazy. Can't she see my life is about to end? Can't she feel the tension in the air?

"Ah!" Weis says, a wide grin spreading across his face as he slaps his hands on his knees enthusiastically and stands up, "Let's eat!"

I remain in my seat, too stunned to move. I can hardly breathe. I can hardly think straight. Snot is running down my top lip and my heart is pumping wildly in my chest. How can they expect me to sit down at a table and eat?

"Schmidt," Weis' voice calls from the corridor, "Follow me."

I do as I am told, though my brain is temporarily disconnected from my body. I do not even recall walking into the dining room, and yet here I am, in a richly decorated space, a candlelit table featuring three plates of delicious smelling casserole.

I sit down where Weis tells me to, then watch carefully as he and his daughter take their seats.

"This looks beautiful, Frida," Weis tells his daughter, who smiles and blushes before casting a quick glance at me.

Are they *insane*?

How can they sit here with me, a Jew, and pretend like I am one of them? Professor Weis *hates* Jews. He teaches about their inferiority, about how to spot them through their 'subtle deformities'.

And yet, here he is, knowingly hosting one. How long has he known?

"Since that first day," he says, and I realise I've asked the question out loud, "When I called you to the front and took your measurements."

I frown, are his ridiculous theories true then? Did my 'flat head' give me away?

"Eat," he orders, before cutting into his meal.

I pick up my knife and fork, though I know I will likely throw up if I eat even a morsel, no matter how good it smells.

Perhaps it is poisoned...

"Did…" I begin, unsure if I want to know, "Did my head – the measurements. Were they consistent with that of…"

Weis and his daughter exchange a glance. She is no longer smiling, though she continues to eat in silence. The professor inhales deeply through his nose as he chews, then he puts down his knife and fork.

"My dear boy," he says, "I knew you were a Jew not because of any silly measurements. I called you up there that day to protect you, to help shape your image as the 'perfect Aryan'," he chuckles and shakes his head, "No, it wasn't your head shape which gave you away."

"What then?" I ask, my panic rising again.

Frida wipes her mouth with a napkin, before looking directly at me, "What my *papa* is trying to say," she says, "Is that he knew straight away that you are a Jew because, like you, we are also Jewish."

Weis grunts slightly under his breath, and I look at him.

"What?!" I gasp, incredulous.

He nods at me, a look in his eyes conveying a mutual understanding. And I, overcome with relief, shock and dread, lurch and vomit all over his beautiful maroon rug.

Annika

<u>The Netherlands, Giethoorn</u>

He looks older, more haggard.

I guess being tortured will do that to you.

"Meyer," I say, half in exhale.

He turns to face me, and I get a full view of how he has changed. His formerly clean-shaven face now sports a black stubble over his cheeks and chin. His dark hair hangs limply over his ears, like strands of black liquorice. His green eyes, though still piercing, appear to look right through me, and a flash of something resides in them. Some hurt that remains despite his release. He has a pink scar down his temple, at least three inches long, fresh and angry.

"What happened to you?" I hear myself say, reaching up to touch his scar.

He flinches briefly, then throws the gun down into the mud and goes over to where Marta is lying on the ground. I notice a slight limp in his step.

Meyer heaves the dead German off of Marta, then shakes her gently by the shoulder, "Marta," he whispers.

Helga and I are beside them now, ready to help Marta and get her cleaned up and out of here before authorities come running.

"We have to go," Helga says, her voice steady but for the hint of remorse I am sure only I can hear. She looks over her shoulder into the darkness when Marta fails to respond.

Meyer shakes Marta again, more roughly this time, and I want to tell him to be gentle, that she's likely in agony after the attack, but then a sound escapes him, a sound of sorrow I had not expected to hear.

"Marta!" he says again, angrily now, his deep voice cracking.

"She's dead, Meyer," this from Helga, and my head snaps to stare at her, dumbfounded.

We hear the screech of a whistle in the distance then, followed by calls in German.

Helga grabs me under the arm and heaves me up, "Let's go!" she says, a command.

I'm torn. Between dragging Marta with me or leaving her here to be discovered. And I sense Meyer is in similar turmoil as he straightens up but remains rooted to the spot, staring down at his friend.

"*Meyer!*" I hiss, then wave my hand at him to follow.

He looks at me, then back at Marta on the ground, her neck bruised and broken, her lids closed, as if she's asleep. My stomach drops with guilt and misery, but I know we cannot carry her *and* run.

The shouting in the distance is growing nearer, and Helga pulls at my arm, "Come *on!* We can't do anything for her." I know she is right, but her tone is harsh, nonetheless.

She tugs at me again and then we take off running.

A gunshot sounds behind us, and I look back to see Meyer ducking down at the sound, then turning on his heel and running after us. There is no sight of the Germans yet, but they cannot be far if they fired.

Can they see us in the moonlight?

"This way," Meyer's gruff voice calls, now beside us, faster than us even with his new limp.

We follow him down a path in the mud likely formed by nature, foxes and deer taking this route from the wilderness to the river for a drink. He grunts under his breath with every step on his busted leg.

"Where are we going?" I pant behind him and Helga now.

Neither of them answers me, though I know Helga doesn't know either.

We're away from the riverbank now, running through a grassy field and into a small cluster of trees on the outskirts of town.

Meyer stops and turns to look over my head.

"They'll find us here," I say, breathing heavily.

"Catch your breath," says Helga, clamping her hands on my shoulders, "We're not far from home. We can cut –"

"You're not going home," Meyer interrupts, turning an angry face at my sister, "That was a raging fuck up, and with Marta dead for them to discover they will make the connection to all of us."

"But they don't know about us," I protest, "Why can't we go home?"

I am suddenly fearful for my mother. If it isn't safe for us to go home, then she is in danger.

Meyer turns his sharp eyes to me.

"Our mother…" I whisper.

"I will send a message through the network to have her protected. She can lie low with Pieters."

"What about us?" Helga says, "Where will we go? We can't stay with you! Your place will be the first they raid!"

He pushes past her then and continues through the trees, "Follow me," he says.

I start to follow but Helga holds me back, "Ani, I don't like this," she says, "He's the last person we should be seen with."

I frown at her, "He saved us, Helga. If you'd have taken that shot sooner Marta may –"

I break off, but Helga flinches all the same. She knows what I was about to say.

She nods her head slightly, accepting her fault, then inhales.

"Come on, then," she says, as if neither of us had spoken, and we follow Meyer through the darkness.

*

To my utter surprise, Meyer takes us through parts of town I would have thought we'd need to avoid.

"Hide in plain sight," he mumbles at one point, as though he can read my mind. And I figure he isn't wrong. The Nazis aren't looking for us in town just yet. They are all searching the area near the river.

We keep to the shadows, sneaking down backstreets only us locals knew of, and shrinking back into shadows at the sound of booted footsteps.

We stop briefly at a house that appears abandoned, and Meyer knocks twice. It opens a crack, and he mutters something through the door before hurrying us along again.

"Pieters," he confirms as we scurry away, "Your mother will be just fine."

It has only been mere minutes since the attack, and yet we appear to be heading back down towards the river.

"What are you doing?" I whisper at him as loudly as I dare, "You're going straight to them."

He ignores me, and I begin to think maybe he's crazy.

We speed-walk down the path to the river, then turn left towards the barges, where we accelerate into a jog. I relax slightly. Perhaps we're to hide out at the meeting point, the abandoned flatboat on the edge of the stream, until we come up with a more solid plan?

Meyer is at the lead, Helga and I closely behind, and I prepare myself for the ten-minute journey along the muddy path, when suddenly Meyer turns and steps onto a boat I recognise all too well.

"Come on," he says, offering me his hand.

I blink in confusion. What is he doing? But I take it and let him pull me onto the bobbing barge.

Helga has climbed on by herself, and when she looks around, she releases a small laugh.

"*Papa's* boat."

I recognise it too, of course. But why would we go here – just another abandoned flatboat – when one that we know is secure is but a moment's jog away, and further afield from the scene of the crime?

Meyer knocks, the same secret knock he did at Pieter's house, and I open my mouth to tell him that nobody lives here anymore, when the door suddenly swings open and I am met with a moustache and two blue eyes I thought I'd never see again.

Meyer enters into the darkened space.

"Get in, Ani," my father says to me, as though we'd only parted ways yesterday.

I stand there staring at him in disbelief. He has some nerve.

"Helga," he says, turning to his eldest. And she nods and enters without question.

"Ani?" he turns back to me, extending a hand, and then Meyer appears beside him.

He nods at me. His lips twitch with a small smile of encouragement, and I realise how ridiculous I am being, how childish. With a deep breath, I look at my father – who I haven't seen in years – and I hurriedly step into the past.

Chapter 11

Alma

<u>Poland, Auschwitz</u>

Because of her language skills, Esther had acquired a job as a secretary to one of the SS officers shortly after her arrival here. Which I guess is how she has survived for so long in these harrowing conditions.

"I was working in Kanada with Trudi and Gita when he overheard me singing in French," Esther whispers to me one morning as we stand in line for soup.

We aren't allowed to talk, and if one of the *kapos* overhears us, we will surely be punished. But sometimes, to distract ourselves from other risks to our lives – such as, in this case, the growing cold of autumn – we dare to whisper amongst ourselves whenever possible. After all, it is the simple things that nourish a soul, and when food is scarce, you have to take anything you can get.

"Singing?"

"Just singing to myself," she says without turning around, "It helped to pass the time and to take my mind off what I was doing."

"What did you do in Kanada?" I whisper.

"It's where the people's belongings get sorted," she explains, her tone suddenly heavy, "People's luggage and clothes. That's where they get sifted through and searched for anything of value to hand over to the Germans."

"Dead people's belongings?" I ask, disturbed.

Esther clears her throat, "After a while, you switch off to what you're doing. The most difficult part of that job was knowing that the last person who had touched the items

inside the suitcases was probably already dead. But it was children's possessions that were the toughest. Toys, blankets, little leather shoes – when I came across them, I would cry. I knew I had to turn my mind off to it. Focusing on it would've driven me mad."
We share a look.

"It was a good job, though," she continues, "Safer than some. Indoors, so you're out of the cold or sunshine."
I nod sombrely, my back and arms aching with the strain of my work carrying cadavers up and down the camp all day. I blow into my cupped hands and stomp my feet. It is only the end of September, not yet winter. But already we can feel the change in weather against our exposed skin.
As we inch closer to the pot, I lean to the side. There are only three ahead of us, and my stomach rumbles in anticipation of the meagre meal.

"How can you do it?" I ask her, referring to her secretarial job, "How can you work so closely with one of them each day?"
Esther shrugs, "It's the best position I have had in here, I'm not going to look a gift horse in the mouth! I am sitting down most of the day, filing paperwork, typing up letters. He's good to me."
That surprises me, and I frown. She steps forward and presents her bowl to the prisoner in charge of the servings. I notice they exchange a smile, and the server dunks the ladle deep into the pot and swirls it around to get some of the vegetables that have sunk to the bottom. My mouth waters to see Esther's portion includes a potato, and I almost cry out with excitement to think I might be so lucky. I step forward and present my bowl, and watch intently as nothing but watery soup is poured in. I follow Esther out of the queue, disheartened, my head bowed in worry. I received even less at dinner last night, and I don't know how long I can survive on such measly scraps.

"Here," Esther says, breaking her potato in half and passing me a piece, "It's only because I know her."

I look up at her with tears in my eyes, "*Merci*," I mumble, my heart fluttering with gratitude.

"Don't wolf it down," she says, "Savor it."

I nod.

Two SS officers walk past us then, one of them kicking a prisoner to the ground for no apparent reason.

I scowl over at them.

One of them must feel my glower, because he turns to me, and I quickly rearrange my face.

I look away and down at my watery soup, certain there is dirt floating around on the bottom of my bowl. The potato piece is floating in its centre, looking simultaneously like fodder I wouldn't have deemed good enough to feed our pigs back at home, and a gourmet meal; my starved mind and body fighting with reality and logic.

Trudi and Esther are teaching Gita and me some German. Gita and I have never really interacted before apart from with grunts and hand gestures, since she is Polish and I French. But as the weeks have gone by, we've been bouncing new words back and forth at one another as we learn them, giggling at our pronunciation of the harsh language.

Of course, we picked some words up faster than others, words we hear shouted all around camp on a daily basis.

Nein – no.

Raus – out.

Schnell – Quick.

Jude – Jew.

Schnauze – Shut up.

Trudi gives us a new word every day and a sentence on how to use it. And in the evenings after lights out, as we all huddle tightly together against the cold, Esther whispers German lullabies. She says it is to help us sleep, but I figure it's her mothering nature needing to come out in those vulnerable moments, where her mind is no longer occupied and memories of her son shine through. Afterwards, her cheeks are always wet with tears, and I wonder if they were lullabies her little Josef used to fall asleep to.

After a while, the songs start to make sense in my head, their stories becoming clear in my imagination, their repetitiveness helping me to understand.

'*Schlaf, Kindlein, Schlaf*' is my favourite, which at first had been nothing but gibberish, but I quickly learned is about a father who tends the sheep while the mother shakes a dream from a tree for their child. It reminds me of when I was a little girl, when my *maman* would rock me back to sleep in her arms after a bad dream, singing *Clair de la lune* in a hushed voice.

"*Rrrr – Raus,*" Trudi says beside me now, rolling the 'r' as if she has phlegm in her throat.

I repeat after her as best I can.

"*Gut,*" she says, and I grin despite my surroundings.

We are at roll call, whispering amongst ourselves while standing perfectly straight and looking ahead, awaiting the call of our numbers.

Suddenly, a number is shouted out twice, three times, and I gasp. I recognise it.

I look left to right, "Where's Gita?" I ask quietly.

A soldier orders three prisoners near the end to go look for her, and I watch wide-eyed as they hurry into the barracks. *Has she died in her sleep?* I am ashamed to say I didn't even notice…

Shouting comes from inside the barrack then, high-pitched wailings that I recognise as Gita. I am momentarily relieved when she emerges from the hut with the other prisoners following behind. But uncertainty is etched onto their faces as Gita continues howling, and my chest clenches with dread. Snot and tears run down her face, her eyes bloodshot and her face manic. She half walks, half stumbles towards us, then suddenly rounds at full speed and takes off running.

The Germans shout, ordering one another to shoot her. Gunfire sounds and many of us cry out and fall to the ground covering our heads. I look up, my curiosity too strong not to, and I breathe a sigh of relief to see she hasn't been shot.

"She is headed towards the fence," someone mumbles beside me, their voice coated with awe and wonder.

The shouting continues all around me, but Gita is still running, and then, as if carried by an invisible angel, she launches herself into the electric fence. I flinch and cover my mouth with my hands, stunned by what I am seeing: her body jerking sporadically about, her skin searing off right in front of me.

A young woman choosing to take her own life, rather than live another day in this nightmare.

<u>Germany, Plön</u>

"So, you're Jewish?" I finally ask, after I helped Frida clean up the mess I had made on their rug.

My face had burned bright red as I'd knelt beside her, protesting until the very end that I should do it myself. But Frida had insisted she help. She hadn't even seemed to mind.

Now, once my thoughts have stopped spinning and I realise I'm not in immediate danger, Professor Weis and I have retired to his study once again.

He nods at me slowly, then smiles up at his daughter when she comes in with a tray of tea, "Camomile," she says to me gently, her hazel eyes meeting mine, "To soothe your stomach."

My ears tingle with embarrassment to notice her eyes are so very different to Weis', whose are as black as the night. But I return her smile, feeling strangely awkward under her gaze.

"My mother was a Jewish Pole," Weis answers me now, "She did not live long enough to see the world go to shit like this, thankfully. My wife, Frida's mother, was also brought up Jewish."

I sip my tea as Frida takes a seat beside me on the sofa. Weis is facing us on his armchair.

"And where is your wife?" I ask.

Weis casts a glance at Frida, and I sense a sadness take over.

"She left us," Weis says, "Many years ago. Back in '38." I nod slowly, unsure how to respond.

Judging by Frida's appearance, she couldn't be any older than me, perhaps even younger, but I would guess no younger than sixteen. Her mother must've left her when

she was around ten or eleven. I wonder how a person could suddenly leave her partner and young child. Especially at a time such as this, where, since the mid 1930's, Jews were being targeted and cast out. Surely a mother would want to be with her child. To protect her in any way she could. It doesn't make any sense to me.
But then again, not much does nowadays.
"I'm sorry," I say, shooting Frida beside me a sympathetic look.
"We don't dwell on it," Weis replies for her.
I smile tightly at him, though I can't help but note his tone, which contradicts his statement entirely.

Following my discovery about Professor Weis and his disclosure to knowing my secret, he and I keep each other's confidence, externally appearing to have no more of a relationship than that of a professor and his favourite student.
He continues to invite me round for dinner once a week, and often offers to accompany my class on the regular hiking weekends sponsored by the Hitler Youth. He does so, he claims, to 'keep an eye on me', and to make sure I am not discovered.
Though he is a Nazi and a Eugenics professor, who makes his living teaching impressionable young men that Jews are inferior in every way, I feel strangely safe around Professor Weis. I figure he can't possibly believe all those things he spouts, since he, his wife and daughter are all secret Jews.
It makes me consider just how many more sympathisers there might be at this school, and throughout the rest of Europe. Hidden among the monsters, passing for Nazis but really aiding those they are taught to hate.
After three consecutive weekly dinner invitations to Weis' house, Otto and the other boys begin to remark on my close relationship with the professor. All of them are no

doubt jealous that I am getting special treatment from someone they so admire.

But I pay them no heed. Because though they joke about my being a 'teacher's pet', I have an ulterior motive for accepting Weis' continued invitations to dinner beyond that he is protecting my identity.

And that is to see his beautiful daughter.

I knock on the door to Professor Weis' house and let myself in after Frida's voice calls to me that it's open.

It has been four weeks since Weis had first invited me to dine with him, four weeks in which he has kept my secret, and I have kept his. And in that time, I have grown more and more enamoured with Frida.

How could I not? She is polite, pretty, friendly, and an amazing cook!

I shed my jacket. It is a cool afternoon, the first signs of a promised Autumn chiming in the air, an aeolian sound that brings with it nostalgia and a humming comfort in my stomach.

"*Hallo*," Frida says as she comes around the corner with a smile on her lips, her almond-shaped eyes crinkling.

"*Hallo*," I reply, my throat constricting at the sight of her, standing before the evening sun as it shines through the window.

A heavy silence sits between us, and I point towards the professor's study.

"Is he – ?"

"*Papa* isn't here yet," she tells me, and an unease descends over me.

"Oh, *Entschuldigung*," – sorry – I reach for my jacket and prepare to leave, "I am too early."

"*Nein, nein*," she says, taking a step towards me, "You are not. *Papa* is running late."

I nod slowly and stuff my hands in my pockets.

A bubbling sound comes from the kitchen and Frida turns towards it, "I have to go," she says, then hesitates, "Actually, could you come help me?"

My eyebrows shoot up, glad to be of use somehow, and I follow her into her domain, realising I have never stepped foot in the kitchen before. Which leads me to think I haven't stepped foot in most of the rooms in this house besides the professor's study, the dining room and the hallway.

"It's just this pot," Frida tells me, "It is quite heavy once it's full."

I look at a large steel vessel filled to the brim with water and potatoes. She isn't lying, it does look heavy.

She turns off the stove and covers the pot with a lid, then hands me a tea towel.

"Could you bring it to the sink?"

"Of course," I mutter, taking the tea towel and carefully lifting the heavy container.

I wonder how she would have done this without me or the professor here to help her.

My God, this thing weighs a ton!

I try not to reveal how much of a struggle this is to manoeuvre, keeping my face as expressionless as I can, but I release a low grunt as soon as I set it down.

"So," she says casually after I plonk the pot down a little less elegantly than I'd hoped, "What's your real name?"

I turn to her with a frown; I hadn't expected her to ask that. In all the times I've been here, she and I have hardly spoken past pleasantries, the professor usually taking the lead on the topics of discussion.

"My name?" I parrot like a chump.

She grins at me, "You don't want to tell me."

"No, no, it's not that," I say, a little flustered, "I just – I haven't told anyone here my real name. It's probably safer for all of us that I don't."

She shrugs, then sidesteps me to gain access to her pot, "No matter," she says, and I watch as she pours the hot water into the sink, the potatoes tumbling out and being caught in a sieve. She squints and tries to avoid the steam that snakes into her face.
I go on to help her mash the potatoes while she checks on the Vienna sausages in the oven.

"What do you do when you're not…in here?" I ask Frida after a moment.

"I used to attend the League of German Maidens," she says, folding a tea towel in half.
I nod, Hitler Youth, but for girls.
She straightens up to stand beside me and rolls her eyes, "That's where I learned to cook and sew and…all the necessary accolades that constitute to being 'the perfect German wife.'"
Her tone makes it very clear how she feels about that.
She sighs, "I was just like you, hiding in among them. But *Papa* got paranoid about a year ago and got me to finish early."
She adds a splash of milk to the potatoes, and I mash some more.

"But you're glad about that, right? That you no longer attend?"
She exhales a gentle laugh, and I look away, my cheeks burning at the sound.

"Oh, yes," she affirms, "I hated it there. There's so much more to life than being a *Hausfrau*."
A hint of something in her voice catches my attention, and it makes me think: but isn't she being exactly that, except for her father?
Pity for her sprouts within me. And I keep my notion to myself.
She reaches into the bowl now and swipes a finger into the mash before bringing it to her mouth to taste.

To my horror, I cannot help but stare. And to my surprise, she does not avert her gaze from me as I do.

For a second, she and I watch each other: me holding the masher in my hand, my Adam's apple bobbing up and down like a drowning sailor as I swallow hard. She, innocently taunting me with her allure.

I clear my throat, as if my body has just switched back on after short-circuiting, and look away.

"Er, right," I say, shaking my head at myself for sounding like a buffoon, "What about – what about your mother? Tell me about her."

I can sense the change in atmosphere immediately, and Frida turns from me to stick her hands into oven gloves.

"She left us," she says, "What else is there to say?"

She takes the sausages out of the oven, then closes it with her foot in a motion that suggests she has done it hundreds of times before.

"I just thought, maybe, that you'd like to talk about her." Frida shrugs, her mouth turning down as if to say, *Not really*. But then she speaks.

"She fled to England," she says, "At least, that's what *Papa* told me one morning, when we woke up and she wasn't there. She left a note, saying quite simply: 'I cannot risk it here. Don't search for me. Love, *Mama*.'"

She shrugs again, "I haven't seen her since. I was eleven."

"Wow," I mutter, turning to face her, "That's rough."

Her eyebrows twitch like she's trying to appear indifferent, but the line of her mouth says otherwise.

"Here," she says, handing me the tea towel.

I take it and wipe my hands, leaning my hip against the kitchen counter.

"But the professor," I continue, feeling completely at ease around her, despite the deep conversation, "He's a good father."

I say it as a statement, but Frida still replies.

She beams at me, "He's the best father anyone could hope for," she says, her eyes shining with adoration for him. I smile thinly at her.

"Does it bring you comfort to know that she is safe, at least?" I ask, thinking suddenly of Mia, shot dead by the Nazis back in Le Chambon. And of my own parents back in Lodz, and how I have no idea if they are alive or not. At least Frida can rest easy knowing her *mama* isn't dead. Frida inhales deeply as she thinks, her head cocked to one side. She pulls her long plait over her shoulder and starts to play with the end.

"Yeah…" she says slowly, "Of course it does. I know that we are both lucky compared to many. She saved herself by going to England. And *Papa* is saving me. Sometimes I just wish she'd have found it harder to leave her family behind. To leave me behind."

We stand facing one another, two feet apart; her confession having offered me a glimpse into her soul, her deepest laments. She looks up at me with a small, unsure smile, and I sense a sudden shift in her usually confident nature. I want to tell her that her mother was a fool for leaving her, and that she is missing out on knowing how wonderful her daughter has grown up to be. But that feels too forward, too sappy. So, I return her smile instead, our eyes meeting companionably, and I hope I am able to convey to her that she should not feel at fault for her mother's flaws.

We hear the front door opening, and Professor Weis calls into the house, apologizing for his tardiness.

Frida and I both turn at the sound, then look back at one another, feeling like a strange spell has been broken.

Weis exhales out in the corridor, the heavy sigh of a man returning home after a long day.

"What's for dinner?" he calls.

I clear my throat then, desperate to tell her something about myself in return for her honesty before her father invades the moment further.

"Abel," I whisper to her, adrenaline rushing through me as Weis' footsteps grow closer.

I feel dizzy to speak it – my name – not having breathed life into that part of myself for months, a segment of my existence I feared would never again come to be, though he is me.

It feels good to remember who I really was, who I really *am*. Even if just for a moment.

"My real name," I say, as her face turns to me and her hazel eyes find mine, "is Abel."

Annika

<u>The Netherlands, Giethoorn</u>

My past and my present collide as we all hunker down in my father's flatboat, my old home.
We are crouched on the dusty floor with nothing but a candle for illumination. The built-in kitchen and furniture of the barge have not changed one bit since last I saw it, save for the fact they're now covered in dirt and grime.

"What are you doing here?" I whisper at my father, who, I notice in the dim light, has greyed significantly. Not only at his temples but in his complexion in general.
He glances swiftly at Meyer, as if asking for permission to speak, but then answers without waiting.

"I've been in Germany," he tells us, running his fingers over his moustache, "I left the week after you two and your mother moved out."
I frown at Helga, who frowns back, "Why?"
Meyer shushes us all of a sudden, then licks his thumb and forefinger and puts out the candle between us with a *hiss*. The smoke curls up and we are engulfed in darkness. I crane my neck to listen, tuck my hair behind my ear and try to focus past our uneven breathing.
Shouts, coming closer.

"We should have gone to the abandoned barge on the end," Helga argues quietly.
Meyer shakes his head, "Compromised with their discovery of Marta."
The accusation hangs in the air, and I can almost feel Helga's guilt as it weighs on her conscience.
Dogs bark in the distance.

"They have their hounds out," our father says, his shining eyes darting left to right in the gloom.

Meyer nods slowly, "We went through town, they'll track our scent in circles."

"What do we do?" I whisper, so quietly I think no one has heard me.

But then Meyer reaches across the shadows and takes my hand. And I feel my throat constrict a yelp.

"We settle down," he replies, his voice soothing in the darkness, "And wait out the storm."

For three hours, we lie on the floor of my old family home, adrenaline rushing through our bodies. I can almost *hear* Helga shaking with nervous energy beside me.

We move as little as possible to avoid rocking the boat, the still night air granting us no room for mistakes. Without even a breeze outside, an abandoned flatboat causing ripples in the water would only attract unwanted attention.

As a result, my legs have gone numb, my shoulders ache, and Meyer has held my hand for much longer than necessary. I tell myself, as we wait and wait to either be found or be in the clear, that it is only to avoid unnecessary movement why he has held on for so long. Because the alternative is ludicrous.

We haven't seen each other in over a year, during which time he has endured unknown horrors at the hands of the enemy, and I have gone from a gangly girl to ganglier young woman.

We are both broken in our own way. Surely his reaching out is no more than one member of the resistance reassuring another during this terrifying moment. His friend has just this night been killed, for God's sakes. He wants no more than some comfort.

"I think we're clear," my father's voice whispers now, breaking into my thoughts and propelling me towards others.

Namely, where has he been and what has he been doing for all these years?

I roll onto my back and slowly sit up. Helga dusts herself off and helps me stand. My legs tingle like fire ants have entered my circulation, blood rushing through them again after hours of stillness.

After a moment, while our father peers out the small window and Meyer reaches into his pocket for matches, Helga and I look around ourselves properly, memories washing over us.

A nod from our father alerts Meyer that it's safe to relight the candle, and as he does so, I find myself watching him. I sense Helga looking at me and quickly avert my gaze to her. She throws a question at me with her eyes, flicking them to Meyer; and I look away embarrassed, shaking my head.

"What's the plan?" father asks Meyer in a hoarse whisper.

"You stay here with your daughters until you receive the all-clear."

The men nod at each other, and Meyer heads towards the door.

"What about you?" I ask, the question rushing out before I am able to stop it, "It's not safe for you out there." Meyer throws me a look from over his shoulder, with a twitch of his lips that I assume is supposed to be a bolstering smile. It does nothing to alleviate my dread.

"Two days, Lange," Meyer calls to our father, addressing him by our surname, "If you don't hear from anyone by then, you move them out."

Father nods and Meyer steps out onto the boat deck, quietly closing the door behind him.

"Don't worry about Meyer," Father tells me as I stare at the closed door, "That man is like a cockroach. Nothing will kill him."

We sleep for the rest of the night, or try to, anyway.

I blame father's snoring for keeping me awake, though I know it has more to do with the recent events. It feels like a whole lifetime has passed since we left to lure that monocled officer out of the hotel.

Helga didn't sleep either. I can tell by the dark circles under her eyes that she, too, has been going over the attack again and again.

"You okay?" I ask her gently, as she and I sit up with the dawn. She has her back pressed against the wooden wall, her eyes downcast as the sun coming through the window shines on her face, illuminating the world and yet failing to lessen her pallor.

"She's dead, Ani," she says eventually, "I hesitated. And Marta died because of it."

I shake my head and take her hand in mine, "No," I tell her, though I'm not sure I believe it myself, "That German killed her. None of this is your fault."

She turns away from me and sniffs, "Yeah…"

We sit in silence, our father's snoring having ceased for a moment. I look over at him, but he appears to still be asleep.

"What do you think he's been doing in Germany all this time?" I ask my sister, hoping to distract her.

She shrugs and follows my gaze towards him: a tall, lanky man, with greying hair in need of a trim.

"He looks so different," I mumble.

"War has changed us all," Helga replies monotonously, and I turn to watch her.

"Helga?"

"Hm?"

I want to ask her not to let last night affect her, to not dwell on something that she cannot change.

But that would be foolish. Because this war, what has happened to us since, and what we have done in order to survive it, what we have become, has of course shaped us into something we would never have been in different circumstances.

I look away, "Nothing," I say instead. Then add, "Just know that I'm here for you. No matter what happens, we will always have each other."

But I take little comfort from the weakness of her smile.

Chapter 12

Annika

<u>The Netherlands, Giethoorn</u>

When our father finally wakes, he rummages through a bag under the table and pulls out a tin.

Helga is up in a flash, a burst of energy fuelling her at the wonderful sight.

"Peaches?!" she exclaims, her face brightening with a smile I haven't seen in a long time.

"*O, mijn god*," I whisper in astonishment, my eyes wide and my mouth watering.

"Where did you get that?" Helga asks.

"I brought it back from Germany," our father offers vaguely, "Here."

He hands Helga the tin, then pulls out another and I snatch it out of his hands, hunger eclipsing my manners.

Helga has already found a knife to open it with and has torn away the top of her container, and I quickly follow suit.

The peaches taste better than anything I have ever eaten. The juice fills my mouth and sates my thirst as though this old beaten-up canister is the Holy Grail itself. The fruit fills my shrunken stomach with such deliciousness I don't even mind when it gurgles in protest at the suddenness of my intake. We eat like ravenous animals. Nothing about it is graceful.

Helga lets out a burp, and I laugh like I haven't laughed in months – *nee* – years!

"Thank you," I tell Father afterwards, licking my fingers for any last drop of the peach juice that clings to them.

He smiles and nods at us as he eats his own peaches with more self-control, "It's the least I could do."
And suddenly, we are back in reality. Back to wondering where he's been.

"What happened, *Papa?*" this from Helga, her use of the endearing term for our father sounding weird on her adult lips. Not because we are too old for such terms – we still call our mother *Mama* – but his absence has caused a detachment for me.
Father's mouth twitches, and he looks away ashamedly, shaking his head.

"They were strange times," he mutters.
Helga and I share a look, "They still are," I counter.
He meets my gaze for a moment, then exhales, "Your mother and I…we didn't see eye to eye afterwards."

"After what?" I ask.
He frowns at us, "She didn't tell you why…?"
A heavy exhale, "Something happened to one of the Jewish families we were sheltering. After they left us and made their way to the next checkpoint, they were caught by the Nazis, tortured for information and killed."
His face flushes with the memory.

"We couldn't afford the risk of staying here," he continues, looking around, "That's what I told your *mama*. But she…she refused to leave Giethoorn. She took you away from the barge, at least. For that I am glad. But I couldn't stay."
My chest pinches with resentment. Though I can understand his fear.

"It had nothing to do with my love for you," he says, "But you had your mother, and I knew that you three would be safer without me. If the family revealed that it had been a household of four who'd hidden them, at least with my leaving, you had an immediate camouflage."
Helga is nodding, taking in all the information with no apparent level of emotion. I wish I could be as indifferent.

"So, that's why you left," Helga states, "That's the whole story."

She looks at me and smiles tightly.

"*Mama* didn't tell us about all that," I say.

Father is nodding when we look back at him.

"Why Germany, though?" Helga asks then, "Why go there?"

He shakes his head and shrugs, his palms facing up, "I guess I thought it would be the safest place to be. I didn't think Germany would necessarily be searching for Dutch resistance in their own country."

A moment of silence befalls us as we digest everything we've learned. I assume *Mama* didn't tell us about the family that had been captured because she didn't want to scare us. Or maybe she didn't like to admit that fleeing might have been safer for all of us.

"So…what did you do in Germany for all these years?" I ask.

He starts to scratch at his arm, his face twisting at a memory.

"It doesn't matter," he mumbles, "What matters now is that I am back. I've been back and aiding the resistance for weeks."

"Weeks?" Helga asks sceptically, looking around the dirty kitchen.

"Well, I haven't been living *here*," Father replies, understanding the judgement in Helga's expression, "I only just returned here two days ago. Cleaning hasn't been at the top of my priorities."

Helga scoffs, "So…what will you do in the resistance?" she asks, "Now that you're back."

He snorts a nervous laugh, "Well, it was certainly interesting to come back and see young Jakob in charge. Years ago, it was his father who your mother and I received our information from. Hans Meyer. Jakob Meyer was just seventeen last I saw him."

"Seventeen?" I frown, "But that would make him only twenty-three now."

"Yeah?"

"Well, I mean, it's just – it's young," I babble, "Younger than we thought he was, right Helga?"

Helga nods, though her eyebrow is cocked at me, "*Ja*, younger than we thought. But he *looks* about thirty."

The teasing tone isn't lost on me, and I glance at her sideways.

Then she returns her attention to our father, who has since leaned back against the wall, a sofa cushion propped behind his head, "How did he take over from his father?" she asks, and I settle down beside her on the floor, fighting the bubble of excitement in my chest to hear more about Meyer.

"Well, same way most sons take over from their fathers," he says matter-of-factly.

When neither of us shows an inkling of understanding, he elaborates.

"You know Pieters?" he asks, and we nod, "Well, Pieters and Hans Meyer were the men at the top for this region. There are no leaders in the resistance. But some have more contacts than others. And they were the ones who helped coordinate efforts, and provide support to other resistance groups if needed, including things like financial resources, information, you know? But when Hans was captured and sent to a concentration camp –"

"A concentration camp?" I interrupt, stunned.

Father nods, "Just weeks before your *mama* and I went our separate ways," he says, as if it's old news. Which, for him, I suppose it is, "Well, when that happened, his son Jakob took his role, I guess. I was no longer here by then, but it makes sense. Despite the boy's young age. Well, he's a man now. And look, you two started young yourselves."

He goes on rambling for a bit, but I tune him out.

My stomach is churning, likely because I am no longer used to the amount of sugar that was in those canned peaches.

My mind is buzzing with everything my father has said, the overload of information has given me a headache.

"I think I need to lie down," I mumble, standing up and walking into the back of the barge where mine and Helga's bedroom used to be.

"Is she okay?" I hear my father ask.

I push open the door to a room I no longer recognise, with nothing but a tatty mattress on the floor, and I don't wait for Helga's response before closing the door behind me.

What a terrible world we live in, I think, as I sink down onto the mattress, unbothered by its musty smell.

I think of what little we have actually achieved by going after individual Nazi officers, and how much of ourselves we have given up in the process of 'resisting.'

Meyer's father was sent to a concentration camp, a worker camp, to endure harrowing conditions. In truth, he was likely dead.

My family is torn apart.

Helga hasn't been the same since that first face-to-face kill.

Meyer has undergone severe interrogation and torture.

Marta is dead.

And I?

I think I am falling for a man whose likelihood of survival through this war is slim. Hell, *any* of our survivals through this war is slim!

With a shuddering breath, I close my eyes and hope for dreams, reality being too heavy to bear.

And I realise, just as sleep takes me, that our father never *did* answer my question about what he has been doing in Germany for all these years.

Wolfgang

<u>Poland, Auschwitz</u>

  Bit by bit, I like to think that I have done as much as I can to help the prisoners without drawing attention to myself.

When a prisoner is prescribed a beating, I volunteer if I am nearby, knowing my blows will be far less wounding than came from a camp *kapo*. The *kapos* are prisoners assigned to supervisory positions in the camps, and they are sometimes more aggressive than the officers themselves, as if to somehow show their loyalties to the Nazi regime.

When *Mutti* sends me care packages with food, I discretely hand the items out at random to those who appear to need it the most.

My reputation among the prisoners grows positive, some nodding ever so slightly at me in thanks when we cross paths.

But it is still not enough.

And this was made clear to me every single day.

This morning, as I make my way to the central SS administrative building, I hear a baby crying. It is not an uncommon sound, many women arriving from the trains with babies cradled in their arms or young children hanging from their hands. I search the origin of the sound, nonetheless, somehow drawn to it, feeling its despair. I see it then, the child, wrapped in rags, lying on a ramp attached to the opening of one of the trains that arrived just moments ago, spewing out more prisoners. My brows twitch with unease, uncertain of what I should do. But my feet take me towards it, my conscience unable to simply leave it there. A mother must've left it behind, perhaps knowing that women with infants were sent straight to the gas chambers. I can see its arms flailing, protesting the only way it knows how at being left behind, unaware of where it is. Just a few feet away, my stomach drops with dread when another SS soldier reaches the baby first and grabs it by its leg, holding it up.

I stop in my tracks, my blood running cold at the realisation that I am too late – though I cannot think of what I could've possibly done to save it had I reached it first.

I close my eyes and turn my back on the scene before the shot rings out, ceasing the baby's cries. And I immediately regret my cowardice. I should have made myself witness that poor child's final moment. My full attention was the least I could've offered it. The image of its inhumane death should be my burden to bear.

I walk away, swallowing down the lump in my throat, loathing weighing me down. I am filled with outrage, my throat burning with it, and I nearly double over to vomit where I stand. But I force it away, focus instead on my rising shame in my countrymen. I simply cannot understand how they can do this to people – to *children*.

Moments later, I am standing before my superior, fuelled with anger by what I have just witnessed.

"I need an assistant," I tell him, more aware than ever that I need to do more for these people, even if my own life depends on it.

He looks down his nose at me, his round-rimmed glasses making his eyes look bug-like.

"*Warum?*" – why? – he asks.

My work is mainly administrative here in Auschwitz. My insubordination over the years had demoted me to a more clerical position, one which I certainly appreciate more than what I was made to do previously. To me, it had not been a demotion at all, but a prize for a job badly done. Though I would not admit this to anyone but myself.

"The paperwork is getting away from me," I say, "It's piling up, and I need someone to organise."

The *Hauptsturmführer* shrugs, "You'll have to find someone in this shithole that can actually type. And in German, of course."

I nod, though I don't care either way, since helping me to type up all the items that had been salvaged from Kanada is hardly something I need to burden anyone else with. It is only a cover story, so that I am granted my request. As long as they can dust and empty the bin under my desk, they will have a safe job with me.

Alma

<u>Poland, Auschwitz</u>

I wake up to screaming and the next moment the SS-*Aufseherin* smacks me on the legs with her metal rod.
I cry out in pain and hold my shin, but scramble out of the bunk.
"*Raus! Raus!*"
The *Aufseherin* – a female SS guard who oversees the women's blocks – and the *Blockältesten* – Jews in charge of the barracks, who were sometimes worse than the German guards – were beating our beds with their rods to get us up.
They shove us out of their way, some women falling to the floor, before yanking the ratty blankets off our wooden beds and sweeping off the straw.

"They're looking for contraband," someone whispers to another near me, and I can hear the tremor in her voice.
I follow everyone to stand against the wall, but I cannot help but wonder what contraband there could possibly be. When we live with nothing but the clothes on our backs and the wooden clogs on our feet, what do they expect to find?

"The book," a woman beside me whimpers to her friend then. I look at her and realise she must work at Kanada, because she, like her friend, have been allowed to grow their hair long. Everyone else, me included, have their hair shaved off every three months. Many envy those who work in Kanada for that, and many other reasons.
I try to meld into the crowd, realising I am in the frontline, and right next to the culprit at that! But the women behind me do not budge, none of them wanting to swap places with me.

The *Aufseherin* comes towards us, holding up an item. And sure enough, it is a book.

"Who sleeps in that bunk?" she asks, pointing to where she found the item.

The woman next to me is shaking so hard I doubt the *Aufseherin* even needs her to step forward and confess. But she does, nonetheless. As do the four other women who sleep with her on the bunk.

"Which one of you stole this?"

None of them fess up, and the *Aufseherin* doesn't hesitate to hand out punishment for their silence, raising her metal rod and smacking the one near me hard in the face.

She cries out and I shrink back in shock, her blood splashing my cheek and something hard knocking me on the forehead. I lift my hand to wipe my face, and look down at the ground to see one of the woman's teeth.

I straighten up slowly, my heart beating wildly in my chest, and close my eyes to stop myself from retching. But it is too late, and I double over and heave, though nothing comes out.

The woman is a crumpled mess on the floor, a hand over her face, blood seeping through her fingers as she blubbers frantically. Her nose is no doubt broken. Her teeth smashed in.

Given the other four women who stepped forward have short hair, the *Aufseherin* must've guessed that she was the culprit who'd stolen the book from Kanada.

"Does that stir your memory?" she barks down at her, grabbing her by the hair and dragging her outside.

I don't know why I do it. Perhaps my natural instinct to help has not yet been corroded by the more animalistic instinct to survive, because suddenly I am up and following them out the barrack.

"Hey!" I call, my hand outstretched to stop her.

She must not have heard me, because the *Aufseherin* continues forward and shoves the woman down into the mud. I don't know why I focus on this, but I notice the woman has lost one of her shoes in the chaos. And I think, *What is the point in interfering? Without her shoes, she is dead already.* As was proven by the woman who'd had her shoes stolen my first night here, and who went on to develop sores on her feet that got infected. She died just four days after I arrived. I know because I carried her body to the crematorium.

But the *Aufseherin* turns to me suddenly then. She did hear me after all.

"*Bist du blöd?!*" – Are you stupid? – she shrieks at me, her metal rod raised.

I take a step back and lift my arms to protect myself, and just as I expect the rod to come down on me, I hear a voice.

"*Halt!*"

I peer through my fingers to see the *Aufseherin* look up and drop her rod, before practically bowing to the SS officer standing behind me. But I am too scared to turn around.

"*Oberscharführer,*" she says.

"*Was tun Sie mit meiner Arbeiterin?*"

The older woman looks at me with venom in her eyes.

"*Arbeiterin?*" she spits the word, and I am left reeling, trying to understand their conversation. I might've learned some basic German from Esther and Trudi, but I cannot keep up with these native speakers when they speak quickly.

By now, guards and even some of the women from my block have come outside to watch, and I look to them as the *Aufseherin* and the SS officer continue talking, searching for my friend's faces for comfort.

I think I see Trudi hiding behind some others, smart enough not to draw attention to herself. Unlike me.

"*Ihr zwei,*" the SS officer says, clicking his fingers and pointing.

Two guards come towards us and haul me upright.

The officer walks off ahead, and before I know it, I am being taken past the courtyard, past Kanada and to the administrative building.

This is it. I am about to die.

My throat is dry, and tears are blurring my vision. I am even surprised for a moment that I am hydrated enough to produce tears. And then I think what a strange final thought that is. My *maman* and *papa's* faces come to me, the heartbreaking look my *maman* gave me before flinging herself to safety, my *papa's* words of warning that I should've heeded. I even think of Abel, and how I wish – as I have done every day since – that I had been smart enough to remove my star before being rounded up. I wonder what has become of him. If he is still alive. If he still thinks of me. Or of anyone in Le Chambon.

The officer enters the building, and the guards follow with me sandwiched between them, my feet barely touching the ground as they carry me along. He shouts an order over his shoulder, and I am brought upstairs, to an office. The guards leave after shoving me inside, the officer having taken a seat at his desk.

I am so flustered I do not know where to look, my eyes darting around the room but taking nothing in. I wipe at them, blink the tears away. I will not let him see me cry!

His door is still open, and on it is a name: *Oberscharführer W. Herrman.* The walls are lined with bookshelves which are crammed with folders and files. A swastika flag dons the wall above the desk, and sitting at the desk my gaze finally comes to rest on the SS officer.

And my knees almost give out to look upon the man who saved my mother's life.

Chapter 13

Abel

<u>Germany, Plön</u>

I feel like I am living a double life.

Like I am a schizophrenic with two identities living in one body.

After breathing life back into my old self, I have unleashed a wave of guilt, betrayal, and self-loathing. And I feel like I am drowning.

How could I have allowed myself to feel comfortable here? To feel like part of this community? To feel *pride* in it when I know they were targeting people – *my* people?

It just goes to show how easily a mind is led. Whether young or old, if we are told something often enough, we end up believing it, despite knowing the truth.

What a weak organ the brain is. Or perhaps it is the heart? Whichever organ is responsible for feeling at ease in one's own skin? *That* one is to blame for letting me think I could live as Walter Schmidt.

It is like I've outgrown myself. Or at least, the self I had created in order to blend in in the Hitler Youth.

I am Abel.

Abel!

Not Walter Schmidt.

But of course, I cannot tell anyone. Cannot ever allow myself to let my mask slip even for a moment. Outwardly, I have to make sure I portray a happy-go-lucky young man in the Hitler Youth, proud to be part of something incredible, and willing to fight – *die!* – for the man who has quite literally ruined mine, and millions of others' lives.

Otto and the other boys haven't noticed a change in me. Or if they have, they don't mention it.

I have continued as always. Laughing at their jokes, marching in perfect synch, doing well in class.

But inside, I am itching to be returned to my true self.

And the only person who could ever understand how I feel, is Frida.

"How long did you attend the League of German Maidens?" I ask her now as she and I sit on the grass in the field behind the castle, the perimeter fence separating us, since she is not a student at the boarding school.

We had agreed to meet here following my latest dinner at her home, our private conversation in the kitchen having led to a camaraderie I hadn't realised I'd needed. My attraction to her aside, I am glad to have someone know the real me. After all, what would be the point of surviving this war if, by the end of it, I no longer know who I truly am?

"Three years," she tells me.

I exhale through my nose, "How did you do it? How did you manage to remain hidden for so long?"

She shakes her head and shrugs, "I honestly don't know. I guess they see what they want to see."

I examine her face, her hazel eyes, small mouth and straight nose. Her long, blond hair.

In her case, she appears to be of perfect 'Aryan' descent. The same could be said for her father, except for his dark eyes.

"You know the study of Eugenics is hogwash, don't you?" she says, like she could hear my thoughts.

I do, though I cannot help but think of my own black hair, my dark eyes. Hitler Youth's brainwashing has begun even to affect me!

The sun is shining down on us, though Frida is half covered in shade by the row of ash trees that surround the castle.

I squint up at the sky and inhale deeply, thinking for a moment how I wish none of this had ever happened, and that I'd never come here.

I return my gaze to Frida, ambivalence tapping at my heart to think that, had I not, I would never have met her. My two realities battle within me again, my conflicting emotions tearing me up inside, and I hang my head. It's all too heavy.

"What's the matter?" Frida asks, scooting closer to the fence.

I turn my lolling head in her direction. She has wrapped her fingers around one of the rails and is leaning her temple against it, her expression calming.

"Nothing," I tell her, "Just the clash between Walter and Abel in here," I tap on my forehead.

The corner of her mouth quirks into a lazy smile, and I cannot help but think how pretty she is.

"Maybe it's better that you keep them apart."

"How do you mean?"

"Keep them apart," she repeats, shrugging easily, "You spent the past year with Abel locked up entirely, where did you keep him?"

I shake my head. I don't know.

She reaches through the fence then and rests her hand on my knee, "Abel," she whispers, her tone guiding. As if to say *Stop being so obtuse.*

I look down at her hand on my knee, and fight with all my inner strength not to burst into flames. I can feel my ears burning and my throat running dry, and I lift my gaze back up to meet hers.

"Where did you feel from then? When I called you by your true name? In your heart, or your brain?"

I couldn't very well tell her that when she touched me, I felt with neither of those organs. But I push past those immature thoughts and raise my hand to my chest.

"In here," I whisper back at her, pleased as she nods her approval. She retracts her hand from my knee.
It feels cold with her retreat.

"Then there you have your answer," she says, "Keep Abel safely in your heart, and Walter at the forefront of your mind. You do not have to forsake one for the other. Simply keep them separate until the day comes that you may free Abel once again."

"Do you really think that day will ever come?" I find myself asking.
She sighs, a hint of sadness coating her intake. Then she blinks at me and forces a tight smile.

"All we can do is pray for that day. And if it does come, remember to return to our roots."

This time, it is Frida – not Weis – who invites me to their home.
By now, we are both very clear about our feelings for one another. We've shared enough lingering glances across the dinner table and had enough charged moments scattered in between that there is no need for words. And with the touch of her hand on my knee followed by her invitation to come over, I know that something amazing is about to happen.
At my knock, she opens the door almost immediately, like she has been waiting for my arrival, clearly as eager to see me in private as I am to see her.

"Hi," I breathe.
She looks beautiful, her golden hair is loose and tousled over her shoulders, her smile pouted with mischief.
She pulls me inside by my hand, and I worry that she'll notice how sweaty they are. If she does, she appears not to care; and I am immediately at ease.

Frida leads me to the living room, where she sits down on a floral sofa decorated with burgundy cushions on either end. I sit down beside her, as closely as I dare, always observing her to make sure I do not overstep.

I risk a glance at Frida and find her shifting in her seat so that she is sitting closer to me, playing with her hair in a way which makes my skin tingle.

"It's hot," I say, meaning the weather, realising it sounds like an intimation.

She smiles and nods, "Summer is still clinging on."

I exhale with relief that she understood my meaning.

"And your father? He is well?"

"Yes, all well."

I nod, unsure for a moment how to continue this small talk. If I even should.

"My friends," I say, "Otto especially, he is very jealous…"

I trail off, aware that I am but stalling, and that she likely does not care about such mundane topics. Not when we both know what I have been summoned here for. Today of all days.

A silence ensues, and it feels suddenly electric, as if there is something growing between us that could only be snuffed out by hedging closer. Our thighs touch then, and a breath catches in my throat.

I sweep a lock of her hair from her face, "May I?" I utter, fearful that the moment will burst like a bubble if I speak too loudly.

She nods, ever so slightly, and when her eyes flick to my lips, I close the gap between us.

I've never kissed a girl before. And when our noses bump together and I accidentally bite her lip, she giggles, amused.

We pull apart, grinning nervously, and I rub my hand over my face at my inexperience. But it isn't awkward or embarrassing. Not at all. Because it is Frida.

We kiss again, slower this time, our bodies and minds relaxing into it. And before I know it, my hand is on her thigh, and her arms are around my neck.

I become hot, ablaze with senses that feel suddenly too big for my body. She smells like apples and cinnamon; she tastes like spring. On occasion, she makes a soft little sound at the back of her throat that drives me crazy with desire.

I stop, gasping for air. I must stop before we get carried away. She is too special to have anything further happen in this way. But boy, I want her, no question. And she clearly wants me, too.

"Wow," I sigh, and she smiles shyly.

I move away, extremely aware and embarrassed by my obvious excitement. I grab a cushion and cover myself.

"The bathroom?" I enquire, hoping to splash water on my face and neck, and to quash my growing urges.

She points behind her, "Door on the left," she says, and I feel superhuman at the sight of her flushed cheeks and blissful smile.

I did that!

And it feels incredible.

I head out of the living room as if I am floating on air. Never have I felt so alive. And I can only hope that Professor Weis will approve of me courting his daughter.

I make my way through a corridor I have never been down before. There are pictures hanging along the walls, some of Weis and his family, some of him and who I assumed is his wife, some of only Frida through several stages of her childhood.

They appear happy. I would never have guessed from those photographs that the beaming woman in them would one day abandon her loving husband and daughter. I guess one snapshot of someone's life cannot define a person's inner turmoil.

Finally, I arrive at the end of the corridor. But to my surprise, I find two doors on the left, side by side. With a shrug, I reach for the handle of the first and pull it open, revealing a dark room which I can immediately tell is not the bathroom. Much too big. And isn't that the outline of a bed?

But before stepping back and closing the door behind me, curiosity takes over when a giant red swastika flag catches my eye.

I squint into the darkness.

This has to be the professor's bedroom.

I look over my shoulder, and then, before I can talk myself out of it, I step inside and switch on the light. A bright yellow glow washes over the room, revealing a rather disappointingly decorated space containing nothing but a bed, a dresser and that godawful flag.

Dissatisfied, I turn to leave, feeling ashamed for having allowed my curiosity to break the professor's trust. I have no right to be in here, in his private chambers.

But suddenly, something strange catches my attention, and I narrow my eyes at the bed in the far corner.

What is that?

I move closer, cock my head to one side. I am standing over the bed now, frowning. On its headboard is a strange etching. I run my finger over it.

Three lines. Like the roman numeral for the number 3, spearheaded by a single name: *Josef.*

I frown. Who is Josef? And why would the professor have names and numbers etched on his bed?

"What are you doing in here?"

My blood runs cold at the unexpected voice behind me. Not because I have been caught out, but because so many tiny little awful details suddenly click into place.

Annika

<u>The Netherlands, Giethoorn</u>

Finally, the secret knock sounds almost 48 hours after Meyer left the barge, and our tense shoulders relax.
We'd been getting antsy to think we would have to leave without hearing from the resistance.

"Where would we go?" Helga had asked our father the night before, "If we do not receive word?"
He'd swallowed hard, "Through the woods to the nearest town. From there we'd have to find a way to England. But I don't think it will come to that."
We'd stayed up all night awaiting that knock, knowing that if it did not come, our lives in our homeland would come to an end.
So, I breathe a sigh of relief to hear it now, and Helga beside me sits up straight.
Father opens the door a crack and exchanges whispers with someone, and I crane my neck to see if it is Meyer.

"It won't be him," I hear Helga say.
I snap my head around, "Who?"

"Don't play dumb with me, Ani," she says, grinning, "You like Meyer?"
I shush her sharply, slapping her arm, "I don't like anyone. What good is 'like' at times such as these?"
Helga shrugs, "At least one of us has something positive come from all this."
My eyebrows furrow and I open my mouth to speak, but suddenly our father is walking towards us, the door closed behind him.

"Good news," he sighs, "We are to convene at the barge in an hour. Meyer and Pieters will meet us there."

"Is *Mama* alright?" I ask when he mentions Pieters.

He nods, "If Pieters is meeting us then he has not been found. Which means your mother is safe."

An hour later, with the bright sunshine beating down on us, Father, Helga and I are walking from one abandoned barge to another, maintaining a steady pace along the muddy path so as not to attract attention.

"You think they're still searching for us?" I ask quietly, though there is no one around.

"Make no mistake," Father mumbles, squinting against the sunlight, "The town will be crawling with Germans. People will have been dragged out of their homes and questioned for any information."

My stomach lurches with guilt and fear.

At the meeting point, we enter swiftly, cramming ourselves into the flatboat as well as we can.

I blink to adjust my vision to the darkness, its gloomy contrast to the outside blinding me momentarily.

I notice Pieters first, sitting on the ratty, built-in sofa in the dark. Then I see Meyer leaning against the kitchen counter, his lanky frame at an angle and his arms crossed over his chest.

I find myself almost smiling at the sight of him, and I think how, if not for these awful circumstances, I would no doubt have blushed like a silly schoolgirl to be near him.

I wonder briefly what my life would have been like as a normal teenager and young woman. Certainly, I wouldn't know how to shoot a man while riding a bicycle, nor that tulip bulbs are edible and that by grating and boiling them into a soup one can avoid starvation for another day.

No doubt I would've learned, through trial and error, how to flirt with a boy I liked, how to kiss. Maybe I would have learned a new dance rather than how to load a gun. Or if red lipstick suited my complexion, rather than how to make a dress out of an old curtain.

A nod from Pieters as we enter is all the greeting we get before being thrown into the deep end.

"They aren't looking for us," he says, shooting Meyer a quick glance, "They are officially looking for two young women luring men out at night. We cannot continue as we have."

"What's next, then?" Helga asks, detached, icy.
A dizziness overcomes me.
What else can we possibly do?
What more will be expected of us?
We've already given so much of ourselves. I worry that to do more will cost me my soul, as it already appears to have cost Helga's.

"It's no longer safe here," Meyer says now, glancing at me with an expression I cannot place.
Sadness?
Concern?

"But," I begin, "But why summon us here?" I look from Meyer to Pieters to my father, "You said that if we got word, we would be safe, that we wouldn't have to flee."
Father opens his mouth to speak, but Pieters cuts in.

"It's only to keep everyone safe for now. They are looking for you, they will have ransacked your home by now and you will receive no rations at the shops. Your mother is safe as long as she's with me. The best course of action is to move you both to a new location. You can continue your work there."
Instinctively, I reach for Helga's hand, "But you won't separate us, will you?"
Pieters shakes his head, "No, you are both to go together. Your father will stay, however. He is not compromised. And we need all the help we can get."
I look to our father, feeling suddenly like this is some great injustice. We have only just been reunited with him! Haven't even had enough time together to know where he's been and what he's been up to.

"*Papa?*" I hear myself mumble, tears pricking at my eyes. Exhaustion, anxiety, tension, hunger. It is all too overwhelming. And I lean into him as the tears fall.

He wraps his arms around me, and I notice he is unsure of how to place them around the body of this daughter of his that has changed so much since he'd last held her.

This only makes me feel more distraught, but before I make an even bigger spectacle of myself, I pull away and wipe my face with the palm of my hand.

Helga puts an arm around my shoulders, and I press my lips together tightly.

"What about *Mama?*" I ask after a moment, "We need to say goodbye."

Pieters shakes his head, and the knot in my stomach tightens.

"There is no time, and it isn't safe."

"But –" I say, before Helga interrupts me.

"When do we leave?" she says, stoic and impassive.

I can hardly believe her indifference.

Meyer pushes himself upright off the kitchen counter and grabs his jacket from the side.

"Right now."

"Where are we going?" Helga rasps, as we slip out the perimeter of the village where we grew up. Giethoorn: the only place I've ever known.

I look back over my shoulder for one last glance at it in its full splendour, a lump forming in my throat to think of my parents, who we are leaving behind without having had a proper goodbye.

We might never see them again.

We might never see Giethoorn again –

"Arnhem," Meyer's gruff voice says as he walks ahead, "Some ninety-five kilometres south."

"Arnhem?" Helga parrots, "Why there?"

"There are people who will help us," he replies.

His tone is clipped, like he's cut around each word, trimming all emotion out of his speech. I know better than to add to the questions. I let Helga do the talking.

"How long will it take?" she asks, just as I shift the rucksack on my back a little.

The straps are digging into my shoulders already, though the bag itself only contains one change of clothes, a blanket, a water bottle and a stale loaf of bread. But my body is weak from the many months of little nourishment, though I'm not about to complain just moments into our travels.

When Meyer doesn't answer, Helga looks at me.

"You okay?" she asks quietly, and I nod, trying not to think about how our rations were barely enough for one journey, nevermind a return.

"If all goes well…" Meyer says after a beat of silence, "We should be there in three days."

Dread prickles my skin to think that we might be caught on our way. What would happen to us if we were?

"What if we are spotted, Meyer?" Helga asks, "Do we disperse, surrender – ?"

At that, Meyer stops and turns to face us with an exasperated exhale, the sun behind his head. And my heart jumps to my throat at the sight of him, striking despite his raggedness, or perhaps, because of it.

"You know," he says, tightening one of the straps on his shoulder, "We should really conserve our energy by not talking."

A smile threatens to pull at my lips. I press them together to keep it in.

"You're right," Helga says, jerking her backpack higher and walking ahead.

Meyer lets her take the lead for a moment, and I wonder how long she will pretend to know the way before hanging back again and allowing him to advance. We aren't exactly following a path or a road, and Meyer is the only one among us who knows the way.

I shoot him a rueful glance as we continue, almost in apology for my sister, and he falls into step beside me.

As suggested, we hike on in silence for a while and none of us dare to stop even for a drink of water as we walk along the riverbank into the unknown.

After a while, we separate from the stream and head up into a grassy field. Each step feels measured as I put one foot in front of the other, growing unsteady sooner than I hoped. But I push on, hooking my thumbs underneath the straps of my bag to alleviate some of the pressure against my skin.

I try to focus on other things. The chirp of birds as they fly overhead. The flap of their wings. The rustle of the grass against my legs.

Meyer's breathing.

I steal a glance in his direction, disguising it by appearing to take in my surroundings. He catches my eye, and I quickly look away, my cheeks burning, mortified for being caught out.

Eventually, Helga slows down and Meyer takes the lead again, before steering us into a wooded area. Among the trees, the temperature drops noticeably, but at least we are no longer out in the open.

We walk for a long time, until finally, he stops.

"We'll camp here tonight," he says, taking off his backpack with a grunt.

"Here?" Helga counters, looking around, "Now? But it is not yet nightfall."

"Trust me," he replies, "We're secluded here, and we'll need our full strength tomorrow for another long day before we reach the first checkpoint. By the time we have set up and cooked dinner it will be dark, and you'll be ready for sleep."

Helga doesn't argue, and I for one am glad. My feet are throbbing like they have their own heartbeat, and I'm happy to shed the bag off my back.

"I'll gather some kindling," Meyer says, walking off.
I watch him, my unease growing the further he goes.

"He'll be fine," Helga mumbles beside me as she massages her calves.

"I know," I reply, "It's just…"

"Scary?" she finishes for me.
I nod, "It feels weird leaving our home. Like…like my body and my soul are disconnecting the further I go, you know? Like I'm losing a sense of who I am without my roots."

"Our roots are still there," she says, shrugging casually, as if this outing is like any other activity, "We're just going on an adventure."

"*Ja*," I mutter, unbuckling my bag and pulling out my blanket, "An adventure."
When Meyer returns, he builds a small fire, around which we unroll our blankets.

"Here," he says to us, holding out two sticks, "To skewer the meat."
He pulls out a lump from his backpack and peels the cloth away to reveal four sausages, and Helga and I practically squeal with delight.
My mouth waters. The last time we ate sausages was over a year ago, when the butcher's wife took pity on me. I think of her fondly now, remembering the taste of them. She may very well have saved our lives that day.

"Where did you get those?" I gape, never taking my eyes off of them as he stabs one onto the end of a stick.

"Your *mama*," he says, "She camped outside the butcher's for two nights to make sure she got the best things for our travels."
Tears well in my eyes, and I grin at my sister half in happiness, half in sadness.

"She will be alright," Meyer says after a moment, realising perhaps that we need to hear it, "She's tough, your mother."

A breathy laugh escapes me, and I wipe my tears away with my sleeve, "That, she is."

I take out the loaf of bread from my bag and break off three pieces. We eat our meal in silence as the fire crackles between us, savouring every mouthful as if it might be our last.

I chew extra slowly, fighting with myself not to scarf it down.

We each eat one sausage, and then Meyer cooks the fourth and I almost cry with appreciation when he breaks it in half and hands one part to each of us.

I gift him a grateful nod, but neither me nor Helga has it in us even to pretend to be polite and offer our half to him, we are so starved. And I guess he wouldn't have accepted it anyhow.

Once we are fed, watered, and warm, we sit in companionable silence for a while and wait for the fire to burn down to embers. Then Meyer picks up his backpack and heads to a nearby tree, where he makes himself comfortable.

"You'd best get some shut eye," he says, pulling a gun out of his bag, "I'll take the first watch. Tomorrow, we'll be at it again, bright and early."

Helga and I don't argue, welcoming the respite, and we arrange our blankets next to one another's in the hope of catching some sleep. But it doesn't come easily, some lump or root digging into us no matter how we lie. And though there is a bed of leaves beneath our blankets, we shuffle about for some time, mumbling complaints until we give in, resigning ourselves to an uncomfortable rest.

Alma

<u>Poland, Auschwitz</u>

"*Du...*" – You… – I whisper, forgetting myself for a moment.

The Nazi stands up sharply, and I cower, reflexively raising my hands above my head.

But when he reaches around me and closes the door with a quiet *click*, a strange sense of safety settles over me. Which, given my company and my location, is the most unexpected oxymoron.

"*Setz dich,*" he says, and I take a seat.

He walks around me for a moment, a time in which I gather all my strength and dare to look him in the face.

I hadn't noticed before, not while on the truck here, nor when he had urged me into silence on my first day in this hellhole, but he has an inch-long vertical scar above his upper lip, which pulls one side of his mouth up ever so slightly.

A war wound perhaps. Or something he'd been born with, like a cleft lip?

"*Sprichst du Deutsch?*" – Do you speak German? – he asks, sitting down at his desk again, facing me.

At this, I am relieved to be able to say, "*Ja.* But only a little."

He nods, a frown between his brows, "How?" he asks, "You were detained in France."

So, he remembers.

I wonder if he is haunted by his actions. If he remembers where everyone he's taken had come from.

"My friends," I say slowly, unsure if I should share this information, "They have taught me what I know."

I'm aware that my German is not very good, that I have misspoken at least once, and that my accent is laughable.

But he appears to understand me, just as Esther and Trudi understand me.

He smiles then, just a twitch on one side of his mouth, finding amusement, no doubt, that I deem my desperate relationships in here as friendships. And my hatred for him and his kind flares up again.

"You have made friends?" he asks, perching on the edge of his desk and meeting my gaze.

His eyes are a deep shade of blue like the heart of a flame. I shift in my seat, uncomfortable to have noticed.

"*Ja*, good friends," I tell him, raising my chin, readying myself for his mocking laugh.

But he only nods instead, his smile quirking higher.

Is he…happy for me?

He twists and takes a cigarette from an open packet on his desk, lights it, and takes a deep drag, squinting against the sting of the smoke as his expression changes to seriousness.

"You are to work here now," he says, changing the subject. He blows two twin streams of smoke out his nostrils, and for a moment, I think I misunderstand him, "What was your position?"

I gawk at him, then blink, "Uh…*Leichenkommando*."

I see a slight but noticeable tic of distaste cross his face, "You'll find working for me much easier," he says, getting up and walking around the desk.

"You will empty the bin, organise paperwork, clean my windows, dust, that kind of thing," he says, looking out the window with his hands clasped behind his back, his cigarette dangling between two fingers.

I nod, tears pricking my eyes to understand what he is doing.

What I don't understand is: why?

He turns to me, his eyes finding mine, "Why?" he asks, and I flinch, realising I have spoken aloud.

He takes a step towards me. His desk – and the world – is between us, and yet somehow, despite myself, I feel myself leaning closer.
He stubs the roll-up out in a metal ashtray on his desk, then looks at me.

"Because," he whispers earnestly, a hint of remorse cracking his voice, which I realise I am not surprised to hear, "Not all of us are monsters."

Chapter 14

Wolfgang

<u>Poland, Auschwitz</u>

Her eyes, a brown like the richest, darkest chocolate, shift to mine and I see a sadness in them that almost takes my breath away. What have those eyes seen that makes them hold such anguish? I don't need to wonder, because I know. I have seen the horrors. I have *been* the horrors.

"There is another Germany apart from this one," I mutter when she does not respond, though I am not sure what I expected her to say.

My voice is heavy with the truth, a truth I wish I could spark life into simply by uttering it. But I know to achieve that Germany again requires more than breathy promises, it requires actions.

I think of the people I have met along the way who, like me, are taking dangerous but necessary measures to return the world to normality. And I can only hope that we are collectively doing enough, a little here, a little there, to one day come out of this darkness.

Her jaw sets rigidly, like she is struggling to believe me. And I cannot blame her. If I stood where she stands, I wouldn't believe me, either.

I show her what her new duties to me will be.

No funny business, not like some officers do with their chosen helpers. Just light cleaning and tidying. A simple enough excuse to get her out of the cold and grime of Auschwitz.

I leave her alone after a moment, closing the door to my office behind me and making my way down the corridor.

She will not be disturbed. I have made no friends here and am of little importance in my sector. As long as I report to my supervisor, neither I nor my office will be sought out by anyone.

She can rest there, she can breathe. And if my plan works out, she will be the first of hopefully many that I will smuggle out of here.

Alma

<u>Poland, Auschwitz</u>

"Be careful," Esther tells me after I explain what happened the day before, then she hurries to take her turn to use the lavatory.

I watch her go, not needing to ask what she meant. Being near them gains us warmth, a lighter load, the possibility of extra food. But it also puts us…well, near them.

"He's taking advantage of her," Trudi adds quietly behind me, and I turn my head to listen, "Her officer, who Esther works for – Neumann – he's been raping her for weeks."

"What?" I gasp incredulously, "But she told me he was good to her…"

Trudi shrugs, "We do what we must to survive."

By the time it is my turn to enter the lavatories, I am so desperate I almost don't make it, and I thank God I didn't need to use my bowl while waiting in line. Only last week, a man behind me had been shot in the head for relieving himself on the wall by the lavatory, unable to hold it any longer.

I wish I could say that I cried out in shock and maybe shed a tear to witness his brutal demise. But death is so common to us now that we simply stepped over his body and continued standing in line as his head squirted blood from the bullet hole.

But Trudi's words ring in my ears as I make my way to the administrative building.

A group of guards walk past me, one of them holding a stick and hitting prisoners with it as they walk past. I duck my head and detour around them. A woman screams behind me, followed by the sound of wood beating down on flesh once, twice, three times. I stop counting, but I dare to look over my shoulder at them. One of them laughs as another smokes a cigarette, watching the woman's torture as though it is a show.

Disgust and hatred curls my lip and boils my blood, and I cannot *possibly* imagine allowing one of those creatures to touch me in exchange for an extra crust of bread, or another day in this place.

How does Esther live with herself? Especially given what their hatred has caused her to lose. Truthfully, I think I would rather *die* than let any of them lay an intimate hand on me. I'd sooner take a beating than allow anything else!

The workday begins at 4.30am in the summer and now at 5.30am in the autumn.

We are woken with the sound of an alarm and made to tidy our living quarters to the best of our abilities. Then we have about thirty minutes before the second alarm notifies us to present ourselves at roll call. And in that time, if you fail to relieve yourself, you are not allowed another bathroom break until nighttime.

Every morning after roll call, I walk with Esther through the filth and misery of Auschwitz to the administration's building.

Esther and I are referred to as *Lagerprominent* – an inmate with a 'good' job. The other inmates look at us with yearning and even jealousy when we walk past them, Esther donning a green triangle on her uniform to indicate her position as *Schreiber* – secretary.

I try not to look at them as we make our way past those less fortunate people on *Leichenkommando* hauling dead bodies, on *Baukommando* building new barracks or latrines, and even past people who unknowingly stand in line for the gas chambers.

Of course, we know we are incredibly lucky, and yet I cannot say that I ever feel what I felt back then, when I was happy. But sometimes, something would touch the place where that feeling used to be, a touch as slight and swift as the brush of a moth's wing in the dark.

I just have to hold onto those rare moments, and hope they see me through.

Each morning over the course of the following week, I have found his office empty upon entering, and I set about tidying the papers on his desk, dusting, or emptying his bin. I don't know where he spends his mornings, but by 9 o'clock each day, he enters and nods his head in greeting before sitting down at his desk to read through the morning reports.

Today is no different. And as he eats his breakfast at his desk – a muffin and a coffee from the SS's canteen – the smell of the coffee makes my stomach growl. I inhale the aroma as discreetly as possible, its smell alone being a long-forgotten treat.

But then, he does something unexpected.

"Eat," he mumbles out of the blue, and I turn from the bookshelf where I'd been dusting, thinking I've imagined the beautiful word.

I look down at his desk, my mouth watering at the sight of a half torn off muffin on the edge.

And yet I dare not step closer.

When he sees me hesitating, he pushes it further towards me still, and like the pull of a magnet, I take a tentative step forward.

My eyes flicker from him to the muffin and back, wary that this may be some sick test. But once I stand before it, it's moistness teasing me, I cannot control myself, and I think: *Even if this leads to me being shot in the head, to taste a blueberry muffin one last time, would be worth it.*

I stuff it into my mouth like a greedy child, enjoying every part of it: its soft texture on my tongue, its sweetness awakening my taste buds.

This, right here, is Heaven.

Once I've swallowed it, I open my eyes carefully, certain that this is the end.

But, instead of staring down the barrel of a gun as I feared, I see him casually reading through his reports, as if nothing unusual has happened.

Every morning since, he repeats the process.

Sometimes, I eat only a little and hide the rest up my sleeve when he isn't looking, so that I might share it with Esther and Trudi back in our barracks.

They weep the first time I bring them a piece each. But soon enough, they grow simply to expect it. Like it is his due for how we are being treated in here.

"Morning," he says today, breezing into his office and flashing me a smile, and my mouth salivates in anticipation of the delicious treat.

I look up from scrubbing the floor on my hands and knees.

"Morning," I repeat, dropping my gaze immediately when the kindness in his face makes me falter. I pray he mistakes it for exertion.

It still feels so completely out of place, to see good in someone wearing a Nazi uniform.

A knock at the door suddenly makes me jump, and I drop the scrubbing brush into the soapy bucket. It *plops* loudly, creating a small puddle on the wood floor.

Herrman flashes me a look and I get up and scurry towards the bookshelf in the corner, turning my back on the door and pretending to dust the books on a shelf.

"*Oberscharführer* Herrman," the deep voice says behind me in greeting, "The file, as requested."

"Thank you," he replies.

A moment passes, then, "So, is she working out?"

I can practically feel their stares on my back.

"Indeed," *Oberscharführer* Herrman replies, before adding, "As well as can be expected."

My stomach drops in disappointment at his tone, though I know that he must play his part.

The other man scoffs, "These *Drecksjuden* are all the same."

I hear Herrman clear his throat then, "*War's das?*" – is that all?

The man mutters a sound of affirmation, and I exhale slowly in relief. But then his bark makes me jump, "*Ach!* Look at that!"

I freeze. Does he mean me? Should I turn and look?

"Look at the mess that animal has created. Soaking wood like that will ruin it!"

He grabs me by my arm and whirls me around, "*Bist du dumm?!*"

I stare wide-eyed at his red face, pressed so closely to mine that I can see each of his pores.

"*Scharführer* Schulz!" Herrman calls from over his shoulder, and he tears his eyes from me, "*Genug*, I will deal with her."

He shoves me away, as if *I'd* invaded *his* space, and I make myself as small as possible.

Over the rushing of blood in my ears, I hear footsteps and the door closing, but I do not dare look up.

I am trembling so hard my bony back rattles painfully against the wall. With my eyes closed, I inhale slowly to settle my nerves when suddenly a hand clasps my shoulder, and I cry out in panic, my arms covering my head.

"It's alright," says the voice, and my pounding heart begins to slow.

I look up and see Herrman standing over me, his palms facing forward in surrender, "He's gone."

Too frightened to believe anything but my own senses, I scan the room, my eyes flitting to all the corners until I am satisfied he is telling the truth.

"He's gone," he repeats, and I regard him as he looks down at me not with pity, but with shame.

I am still shaking, and yet, when he offers me a hand, I take it. It is rough but gentle, his long fingers brushing my wrist as he hauls me upright. He takes a step back as soon as I'm up, supposing that his proximity would make me feel uncomfortable, threatened.

But to my utter disbelief, I find that it does the complete opposite.

One afternoon, I and thousands of others are forced to stand in silence in the courtyard to watch a public hanging.

A full ceremony is performed, where we all stand facing forward, and the SS guards line up in perfect precision with their guns over their shoulders and marching drums strapped around their necks. In among them, I spot Wolfgang, and my heart drops. He stares straight ahead, never once making eye contact with me or any of the prisoners. I imagine he is as torn up inside as we are. But from Wolfgang's face alone, I would not be able to tell that he is against what is happening. And it makes me wonder if there are any other SS officers standing before us that are as horrified by their peers' actions as we are. Somehow, I doubt it, though I want to believe it to be true. Surely Wolfgang cannot be the only one with a conscience.

Two mobile gallows are moved into position then, their wood wheels squeaking eerily. There is one for each doomed man, and we know then that two people had attempted an escape. And failed.

The two prisoners are announced – by their numbers of course, and not by name. Because here, we have no names – and the rest of us can do nothing but watch as they are brought out, bloodied and bruised. I don't recognise them, not from my life outside of Auschwitz, nor from my life within. And the not knowing makes it all the worse. There are just *too many* of us in here, from all over Europe, to know everyone. And most of us aren't here long enough to form a connection.

A *kapo* ties their ankles and thighs with rope, then places a noose around each of their necks. One of the men, a teenager really, a boy, stares up at the sky in his final moments, his eyes wide like a frightened deer. While the older man looks down at the ground, exhausted, dejected, perhaps ready to meet his end if all that is left is this.

I wish I could say they meet their end swiftly, but that would be a lie. Their necks do not snap, their spines do not dislocate. Instead, they die slowly, their feet twitching and their faces turning red. Their eyes and their neck muscles bulging. They both wet themselves. It is a truly grotesque sight. But anyone caught looking away is punished. So, I keep on looking, ignoring the tears that stream down my face.

Afterwards, the Nazis pin signs to the corpse's chests, the words written as if the dead men themselves are warning us:

Because we tried to escape.

The enemy wants to teach us that to escape is lunacy, that to attempt it is suicide.

We continue forbidden to look away. For an entire hour we are made to stand in silence, staring at the two dead bodies swaying in the wind. I focus not on their faces but on the sign on their chests, the words swirling in my mind. But, as my fear evolves into rage, I draw a different lesson to the one the Nazis tried to instil in us. And I realise: the danger is not in trying to escape. Nor is it in trying and *failing*.

The real danger lies in becoming dormant, and in never attempting to escape at all.

Abel

"What are you doing in here?"
I whip around, my heart beating so wildly to have been caught that I do not even register who has spoken.
Relief floods my senses to see Frida standing in the doorway.
Of course it is only Frida. Her father is working late.
Oh God, her father. The professor who I've trusted, who is himself a Jew, and the father of a Jewish child.
He is the one who killed those children in the winter of 1938.
Little Josef.
They say he is likely dead.
Oh, mein Gott...
I can still hear my parent's conversation when they thought I'd been asleep. The little boy from our village that had been targeted and subsequently killed. The final straw that had led to our relocation to Poland all those years ago.
Does Frida know?
Is she complicit?
I frown at myself, of course she doesn't know. How could she? She'd been a child when this happened.
When this happened…
Was it *still* happening?
"Frida," I gasp, hurrying towards her, "Your father –"
She takes a step away from me and back out into the corridor.
"You have to get out of there," she says, pulling me by the hand, "*Papa* is very particular about his room. *I'm* not even allowed in there."

I take one last glance at the headboard. The three neat lines, the carefully etched name of a dead boy.

She closes the door behind me.

"What were you doing in there?"

"I was looking for the bathroom."

"But once you realised that was not the bathroom, what –"

"Frida," I interrupt, holding her by the shoulders, "Are you telling me you've never been in there? You've never seen?"

She frowns, and a hint of worry flashes across her face.

"Abel, you're scaring me," she says, "What did you see?"

She doesn't know.

"Oh, God," I breathe, turning from her and running a hand down my face, "Your father. Professor Weis. He –"

"Helloooo?"

The professor's voice cuts me off, and my blood turns to ice in my veins.

Frida shushes me and pulls me into the bathroom, the very room I had needed all along, when I had kissed the girl of my dreams and needed a minute to compose myself.

That feels like another lifetime ago.

She presses her hand over my mouth and pushes me against the closed door.

"Listen," she whispers, "I don't know what you found in there, but you cannot let on that you were in his room! He will never forgive me –"

I move out of her grasp, "*Frida!*" I hiss, "We need to get out of here! It isn't safe!"

She flinches as if I have struck her, pure confusion etched upon her lovely face. Can I really break her heart by exposing her father's secret to her?

"Frida?" Professor Weis calls down the corridor.

"I'm in the bathroom, *Papa!*" she replies, before turning to flush the toilet and running the water in the sink.

His footsteps retreat and for a moment she and I are both still. Then, with the water still running, she takes my hand in hers.

"Listen," she whispers harshly, "Whatever you saw, it cannot be as bad as what you think. My father is a good man –"

"I have to go," I tell her, whirling around and opening the door.

She slams it closed before I can leave, "Not that way!" she hisses, then turns and opens the bathroom window.

I don't even have the mental capacity to argue or protest, my brain still reeling over what I have just discovered.

I climb out the window, which thankfully isn't high up, and tumble out onto the lawn.

And then, as if I haven't just left the girl I like alone with a murderer, I go back to the boarding school.

I cannot sleep.

My mind is spinning, unable to determine what would be the best thing to do with this new information.

I toss and turn for hours in the dark, my sheets getting tangled between my legs and my skin feeling hot.

Eventually I get up, my thoughts too twisted to make sense of them, and I know I will not find refuge in slumber until I act.

I pull my clothes on and pack a spare shirt in my backpack along with my water bottle. I don't know why, but I am letting my feelings guide me. With my boots tied and my bag secured firmly on my back, I pop open my window and climb out.

"Walter?"

I freeze at Otto's voice, laced with sleep and accusation.

"Where are you going?" he asks. I can faintly see his silhouette sitting up in bed. Then his head goes up and down in a slow nod, "Ahh. To your lady friend."

I can hear the grin in his tone, so I say nothing and let him assume.

"Go, my friend," he says, "I'll cover for you."
And before I drop off the windowsill from my first-floor window, I see Otto getting up to rearrange my bed so that it looks like I am still sound asleep underneath the covers. I feel a stab of guilt pierce my insides for not saying goodbye, and I wonder if my subconscious knows something I don't.

With a handful of the smallest pebbles I could find in my hand, I toss one and then another to the window that I hope is Frida's bedroom.
The cold night air tries to snake its way underneath my clothes, but I am too anxious to feel it, my skin buzzing with nervous energy.
When she doesn't appear at the window after the third pebble, I look around myself, terrified I am being watched by someone in the darkness. Are Weis' beady eyes on me right now? Peering around the corner of the house or from the gloom of his own bedroom window? The bedroom where he keeps proof of his grotesque actions against innocent children?
The Yeti, that is what I remember the newspaper article calling him. As though he were some mystical being, a mysterious snow creature. But he isn't either of those things. He is not mystical or mysterious. He is nothing but a cowardly, self-hating, pathetic little man.
Anger makes me throw the fourth pebble a little harder than I'd intended, and I flinch as it *pings* off the glass.
But sure enough, a light comes on inside the bedroom, and my spirits lift at the sight of Frida.
I can see her brows scrunch together in confusion and her lips form the shape of my name before she opens her window.

"What are you doing?" she calls out quietly.

I beckon her down, "I need to speak with you."

"*Now?!*"

I nod, unable to explain any further.

To my surprise, she comes downstairs, closing the backdoor to the kitchen behind her quietly.

She is wrapped in a thin gown, her arms crossed over her stomach against the cold.

"What's wrong? Abel, you cannot be here!"

I take her hand, "Frida, you have to listen to me. I couldn't sleep knowing you were unsafe –"

"Unsafe?" she tears her hand from mine, "What are you talking about? Have you gone completely mad?"

"Your father," I splutter, no longer able to contain what I know, "He – He…"

"Oh, please, Abel," Frida scoffs, "My father would never hurt me."

"He is the Yeti!" I hiss.

"The what?"

"Have you never heard of him?"

Frida looks at me like I am insane, though it is she who has been living under the same roof as an actual madman.

"You don't know…" I say, realising her father must've kept her completely in the dark.

Suddenly, the light in the kitchen is switched on, and my organs turn to liquid in my body.

I duck down and grab Frida's hand, and then I run as fast as I can.

Frida calls out in panic behind me, but she keeps up with me as I half drag her along.

"FRIDA!" I hear Weis call from the house. And to my horror, Frida calls back.

"*Papa, hilfe!*"

Help?

She is really calling for help? From *me?*

I take solace in the knowledge that Weis will likely have to put on shoes and maybe even get dressed for the night before he follows us. Perhaps he will even stop to retrieve a weapon.

I feel sick at the thought of it.

I lead us off the road and into some shrubbery, pushing Frida ahead of me now to make sure she doesn't escape me and return right back to her true captor.

She shrieks and cries as the branches of trees hit her in the face and the rocky ground no doubt slices her feet, but I know what the alternative is, so I push her forward and down into a ditch where I hold her steady and cover her mouth.

I am breathing heavily and so is she, but I try to listen as intently as I can in case he is hot on our heels.

Frida bites my hand over her mouth.

I inhale a hiss.

"*What* are you doing?!" she asks angrily, and I beg her to stay quiet.

"Your father is dangerous!"

"My father is a good man!" she argues, "I don't know what has gotten into you, but he has been nothing but kind to you! *Hiding* your identity, hiding ours! What could he poss –"

"Your father is responsible for at least four Jewish deaths!" I tell her, "Four *children*."

Frida stares at me, her mouth hanging open where I interrupted her midsentence.

"He is the Yeti," I continue, trying to whisper, "You may not have heard of him, but he is real, and he is your father. Four Jewish children mysteriously vanished in the winter of '38 in the town I grew up in."

"What town did you grow up in?" she mumbles, as though she is conserving all her energy into not freaking out.

"Kaltenkirchen," I mutter, knowing that this will be the defining factor to make her realise I am telling the truth. Because I know it will be the town she used to live in with

her father and mother, before her mother, too, mysteriously 'disappeared'. In truth, since discovering the etchings on the headboard, I no longer believe her mother to have simply left her daughter behind. No doubt, she was one of Weis' victims as well. Perhaps even his first.
Frida's chest concaves with deep and panicked exhales then, her face contorting when she finally accepts what I have told her.

"I grew up in Kaltenkirchen," she blubbers, her hand flapping against her chest, "We moved when – when –"
I nod but we don't have time for this, so I grab her hands and will her to look at me.

"I will keep you safe," I tell her, "But we need to go. Now!"
She nods, though her stare is glassy with shock and a newfound terror as she realises the man she has adored all her life is not what he seems.
We get up slowly, careful not to make too much noise, hopeful that Weis has taken a different direction, when suddenly a *bang!* bursts around us, illuminating our surroundings and the face of the Devil for but a second. It splits my ears, and I fall to the ground in terror, pulling Frida to me protectively. With my hand cupping the back of her head, I hold her against my chest to break her fall as we tumble down the ledge. We crash to the ground and the air is knocked out of me as I take the brunt of the collision on my back.
I am certain I have been shot, and I lift my hand to my face to inspect it. My palm is coated in a slick, black liquid, and I press it to my side where the pain pulsates.

"Frida!" Weis' voice rasps angrily.
He's on top of us now, peeling Frida off of me. He is freakishly strong.
I try to keep a hold of her, but he punches me in the face, and I see stars. I shrink away from him, my hands

covering my eye. I can already feel it throbbing under my closed lid.

"Frida!" he calls again. And I am suddenly alarmed when she does not reply.

I scramble up, my one good eye searching the scene before me.

Weis is on his knees in the dirt, his pistol behind him and his daughter in his arms as he shakes her in desperation.

"No," I whisper, realisation hitting me right between the eyes.

I look down to my side where I was sure I had been shot when the gun had gone off, but there is no blood. I lift up my shirt, only to find a red raw scrape, the skin around it angry and already forming a bruise. But no bullet hole.

Weis is crying now, loud, snotty sniffles coming from him as he presses Frida's limp body against him. They are covered in blood. Blood I now realise is not mine at all, but Frida's. I don't know where she was hit, but she is staring blindly ahead, unfocused and distant as Weis looks down at her, his hand cupping the back of her head just as I had done moments ago to protect her from the fall.

"She's dead," I hear myself say, and Weis snaps around to face me.

I expected hatred, a twisted, gruesome face filled with contempt and blame. But I see only a broken, mortified man.

"I didn't mean to," he says wetly, his mouth caving open as another sob escapes him and he turns back to his child, pressing his face to hers.

His pistol glints at me in the moonlight then, and I do not wait for him to regain his composure. I reach for it and point it at him just as I had been taught to.

He doesn't even flinch, continuing merely to rock Frida's lifeless body back and forth and wailing like a wounded animal. I think of how close we are from the boarding school and his neighbours, and I think someone must've heard the gunshot at least, if not his bloodcurdling sobs.

"Why?" I hiss at him, my anger taking centre stage in the concoction of emotions I am feeling.
He stops rocking but continues to cry, ignoring my question and pressing wet kisses to Frida's bloodied forehead.
I grit my teeth and press the pistol to his temple, "Why!?"
He shakes his head, his eyes remaining closed as he speaks into his child's damp hair. Hair I had not long ago stroked from her face when she'd smiled at me. Full of laughter, full of life.

"It no longer matters," he whimpers pathetically, "I have done what I set out to do."

"What?" I spit, my face twisted with raw fury.
He shakes his head like I wouldn't understand. And he's probably right. Who could understand a crazed mind?

"They were practice runs," he whispers, more to himself than to me, as he looks down at his daughter and gently closes her lids over her unseeing eyes, "Just practice runs…"
I lower the gun then, realising what he means.

"You – You've done what you set out to do?" I repeat.
He turns sharply to me then, never letting go of Frida, "But I couldn't do it! I wasn't going to do it. I c – *couldn't*. Not to her. I wanted to. To put us out of our putrid misery. Both of us. But I couldn't. I had to practice. To get a feel, to make sure I didn't do it wrong, didn't hurt her."
He is rambling, words spewing out of him like he has just cracked. But he'd cracked long ago. Of that, I am sure.

"Did you kill your wife?" I ask him now.
He looks away, back to Frida, and I think I detect a hint of shame, "I didn't mean to," he says again. And I wonder if he is talking about Frida again, or of his wife.
I watch them for a moment, father and daughter, rocking back and forth as though she were his straitjacket.

I raise the gun to his temple again.

"You're a monster."

He turns to me then, practically dropping his dead child in a heap on the ground. But his face is not twisted in hostility, he is not lunging for me or for the weapon. His face is open and inviting, his mouth curved up in a grotesque smile as he crawls towards me, pushing his forehead against the barrel of the gun.

"Oh yes," he begs, "please do it. Do it. I didn't mean to. Not like *this*. I deserve to die."

I take a step back and then another, surprised by his disturbing shift in behaviour. But he crawls after me, not intimidatingly, but to keep the gun aimed at him. It is eery all the same.

He *wants* me to kill him.

"I practiced. I had it all planned out. We are Jews…we aren't pure. So I was going to end us all. Better by my hand than what they do to people in the camps."

I think back to the ghettos, to people being starved and left to die from cold or disease. But I frown.

"What happens to people at the camps?" I ask.

Weis laughs. It sounds disturbing, given the setting.

"Jews, especially women with young children, are sent to gas chambers as soon as they arrive there. If you're lucky, you're allowed to live. To work. You're shaved, you're given a number. You're no longer a person. You work…But everyone dies there. Everyone dies."

My stomach churns. I hadn't known the extent of it. We were not told of these things in the Hitler Youth. We weren't told of the horrors, the negatives, only of the greatness of Germany, the greatness of the Reich.

My energy seeps out of me and my arm drops to my side. I cannot kill him. I cannot kill anyone. I am not like them.

"No no," Weis says, scrambling forward. He takes my hand and presses the gun to his head, squeezing his eyes shut, "You have to," he says, "It's part of the plan. If Frida is gone, what else is there for me?"

I push him away from me, disgusted, and toss the gun to the ground.

I look back at Frida, lying alone and cold behind us, her gown drenched in blood, her hair matted against her scalp. Sadness washes over me, so deep and powerful I feel like I cannot breathe.

It reminds me of the last time I saw my sister Mia.

"If you want to die so badly," I gasp, continuing to stare at Frida, the first girl I think I ever loved, "You'll have to do it yourself."

His eyes flick to the pistol, and he reaches for it like a starved man reaches for a loaf of bread. I turn as I hear the cock of the gun, but I am not scared for myself. I know he will not shoot me. I head into the night, away from him, from his daughter, from the Hitler Youth. And just as I disappear into the shadows, he pulls the trigger on himself.

Chapter 15

Wolfgang

<u>Poland, Auschwitz</u>

I try not to look at her as they all stand staring up at the hanging dead bodies. But every now and then my eyes slide to where she stands beside two other women, one of which I recognised as Erich Neumann's secretary.

I know this game, this performance. It is just another show put on to enforce our power over the masses; and because we hold the guns and the keys to the gates, they believe us to be in charge.

How ironic it is that, actually, the prisoners outnumber us 10 to 1, and that if they all rose up against us, we would probably lose. It is why they are kept malnourished, weakened, so that they don't have the energy to overthrow us. It is why those at the *Judenrampe*, where prisoners are belched out by the hundreds as they arrive in the cattle trains, are told to lie to maintain order. It is why they use a green military van with a red cross painted on it, suggesting a medical vehicle to take away those that are sick 'for disinfection'. Given the horrific conditions of the trains people arrive on, it isn't hard to believe. The Nazis stationed there take pride in the fact that there is no hysteria upon people's arrivals at Auschwitz.

It is not some cruel or elaborate joke – not mostly – but the deception has a clear and rational purpose: Hitler needs the concentration camps – his killing machines – to run smoothly and without disruption. There is no room for delay caused by panic, or worse, rebellion.

*

I hadn't yet been stationed here when the first unsuccessful prisoner escape had taken place, but I heard the stories in the canteen, when my fellow SS soldiers boasted about how they'd caught him.

He'd been an older man. An Austrian Jew. I had tried to learn his name, but the soldiers telling the story hadn't known it, or they hadn't cared to remember it. It had happened in 1942, and I learned that he'd been here but a month when he'd attempted his escape. He was of course killed for it.

Others had followed, one even trying to get smuggled out by pretending to be a corpse in among a wagon of dead bodies.

Suffice to say, all those that were caught were given humiliating deaths.

And as for those that succeeded in their escape…well, nobody spoke about them.

"*Guten Morgen,*" I say, as I do each morning when I enter my office to find her cleaning one corner or another. She mumbles a reply but does not meet my gaze.

I sit at my desk and sip my coffee, then present her with the sandwich I had brought from the canteen.

"I thought you might be getting sick of the muffins," I say, realising as soon as the words left my mouth how thoughtless I sound. Given the food the prisoners receive, which is meant to be *Ochsenschwanzsuppe* – Oxtail soup – but is mostly warm water with rotten vegetables floating inside, I am sure the muffin is like a piece of Heaven to her.

But she stands up swiftly nonetheless and hurries to take the sandwich from me as if I'd just offered her a thousand Reichsmark.

"*Danke,*" she says gratefully, same as she usually does, and her brown eyes slip to mine briefly. Sometimes she reverts to her mother tongue and mumbles '*Merci,*' and when she does, I cannot help but wince at how it sounds like she is asking for compassion.

I watch her eat for a moment, pleased to note that her skin has begun to lose some of its pallor, a hint of healthy pink having returned to her cheeks. But then something catches my eye, and I stand up, "How did you get that?" I ask, pointing at her cheekbone, where an angry red welt seeps. Her hand flutters up to cover it, and she turns away.

"Oh, it – it's nothing."

I'm around the desk in an instant, standing before her so she cannot hide.

"Let me see," I say, forgetting myself for a moment. She drops her hand, and I see her jaw clench before she raises a scowling face at me.

"It is nothing," she repeats, her voice stoic, "It is no worse than what any of my fellow prisoners receive."

"But you are under my protection," I reply, "No *kapos* are to –"

"Under your protection?" she scoffs, and I feel a strange stab of pride for her at how she is standing up to me. I only hope she doesn't dare to speak like this to anyone else within the camp. She would be shot without hesitation.

"How can you protect me from this? Why do you even want to? You don't even know my name! I am nothing but a number to you people."

I'm taken aback by this line of questioning, this outburst. I thought I'd made my stance in all this perfectly clear.

"This isn't right," I say as a way of explanation. Because it really is as simple as that.

She shakes her head, "It's not. But what can *you* do about it? Apart from smuggle me food?"

Her eyes flash with regret as soon as she says it.

"I'm sorry…" she mumbles, turning away.

"No," I counter, taking hold of her arm to stop her, it feels so fragile in my hand, "I haven't done much. But I am trying to figure out a way to get you out. To get more out after you, too."

She stares at me in disbelief, "What? To get me out?"

I nod, "But I don't know how, yet."

She holds my gaze, but then her expression falters, and the hope in her eyes is puffed out like the flame of a candle in a storm.

We stand facing one another for a moment in which she stares down at the floor.

I nudge her hand, the one holding the half-eaten sandwich.

"Eat," I say, the reminder sounding awfully like a command, "Please."

I offer her the seat at my desk, taking my cup of coffee as she finishes the best meal she will have all day.

I watch her as she chews slowly, guilt running me through like a spear to see her tear up at the taste and texture, knowing she hasn't tasted chicken or butter for months.

"Who did it?" I say after a while, when she has nearly finished eating.

She shrugs, "*Die Lagerälteste,*" she says, "I didn't make the bed well enough according to her."

Bettenbau – a way to make the bed following strict rules. It was a common excuse for dishing out beatings.

"I'll deal with it," I tell her, and she looks up at me.

After a long moment, where I think she will ask me why again, she simply nods, "Thank you."

I smile at her. A tight smile. Not one of joy or assurance, but one of apology.

"It's the very least I can do," I say. And I mean it.

She and I go about our day after that, and I find I am warmed by our interaction. One that I felt had long been overdue since her employment with me began.

But something niggles at me for the entirety of the day, and I keep stealing glances at her as she sweeps the floors and cleans my windows free of the daily ash that sticks to them from the outside.

When my working day comes to an end and I dismiss her of her duties, she is nearly out the door when I realise what it is that has been playing on my mind.

"Wait!" I call out, causing her to flinch. But she turns around to regard me, her bony chest rising and falling unevenly as I stand and make my approach.

"Something you said earlier," I say, and she regards me curiously, "You're right."

"What?" she gasps, "What did I say?"

I sense in her voice the same thing I noticed earlier: a distinct lack of fear, of tremor. I don't know whether to be glad for it or concerned.

"I don't even know your name."

To my surprise, her lips curve into a slow smile.

"Alma," she tells me, "Alma Mia Basson"

I present her my hand, and she looks down at it between us and laughs. She actually laughs. Just a small, fragile sound. But a laugh, nonetheless. And it causes a spark of rapture to burst within me.

She takes my hand and shakes it.

"Nice to know you, Alma Mia Basson," I tell her in earnest.

And just when I thought the day couldn't get any better, she drops her gaze, almost shyly, and says, "Nice to meet you, Wolfgang Herrman."

Alma

"He isn't like the others," I tell my friends in hushed whispers.

I notice Trudi and Esther share a look.

I *tut*, "I know I sound naïve," I whisper, insistent "But he is not. He saved my *maman*. He saved me, my first day here. And he is saving me again."

Esther shifts slightly, no doubt uncomfortable with my tone. I hear it too; I am defending him.

"And he hasn't laid a hand on you?" Trudi asks, her eyes sliding to Esther briefly.

I look away, "Not once. Not in anger nor in passion."

I choose not to divulge him helping me up, comforting me. Somehow, I don't think they'll understand.

Esther frowns, "You're lucky then. Perhaps your knight in shining Nazi uniform will bring an end to this entire war, and maybe even kill Hitler himself just to keep you safe."

I don't appreciate the heavy sarcasm, "He is doing what he can for us. I cannot imagine he would go unpunished if he was caught aiding us!"

"Oooh," Esther mocks, "Poor Nazi. Might he get a stern talking to?"

I feel my whole face burn hot with frustration, "You speak as though they are all alike."

"They *are* all alike," she hisses back, trying to stay quiet through her anger, "Whether this one gives you a muffin – sorry, half a muffin – or not, he is still a killer. He is still a Nazi. And he is still part of the problem!"

I shake my head in disbelief, "Listen to yourself," I say, "You lump them all together just as they have lumped all of *us* together for being Jews. We must be better than them if we are to maintain our humanity."

Esther goes silent and folds her arms over her chest. But I can tell by her expression that I have made a valid point.

"I'm going to sleep," she says, turning away from me. I spoon her, my frustration soon forgotten. I cannot blame her for hating every last one of them. It *is* easier that way. But I also cannot deny that flicker of hope glinting within me; like a tiny, budding flower that has sprouted from the wasteland that has been my soul since the beginning of this war.

I hadn't known what to do with it at first, and this place has made me want to squash it before I become disillusioned. But the truth is, when I think of his scarred smile and the warmth in his eyes, when I imagine the touch of his hand in mine, the brush of his fingertips on my wrist, I can no longer ignore the conflicting feelings in my heart.

Annika

<u>The Netherlands, somewhere</u>

I wake to Meyer shaking me gently by the shoulder.
The light of dawn peeks through the trees, and I look up
into his tired face and realise he stayed up all night so that
we could sleep.
"You should've woken one of us to take the second
watch," I tell him.
He only shrugs, "I don't really sleep anyway."
As I stand and stretch my limbs I wonder if that's true, or
if he's trying to make me feel better. I watch him
cautiously, and I decide he's serious.
"Why not?" I ask, looking around for my sister and
noticing she isn't here. Her bag is, though, so I know she
has gone for some privacy in the woods.
"Torture leaves behind all kinds of fun aftertastes," he
grins at me.
I don't return his smile.
He stands and heaves his bag onto his back. I follow suit,
only for one of the straps to snap at the seam.
Meyer *tuts*, "Here," he says, and he reaches for the strap.
He's standing right in front of me, so close I can feel his
breath on my forehead as he ties a knot into the strap to
secure it. I look up at his face as he works. His black hair
falls over his forehead and curls behind his ears. It's in
desperate need of cutting. His cheeks are covered in
stubble, and I notice there's a patch by his chin that
blooms a handful of greys. The scar at his temple still
stands out, tender and raw skin wrinkling as it continues
to heal slowly.
With him standing so close that I can smell his skin, a
mixture of leaves and damp dirt, an intense urge to touch
him overcomes me, and I raise my hand and brush the hair

from his eyes. His gaze falls to me, and I meet it as I gently run my thumb along the line of his scar, all the way down to his jaw. He flinches slightly, and I know it is still sensitive. But he doesn't retreat from my touch.

"What did they do to you?" I whisper, and I'm reminded of having asked the same question once before, when I first saw his scarred face following his return.

I search his eyes for an answer when his mouth does not offer one. But I see only myself in their emerald reflection.

"Am I interrupting?"

Meyer and I break apart at my sister's voice behind us. He clears his throat, and I reach for her bag and pass it to her.

"Ready?" I ask, as if nothing at all has happened.

She takes it from me and flashes me a knowing smile before walking ahead and shaking her head.

I run a hand through my hair, realising most of it had come loose from its braid during the night, and exhale heavily to calm my pounding heart. But when I cast a glance at Meyer beside me and he throws me a subtle smile, I know that I am not the only one who has been harbouring secret feelings for the other.

We reach the first checkpoint, as Meyer calls it, and I am surprised to see it is but a homely little cottage occupied by an elderly couple. I had expected an underground bunker or an abandoned cave. Certainly nothing quite so…ordinary.

Meyer smiles at the couple when they open the door, introducing us like they are lifelong friends. They wave us inside.

"I imagine you are just exhausted!" the grey-haired lady, who Meyer introduced as Mrs van de Meer, says, pushing me and Helga down onto their sofa and insisting we take off our backpacks.

We do as we are told, not wanting to be rude, though I become immediately hyper aware of the distance between me and my bag, since it contains the only food we have left for the journey. She hangs the bags up on hooks by the front door, and I relax a little. There, at least, they're easy to grab in case we need to make a quick escape.

Mrs van de Meer hurries away into the kitchen and returns moments later with a teapot and cups, which she distributes accordingly.

"Fruit tea," she says, pouring me a cup, "Or as good a substitute for tea as we can get. I dried the berries myself from our garden."

I am so grateful for the sweet treat, I thank her with a bright smile, and Helga bows her head at her as if she were the Queen herself.

"We will only need to stay one night," Meyer says to Mr van der Meer as Helga and I sip our tea and sink into their shoddy, yet comfortable sofa, savouring the cosiness.

Mr van der Meer nods casually, "Whatever you need, Jakob," he says, and I smile to myself from behind my cup, enjoying the sound of Meyer's given name out loud.

"The Nazis aren't due to come by for another week," van der Meer goes on, "They come, they take what few provisions we produce, and they go. We've never had a problem with them. They don't suspect."

"I'm glad to hear it," Meyer says, leaning forward and taking his cup, smiling at Mrs van der Meer in thanks before shooting a quick look in my direction.

My cheeks blush despite myself. His regard almost causes me to forget we are fleeing from the Nazis. That we are at war.

"It'll be hard to get into Arnhem, Jakob," Mr van der Meer says now, stealing Meyer's attention, "We've heard whispers of Allie plans."

"Operation Market Garden?" Meyer replies, "I've heard of it."

Van der Meer nods, "The place will be crawling with the enemy."

Meyer sighs, finishes his tea and turns to me and my sister.

"Then I guess we'd better make sure we aren't caught." And just like that, I am firmly reminded of our circumstances.

Compared to what we've been surviving on back at home, we enjoy a bountiful feast at the van der Meer's.

A roasted chicken – plucked from their pen for this very occasion – graces the centre of the dining table, and bowls of delicious smelling vegetables from their garden surround it. My plate is a rainbow of colours, and I cannot remember the last time I have eaten so well.

After dinner, Mrs van der Meer shows us to the barn outside, where freshly strewn straw lays in the far corner.

"We used to have a horse and some goats," she tells us, "But that was a long time ago. Now this barn houses people, whenever they need it."

"*Dank u wel,*" Helga mutters, "This will be perfect." I smile gratefully at the older lady as she hobbles back to the cottage, then carry my backpack to the far corner.

"We'll have to huddle together to stay warm," Helga says, a hint of insinuation hiking her voice at the end.

We make up a little nest, two of our blankets laid out on top of the straw and one set aside to cover all of us horizontally. It is the best we can do with what we've been given and what we've brought, but Helga is right, with our shared body heat we should be fine.

We settle in, and to my surprise, Helga doesn't wrap her arm around me like she normally does, and she doesn't spoon me either. Instead, she turns and presses her back against mine.

I feel exposed suddenly, but I say nothing while Meyer arranges his backpack as a pillow by my head and then lies down beside me.

"Welterusten," – Good night – Meyer mumbles, lying on his back. He doesn't close his eyes, but fixes his stare up at the wooden beams of the barn.

"Good night!" Helga replies enthusiastically, and I feel her shifting ever so slightly away from me.
My ears begin to burn with embarrassment. What, exactly, is she trying to achieve?

"Good night," I mutter under my breath as I shift onto my side to face Meyer.
He must sense me watching him, because he turns his head to me.
He smiles, warmly, calmly, as though we have not a care in the world. As if we are not spending the night in some kind strangers' barn on top of some scratchy hay.
Neither of us looks away for the longest time, a strange sort of silence unfolding between us which might as well have held an entire conversation, his eyes conveying to me that within the blackness of the world, we appear to have found a sliver of light.
I smile back, my heart feeling light despite all the heaviness bearing down on us.

"You will sleep tonight?" I whisper, though I doubt Helga is asleep yet.

"For as long as my subconscious allows."
He says it with a hint of humour, but I look away, saddened by the reminder of what this war has put him through, what it continues to put him through.

"Do you ever worry they will come after you again?"
He inhales, considering the question, then releases his answer in a hurried breath, "All the time."
I don't need to ask why he continues doing what he's doing, because I know. It is the same reason any of us would give.
He shifts onto his side slightly, facing me, "What are you thinking?"

I am taken aback by the forward question. We have never spoken so directly to one another.

But I am not sure how to answer, because in my mind swirl many things, same as they have done for days.

Will I ever see my parents again?

Will we make it to Arnhem?

If we do, what is expected of us there?

How long will we stay?

Is Helga ever going to recover from all the things she has seen?

Can I allow myself to fall in love at a time like this?

I settle for ambiguity, shrugging one shoulder, "Too many things."

He smirks, returns to lying on his back, "I know the feeling."

A comfortable silence settles over us, in which time I am sure I hear Helga's quiet snoring.

I feel brave all of a sudden, as though her drifting off to sleep has gifted Meyer and me a new level of privacy. But before I can bring myself to move closer, he reaches underneath the thin cover and takes my hand in his, and I let him intertwine our fingers. They slide together easily and a thrill flows through me at his touch. And when his body relaxes and he sighs contently, I find joy in the simple sound, knowing that I am responsible for it. I do what feels natural then, no longer caring for caution, no longer fearing rejection. I know exactly where I stand with this man. And so, I scooch closer, lie my head on his chest, and allow myself to fall.

Wolfgang

<u>Poland, Auschwitz</u>

By now, many within Germany – military leaders and ordinary citizens alike – recognise that Germany is heading towards defeat.

But not Hitler. He and his close advisors refuse to acknowledge it, clinging to the belief that the war could still be won. But the Reich's inability to control the air and sea, coupled with increasing Allied bombing raids, has begun to deteriorate morale.

The Allies' extensive bombing raids of Germany's cities continue to cause widespread destruction and firestorms, leading to significant civilian casualties and homelessness. Bamberg, where my mother continues to live, is also targeted, but thankfully, it is not too badly damaged, and my mother has confirmed she is safe. For now.

But still Hitler does not accept defeat.

It is May 1944, and though Germany has been facing more and more losses of late, the concentration camps continue as they have. Hundreds and thousands of people arrive every day by trains, and most of them are being selected for the 'showers.'

The smoke rises incessantly from the crematorium, ash falls onto the ground, onto people's shoulders and their hair, even, I have seen, in their soup bowls as they eat.

I am doing my morning rounds, making my presence known to the prisoners as they go about their duties, some of them digging trenches, some of them building new barracks, some just about hanging on by a thread.

I brush my fingers over the three biscuits I have hidden in my pocket – *Mutti's* latest treats from home – and stealthily distribute them to three workers who desperately need them more than I.

Two of them flinch at my swift approach, but once they notice the precious wafer in my hand, they reach out and stuff them into their mouths. The third man already knows me for an ally, and he bows his head at me and whispers 'God Bless you' at my retreating back.

I am too ashamed to accept his gratitude, and walk away briskly.

I make my way to the SS canteen to get my coffee and breakfast, my mind clouded by my growing unease, when suddenly I hear the strangest sound.

I look up into the blue sky, shielding my eyes from the rising sun, trying to locate the noise. Overhead, the strange hum grows louder, until suddenly it is right above us.

"A plane!" many shout in various languages, some raising their hands as if in greeting.

They're not wrong. A Mosquito plane, if I am not mistaken.

It zooms overhead, disappearing as quickly as it came.

Those types of planes are used for either bombing or reconnaissance, I think, as I hurry to the canteen, my head hanging low, *And since it didn't drop a bomb over us...it is safe to say that that plane just took aerial pictures of Auschwitz.*

I grin to myself. There is hope.

The world will soon know what is happening here.

Not long after that, Heinrich Himmler suddenly orders for the liquidations of ghettos to take place, leading to a mass influx of new prisoners at Auschwitz.

"I hear Chelmno got a lot of them," I overhear one officer tell another as we wait in line at the canteen one day, "Some 25,000 were eliminated upon arrival and burned."

The other officer blows a breath out of his mouth, "Can you image the smell!"

And they laugh. They laugh. And I shake my head.

But we go on to receive far more than Chelmno. Some 67,000 prisoners from the Lodz Ghetto are belched out of the cattle trains just some days later. Two thirds of them are immediately sent to the gas chambers upon their arrival. Men, women and children. Their bodies are burned in pits. All evidence of their existence is simply gone. Destroyed.

I can do nothing to stop it, not even to spare *one*.

They want all those people eliminated.

And I realise with sudden clarity that things will only get worse before they get better. Because Hitler must finally have realised that the Allies are closing in around him, and he is trying to erase all evidence of what he set in motion.

Abel

I walk all night following my confrontation with Professor Weis, the Yeti.

I still can hardly believe I stumbled upon Germany's mysterious child killer by chance. Nor can I believe that he had committed his heinous crimes when he *himself* was a Jew. But, if I understood his manic ramblings correctly, it was precisely *because* he was Jewish that he had set out on his twisted path, a path which had led him to kill his own wife, and planning to kill his daughter and then himself.

I didn't mean to. I couldn't.

His panicked sobs ring in my ears as I walk through the darkness, and I try not to think about how my interference might've been the very thing which had forced his hand, in the end. Maybe…he wouldn't have been able to go through with it. Maybe, I am somehow responsible for her death.

I cannot linger on such thoughts. That kind of guilt would consume me. To have her blood on my hands when I had tried to *save* her…it is too caustic to bear.

And yet – if Weis is to be believed – apparently, he had planned his family's end in an effort to *avoid* their suffering.

Better by my hand than what they do to people at the camps.

What a sick individual he had been. Or maybe – just a terrified, pathetic man.

With my false German identity papers proving that I am Walter Schmidt, and my Hitler Youth uniform, I am able to travel through Germany freely, and I will take full advantage of this while I can. Before the authorities are informed of my getaway.

Fleeing from the Hitler Youth is a punishable offense, especially now that Germany is losing their upper hand in the war following the Allied forces' success at Normandy. I will have to be careful with what story I give if questioned.

I make my way to the Plön train station with the intention of getting a ticket to Poland, only to realise I have no money. I try to haggle with the ticket salesman, offering what little I have, but he isn't interested, all but laughing at me. And when I insist, his expression darkens. I make myself scarce before he calls over a police officer to take me away.

Luckily, I manage to haul myself onto a freight train out of Plön. I have no clear idea where it's going, but I am simply glad to be getting away from here. There will be much police activity in the hours to come, when Professor Weis and Frida's bodies will be discovered, followed, perhaps, by the realisation of my disappearance.

I wonder if they will connect the two events.

I may have to ditch my identity as Walter Schmidt. Though I doubt walking about without any papers at all would be much safer.

I jump off the freight train at dawn, when it stops at its destination, and as I look around, I know I am in Berlin. Memories of when I was last here invade my mind, and I am transported to a time not that long ago, but which might as well have been from another life.

The train station doesn't look the same, however. Huge chunks have been blown away from when the Allies began targeting Berlin in November 1943. In fact, as I look around, I am surprised my train even made it in. But despite the devastation, I am able to make my way to the arches where Mia and I had been directed to, way back when we had fled Poland and made our way to Le Chambon. I wonder if the moustached man who helped us get to our next stop is still around, if he is still helping Jews escape out of Berlin.

But I am not trying to retrace my footsteps back to Le Chambon. I am trying to get back to Lodz, back to where my parents and Aunt Ayla will hopefully be waiting, just as they had promised.

I take one last look around the station and decide there will be no successful escape out of here via train, not only for my lack of money but also for its lack of any surviving tracks save for the one I arrived by.

I straighten my back and loop my thumbs under the straps of my backpack on my shoulders, readying myself for a long journey, then head into the streets of Berlin, hoping to find a way out of this false life and back to where I belong.

Chapter 16

Annika

<u>The Netherlands, Vierhouten</u>

We make it to our destination on the third day of our travels, some twelve hours after we waved goodbye to Mr and Mrs van der Meer and their cottage.

And to my surprise, we do not stop at the city of Arnhem, but in the middle of the forest near the village of Vierhouten.

"Where are we?" I hear Helga ask quietly as we approach what looks like an animal's lair, if the animal was smart enough to use tools and build an underground hideout.

Meyer is about to reply when a man dressed in a brown jacket and trousers emerges from the dark entrance.

"Jakob Meyer!" the man calls, his arms outstretched, his leathery face warm and inviting. I say 'calls' but he speaks in a throaty whisper, like he's trying to make his low voice stretch further without actually speaking up. He claps Meyer on the shoulder, "Who have you brought?"

"De Boem, this is Helga and Annika Lange," Jakob murmurs.

The man's eyes grow wide, "The Giethoorn sisters? I have heard so much about you."

He shakes our hands enthusiastically, "Welcome to the Hidden Village."

He turns and leads the way inside his underground hut, the entrance marked by a row of neatly lined logs on either side of the doorway.

Inside, once my eyes adjust to the underground dimness, I am surprised to see a simple yet cosy little home, with a wooden bed in the corner, a wooden table and chairs at its centre and even a little bookshelf. The ceiling and walls within are held up by wooden beams which you would never believe to be there from the outside, the exterior looking simply like the forest ground.

"It's not much, but we are safe here."

"'We'?" Helga asks.

De Boem nods, "There are several dozens of people living in this forest."

My mouth hangs open, but before we can enquire further, he waves his hand over his shoulder and leads us back outside.

"Come!" he whispers hoarsely, "Opa Bakker and Tante Cor will want to meet you."

He takes us slowly through the trees, and all the while I am scanning around myself, wondering how so many people are hiding here.

"In here," De Boem mouths, presenting us with another hole in the ground.

One by one, we follow him inside and almost immediately we hear a woman's voice.

"Jakob!" she squeals quietly. She has grey hair in a long plait down her back.

She folds Meyer into a hug, and I find myself smiling.

I feel someone tugging on my dress then, and look down to see a little boy staring up at me.

"Hi," I say, but he scurries away, hiding behind the woman's legs.

She laughs, a hushed sound, "Herman is a little shy," she explains in a similarly husky whisper as De Boem, "He arrived here all alone last year. Hasn't spoken a word since his arrival. We don't even know how he found us."

My smile vanishes in pity for this poor boy, but before we can linger on it, the woman thrusts a hand at us.

"Cornelia," she says, "But call me Tante Cor. Everyone does. This is my husband Dionisius. Call him Opa Bakker."

"Aliases," Meyer explains when he notices our confused faces.

"Come, let us show you around!" Tante Cor exclaim-whispers, waving her arm for us to follow.
We tail her outside, the corners of my mouth curled up at how incredible this is.

"The village was De Boem's idea," Tante Cor tells us quietly, sensing our curiosity as we walk through the trees, "Since June 1943, we've hidden stranded Allied pilots and people fleeing from persecution – Jews, resistance, anyone who needs it."
We stop when we reach another underground hut where a man sits outside on a wooden stool before a small fire. He nods his head at us as he turns a fish skewered on a stick. We move along.

"We manage the village, providing shelter and support. The number of inhabitants varies, some people choosing to move on after some time. But we've housed up to a hundred people here at one point."

"A hundred!?" I splutter in surprise, looking around yet again, trying to find all these hidden homes. But it is impossible. Unless you know where they were, there is no way of finding them.
Tante Cor grins, taking her husband's hand in hers and flashing a companionable look at De Boem beside her. They are clearly proud of what they have built here.

"The village consists of four forest sections, separated by barriers," she continues, "Residents are allowed out during the day but only in their own section. And there must be absolute silence."
I nod, understanding their husky voices

"For over a year," De Boem says now, continuing the introduction, "The Hidden Village has remained undiscovered by the German occupiers thanks to the resistance and the local's silence."

He continues walking and we follow them to another hut, one where three young children are silently playing with sticks and leaves as a mother watches from their hut's entrance, a baby in her arms.

"Supplies are delivered at night to a designated location by local farmers. We also go on supply runs, and we bury food in deep holes to keep it safe and cool. We pick mushrooms and berries...There is no hunger here."

I hear the pride in his voice, and a surge of it rises in me, too. This place is truly remarkable. Though, I don't understand what it is we will be doing here.

"This is yours," Tante Cor says then, presenting us with a hut a hundred feet from the one where the children quietly play.

I look at Meyer, "Ours?"

He nods at me and Helga, "Arnhem is close by. Operation Market Garden is underway. The Allies plan to cross the river Rhine and advance deep into Germany in a bid to end the war. Our new assignment is to help here, however we can."

The three leaders step away.

"We'll leave you to get settled," Tante Cor says with a smile, and we are left alone.

"I thought we were to go *to* Arnhem," Helga says as soon as they are out of earshot, "We left Giethoorn to continue our fighting. Not to hide away in a forest!"

Meyer ignores her and walks into the underground hut.

My sister turns a stunned face at me, and I am left torn as what to do. I am spared having to choose a side when Helga storms after him and I follow.

"Meyer!" she hisses, "I want to fight! I don't want to be here, hiding with the children and the old folk."

"You'll do as you're ordered to," he counters, and I know better than to interfere. I make my way to the far end of the small hut and place my bag on one of the two wooden beds. I know his answer will not go down well. Helga's eyes bulge.

"I have not left my family behind – my *home* – just to squirrel away in this forest! I thought we'd be stationed in Arnhem, that we'd be continuing our targeting of Nazi soldiers and generals. Please tell me this is a pitstop."
Meyer dumps his bag on the floor by a wooden beam, "It's not a pitstop."
I know his calm tone is only adding fuel to Helga's fire, rather than quenching it.

"What are we to do here?" Helga asks now, crossing her arms over her chest.

"Tomorrow, De Boem will assign us posts in the village. Everyone has a role to play here."

"So, what? I will be made to care for the children? For the wounded Allied pilots?" Helga asks, as though this were somehow not an admirable purpose.

"Is that what we are to do?" I ask then, intrigued.
Meyer looks over at me, his expression softening to hear the delight in my voice. I *would* rather care for people than be in constant danger.

"I don't know yet," he admits, "But whatever we are to do here will not include shooting Nazis at point blank," he turns his attention back to Helga, "I would've thought you of all people would appreciate that."
That leaves Helga stumped, and she turns away from him and goes to sit on the bed where I stand.
It is no secret that Helga has struggled with our part in the resistance for some time. Hell, we've *all* struggled in our own way. None of us really *want* to be killing people, even if they are Nazis. But everyone in the resistance at Giethoorn knows of Helga's nightmares, of her inability to make the shot that might've saved Marta. No one begrudges her of course, but they know of it all the same.

"This place," Meyer continues now, taking a tentative step towards us, "It will keep you both safe. It will help you heal, Helga. And it is a worthy cause in the resistance."

Helga stares him down for a moment, then turns to me.

I smile at her, "I want to stay," I tell her.

Her mouth twitches, but eventually she nods.

It is September 1944, and daily life in the huts is tough work, not only due to the physical side of things but also the mental. It is honestly surprising how draining *not* speaking for many hours of the day can be.

"We are hidden, but that doesn't mean we can whoop and cheer and make our location known," Tante Cor explains that first morning, when we're assigned our positions, "Whenever possible, we speak using our hands, and whispering is preferable. Voices carry."

It makes sense, of course, there are dozens of people living within this secret village. We can't all just chatter and go about our day as though we aren't still at war. As if most of us aren't being hunted.

I am assigned to watch over the children, which I am extremely grateful for, especially when Helga is assigned the night watch. I feel bad for my sister. I cannot imagine the tedium of that post. But at least the camp is always quiet enough that Helga has no trouble sleeping during the day.

The days are long, but the seven little ones I am in charge of are all so well behaved, and the woman I work with is very kind. Her name is Hanna, and three of the seven children in our care are hers.

"My husband brought us here some months ago," she tells me on my first day, her baby boy latched to her chest as he feeds.

"Have I met him, your husband? What post is he in?"

Hanna smiles sadly, "He died shortly after we got here. Infection."

But then she turns a beaming face to little mute Herman, as he presents her with a picture of a forest.

I look down at her baby as he suckles at her breast, his pink eyelids closed and his cheeks rosy. Sadness pinches at my heart at the sight. He will never know his father. And a bittersweet truth comes to me: even with so much death around us, life, inevitably, goes on.

The long days are made more bearable through organized activities: reading to the children, even having quiet dances in Hanna's hut, or the occasional walk about in our sector, searching for mushrooms. Anything that we could think of to keep their young minds occupied and ours from growing weary.

On our twelfth day here, Helga and I cross paths – same as we do every morning, she at the end of her duty and heading for bed, and I at the beginning of mine – when we hear hushed voices calling from among the trees. Helga grabs me by the arm and tugs me down into the darkness of our bunker, and we scan our surroundings.

"Quick, quick! Bring him to De Boem!"

"Meyer," I tell Helga, recognising the voice, and I hurry towards the sound.

"Ani!" my sister hisses after me, but I pretend not to hear her.

She doesn't follow me.

Not thirty feet away from our new home, I spot Meyer and another man carrying a uniformed soldier further into the forest and towards De Boem's hut. The three of them stumble forward, the soldier limping terribly, his trousers completely soaked in blood.

I rush towards them.

"Let me help," I offer, and the old man on the soldier's right, the one who'd nodded at us on our first day as he cooked fish, peels the soldier's arm from his shoulders and I take his place.

The man weighs a ton, but I grit my teeth and haul him forward.

"Who is he?" I whisper to Meyer, catching a glimpse of the soldier's bloodied face as I look over at him.

"British pilot," Meyer says, and I wonder how he knows.

"The wings brevet on his jacket," Meyer elaborates.

The pilot grunts in pain and I try to hold him steady.

De Boem and Opa Bakker race towards us then and take the pilot from us, taking him the rest of the way with much more ease. I fall to the ground, immediately fatigued from the short burst of labour. My body is not yet recovered from the many months and years of slowly wasting away in Giethoorn.

Meyer sits down beside me in the dirt, our backs pressed against a tree, and he exhales like he's in pain. I look at him.

"Are you hurt?"

He shakes his head, "Nothing new."

I think of the limp he sported the night that Marta was killed. I wonder if his leg still ails him. I wonder if it would be too forward to ask.

We watch the pilot be brought inside a hut where a Jewish medical student resides. He will be taken care of as best as we can offer.

"Where did you find him?" I ask.

Meyer doesn't look at me when he answers, "Operation Market Garden is proving unsuccessful," he tells me, "German forces are overwhelming the British defenders. The Allied intelligence crashed."

"What does it mean?" I whisper, this time not to avoid detection, but to hide the fear in my voice.

"It means the plan to liberate the Netherlands is failing," he says, turning his piercing eyes to me, "It means I am glad we were not stationed at Arnhem."

His tone is tender, and I hear the unspoken words.

"We are safe here," I assure him, though I know it isn't entirely true. Because nowhere is completely safe. Not while Hitler lives.

He reaches for me then, his hand cupping my cheek. It is stained with blood and dirt, but I don't even mind.

"I'll make sure you stay that way," he whispers, "Safe." I raise my own hand and place it over his, press my cheek into his palm.

"Meyer –"

"Don't," he interrupts, "Don't call me that. You know I want to be more than just Meyer to you."

A smile twitches at my lips, and I hold his gaze as he slowly leans closer, closing the space between us.

His lips touch mine so softly that I am almost disappointed. I have been yearning for his touch for so long that his tenderness causes my body to burn for more, though I have never experienced any act beyond it.

Feeling suddenly brazen, I shift closer, so that my body and his are almost touching, and I press my lips to his with more urgency, conveying to him that I want this, that I want him, and that he does not need to continue to be so cautious.

Haven't I proven to him, to the resistance, that I am not as fragile as I appear?

I move my lips over his, parting them to invite him in, and I am reminded of my first kiss. That night when I had lured the Nazi general out of the hotel, and when he had forced his vile tongue into my mouth.

But this is different. So different. And when Meyer's tongue meets mine, I feel my body come alive, and I all but melt in his arms.

"Meyer."

Tante Cor's voice above us causes us to break apart. We scramble up, remembering our surroundings.

"Return to your post," she says.
But her face is not stern. In fact, it's almost sympathetic, her air glinting with understanding.
She walks away, and Meyer takes my hand in his. He brushes his thumb over my knuckles once, and then, without another word, we go our separate ways.

That night, Helga and I cross paths at the entrance of our hut once again as I return from my undertaking and she goes out to begin hers.
Same as every evening since our arrival here, I set about preparing mine and Meyer's meal, which usually consists of berries and mushrooms, or dried meat provided by the local farmers that supply the village.
But tonight, it feels different. *I* feel different.
I am alive with a buzzing excitement I have never felt before. And the moment that his shadow looms in the hut's entrance, I know that he feels the same.

"Ani," he whispers. My name has never sounded so beautiful as with the sound of his hushed voice.

"Jakob," I reply, tasting his name on my lips for the very first time and realising I like its flavour.
We eat our dinner in charged silence, and I am unable to stop looking at him.
Once our plates are cleared – which doesn't take long given that I'd been too impatient to have paid much attention to it – he stands and walks around the table towards me.
I allow him to guide me, in every sense of the word, as he takes my hand and leads me to his wooden bed, which is on the opposite side of the wall to the one I have been sharing with Helga. He kisses me. Slowly at first, as he peels my raggedy jacket off my shoulders and it slips to the floor.

Strangely – or perhaps, not so strangely – I do not feel uncomfortable or embarrassed, and I run my hands underneath his shirt, my fingertips grazing the few hairs around his bellybutton and feeling the residue of muscle that still lingers despite our undernourishment.

As my dress slips from my body and he lays me gently down on the hard bed, I think about how every terrible thing that has happened to me has been worth it for leading me to him, to here, to this moment.

And tonight, as Arnhem is bombed and the world crumbles all around us, Jakob Meyer makes love to me. And for just one night, I am not part of the resistance, nor hiding from the Nazis. I am not plotting to entrap the enemy, or fearing for my sister's wellbeing. Tonight, I am nothing more than a young woman in the arms of the man she loves, and she is living the life she deserves.

Alma

<u>Poland, Auschwitz</u>

After a while, it is no longer enough that I simply clean and tidy Wolfgang's office, so he sends me on errands to keep up the façade that I am his little slave.

He sends me for cigarettes at first, then to deliver a message to a junior officer of his. I never encounter any trouble. Every one of them knows who I was working for. One day, Wolfgang requests I get him a coffee from the canteen, and once I step over that threshold into *their* world, I am stunned by what I see.

The main camp at Auschwitz is like a little village. There is the canteen of course, where officers get their thrice daily meals – and where I cannot help but stare at all the various cakes and pastries on display as I walk past – but there is also a cinema and even a theatre hall where musicians perform for the Nazis' entertainment.

It is like torture, being granted this knowledge that all this food and comfort is but a stone's throw away from where people are starving and being worked to death.

There are others like me, *Lagerprominente* who are privileged enough to be accepted among *them*, and I often spot one or two on my way to the village. I nod at them in greeting sometimes if no officers are about, but more often than not, we pretend not to see one another, too fearful to draw attention to ourselves while in the lion's den.

Today, as I make my way to the canteen on an errand for Wolfgang, the mouthwatering scent of freshly baked bread and coffee surrounds me. I inhale as subtly as I can, imagining how the soft bread would feel on my tongue, how the coffee would taste on my lips.

I stick close to the walls to avoid the officers at the tables, and make my way to grab Wolfgang's coffee, when I see Esther. She is sitting on an officer's lap at the centre of the canteen as he paws at her breasts, laughing and hooting at the colleagues that surround him.

I freeze to the spot, my eyes wide at the sight of her, her grey dress torn off one shoulder, her face stony and expressionless as her officer – her *kind* officer – gropes at her exposed chest.

"I show you a good time, don't I, *Schätzchen?*" her officer – Neumann – jeers.

I see her lips moving in response, but it is so low I cannot hear.

The other officers laugh like drunken oafs however, pleased perhaps with her answer, or with her vulnerability. Probably both.

Another officer reaches across the table and runs his hand up her thigh, "What's so good about this one?" he asks Neumann, "Does her cunt taste sweeter because she's German?"

A guffaw erupts and Esther's head lolls to the side. She sees me then, and I am strangely ashamed to have been caught witnessing her abuse. I swallow, my mouth feeling dry suddenly when I see a tear glistening down her cheek.

I hurry to retrieve the coffee I have been sent for, hanging my head, unable to do anything that would aid either of us.

I wait behind a handful of guards, all of them sniggering at what is happening at Esther's table, and all I can do is try to ignore the sounds.

But then I hear a scream. Just a short scream, a yelp, like it was cut off halfway before being expelled, and my head snaps towards the cry.

Pressed face down over the table with her arms held steady at either side by two Nazis, Esther's officer stands behind her, fumbling with his belt with one hand and lifting her dress with the other.

My blood rushes to my feet when her bare bottom is suddenly out for all to see, and four or five other men stand behind her with disgusting smirks on their faces as Neumann readies himself to rape her as the others watch. A croak escapes me, my hand reaching out and my feet falling before one another, and before I know it, I call out for them to stop.

All of them – in fact, everyone in the canteen – turn to look at me. And I am suddenly acutely aware that my interference has saved no one, and that all I have done is given these vile men just cause to not only gang rape one Jew today, but also to kill another.

Wolfgang

<u>Poland, Auschwitz</u>

I don't know what is taking her so long, but something tells me it's not good news.

I hear the shouting before I even open the door to the canteen, and straight away, the hairs on my arms stand to attention.

I burst through the door and scan the room.

"What is the meaning of this!" I bark to the *Unterscharführer* bent over a coiled-up prisoner on the floor. His arm and closed fist stop mid-air at the sound of my voice. He turns towards me, and I notice his cheek is sprayed with blood.

He straightens up, gingerly opening and closing his fist, stretching out his fingers. His knuckles are bloodied.

"*Dieses Tier hat es gewagt, mit mir zu sprechen!*" he spits.

I look down, and sure enough, as I had feared, it is Alma. I raise my chin and force myself to appear nonchalant as I make my approach, but I clench my jaw to suggest that he has stepped over the line.

It might sound unbelievable, but there are rules at Auschwitz.

An officer can beat or kill any prisoner they want to; there didn't need to be a reason. But he could not simply kill a *Lagerprominente* without cause, especially if that privileged worker is assigned to an officer of higher rank than the officer doing the killing.

"This Jew is mine," I say, keeping my tone low, icy. In my experience, speaking with quiet ire with these types of men works better to intimidate them than shouting.

Neumann, who was dishing out the beating, takes a step back, casting a glance at some of his colleagues before lowering his head. But his face shows no remorse, only frustration at being interrupted.

I look down at Alma on the floor. Her short hair is caked with blood, her left eye already swollen shut and sporting a deep purple bruise. There are red marks all over her arms. I dread to think what welts are hidden beneath her clothes.

I inhale deeply through my nose and look around the room, at each of their faces. Some of them are still wet behind the ears, not yet having seen their twenty-first winter. And already they harbour evil inside them. They may not have been the ones bloodying their knuckles, but I'd wager not one of them *wasn't* enjoying the show.

"Someone clean this up," I say, clicking my fingers at the mess on the floor, all the while fighting with everything inside of me not to shoot every single one of them in the face. To do so would be embracing my own demise. As well as losing all hope of saving Alma and anyone else that might follow.

"*Du!*" I bark at a trembling female prisoner in the corner, "Pick her up."

"That one's mine," *Unterscharführer* Neumann says, stepping towards me.

I remain where I stand, allowing him to invade my personal space. Quite casually, I take a cigarette out of my breast pocket and light it, taking a deep drag before deliberately blowing smoke into his face.

"You'll have her back, as soon as I'm done with her," I say, my expression unperturbed.

I let him think I will have my way with his plaything. In whichever manner his sick mind wants to believe.

Then I walk towards the door, casting one quick look over my shoulder to see Alma's friend peeling her off the floor and wrapping her limp arm around her shoulder.

I hold the door open for them and as they walk past, I curse myself for a fool. Her association with me is not enough to protect her. Not here. Every day she is at risk of a random selection, of infection, of disease, of some officer not liking the way she looked at him. And every day that I postpone what I know I must do increases the chances of her ending up like so many others.

There is nothing for it. In order to save her, I have to let her go. And though it pains me, I have to do it now.

Abel

<u>Poland, Lodz</u>

I stand before the door to my Aunt Ayla's home, unable to bring myself to knock.

It is October 1944. Five years since my parents bundled me and my sister out of this house to save us. Just five years. In that time, I feel like I have lived multiple lives, and yet only one of them has brought me back here, to my roots.

A memory drifts in my mind of a conversation my sister and I had not long after arriving at Le Chambon. Where I had made my disdain for our escape well known.

I can still hear her voice in my head, the only thing that is left of her.

We do not know that they are in the ghetto. They, too, could have escaped.

I'd scoffed at her and the way she always saw things with a hint of light, when in reality, all the light had gone out. I had known it then. And yet I find myself hoping for a spark to reignite as I ready myself to knock on the door of the last home we all shared as a family, praying that I will see their faces again.

I raise my fist and rap my knuckles against the wood, then stand back, bracing myself.

The door swings open.

"*Ja?*" says a young woman as she dries her hands on her apron.

I force a smile, though I feel like I've been punched in the gut.

"*Entschuldigung,*" I say, "I am looking for someone."

She takes in my uniform, but does not seem intimidated by it.

"Who?"

My mouth opens, no sound coming out. How could I ask for the previous inhabitants without making it clear that I know them?

"Have you lived here long?"

She frowns at me, "Who wants to know?"

"Schmidt," I tell her, "Walter Schmidt."

"Schmidt?" she echoes, "Perhaps you are at the wrong house. This house was reclaimed by the Reich in 1941. Rats lived here before we moved in."

So, they were made to enter the ghetto, just as I'd suspected.

I smile at her, cursing myself. Of course they weren't still here, simply waiting for our return.

My return, I remind myself. Only *I* would ever be returning, if there was even anyone left to return to…

"The rats, yes," I mumble.

She looks up and down the street casually, "They're all gone now, thank God."

"To the ghetto…Where they belong," I add quickly.

She frowns at me, her blue eyes narrowed, but then a baby's cry erupts from within her house – my aunt's house – and she turns her head towards the sound.

I begin to move away, when her voice calls me back.

"You know the ghettos have all been liquidated, right?" she says, her hand on the door, "Lodz Ghetto has been out of use since August. Everyone was sent away, those who remained…"

My face grows hot, "Sent away? Away where?"

Her frown deepens, "I don't know," she says, her voice hitching, frustrated. She begins to close the door, her baby's wails getting louder, but I smack my hand against the wood, stopping her.

"Where?"

She stares up at me, bewildered, and I realise how I must appear to her: a strange man, towering over her with desperation and a hint of anger in his eyes. I realise suddenly I must look a mess, my hair dishevelled, my cheeks in need of a shave, a black eye from when Weis had punched me.

But I don't back down.

"Away," she stutters, "Probably to those worker camps everyone talks about."

I falter at the news, and she seizes the opportunity to close the door in my face.

My throat closes, and I struggle to breathe as I walk away. If they are at a camp, there is no way my family has survived. That is, if they hadn't died in the ghetto…

I feel nauseous.

My hope had already been thin when I made my way here thinking that the worst possible place they could be is the ghetto. I'd imagined finding them somehow, smuggling them food through a fence and maybe helping them escape. During my journey here I'd envisioned countless scenarios of me looking into the faces of emaciated strangers, hoping to discover my mother's eyes, or hearing my father's voice. I'd thought that, even if starved or diseased, I would recognise them, I would aid them, and I would set them free.

But of course, they aren't here. Of course they aren't alive. Only a miracle of God might've spared them. And I guess they already used up that miracle when they sent me away.

Chapter 17

Annika

<u>The Netherlands, Vierhouten</u>

I walk around grinning like a fool.

But we are at war.

I stop and listen to birdsong as though I've never heard it before.

But we are at war.

His lightest touch or briefest glance makes me blush like a schoolgirl.

But. We are. At war.

I can never forget it. No matter how happy I am, I am constantly reminded of it by those who arrive in the dead of night looking for aid, or by the faint sound of bombs dropping in the distance.

By now, just a month after our arrival at the Hidden Village, word has reached us that Operation Market Garden has been unsuccessful, the Allied forces suffering heavy losses and failing to secure the planned bridgeheads in Arnhem and other major cities.

But life in the forest continues, and we are always busy, its habitants reaching near a hundred people, some of which the resistance can smuggle out swiftly, while others have to stay and recuperate.

I stay because I wouldn't leave without Jakob.

And Helga stays because she wouldn't leave without me.

Our duties have changed a little, the leaders understanding that Helga craved a more hands-on approach in the resistance.

Much to her delight and my angst, she has been allocated with the small group responsible for procuring supplies, meaning she will be sent out on covert runs to collect ration cards and meet with smugglers. And I cannot help but be on edge.

"I don't like this, Helga," I tell her the morning she is to begin her new charges, "It will be dangerous!"

Helga's mouth rises into a mischievous half-smile, "Good! I'm sick of sitting around in a tree or in the bushes during night watch."

She doesn't say it, but I know she is glad to detach herself a little from me and Jakob.

I know she approves of us; she's made it pretty clear that she wanted this for me again and again. But now that it's actually happening, I think she finds it hard that despite this war, my life is moving forward, while she remains suppressed, a young woman who has seen too much and forgotten that there is life outside of the fighting.

I cannot talk her out of it. Nor can I go against what the leaders have decided.

"Be careful, okay?" I tell her, taking her hand.

She *tuts,* "Ani, stop that," she says, "Come on, give me some credit. Have I ever given you reason to doubt me?"

I think of her screaming in her sleep, the nightmares that haunted her for months. I think of her easy laugh, a sound that trills now only in my memory. She won't admit it, but this life we have led has altered her. Made her into someone who seeks out danger but who is unequivocally unable to face it, despite the bravado she puts on.

But I have to trust her. After all, she is my big sister. She has always been the one to protect me; so without me present, surely she will be able to protect herself.

"I'll see you later," I tell her, squeezing her hand goodbye before she heads out the door to her first assignment outside of the forest. Her first assignment without me.

And as I watch her go, the pit in my stomach grows heavier and heavier; but I ignore it, telling myself that she is strong, capable, and savvy. There is no need to fear for her.

But then, if that is true, why do I suddenly feel like our roles have been reversed?

Life in this magical forest is peculiar. Though we are away from all we know and love, living in holes in the ground and speaking not twenty words a day, it is the happiest we've been since the start of this war.

When Helga returned from her first supply run, I barely noticed her dirty clothes and her sweaty brow, my focus was entirely on the accomplishment sparkling in her eyes like stars on a clear night.

"Did you miss me?" she joked, having only been gone a day.

I am happy for her, and she in turn is happy for me. We are exactly where we need to be.

Today, I wake to Jakob slowly sliding his arm out from underneath my head, and I crack open my eyes. There is not a single ray of sunshine peeking through the wooden slats of our makeshift walls and ceiling.

"Where are you going at this hour?" I whisper sleepily, trying to nuzzle closer to him.

I feel the warmth of his hand on my shoulder, the brush of his knuckles on my cheek.

"Wood chopping duty," he whispers back.

"Now?" I groan, though I know it is safest to chop wood before the sunrise, to avoid detection during the day.

He kisses me on the temple, and I welcome the scratch of his stubble against my skin. He climbs out of bed, leaving me feeling cold and weirdly empty.

I've taken to sleeping in his bed since our first night together. It is *our* bed now; Helga having gained that extra wriggle room in her own wooden bed since my move across the room. It had felt natural, an unspoken progression to our circumstances. Jakob and I may not be married – and the outside world may very well judge me for that someday – but in promise at least, we are committed to one another. And that is good enough for me. For now.

I watch through slitted eyes as he pulls on his boots and grabs his jacket from the back of a chair before heading out the door. There's no need for a goodbye, we will see each other when he comes back for breakfast in a couple of hours, before we all head off to our posts for the day. And yet I miss him already, my body aching to be near him. I pull the blanket over my head and force myself to go back to sleep, telling myself to get a grip.

"Get up, get up!"

I bolt upright and look about our small dwelling.

Jumping out of bed, I pull clothes over my head and push my feet into my boots. I glance towards Helga to ensure she is doing the same.

"What is it?!" she asks.

"Someone saw us," Jakob rasps, shoving my jacket at me, "We have to go. Now!"

He grabs my backpack and stuffs some food inside, anything in grabbing distance. Then he thrusts it at me, and I put my arms through the straps.

"Is it the enemy?" Helga asks, ripping her blanket off the bed and stuffing it inside her backpack.

He does not need to answer. Who else would it be?

Jakob grabs a small axe off the side and takes my hand.

"Let's go," he says, and Helga and I share a worried look.

We have been found.

The village has been discovered entirely by chance.

"Two men," Jakob tells us and the leaders at De Boem's hut, "They appeared as if out of nowhere."

"Nazis?"

My stomach drops when Jakob nods.

"They were carrying hunting rifles. Probably out looking for game. They didn't expect to find us. They were more surprised than we were."

"Are you hurt?" Tante Cor asks, and I immediately scan him for any wounds, suddenly frantic.

"They took some shots but missed," he assures.

"They've no doubt gone for backup," Opa Bakker says, turning to De Boem, "We need to flee."

Helga nods in agreement, seizing my hand, ready to go.

"We need to warn the rest of the village," I protest.

"We need to *run*, is what we need to do!" Helga counters, pulling me out the door. But I stand firm.

"The children, the elderly, the wounded," I argue, "They'll need our help."

Tante Cor, De Boem, and Opa Bakker are already heading out, and I follow them, "We'll split up and get everybody out. Don't worry, Annika. They'll be safe."

And they scurry off into different directions, ducking into the nearest huts to warn those within.

"We need to help them!" I insist, to which Jakob and Helga share a torn look.

Helga opens her mouth to protest, but Jakob cuts her off.

"Let's hurry," he says, "No good can come from dawdling in between decisions."

We take off running to the west, the three leaders having gone off in the other directions. At the first hut, we burst inside without ceremony.

"Get dressed! The enemy is coming, they found us!"

Immediately, the two women housed inside grab their gear and head for the exit. They must've only arrived a short while ago, their bags are still packed and ready to go.

We watch them scurry away, and I turn towards the next hut up ahead.

"Dr. Stern!" I call, nearing the young medical student's hut. He isn't a doctor, since his studies were interrupted by the war, but I refer to him as doctor, nonetheless. It's the least he deserves for how well he's cared for the wounded pilots and deserters during his time here.

I enter the dark hut, Jakob closely behind. Helga remains outside, keeping watch.

"What is it?!" comes the young man's voice, laced with fear.

"We need to get the wounded out," Jakob says gruffly, "Can they walk?"

I look down at the three occupied beds at the centre of the underground bunker. One man sits up, a German soldier that arrived the week before. He looks at us sheepishly, in the same way he has done all week, his guilt for the part he has played in this war shining through.

"I can walk," he says. How he speaks our language I do not know, nor do I have time to wonder.

"Alright," I reply, and I look down at the other beds as he makes his way out.

On one bed is a British pilot, shot down during the failed Market Garden. He landed via parachute not far from here, and dragged himself into the woods to hide, one of his legs having broken from the rough landing.

On the other bed lies a young girl, no older than three or four. Her cheeks are red, and her hair is matted with sweat. I recognise her from my duties at childminding, she'd arrived just two days ago. What was her name?

"Fever," Dr Stern says beside me, explaining her ailment.

"I can carry her," Jakob says, taking the girl into his arms. She is floppy, and continues asleep, her head resting on his shoulder.

The pilot has pushed himself up on his elbows, concern painted across his face. He is looking back and forth between us. Then he rattles something off in English, a language I do not know.

But Dr. Stern replies reassuringly.

He turns to us, "He cannot walk alone. But I will help."

Jakob nods once and begins to head out the door when Helga bursts in, her face wild with panic.

"They're here!"

A loud explosion blasts somewhere nearby all of a sudden, and dirt rains down above our heads.

"We're too late," I whisper.

"We cannot stay here," Jakob says, "We're sitting ducks!"

Helga looks at us, at our burdens: Jakob carrying a child, the doctor holding the pilot upright, the pilot's arm over the doctor's shoulder. And I see the choice she has made through her expression.

"No," I hiss, "We cannot leave them!"

Gunfire goes off somewhere to the north, and we all jerk down instinctively.

"If we don't dump them, we will *all* die!" Helga argues as we're huddled down on the ground inside the bunker.

"How far are they?" I whisper to Helga.

She shakes her head, "I didn't see them, I heard dogs barking and I ran in here."

"We may dodge them if we go now," Jakob says, shifting the little girl in his arms.

Irene, I remember then. The little girl's name is Irene.

I look at them, my sister and the man I love, and a small child, and I make a decision.

"Stay here with the pilot, Stern," I say over my shoulder, "You cannot outrun them with him. You have a better chance if you remain hidden."

I can tell the young Jew doesn't want to stay behind, but he nods once and gently sits the injured pilot back down on his bed. He begins to whisper frantically in English to the doctor, but I turn away and pick up the axe Jakob set aside to carry Irene.

We hurry outside, looking left to right before darting from tree to tree in the dewy light of dawn.

Blasts go off at random intervals throughout the forest, followed by sporadic gunshots and shouting. Each time, we flinch and rush to the nearest tree.

"They're throwing hand grenades into the huts," Jakob murmurs behind me, and my throat tightens with terror.

The little girl in Jakob's arms stirs then and lifts her head. She squeals in fright before any of us can stop her, and we huddle behind a dense beech tree, where Jakob *shushes* her gently and tries to bounce her while Helga and I keep a lookout.

"Do you think everyone had enough time to flee?" I whisper, my breathing too quick and my words stiff.

Neither of them replies, because none of us have the answer. All we can do is hope.

"We have to keep moving," Helga says softly, turning back from peering behind the tree, "Head towards Vierhouten. If we make it, we can hide somewhere in the village."

We scramble up as quietly as we can, Irene's little arms locked around Jakob's neck, her sobs stifled. I offer her a small smile, hoping to convey to her how very brave she is being.

We wordlessly signal south and begin to dash through the foliage, the gunfire sounding so distant we are certain we are heading away from danger.

Only for three uniformed Germans to stop us in our tracks, their rifles aimed at our heads.

Abel

<u>Somewhere</u>

I do not linger in Poland. There is nothing left for me here.

I sneak onto the first bus out of Lodz, slipping on board behind a family, and get off at the same place they exit. By some stroke of luck, I manage to hitch a ride with an elderly couple in their car, who cross the border to Dresden in Germany. It is a long drive, in which time I try to make conversation as well as I can, but thankfully they let me sleep for most of it.

I am exhausted. Physically, mentally, emotionally. I could've slept for an age. But soon enough, they drop me off at the Dresden train station, the old lady pressing something wrapped in cloth in my hand.

"For your journey," she says, all maternal, all heart.

They wave goodbye as though we are old friends, and their kindness makes me miss my parents all the more. But also, two other people.

Having no money, I am prepared to hitch another lift with someone, but somehow, I talk my way onto a train to Stuttgart, and I make myself comfortable for another long journey.

I'm not sure where I am going. All I know is that I have to keep moving, for fear that standing still will cause me to fall apart.

Where do I belong now, when everyone I have ever known is gone?

Even before, when Mia was killed and I was taken from Le Chambon to Plön, I could at least pretend that my parents and aunt might still be waiting for me in Poland; though, deep down, I'd known it was a folly.

But now I know it for certain: I am alone in this world.

I should have listened to my gut and saved myself the journey, the heartache, the fresh loss. But that tiny flicker of hope had still burned somewhere within me. I couldn't have ignored it. I'd *needed* to know.

But no more. I've snuffed it out. Now there is only darkness.

What else is left for me here? On this Earth, this world that is tearing itself apart?

I shift in my seat, feeling nauseous.

I realise I haven't eaten in hours, maybe days, and I reach inside my practically empty backpack and retrieve what the old lady gave me earlier.

I unwrap the cloth, gratitude warming my insides at the wonderful sight.

"*Lebkuchen,*" I mumble to myself, astonished.

I bite into the honey-based gingerbread cookie traditionally reserved for Christmas.

"Oh my God," I breathe, the icing sticking to the roof of my mouth.

I try to savour it, each bite taking me back to a simpler time. But all too soon, it is gone, and I lick my fingers clean of every last crumb. I am thirsty, but don't want to wash away the delicious taste of the *Lebkuchen* with my water. And so instead, I rest my head against the window, and close my eyes, hoping for sleep.

"*Papiere!*"

The shouting tears me awake and my hand darts subconsciously to my backpack on my lap, where the documentation I was issued when arriving at the boarding school is safely stored. I should be safe.

But the shouting isn't directed at me.

I look up to see a Nazi officer standing four rows ahead of me, a hand thrust towards a young couple, the other on the hilt of his gun.

The man shakily hands the officer their documents, which he scans with a careful eye. The man looks towards me, a brief yet distinct plea for help reflected in his eyes, and I know immediately that they are travelling under forged documentation.

The officer licks his thumb and smears it over the document, and the woman releases a low whimper.

What follows is hard to watch, but I force myself to, all the same. The way I see it, looking away from the horror is halfway to co-operation.

The man is hauled from his seat as he whimpers, and the officer smacks him in the face with his gun. The young woman is crying loudly now, begging the Nazi to stop. Her tears are streaming, but the officer ignores her and drags her husband behind him by the hair. The woman keens after them, her hands clasped together as she begs. I lose sight of them.

They'll be put in handcuffs and dragged off the train at the next stop, before being formally arrested. Maybe they'll be sent back to wherever they came from. Maybe they'll escape.

More likely than not, they'll be sent to one of the concentration camps. More likely than not, this trip has cost them their lives.

Not once am I asked for documentation throughout the entire train journey, the officers simply nodding their heads as they walk past me, like we are colleagues.

I get off at Stuttgart in the middle of the night and am immediately chilled to the bone. Not due to cold, but due to my complete lack of certainty.

Where will I spend the night? When will my next meal be? Where, even, am I headed?

I stumble my way out of the station, figuring I'll walk throughout the night, when a man rides past me on a bicycle and hops off, leaving it unattended outside a shop.

I don't hesitate, and with one fluid motion I have flung my leg over and am pedalling down the road as fast as I can. I hear the man shouting after me, telling me to come back, but at eighteen years old and with adrenaline pumping through my veins, I am able to zip out of his line of sight in an instant.

I am going so fast that tears stream into my hair, and I let out a *whoop* of success as I turn a corner and then another. It dwindles quickly however, when it dawns on me that I am no nearer knowing where I should go or how to quench the gnawing hunger in my belly.

As I ride around, the city's devastation strikes me. This place must've taken quite a beating from the Allies recently. Everywhere I look, there are burnt cars, blackened with soot, lines of dirty washing hanging from abandoned balconies, bombed-out shops, crumbling buildings, and closed off roads. It all stinks of death, there are piles of rubbish on the pavements. I hear a baby crying in the distance. Dogs barking.

And I wonder if this is what victory looks like.

Alma

<u>Poland, Auschwitz</u>

I wake to a cold cloth being gently pressed against my forehead, and I immediately regret opening my eyes.
Pain bursts through my head, my left eye throbbing as if it has its own heartbeat. I can taste something metallic on my tongue and swallow only to realise that it's me. I can taste myself. My own blood in my mouth.
Where am I?
What has happened?
Esther's face is in front of mine, concern etched onto it.
"She's awake," she mumbles over her shoulder, and I realise I am in *Oberscharführer* Herrman's office. But what is she doing here?
I try to sit up but the pain shoots through me, and I fall back where I lay. With one hand pressed to my temple and the other digging into leather, I know I am on his chaise longue, and I feel a surge of ingrained alarm that I shouldn't be on here.
"*Du bist sicher,*" – You're safe – Herrman says then, and I almost laugh.
But then I remember everything that has happened in the last few weeks, and I look in the direction of his voice. I have to turn my head completely in order to see him, my left eye is so swollen.
His jaw is set tightly, and his brows are furrowed; his expression set in a look that is both intense and tender.
My nose smarts and tears prick my eyes at the sight of him. And I remember. I remember it all…
It hurts my head.
"*Shh,*" says Esther, pressing the cloth to my brow again, "You need to rest."

"Esther," I whisper, the blood on my tongue tasting awful. I lick my lip and at the sharp pain I realise that is where it is coming from.

"I'm okay," she assures me, "You saved me."
She doesn't say it, but I hear it in her voice all the same: *For now.*
We know exactly what will happen when she goes back to her officer. How he will brutalise her all the more for my interference.
But I couldn't *not* interfere. It was instinct for me to protect her, someone I have grown to love.
She brings a weak smile to her lips, then looks up. I follow her gaze to Wolfgang, who continues to look at me with that same pained expression.

"You were right though, Alma," Esther says, so quietly I think I have imagined it, "He isn't like the others."

Drifting in and out of consciousness, I dream I am back at Le Chambon, in my *maman's* arms.
I can smell the aroma of her cooking, taste the sweetness of our garden's cherry tomatoes on my lips, feel the spill of their juice on my chin. I can hear her and *Papa's* laughter as they slow dance in the kitchen after dinner, see the spark in *Maman's* eyes when *Papa* leans in for a kiss after a long day apart.
But then other images invade my mind. Two men hanging by their necks, their eyes bulging out of their skulls, their tongues purple and swollen; the frozen stiff corpse of a woman who'd died in the night; a man's head squirting blood after being shot for failing to hold his bladder; Gita's jerking body as she electrocuted herself on the perimeter fence.
I wake again to find only Wolfgang in the office, and my heart jolts in panic at Esther's absence.

"Where is she?"
My jaw hurts as I utter the words, and I wince.

"She had to return to her duties," he mutters, leaning forward in his chair, "It is almost time for you to leave, too."
Evening roll call. I must have slept almost the whole working day.
I try to sit up, my entire body aching at the movement. Wolfgang takes me by the elbow and helps me up, coaxing me gently with soft words of approval. He seems satisfied when I can stand.

"No more errands for a while," he chuckles grimly, and I try to smile, knowing he is trying to break the tension.
With one eye swollen shut, it is hard to find my balance, but I manage to slowly make it to the door, my body hunched over in pain and my arms crossed over my chest like they are the only thing keeping me together. But I feel his hand on the small of my back, sense his body beside mine, a steady support, and I know it is more than my own will to live that is keeping me going. But also *his* will for me to live.

"Wolfgang," I whisper as I turn to him, my voice a strange croak in the back of my throat.
I don't know what I planned to say. 'Thank you' feels so grossly misplaced, so infinitesimal.
But I do not have to say anything, because he quirks his scarred mouth into a downcast smile. A grimace really.

"I have to get you out of here before you get killed," he says, his voice so low I have to watch his lips as they form the words.

"Yes, you do."
He cups his hand around my cheek then, so gently I want to lean into it, but I dare not. Not for fear or pain, but for the knowledge that this can only end in tragedy.
Who would have thought that the man I have been searching for all my adult life, would turn out to be the one man I could not, and should not, want.

And yet, when he slowly leans in to kiss me, I do not pull back, instead closing my one good eye and allowing the rest of the world to melt away around us. Just for one moment.

His lips are soft against mine, tender and cautious, and yet it is the deepest kiss I have ever suffered; as though he is poisoned, and I am his antidote.

Chapter 18

Annika

<u>The Netherlands, Vierhouten</u>

They tie our hands in front of us and push us forward with their rifles.

Two others, a man and a woman I don't recognise, are found and added to our group, but I take comfort in knowing that over eighty other people have managed to get away. I wonder if Dr. Stern and the British pilot escaped. I pray that they did.

Irene is walking beside me. Her hands are not tied, but she holds onto me and sobs quietly as we all stumble through the forest. She knows there is no way she can escape them. I don't know what is to become of us. I don't know where they are taking us, but it slowly dawns on me that this might be the end.

Once out of the forest, I squint against the direct sunlight. For October, it is a bright and sunny day.

We walk for about ten minutes before we are guided up a path to a house on an enclosed field. We are still near the village of Vierhouten, I know that much. What I don't know is what kind of torture awaits us once we get inside that house.

Suddenly, the two who had joined our group take off running, and my stomach drops with dread to know they will not survive.

I exclaim and cover Irene's face with my knotted hands just as one of the officers behind us raises his rifle and shoots the runners in the back. Irene screams at the loud noise, but I press my hands over her mouth and kneel down in front of her, *shushing* her as gently as I can.

She is hauled out of my grasp then and taken inside the house, and the two dead people are immediately forgotten.

"Don't hurt her!" I plead, reaching towards the monster that has taken her.

"Annika!" Jakob calls behind me suddenly, and I feel his fingers reach for me, just grazing my arm. But I ignore him, my legs pushing me to get to Irene.

The sound of metal making contact with flesh, and a pained yell makes me turn around, only to witness the most terrifying scene I have ever been forced to behold.

"Jakob!" I gasp, reaching my tied hands towards him as one of the Nazis holds him down, his knee pressed onto Jakob's chest.

Jakob tries to wrestle him off, but his secured hands are no use, and he grits his teeth against the pain of the brute on top of him. The Nazi laughs and grinds his knee into Jakob, who grunts under the strain, trying and failing to wrench himself free. And then, to my utter horror, the German smashes the hilt of his handheld gun against Jakob's temple, blood oozing from his forehead, and stuffs the gun into Jakob's mouth.

"No! Stop!" I screech, my heart feeling like it will literally leap from my chest. But I am frozen to the spot, afraid to move, afraid to even breathe.

"Where are the others?!" the Nazi shouts into Jakob's face, and I think how ridiculous it is to ask a question when he obviously cannot answer.

Another officer grabs my arm then and tries to haul me inside, while the Nazi above Jakob shouts the question again.

"I can take you to the leader's hut!"

Helga's voice erupts over the commotion; I had almost forgotten she was here. I look up to find her staring directly at me. And in her eyes, I see a flicker of hope, but also an apology. She has made some kind of choice. But in my torment, I cannot see what.

"Helga?" I mutter, thinking she will get herself killed. If she leads them to the huts, they will only find them empty, and when they do, they will kill her.

"I'll take you to them myself," she says, tearing her gaze from me to the man kneeling over Jakob.
The Nazi looks from Helga to Jakob on the ground underneath him, to me.
At Helga's words, I sense hope blooming inside me. Maybe we can escape while they are distracted in the hut? Maybe Helga has a plan?
Jakob is breathing hard around the barrel of the gun, watching me as if nothing else is happening around him, as if all our lives aren't in danger.
Or perhaps…because they are.
I sense it then. Reality. It descends over me like a tidal wave of mourning, a sorrow so great my knees buckle and the guard beside me has to hold me up. We aren't getting out of this. Not all of us. Maybe not any of us. And just as I begin to form the words I should've told Jakob weeks ago, an ear-splitting explosion bursts through the air.
A bloodcurdling scream escapes me, from deep down in my soul, to see Jakob's brains suddenly splattered in a gritty puddle all around him, his eyes continuing fixed on me, lifeless and dull where once there had been so much…love.

"We don't need all of you to show us the way," the Nazi says matter-of-factly, standing up with a groan as though *he'd* been the one to suffer through this ordeal.
I am still screaming, unable to look away from Jakob, his open mouth, the blood spurting from his head. I cover my face with my hands. I am shaking all over, completely unaware that the Nazi now stands in front of me with his pistol raised to my face.

"No!" I hear Helga yell, somewhere in the distance. Or maybe it is I who is distant, floating above myself and this devilish nightmare.

I am vaguely aware of my sister launching herself at the Nazi before me, of two other officers holding her back, one punching her in the gut. She doubles over, coughing violently.

And I? I am still wailing, breathing in raggedly as my throat grows raw, unable to stop.

Hot tears cascade down my face, and I collapse to my knees, the officer letting go of my arm so that I fall in a heap. And I just keep on sobbing, struggling to inhale, choking on my despair. Despair for Jakob bleeding out before me, for Irene somewhere in the house behind me, for the two people lying dead in the grass, for Helga as she tries to get free of her prisoners, and everyone else that has been grotesquely affected by this war.

And then, as if my life has no meaning, no potential, no worth, the Nazi who killed the love of my life presses his pistol to my forehead, and pulls the trigger, silencing me.

Wolfgang

<u>Poland, Auschwitz</u>

On the 7th of October 1944, a revolt ensued.
Having learned that they were soon to be liquidated as part of Hitler's frantic plan to erase all evidence of Auschwitz, the prisoners of the *Sonderkommando* rose up in rebellion. Some two hundred and fifty were killed during the fighting, and guards shot another two hundred after that, even when the mutiny was already suppressed. Those at the heart of the uprising were located some days later, four Jewish female prisoners, all of which were publicly hanged for their disobedience.

The prisoners' time in this place is running out, and soon, no one will be left to tell their tale.
I stole the spare SS uniform a few days ago, the same day Alma was beaten to within an inch of her life. I cannot put her escape off any longer, to do so would mean killing her. But she can't attempt to flee in the condition she is in, either. Not only for the severity of her injuries, but also for the fact that no SS officer has recently sustained such a battering. Her welts would call her out as an imposter before she'd even made it through the gate.
So, we wait. We wait for her bruises to fade and for her split lip to heal. Only her face needs to clear up, everything else will be covered.
But her body aches still, even after over a week of healing. I can tell by how she walks when she carries the mop and bucket from the supply closet, I can hear it in her strained breathing when she cleans the windows. She may have a cracked rib, I think, and fresh rage ignites within me.
But there is nothing I can do.

While I want nothing more than to beat the living daylights out of that snivelling little shit, to have him coughing up blood and begging for mercy, I know I cannot. But I take some comfort in the fact that, *at least*, Alma didn't need hospitalising. Because setting foot inside the onsite hospital was a sure-fire way to get sent to the gas chambers.

Here, a useless worker is equivalent to a dead worker.

Mostly, I try to get her to rest on the settee in my office. But she is too fearful that someone will enter unexpectedly and find her lazing, leading to not only another beating – or worse – but also to me being caught out as a sympathiser.

So instead, she cleans. I do not send her out on errands anymore. I would be stupid to. But even as the tension in my small office builds, I have not dared to kiss her again since that day.

"Thank you," she mumbles now as I hand her the muffin from the canteen, and when I see her hands shaking, I think I will go back and get a warm soup for her, too.

It snowed last night, just a light dusting, but I curse myself nonetheless for having waited this long to send her away. I only hope I am not too late.

"You're welcome," I mutter back, and our eyes lock for the briefest of moments.

She turns away from me and sits on the armchair to eat.

"So," she says, tearing off a piece of the moist cake, "Will you tell me the plan?"

I nod sombrely, my stomach clenching at the idea of her leaving. If successful, I will never see her again. If unsuccessful...

"I have a uniform ready for you," I tell her quietly as she eats, "You will ride out of the main gate on a bicycle. It's as simple as that. SS officers go in and out all the time. I'll be there, to distract the guard with some errand. He will let you through and then go off on whatever mission I send him."

She frowns, "Is that it? No hiding in a box for three days? No elaborate heist?"

I shake my head and lean back in my chair, "The simpler we keep it, the smoother it'll go."

"Hopefully," she adds, a challenge in her tone.

I swallow hard, "Hopefully," I echo.

We're silent for a moment while we contemplate what I have shared, then she breathes a sigh. Her face twinges with pain suddenly, and I sit forward.

"What is it?"

She looks up at me, "Just a pain," she dismisses, "It's nothing."

I watch her stand and follow suit, making my way to the door to fetch her that soup. But with my hand on the doorknob, I hesitate. I don't like to leave her alone.

"This is wrong," I hear her voice behind me, and turn around to see her standing by the window, last night's snow casting an angelic light around her.

"What is?" I whisper, though I know.

She falters, "What is happening here."

I can tell by the look in her eyes that she is not talking about Auschwitz. And yet, at the same time, she is.

"It's wrong," she continues, choosing to step around our feelings, "Your people have done unimaginable things."

"They aren't my people," I mumble back instantly.

I don't need to say it, but it hangs between us all the same, the end to my statement: that *she* is my people.

I turn the doorknob, "I'll be right back," I say, unable to look at her any longer. And I put some distance between us, when all I really want to do is the complete opposite.

Abel

<u>Germany, somewhere</u>

I ride the bike all day, through towns and fields and wooded areas, and never once am I stopped.

At night, I find shelter in a barn and snuggle up to the handful of sheep that lie in the straw, making myself scarce with the first ray of sunlight; lest be met with the barrel of the proprietor's gun for trespassing.

Luckily, I'd found an apple tree soon after leaving Stuttgart and filled my backpack with about a dozen apples. I grab one now and bite into it, some much needed sustenance before another long day.

With nothing but the open world before me as I continue to pedal on the bicycle, I've had plenty of time to think about anything and everything. And by now, I know exactly where I am headed.

Mostly, I thought about Frida, and of the fateful discovery I had made back in Plön. But I try to separate Frida from Weis in my mind. She deserves to be remembered for who she was and who she could have been. Not for the wrongdoings of her father.

I wonder if anyone will ever make the connection that I made? Once the police found the bodies, they will have investigated the house. Did they put two and two together when they discovered the strange etchings on his headboard? Or would Weis' crimes be forgotten and lumped together with the bigger atrocities that are taking place all over Europe? *Were* they even separate crimes?

The sun is setting as I reach the town of Müllheim near the borders of Germany, and I make my way towards its train station.

With another apple clamped between my teeth, I lean my bike against the wall and observe the station. There is no way I'll be able to cross over to France with just me and my stolen bicycle, I would need all kinds of permits to be let through. So, I am hoping that luck will be on my side once again, and that I'll manage to board a train.

I hang about at the station for hours, remaining hidden behind a wall or among the crowd so as not to attract unwanted attention. Night falls around me, chilling me to my bones, and I stamp my feet and blow into my cupped hands to keep from freezing. I wait and wait for a train to arrive that will take me to France, but any time one does – which isn't often – guards with growling dogs secure the doors. I don't dare to try and jump on without a ticket. I cannot afford to be arrested so close to my destination.

And then, just before ten o'clock at night, a freight train blows its whistle. I observe it, and something inside me urges me to chance it. Even if only to get out of the cold for the night.

I don't second guess myself, seizing the opportunity, and I hop on an open carriage as it starts to pull away. I scurry deeper inside and hide in the darkness behind some wooden crates. Unfortunately, I had to leave the bike behind, but it was either take this risk or be stuck here until the next opportunity arose.

I hope this train will lead me out of Germany. I am done with this country. I wash my hands of it. In my heart, this is no longer my place of birth or my home. But neither is Poland.

The only place I care to go back to now – even if I find that no one I care for has survived – is that small, hidden village in France, where I last felt safe and wanted.

<u>France, outskirts of Le Chambon-sur-Lignon</u>

Everything is grey.
Grey skies, grey clouds, grey roads, grey world. Even I have become grey, caked in dust and sweat and grief.

Luck had been on my side. That freight train having crossed the border into France and travelled south for several hours. I'd hopped off at a town I'd never heard of before, but upon asking for directions to Le Chambon at a bakery, I'd learned I hadn't been far from it at all.

So I began to walk, and I have been walking for hours since.

Rain threatens to spill from the dreary sky at any moment, but I take comfort in the sight of the woods that surround Le Chambon – known as *La Montagne Protestante* – and I know that I am home. And though I am weary, dirty, and cold, I feel a slight bounce in my step at the familiar sight. I have made it. I am *so* close.

No matter what I find there, I think, trying to rally myself, *it is where I will remain*.

I know this as well as I know that my name is Abel Friedman. I will settle down, build a house, make a home, help the people rebuild. Maybe the resistance is still operational. Maybe I could finally join now that I am of age to trek across the mountains to Switzerland. I'd been a boy when I had first arrived here. And since then, I have been dragged up a man.

But darkness descends over me the closer I get, doubt and worry creeping around my heart like the smoky fingers of a poisonous mist. The truth is: I don't know what I will find. Perhaps the Nazis bombed the place to pieces. Maybe all that is left behind are the skeletal crumblings of a long-forgotten village, and the disintegrating bodies of all that got caught in the blaze.

I enter the woods, the woods I had gotten to know so well in the weeks before the raid. It smells the same as it did back then, earthy and wet, reassuring. It makes me think about how, even if all of humanity is extinguished from the planet, nature will prevail. It will always simply go on.

The foliage holds a dewy shine, giving the impression that it has rained recently and it is still clinging onto that last bit of goodness.

As if my thought has summoned it, I hear the *pitter patter* of thick raindrops falling on the treetops above. I look up. A squirrel climbs a tree at my approach, stopping halfway up the trunk to look down at me curiously. I watch it watching me for a moment, but when the rain begins to seep through the trees' protection, it scurries upwards.

I feel the first fat drops landing on my upturned face, and I push forward.

With nothing but my filthy jacket, I let the rain fall onto me. It presses my hair to my scalp and muddies the ground. With every step I take, I am more and more convinced that I will not like what I find. Perhaps it is the gloomy atmosphere. Perhaps it is my jaded soul. But all I know is that every journey so far has led to disaster. In the world we live in, where people turn against their neighbours, and loving fathers kill their own children, how can I expect to find anything but horror yet again?

Slivers of light become visible through the trees then, and I am suddenly overcome with a wild urge to both sprint towards the end of the woods, and to stop dead in my tracks, too afraid to see what I would find.

I settle for a steady pace, trying to ignore the growing knot in my stomach. I carefully emerge from among the trees and out into this miserable void, squinting against the rain as it pummels me. I raise my hand to shield my face and try to focus on what lies ahead.

And then, when it all becomes clear, the world doesn't seem quite so colourless anymore.

Alma

<u>Poland, Auschwitz</u>

My eye is no longer swollen, and the purple-black bruising has evolved into a yellow-green mess on my cheek.

I have never had a black eye before, but as I look at my reflection in the window while I clean Wolfgang's office, I imagine it will clear up in a few days.

Wolfgang is out doing his rounds, same as he has done for two days, covering for another officer at the sorting warehouse, Kanada. Yesterday, he came back with news of Trudi, who is stationed there. One of the *kapos,* a horrible woman known among the camp for manically laughing while she hands out beatings, had laid into Trudi for apparently working too slowly. I saw her bloodied forehead and bruised arms that evening, and handed Trudi the extra blanket that Wolfgang had secretly given me for her.

Esther hasn't been the same since her officer almost led the gang rape against her in the canteen, the same day he almost killed me. She hardly talks to either me or Trudi, turning her back on us as soon as lights go out. I suspected it was because he'd been taking his humiliation out on her following Wolfgang's interference. But when I asked Trudi about it last night as I tended to her wounds, she shook her head.

"He hasn't touched her since," she told me, "she fears he has grown tired of her."

I consider this now as I wipe ash off the windowpanes, trying not to think about how it was a person not long ago. I want to believe that it is a good thing that he is no longer raping Esther. In a normal world, it would be. But in here, it also means she might be thrown out of the security and warmth of his office and back into Kanada. Or worse.

Except, maybe it is good timing. Maybe, when I escape, Wolfgang can recruit Esther to take my place here, and she can be the next person he smuggles out?

I allow the idea to mollify me as I get on with my work.

It is evening roll call, and I am standing among thousands of other prisoners, shivering against the cold. It is early November, and it hasn't snowed since last week, but the wind is cutting, and its chilled claws curl their way through our thin clothing. Some of the prisoners have blankets wrapped over their heads and shoulders, others have no more than the uniform they were given on their first day, and our teeth and bones rattle together so loudly it is like we are a human windchime.

I don't know the people I am standing with, which is often the case, since there is always such a huge influx of fresh arrivals, as well as a vast loss of others.

I listen out for the numbers I know however, as I have done every day since memorising my own, Esther's, Trudi's, and Gita's. Gita's number has faded into the deeper parts of my memory by now, though she has only been dead for four months. But I remember her in other ways. In ways she would have preferred to be remembered.

I holler when my number is called, willing this roll call to go smoothly so that we can retreat indoors that much quicker. Not that it is much better inside the barracks. Without proper heating or blankets, we often wake up with frost crystalised in our hair. That is, if we are lucky enough to wake up at all.

Trudi's number is called, and I hold my breath and pray for her response. It comes in a clear '*Hier!*' and I relax.

Dozens more are shouted out, and I stamp my feet to keep from freezing to death. The guards all wear fur-lined coats as they walk up and down the length of us. Those up in the wooden towers dotted around the camp even hold a steaming mug of something in their hands. I imagine it is the coffee Wolfgang sometimes gets from the canteen. He offered me a cup of it once, but I declined, too scared that one of the *kapos* would smell it on my breath.

The Alsatian dogs that patrol with some of the officers start to whine and paw at the ground, their tails between their legs as they await the end of roll call.

Esther's number is shouted then, and again, I stiffen to listen.

After a beat, I turn my head to the side, shielding my ear from the wind.

Her number is called again, the Nazi shouting it louder over the speaker in case she did not hear, and I clench my teeth together, trying not to panic.

Has she passed out from the cold, or maybe forgotten her number? Has she answered and I have missed it? I turn to look at the guard, but he is craning his neck to look into the immense crowd, his eyebrows furrowed in exasperation.

And then a delicious thought comes to me.

Has she escaped?

Two prisoners are sent to look for her, and I watch them enter our barrack, praying they come out empty handed.

An officer approaches the guard and mumbles something to him. I try to identify him, but it is too dark to see his face.

The guard nods and clicks his fingers at two men in the front row then, and I recognise one of them from *Leichenkommando* – Corpse Squad. They step forward as the officer who whispered something to the guard walks away, *whistling* no less. The whistling officer walks past me, a light illuminates his face, and a chill runs through me.

Neumann.

The two prisoners from *Leichenkommando* run off towards the administration building, as the two who were sent to search for Esther in the barrack return.

They resume their place among us, empty handed. And I exhale with relief, forming a wisp of white mist.

We all stand in silence, with no other sound but the wind howling and the dogs whining. For a moment, I think the whole world has stopped turning.

And then, I hear the two *Leichenkommando* prisoners' footsteps approaching from behind, and some of us – me included – turn around to watch them. They do not return to their posts, continuing instead to awkwardly hobble past us in the courtyard and towards the crematorium.

A low whimper escapes me, though my mouth is clamped shut. I cannot see what they are carrying, too many people stand in my way. But I don't need to see to know that it is a dead body. And I don't need to be a genius to know that *who* they are carrying is the missing number 20556.

Better known by those who she had been close to as Esther. Or…by one little boy who will be glad to be reunited with her in the afterlife… '*Mamaleh.*'

Chapter 19

Alma

<u>Poland, Auschwitz</u>

I haven't slept all night.

Without Esther, the bunk Trudi and I share feels empty – though we are squished together with three other women. The first alarm at 5:30am alerts us to relieve ourselves before roll call, and I do as I am told. The second alarm alerts us to stand to attention in the courtyard once again, and again, I do as I am told.

I feel numb the entire time, cursing myself for having stood up to Esther's officer, cursing Wolfgang for his part in humiliating him further.

We should have known that none of us would come out of this place unscathed. If any of us get out of this place at all.

No one is missing at roll call this morning, and once dismissed, I make my way to the administration building, for the first time, without Esther.

He isn't here.

In Wolfgang's office, I begin by tidying his desk. He is neat and orderly, so there is not much to do. But I go about lightly dusting every surface, nonetheless, focusing on even the most minute speck. I come across a small coffee spill on his desk which has dried during the night, and I hurry to the supply closet to retrieve a bucket and soapy water. I attack the spot with all my might, imagining it is this place and the terrible people within it. Then I get down on my hands and knees and begin to scrub the floor.

It isn't even dirty, but I go at it all the same, washing and re-washing the floorboard until it softens.

When Wolfgang comes in at 9:00am on the dot, his coffee in one hand and a brown paper bag in the other, I am sweating and crying all at once. In fact, I'm pretty sure I have scrubbed some of my own sweat and tears into this very floor.

"Alma," he breathes, closing the door behind him, and it is enough to break me.

I stand – awkwardly, since my side still hurts if I move too quickly – and I fall into his arms.

His broad frame staggers backwards, unprepared for my embrace, though I weigh nothing anymore.

He drops the paper bag to the floor and, with his free hand, holds me to him. I am sobbing now, tears I have been holding in for days, weeks, months. And I let them soak into his uniform. His hand gently cups the back of my head.

"She's dead," I mutter wetly against him.

"I know," he replies quietly.

I look up, caring little for my bloodshot eyes and my runny nose, "He did it," I say, "It was him."

"I know," he says again.

"What can we do?"

He looks at me, his expression one of misery and anger.

"Nothing."

I knew this day would come, but I didn't think it would come quite so soon.

"Here," Wolfgang says after he wiped my face and I have calmed down enough to eat the apple tarte he'd brought me, "Put this on."

I blink down at the SS uniform he has pressed into my hands, and understanding shoots through me.

I am not ready.

"No, no no no," I splutter, pushing the uniform back at him, "Not today, not like this!"

He stares at me, "How then, Alma? There's no preparing for this, no training. We have a plan. You are healed. You have to go before the next snowfall."

I look out the window, a cold finger of dread running down my spine when pale specks settle on the glass.

But it isn't snow. Only the constant fall of ash; and my shoulders sag with both relief and misery.

But Wolfgang is right: my bruises have healed, even if whatever ails me inside has not.

I swallow hard, fearing the tarte will make a reappearance.

"I can't do this," I whisper, suddenly more scared than I have ever felt in my entire life.

He drops the uniform on his desk and grabs me gently by the arms, "Yes you can! And you will! The longer we put this off, the less time you will have before evening roll call. Once they realise you aren't in the camp, they will send search parties after you. They will look for you for three days. If they don't find you by then they will call off the search. And only then will *I* know if you've made it safely away."

Tears spring to my eyes, but I nod my head and pick up the uniform.

"It is the smallest size I could find," he tells me as I hold it before me, feeling sick to think that I have to wear it, this skin of a killer.

I shudder, but before I can talk myself out of it, I turn around and kick off my wooden clogs. My fingers fiddle with the buttons of my grey dress, too shaky to do a thorough job.

The sound of the door closing behind me makes me turn back around, and the sudden emptiness of Wolfgang's office looms over me like a slow-throbbing heartbeat.

This will be the last time I will ever see him, the man who has risked his life for me, for my *maman*, for all of 'us'.

Sadness threatens to engulf me, but I return to the task at hand, ripping the damn dress over my head after failing yet again to undo the buttons. I step into the Nazi uniform without looking down at it, first the trousers, then the shirt and finally the jacket.

A quiet knock at the door sounds then, and I turn towards it, "Yes," I whisper, and Wolfgang re-enters.

He looks at me, drinking me in as though I were wearing an elegant gown, and not a murderer's garb. Though, it is the same way I have looked at him of late, despite him having always donned this identical uniform.

It's peculiar. The rush of warmth that comes from looking beyond the exterior, to find something else entirely within.

He clears his throat, "It fits," he says, and I look down at myself.

I have rolled up the trouser legs and tightened the belt to the last hole, but yes, it fits.

He picks the cap up off the side, the final touch to my disguise, and places it on my head just so. He is gentle, though I am no longer in pain. Not physically, at least.

"You ready?" he asks me, a loaded question.

His fingertips brush the nape of my neck, and I look up to meet his gaze.

How can anyone ever be ready for all of *this?*

But I nod my head, though I'm not ready at all.

Not ready to attempt this crazy escape. Not ready to die if I am caught. Not ready to live in a world as lost as this one. Not ready to leave Trudi. Not ready to leave him.

Not ready.

Not ready.

"Ready."

Abel

<u>France, Le Chambon-sur-Lignon</u>

  "Abel? ABEL!"
Marie's voice is a whisper in the breeze at first, drowned out by the heavy downpour.
But then she is running towards me, her grey hair plastered against her head and her dress soaked through.
Despite my fatigue, I take off running too, my chest pinching at the sight of her – the only mother I have left.
She is crying when she reaches me, and takes my face into her hands.
I notice she is shorter than when I was taken.
  "You survived!" she sobs in French, grinning up at me.
I nod, overjoyed to see her, "So did you!"
The language flows from my lips as easily as though I'd only spoken it yesterday.
  "Come, come," she says, looping her arm through mine and heading back to the village.
Once inside the little house – a house I hadn't realised I'd missed quite this much – a rush of respite washes over me.
  "Pierre!" Marie calls then, leading me towards the roaring fire in the hearth, "Pierre, quick!"
Heavy footsteps come barrelling from the bedroom, "What's wrong?" my adoptive father asks, looking bewilderedly about the small living space.
He blinks when his old eyes find mine, "Abel?"
I nod, running a hand through my sodden black hair, "*Bonjour*," I mumble, unsure what else to say.
He stumbles towards me, stunned to see me, "Abel, it is you!"
He pulls me into an embrace so tight I feel a lump forming in my throat.

"Where have you been?" he asks when he lets go, "Where did they take you?"

But before I can answer, Marie steps forward.

"Let's get him out of these wet clothes first, *amour*, so he doesn't catch a cold."

She looks me up and down, then turns back to Pierre, "Go get him some of your trousers and jumpers. Nothing we have kept of his will fit anymore."

They kept my old clothes.

I meet her gaze and smile down at her fondly, "*Merci*, Marie," I tell her, so many emotions bubbling about within me.

She pats me tenderly on the cheek, "How about some tea?"

Once Marie and I have changed out of our wet clothes, the three of us sit by the fire with steaming cups of mint tea in our hands.

"From our garden," Pierre says proudly, referring to the peppermint leaves.

I raise my cup at him in admiration.

"So, tell us," Pierre says after a moment of quiet wonder, "What happened to you?"

I shake my head, not sure where to begin.

"Well," I exhale, thinking, "once I got you out of the house, I hid my papers in a shallow hole by the backdoor —"

"I found them!" Marie interrupts, "Didn't I, Pierre? After the first rainfall, the soil softened and there was this hole. I nearly broke my ankle walking over it! And inside were these muddy, drenched papers. I'm afraid they're ruined now."

I nod as she speaks of her discovery, disappointed to learn my true identity papers are destroyed. Though I know that one's identity is defined by more than some document.

"What happened then, Abel?"

I tell them about how, without my yellow star or my paperwork identifying me as a Jew, I was thrown into the group of non-Jews and taken away.

"We are so sorry about Mia," Marie interrupts again, gently, shaking her head, "We buried her and Azriel side by side in the graveyard. We can take you there when the rain clears."

I nod, my jaw clenched to keep in the sorrow.

"I would like that."

Then I continue.

"As a German and a minor, I was enlisted in the Hitler Youth."

Marie and Pierre raise their heads in a joint, slow nod. Then they both look at the clothes hanging before the fire, drying.

"Well," Marie says, sipping her tea, "We won't be keeping those clothes then."

We chuckle softly at that.

"Did they treat you well, though, Abel?" Marie asks gently, "Were you alright?"

My throat tightens at the love in her voice, and I think of my mother, and how I am certain she would've liked Marie. Even if only because she cares so much for me. And how much she cared for Mia.

I nod, "I made friends. Believe it or not, the boys at the boarding school are completely unaware about what is going on in the outside world."

Pierre scoffs, unable to believe anyone to be so blind, "All of Germany knows," he argues.

"I don't think so," I counter, though I have no proof.

Pierre finishes his tea and shakes his head, "However did you get back to us?"

I look down at my cup, twirl it around ruefully, "I jumped out the window in the middle of the night," I tell them, choosing not to share my encounter with the Devil and his angel daughter.

"I stole a bicycle," I admit with a mischievous grin, as if it were a terrible crime, "I received a lift from a German couple, took some trains. This last stretch, I walked."
Pierre is nodding at me as if that all makes complete sense, and he opens his mouth to ask another question when I interject.

"I didn't come here straight away," I admit, riding the wave of courage that has appeared out of nowhere. I look them in the eyes, "I couldn't. I didn't even think of coming here until after I checked. I had to check."
Marie's wrinkly hand is on mine then, squeezing gently. They know of what I speak. I look down at her hand, feeling guilty for having had a life before them, as well as feeling guilty for having returned to them. I am torn, conflicted, as I have always been since Mia and I were sent away.

"They are gone," I tell them in a rash whisper, "I thought…I thought if I could find them in the ghetto maybe – maybe I could get them out somehow."
I shake my head, swallow my tears, "But they weren't in the ghetto. There *was* no ghetto. Everyone had been killed or sent away to a concentration camp."
Marie is crying silently, while Pierre hangs his head.

"So, I came here," I conclude.
Pierre looks up at me, and I search his face for disappointment, certain I have hurt him, certain he will think that I see them as my last resort.
And they are…but it runs so much deeper than that.
There is love here, too, despite how ashamed I feel for harbouring it. Like it means I am betraying my real parents, my real family.

"You are always welcome here, son," Pierre says then, to which Marie nods eagerly, squeezing my hand tighter, "For as long as you want to stay here, in this house, in this village, you are welcome."

I release a shuddering breath then, realising suddenly that I've needed to express my guilt for so long. But I've also needed to hear that they understood my uncertainty.

"*Merci,*" I mumble, smiling faintly, unable to find a word strong enough to let them know how much I appreciate them.

But Marie shakes her head and pats my cheek, "No, Abel," she says, looking over at Pierre and then back at me, "Thank *you.*"

Wolfgang

<u>Poland, Auschwitz</u>

My pulse is racing, my palms are sweating. What have I done?

As an SS officer of a moderate high rank, my approach to the *Arbeit Macht Frei* gate results in the guards clicking their heels and extending their arm.

"*Heil Hitler,*" they say, and I nod my head at them in return.

From the corner of my eye, I see Alma slowly approaching on the bicycle I procured for her. And my stomach lurches with nausea.

What have I done? What have I done?

Her cap is low over her eyes, and her face is slightly downcast as she comes to a stop by the gate. I swallow the lump that has formed in my throat.

This has to work. It has to. If it doesn't…

I flick a nonchalant glance at her, then back to the guard before me.

"Well," I say to him, trying to sound authoritative but not too enthusiastic, "Let the man out!"

The guard hops to it, eager to please and to return quickly to find out why I am here.

I take a step back and sigh with exaggerated tedium, making sure that at least one of the guards' attention is primarily on me, and not on the female prisoner that is escaping right from under their noses.

Alma prepares herself to pedal forward again, and once the gate is opened enough for her to slip through, she presses her foot down and dips her head at the guards in thanks as she rides past.

I watch her go, staring at her back as she slowly pedals away.

Was it really that *easy?*

But it isn't over yet.

I had told her to remain as calm as possible for as long as possible, and not to suddenly bolt away at the first opportunity. It would only alert the guards in the towers that something wasn't quite right, and the further she got before they realised anything was amiss, the better.

Her retreating figure grows smaller the further she goes, and deep down inside, a small part of me wills her to look back, just so that I can see her face one last time. But I know she will not. I *hope* she will not. She must not be so reckless. We cannot afford even one slip up.

"*Oberscharführer?*" the guard says then, standing before me. I turn to him and shake my head.

"*Ja,*" I clear my throat, "The new shipment is causing delay. Go help at selection."

The guard blinks at me, then looks at his colleague, as though this were beneath him, which it is. This isn't his job at all. But I continue to stare him down, challenging him to deny me.

"Right away," he says finally, and I exhale the tightness in my throat.

He hurries away and I turn to watch him go, though my entire body is rigid with the need to look back at Alma through the gate. But I take comfort from the silence that follows her departure. There are no whistles being blown and no dogs being set loose. She has made it out of Auschwitz without being caught.

And my chest both aches and soars with that reality.

I burn Alma's grey dress bearing her prisoner number. That way, once the alarm is rung of her escape, they will not know to look for someone wearing a disguise. They will search for an escapee in prisoner's garb.

It is the final thing I can do. The rest is up to her.

I only hope I never see her again.

My breath is knocked out of me at that thought, and I clamp my hands on the edge of my desk and hang my head between my shoulders. I concentrate on my breathing.

I hope I never see her again.

The truth of that statement is so raw and contradictory that my heart clenches tightly. Clearing my throat, I sniff away the emotion. No one can see me faltering.

At 18:55 I exit my office and stand before the administration building, looking out into the courtyard. It is empty right now, but in just – I look at my watch – four minutes, it will be filled with thousands of stick-thin people as they are counted like a herd of sheep.

I light a cigarette and inhale deeply, its smoke encircling me as I blow it out through my nose.

The roll call alarm sounds, and I remain where I stand, watching as the prisoners arrive from all over the camp.

No one pays me any attention. I am just an officer smoking in the shadows.

The guards begin calling out number after number, their patrol dogs pacing up and down with them, and I smoke cigarette after cigarette, awaiting the number I know is missing.

And when it finally comes, all order is lost.

Chapter 20

Alma

Poland, somewhere

I ride away as slowly as I can manage, repeating Wolfgang's warning under my breath that to make a dash for it would only draw attention to me.
I don't know how long I pedal for before I dare to look back, but when I do, Auschwitz is long gone, and I – I am suddenly acutely aware of how alone I am.

The sun is beginning to set, and I know I only have maybe two hours before the evening roll call at the camp will reveal my disappearance.
I need to find someplace to hide, somewhere I can rest my sore muscles. But to stop is lunacy. I have to keep pushing forward and get as far away from here as possible.
I veer off the road when I spot a river, and follow it south for several hours, figuring that to stay near it would be the most logical thing to do, since I have set off on this dangerous journey with nothing but the clothes on my back. I hope to find my bearings soon, but I am getting ahead of myself.
I need to stay focused. One step at a time.

I stop when I can go no further.
By now, the moon is high in the sky, and I think it must be near midnight, but I have no way of knowing. I only know that I ache. All over.
I have been cycling for hours, adrenaline pushing me on.

But now I collapse by the side of the river, and drag the bicycle underneath a shrub, breathing heavily. Sweat begins to prick at my hairline and run down my face, as if stopping has caused more exertion than carrying on would've done.

I lie there, breathing in and out, my hand pressed to my heart until it slows enough for me to sit up.

I wash my face and hands in the river, then drink from my cupped hands as quietly as my thirsty throat allows. It is completely dark, with no artificial light, neither from houses nor cars. Only the moon shines down on me. But I am not foolish enough to think myself far enough away from civilisation to be reckless. So, I don't move more than is necessary.

I look about myself. At the bank of the river, I am surrounded by dotted trees and wild foliage, the grass I'm lying on is as high as my knees and soft enough that I could fall asleep right here, right now.

But I dare not.

Animals call to each other in the gloom, owls and foxes yelling out, like they are warning the Nazis that I am here. It is eerie. And after a moment I scramble up and carefully pick up the bike.

I decide to walk for a bit to spare my sore behind, and soon I come across what looks like a little alcove, two low-growing trees having met and melded together at their crowns. I inspect it cautiously. Underneath, the grass is dewy but soft, and I decide it is probably the best place I will find to lay down my head.

It is cold, and I have no blanket or spare clothing. But at least it is a mild night, with no rain and no wind. And I tell myself that after all I have survived so far; surely I will survive one night underneath the stars.

I wake up several times, not only because I am freezing but also because I keep thinking I hear footsteps, or the sound of dogs barking in the distance.

It isn't yet daybreak, but I sit up nonetheless, too nervous to stay still any longer. I rub at my stiff neck and wince at the feel of the protruding pearls of my spine. A shiver runs through me, and I stuff my cold hands in my pockets.

But what's this?

There is something inside my jacket pocket. It feels hard and…crumbly, and I lift the item to my face. Even in the pre-dawn light, I know exactly what it is, my nose having caught its delicious aroma.

A chocolate chip cookie. A piece of it, at least.

I stuff it into my mouth and begin to cry, throaty sobs escaping me as I retrieve another piece, and then another from the pocket. They taste like childhood, like an early morning sunrise in the summer, and I cry with gratitude and joy. I cry with hunger and exhaustion. I even cry with pure and simple sorrow, for everything that has happened to me. To Esther. To Gita. To Azriel and Mia. To everyone who has suffered and died because of blind hatred.

But most of all, I cry for the love I have found in the most unlikely of places, and how I have lost it.

Abel

<u>France, Le Chambon-sur-Lignon</u>

It is the day after I arrived back at Le Chambon. Pastor Trocmé has come to see me, and I am as surprised to see him as he is to see me.

"Abel!" he gasps when Marie opens the door and invites him inside. He had heard of my return, of course. Word of mouth always did travel fast in this small village.

"Pastor!" I gawk, "How are you – How did you…?"

"How am I alive?" he finishes for me, laughter in his voice.

I only nod as we both sit down by the fire, dumbfounded. The last time I saw him, he and his cousin Daniel were being bundled into the same trucks I had seen Alma and her mother being put into. I still didn't know where they were all taken, but given the pastor's involvement with the French resistance, and smuggling Jews out of the country, I had thought them to have been killed.

"Daniel is dead," Pastor Trocmé says, as if he heard what I was thinking.

My shoulders sag though I am not surprised, "I am sorry, pastor."

He shakes his head, "He will be remembered. With his help, we've smuggled out about 5000 people," he says, beaming with a sad kind of pride.

I nod slowly and watch as he takes the cup of peppermint tea Marie offers him, then she retreats back to her kitchen.

"How did you make it out?" I ask the pastor, eager to hear who else has made it back here.

My chest pinches at the thought of Alma.

The older man takes a sip of his tea, his small, rounded spectacles steaming up slightly.

"Daniel and I were released after just four weeks," he admits with a hint of guilt.

I flinch at the statement, "Four weeks?"

He nods, "We were pressed to sign an oath of loyalty to the Vichy government," he says, sipping his tea again, "I refused. But they released me nevertheless."

I blink at him, stunned. I had not expected this.

"I had to go into hiding for a while, but I was still able to oversee the resistance rescue work. And then," he smiles, putting the cup down on the small table by the sofa, "about three months ago, when France was liberated by the Allies in August of '44, I was able to come home."

"Has anyone else returned?" I ask, "Has anyone else that was taken that night survived?"

He shakes his head sadly, "Since my return, I sometimes drive out of Le Chambon, just around the nearby towns, in case someone is trying to find their way back home. So far, I encountered two refugees seeking shelter, but nobody that we knew from before," he sighs sadly, "We weren't all taken to the same place. Those who were Jewish…I regret to say it, but they were likely sent to a worker camp, a concentration camp."

A moment of silence settles between us, and I think of Weis' words.

Jews, especially women with young children, are sent to gas chambers as soon as they arrive there. If you're lucky, you're allowed to live. To work. You're shaved, you're given a number. You're no longer a person. You work…But everyone dies there. Everyone dies.

"Although!" Trocmé exclaims then, "Lena Basson! She returned to the village the next day, unharmed – well, apart from a badly bruised shoulder."

"Lena Basson?" I ask, forgetful for a moment.

"*Oui!* You know, Alma's mother."

He takes me to see Lena Basson, who envelops me into a tight hug as soon as she sees me.

"Abel! You lucky young man! The horrors you must have faced! You were so clever to tear off your star! I wish we had thought of it, my Alma and I."

She sobs then, and her husband steers her inside the house, sitting her down at the table.

"Come in," he tells me and the pastor, who has tagged along.

We all sit around the table as Lena Basson blows her nose into her handkerchief.

It is gloomy inside, grey and cold, like it's been sitting empty for years. My heart aches for them. I may have experienced my fair share of loss, but I cannot know the pain of losing a child.

I imagine it is ten times more harrowing than the loss of a parent.

"He spared me," Lena says out of the blue, interrupting the quiet chit-chat that had ensued between the men, "The Nazi on our truck, he told me to get off, and so I did."

Monsieur Basson stands up then, rubbing his hand over his face and leaving out the backdoor. I assume he cannot bear to listen to this story again. But I cannot wait to hear the rest.

"What do you mean, he spared you?" I ask, my voice coming out like a soft breath.

"None of us knew what he was saying," Lena continues dreamily, sniffling and pressing the handkerchief to her eyes, "But he nudged me with his boot, and Alma – my brave Alma – I could tell by her face that she wanted to hurt him."

She chuckles softly for a moment, but then the crinkles around her eyes disappear again, "We understood him then, when he bent down and looked me in the eye. I could see in his face how much it pained him to be a part of it. But I refused. For a moment I wanted to bargain, to swap my place with Alma, to save her instead. But I was positioned closest to the truck edge, and there was no time to argue."

Her head hangs and tears fall like rain onto her wooden table.

"I looked Alma in the eyes, pleading with her to forgive me. For being unable to keep her safe. For being the one to survive. But she made me go. She begged me to. So, I flung myself off and fell onto my shoulder. I was winded from the fall, but I was alive, and I made it back."

She looks up and meets my gaze. The despair in her face cuts me like a knife.

"There is not a day that goes by that I don't regret leaving her behind."

Alma

After digging out every last cookie crumb from my pocket and stuffing it in my mouth, I search the rest of the jacket.

In the other pocket I find crumpled up papers, which I carefully unfold and try to read by the light of dawn.

I am squinting down at the documents when a cockerel sounds in the distance, and I jump at the sound. I need to get moving.

Folding the papers and stuffing them back inside my jacket, I stand up and dust myself off before grabbing the bicycle, which I'd laid down in the tall grass to keep it hidden.

I walk it to the edge of the river and drink some water, splashing some on my face. It is cold, but refreshing.

As well as the broken cookies, I found that Wolfgang had hidden some dried meat in my breast pocket. And though my stomach is rumbling, I decide to keep it for later. Who knows how long I will be travelling for?

Carefully, I mount the bicycle and begin to pedal along the small path along the river. My bottom and thighs burn as I sit on the seat, and I inhale sharply through my teeth. But I know I must go on. Walking is just not fast enough, and it would look suspicious if I am seen simply walking my bicycle.

I ride past a small cottage with a barn just minutes into the day's journey and I curse myself for having stopped where I did last night. Just a few more minutes and I could've spent the night inside a warm barn, on a straw bed.

But I push on, there is no use thinking about what could have been.

Two hours later, I am approaching a town, so I steer well clear and go around it.

I've lost the river, but I hope that if I continue south, I will find it again.

It is the sudden downpour of rain that forces me to consider stopping sometime later. I pedal hard, squinting against the rain and scanning the area. I spot what appears to be an abandoned hut in the distance, and I push on, desperate to get out of this wretched weather.

I quickly duck under the hut's porch, shivering in my wet clothes, and cupping my hands around my face to peer in through a window.

There are cobwebs and thick dust coating the glass. I can't see much, but given the lack of light or a fire during this weather, I decide it must be empty.

I try the door, but it is locked, so I hurry around the hut to try the back. Finding that locked, too, I groan in desperation.

I look around myself, frowning at the heavy rain. There's nothing for it. I have to break in.

I bring the bicycle around the back and prop it up against the wall. I hide it underneath a tarp, from the rain and from passersby who might steal it. Then, I take off my jacket and wrap it around my arm before carefully smashing a window with my elbow.

It cracks and then shatters easily, and I carefully force the remaining shards of glass out with my fingers. I climb inside, and I am not elegant with it, landing in a heap on the dusty floor.

I look around myself, fearful suddenly that someone will jump out and confront me. But it is dead silent. Apart from the rain hammering down on the roof.

I find the bedroom quickly – it is the only other room besides the living space – and tentatively sit down on the bed. It isn't clean, there are cobwebs and dust everywhere.

But the mattress and the blanket are dry, and I count my blessings for that.

I unwrap the jacket from my arm and hang it over the back of a chair, hoping it'll dry quickly. Then I peel off my boots and wet trousers and hang them up too, before retrieving the folded documents from my jacket pocket and climbing into the bed in my shirt and undies. The pages are a little damp, but thankfully, not ruined.

There's no pillow, but this is the comfiest bed I have lain on since leaving Le Chambon, and I feel something as akin to comfort seeping through my body.

With the blanket over me and my knees tucked against my chest, I unfold the papers once again. And this time, I can see them quite clearly.

I stare at them, my mind so stunned that, for a moment, I am unable to grasp what I am looking at.

At the top is a woman's name: Kerstin Bolle. Born 14th of February 1922. It holds an official stamp, and underneath the name is the nationality: *Deutsch*. Attached to it with a paper clip is a library card, the same name and date of birth printed on it.

I sit up, understanding jolting through me.

"German identity papers," I mutter to myself, bewildered.

Wolfgang must have procured them so that I may travel home safely, without the possibility of being returned to Auschwitz.

My vision blurs as I look down at the paperwork in my hand, delighted sobs falling from my lips. I press a shaky hand to my mouth, adrenaline rushing in my veins.

I press the identity papers against my chest as though they are a priceless heirloom, precious and irreplaceable. And in some weird way, they are.

I settle down to sleep, warmed by an almost forgotten feeling of security. One I never thought I'd feel again.

I am safe. I am free. And soon, I will be reunited with my family.

Chapter 21

Alma

<u>Poland, somewhere</u>

I wake to the sound of silence, and I know the rain has stopped. I try to sit up, but my tender muscles protest, and I fear I will not make much progress today.

But I have to. I am not safe yet.

Even with my forged papers identifying me as a 'pure' German, there is no denying that I look like a prisoner. My badly shorn hair, my emaciated, filthy body…not to mention the tattoo that will be a part of me until my dying day.

If the Nazis catch up to me here, I am done for.

So I fling my legs out of the bed and scan my surroundings for the first time by daylight.

Facing me on one side of the small room is a chest of drawers, beside it, the chair where I had hung the SS jacket and trousers, in the hopes that they would dry during the night. I stand up gingerly, sucking air in through my teeth as my muscles protest, and run my hand over the uniform, disappointed to find it is still damp.

I look at the dresser, maybe I'll find something in there?

The drawers slide open easily, and my eyebrows shoot up to find them filled with women's clothing. I pull out a warm woollen dress and tights and put them on. They smell musty and are baggy on my shrunken frame, but they are clean and warm. And more importantly, they are not the grey dress I have worn for months as a prisoner, or the SS uniform. In the bottom drawer I find a headscarf, which I wrap around my bald head, and a leather backpack. I take the bag and fill it with an extra dress and tights, almost crying with joy at finding these treasures.

I wonder what happened to whoever used to live here.

With these new clothes, I will no longer need the uniform Wolfgang had provided me with, and I am both relieved and saddened by that fact. But it is safer to leave it behind.

I swing the backpack onto my shoulder and turn to inspect the rest of the room when suddenly I see a skeleton in the corner.

A scream escapes me, and I clamp my hands over my mouth as I stare at it wide-eyed. Sitting on a rocking chair, its head at an incline and with a gun in its hand, I can only assume it was the owner of this house, and that they had taken their own life.

My hands are shivering uncontrollably as I continue to stare at it, then down at myself, wearing the dead woman's clothing. I want to tear them from my body, feeling suddenly like they are itching my skin. To think that I have slept in this very room, with a corpse watching over me the entire night…a shiver runs through me.

I have seen my fair share of death, but this has shaken me. I guess I had thought that, with my escape, I had left all manner of horrors behind me.

How wrong I was.

I stuff my papers and the dried meat from the SS uniform inside the backpack and leave the bedroom, closing the door firmly behind me. I will search the house for anything else that might come in handy for my travels, and then I am getting out of here!

In the kitchen I find mostly empty cupboards, some of them containing only dusty glassware or dead cockroaches. I resign myself to the fact that the house must've been ransacked during the war, either by the Germans or by other desperate people like me.

But then my hand closes around a tin and my heart leaps with hope. I pull it out of the dark cupboard and exclaim with delight. Canned meat. Tearing open every drawer in the kitchen, I'm frantically searching for something to open it with.

I eat it quickly, every mouthful tasting better than the last, and I thank God for watching over me.

I find nothing else of value in the kitchen, much to my dismay, but I spot a jacket hanging by the front door. I take it off the hook and pull on and with one final look around the small house, I head for the backdoor and unlock it.

I ride for a short while until my body cannot take it anymore, and I hop off and walk the bike along a dirt road. I don't know how many hours go by, the clouds are too thick to even tell the time by the position of the sun, but my stomach is rumbling loudly, and I wonder what I will do once my food runs out.

I hear the rhythmic *clip clop* of hooves approaching behind me then, and I anxiously duck down and out of the way, fearful that it could be the SS.

"Woah!" a man's voice calls, and the horses stop.

I look up to find an elderly man and woman sitting on a cart being drawn by two brown horses, and I feel immediately at ease.

The man spouts a question at me in a language I don't understand, but I recognise from his hand gestures that he is offering me a lift. And I don't decline it.

They take me to the nearest town, Wisła, where they drop me off at the train station, though I don't have any money. The old woman points at the station, and I nod in gratitude before gesturing that I will continue cycling. But then she turns to the man, who I assume is her husband, and rattles off at him in their language. The man nods and reaches into his pocket before handing me some coins.

I shake my head, but am stunned into silence by their generosity. And before I can even attempt to thank them, they wave and set off. I stand there, frozen in shock by the kindness of strangers. I don't know how far this will get me, but the gesture alone is a miracle. Because with this money I will probably be able to get out of Poland, and that little bit closer to home.

It isn't a lot of money, but it was probably all the old couple had, and for that I am grateful. I am able to buy a ticket from Wisła on the outskirts of Poland, to Olomouc in Czechoslovakia, but instead of getting off at my stop, I rest my head against the window and pretend to be asleep. Thankfully, I am not disturbed until the train stops at Prague.

From Prague, I continue by bike all the way to the outskirts of Pilsen, where I find shelter in a chicken coop hours after the sun had already set.

The chickens don't mind me, not even protesting when I slurp from their dirty bucket of water before curling up in the straw until the morning.

A rooster crows at the break of dawn and the hens begin their morning chatter, which I take as my cue to leave. Carefully climbing out of the coop and retrieving my bicycle from the side, I search the area for any sign of the farmer before darting away.

I head into Pilsen, certain I will be able to catch a train from there, even if I have to sneak onboard. I hang about the station for hours and eat the dried meat as I wait for an opportunity, trying not to think about how it is the last of my food. After noon, a freight train with open carriages pulls into a platform, so I quickly scramble up from where I was sitting and examine the timetable and the map on the wall. I am fairly certain it is heading into Germany, so I drag the bike onboard and hide behind the wooden boxes just moments before it speeds off.

But I'm not alone.

In the other corner of the carriage, a young family with a small child also finds refuge here. I smile at them, but they are wary of me, and I cannot blame them. Given my hollow cheeks and dark circles under my eyes, I'm surprised the child doesn't scream in horror at the sight of me.

I fall asleep, lulled by the train's motions, when suddenly someone nudges me awake.

I look up in fright, only to find the mother hovering over me, *"Wir sind da,"* – We've arrived – she says, before clambering down with her young child in her arms and hurrying after her husband.

And I throw the bicycle off and dash away in the opposite direction.

Three days have passed since jumping off the freight train in Stuttgart, and I have made it to Lyon, just north of Le Chambon.

But I don't know how much longer I can go on. Since finishing the dried meat, I have eaten nothing but an apple core I found on the side of the road, and a handful of grain I managed to steal from a farm. My vision has become blotchy from sheer hunger. And I think I will likely die before I reach my destination.

My thighs are raw and blistered, my legs are like jelly, my back is hunched and sore. I climb off the bike for the thousandth time and begin to push it along like a trusted companion. Maybe it's time to ditch it...

But whenever I think about leaving it behind, I can't seem to do it. It sounds ridiculous, but abandoning it feels like abandoning my last connection to Wolfgang, the only thing I have left to remember him by.

Night is starting to descend again; bats are flitting about sporadically in the purpling sky, and hedgehogs cross my path every now and then, some stopping to look at me as if to assess if I am a threat or not. I blink back as I walk by.

My stomach rumbles loudly, I feel nauseous and weak. I need to find something to eat, somewhere to sleep.

Are hedgehogs edible?

After some time, when the sky has turned completely black and I am shivering uncontrollably, I think this is it. I tried my best, and I got pretty far. But I don't think I can take another step.

My feet stop working and I sink to the grassy ground, the bike crashing beside me with a loud metallic *clank*. Lying on the ground, I look up at the black sky. It is beautiful tonight, with twinkling stars, and a half-formed moon.

Maybe if I just close my eyes for a second, I will gather enough strength to get back up and continue on. Surely, I cannot be too far from home…

I hear a rumbling sound then, and open my eyes to see two amber lights growing larger. I just manage to raise my arm, but it drives past without slowing down.

My eyes sting like I'm about to cry, but I have no moisture left to produce any tears.

I look over at my bicycle and my mouth twitches. I'm going to die here…

But then, I hear the sound of the car returning. I lift my head and squint at the blinding light coming towards me. This must be it – death has finally found me.

"*Oh, mon Dieu!*" I hear someone say, followed by the sound of heavy footsteps.

"Alma?"

I think I have misheard. I am almost certain that I have. Because…the person whose voice I think I am hearing is surely dead?

I try to lick my dry lips, try to push out the words, but they come out in a raw croak, "Pastor Trocmé?"

"*Oui,*" he replies, and I can hear tears and laughter in his voice.

A sound escapes me, and I feel myself being lifted into his arms.

"Oh my God," he mumbles again and again as he holds me upright.

He bundles me into his small car, wraps his jacket around me and brings a bottle of water to my lips. I drink it, slowly at first, then more eagerly.

"I cannot believe what I am seeing," he mumbles, then walks around the car.

He is about to close his door and drive off when I suddenly remember, "Wait…" I whisper, "The bicycle."

He looks out the windshield, at the discarded pushbike in the grass, "It won't fit," he says simply.

I blink, my starved mind unable to form any words. And even then, I know I could never begin to explain it. And he would never understand.

The pastor frowns, "Alma, you do not need it anymore. I have found you. I will take you home."

And I know he's right. I know he will. I know that I am safe in France. I am fully aware that, with a car, I no longer need that rusted lump of metal and rubber.

But nonetheless, I feel like I am at a crossroads.

Do I leave the awful, horrifying, unbelievable past behind in exchange for a brighter future?

The answer is crystal clear.

And yet, it still pains me to leave it lying there on the side of the road to rot.

But then…I do just that.

"Little Alma Basson," Pastor Trocmé says beside me, shaking his head incredulously as he starts the car, "We thought you were dead!"

And as he pulls away, leaving the bicycle behind, I release a shuddering breath.

"I was."

Wolfgang

<u>Poland, Auschwitz</u>

They searched for three days and three nights before giving up. And when they did, I breathed a sigh of relief so deep, my chest ached with it.
She got away. She was – hopefully – safe. And with the identity papers I managed to arrange for her, she shouldn't face any obstacles.
Now, two weeks later, the pain of her absence has not lessened, though I haven't delayed in filling her position with the next person I hoped to aid.
"Trudi?" I say, turning around in my office chair. She looks at me. "Here," I say, handing her a sandwich.
She thanks me with tears in her eyes and eats it while she cries, same as she has done every day since entering my 'employment' a week earlier.
I chose her for obvious reasons. As a friend to Alma, I want to do this one last thing for her before it is too late.
It is late-November 1944, and now more than ever, I am certain that Germany is about to lose this war.
Instructions were given by Heinrich Himmler that gassing of newly arrived prisoners was to cease immediately and that the remaining crematoria was to be dismantled.
If rumours are to be believed – which I think they ought to be – Soviet forces continue to approach, and our devilish leaders are scrambling to destroy the evidence of their mass killings.
But still, the remaining prisoners in Auschwitz and other camps are not yet safe.
"In Budapest," I tell Trudi now as she eats, forewarning her, "They are deporting Jews and forcing them to march to Austria on foot."

She blinks at me as she chews slowly, "Is that far? From Budapest to Austria?"
I wonder how young she is all of a sudden. With her dirty face and sunken cheeks, she looks to be at least thirty. But devastation ages people beyond their years, and she has seen and endured more than most. For all I know, she is but a teenager.

"Yes, it is far," I tell her gently, "They are death marches. Most won't survive."
Her eyes grow wide then, filled with concern, "Do you think they will do the same thing here? To us?"
I inhale, then nod, "I do. Which is why I need to get you out of here before that happens."

I will do everything exactly as I did with Alma, except I have no way of getting Trudi false papers if we want to do this now. And we *have* to do this now.

"Put this on," I tell her, showing her the SS uniform.
I'd told her about Alma of course. It was how she began to trust me when I had her brought to my office out of nowhere and gave her a position of my *Schreiber*.
She'd backed up against the door at first, shaking her head in terror, no doubt thinking of her murdered friend Esther, and of her 'disappeared' friend Alma.

"I helped Alma escape," I'd clarified before she could panic, and the alarm melted from her face, replaced with wonder.
Since then, I have smuggled her extra food whenever possible, in the hope of building up her strength before her travels. Being from Germany, Trudi won't have to travel quite as far as Alma, but she also hasn't had as much time to increase her body mass before the journey, and I worry for Trudi's success once she is out of the *Arbeit Macht Frei* gate.
She takes the uniform from my outstretched arms, and I go to wait outside.

I am already thinking of the next time I will do this, and if I have enough time before the death marches commence here. Would it be too suspicious if every one of my aids suddenly manages to escape every couple of weeks?

I know the answer to that, but I can't *not* do it for the sake of my own safety. If it were up to me, I would try to free someone every single day.

I knock tentatively after a moment and step inside my office when I hear Trudi's confirmation that she is dressed.

"It won't stay up," she says, bunching the waist of the trousers in front of her with her hand. As a spare, this one doesn't have a belt. In my hurry to steal it before being caught, I hadn't even noticed.

"*Ach!*" I exclaim in frustration, taking off my own belt and piercing a new hole into the leather, "Take this."

She loops it around her waist and sure enough, her trousers stay secured.

She looks up at me, "Now what?"

I try to smile, but I'm afraid it comes across more like a grimace.

"Now, we'll set you free."

It is drizzling. Not ideal, but at least it isn't snowing.

Much like the first time, I approach the gate and begin to speak when, out of the corner of my eye, I notice Trudi ride up and wait to be let through.

There are different guards this time – I made sure of this before choosing this time and day, so as not to alert anyone of my suspicious behaviour.

The man standing in front of me – a boy, really; probably no older than nineteen – looks from me to Trudi, to me again, unsure of what to do first.

"Do you need me to wipe your arse for you, too, boy?" I snarl, "Get on with it!"

He starts to dither.

I had meant to instigate a rushed opening of the gate so that he could get back to me and attend to whatever I needed from him, just as the other guard had done with Alma. But to my dread, he walks towards Trudi.
She has her cap low over her eyes, one foot on the ground and the other on the pedal, desperate to get away, but when the guard approaches and asks for her name, the ground falls out from underneath me.

"Guard!" I bellow, "Let the man out, for God's sake! I have better things to do than stand around here all day in this pissy rain!"
But, disturbingly, the guard only flicks a quick glance at me from over his shoulder before turning his attention back to Trudi.

"Sir," he says to her, "Your name?"
It is then that I realised Trudi is about to die because of my recklessness, that I have failed before I've even had the chance to properly begin.
Trudi has no answer, and even if she did, her voice would give her away for a woman. She can do nothing but raise her head slowly…and when she does, she looks directly at the guard, paying me no attention.

"My name," I hear her say in a clear and steady tone, "Is Trudi Hoffman! Daughter of Peter and Anja Hoffman!" she is shouting now, and the guards stare at her wide-eyed, "Sister of Solomon Hoffman!" she continues, even as they draw their weapons and point them at her. She raises her chin, "And though you may have tried to rid us off the face of the Earth, you will fail –"
The two guards fire a round of bullets into her, and the air explodes with the horrible sound. Her frail body jerks and falls to the ground, where they continue to shoot her already-lifeless body for good measure.

"Enough!" I shout over the noise, "The prisoner is dead!"

But they don't put down their weapons as I had thought, instead turning them on me.

"Hands up, *Oberscharführer!*" the boy nearest to me orders.

I take a step back and hold my hands in the air. But I force an incredulous laugh, as if this is some twisted joke.

"What are you doing? Put down your weapons!"

They do not.

"We have been warned to keep an eye on you," one of them says, "Orders from above, you understand."

My stomach drops.

I have been foolish to think no one would notice.

"Orders from above?" I repeat quietly, trying to make sense of this.

I look down at Trudi, her body bleeding out in the wet, muddy ground, her empty eyes staring at nothing. Then I take in the two men in front of me, their pistols aimed at my torso. And I make an informed decision.

"You have orders to execute me?" I ask, dropping my hands to my sides and straightening up to my full height.

"We were told you would attempt something against the Reich," the man who hadn't spoken yet says, "We never would've thought *this*."

His nose crinkles in disgust, as though the idea of helping an innocent person from certain death is grotesque. They are so brainwashed, so conditioned, that they cannot see that *they* have been turned into the grotesque ones.

And I for one can no longer go on pretending like I am one of them.

I raise my chin and inhale deeply.

"Very well then," I say, reaching inside my breast pocket for a cigarette.

They jerk their guns at me, but I remove my hand slowly and show them I mean them no harm. I light the cigarette and take a long drag, then blow the smoke deliberately at them.

“Kill me.”

And without hesitation – and dare I say, a hint of macabre satisfaction – they do.

Abel

<u>France, Le Chambon- sur- Lignon</u>

The village of Le Chambon continues to be a haven for Jewish refugees, though there are far less people seeking it, now that the war is in its final stages.

The end is in sight, but there is much that needs to be rebuilt, and I don't just mean structurally.

I, for one, have begun to be plagued by haunting nightmares. The kind that wakes you up in a cold sweat, or where you call out in your sleep.

Sometimes, I dream of the night of the raid, where I saw my sister and dozens of other innocent men, women and children be massacred before my very eyes. The guilt that consumes me for not being among them is a strange and irrational one, but it feels as real as any other pain.

Other times, I dream of Frida and Professor Weis, and how knowing them has been both a blessing and a stain on my journey. I don't think I'll ever forget the young girl who made me remember who I am, and who had shown me that even in darkness there can be light.

Marie sits at the edge of my bed with a candle and a glass of milk when I suffer those fitful dreams. She always seems to know when I am having a bad night.

I am grateful to them both. Marie and Pierre have given me much time and space to try to overcome my demons. But they will never quite understand, and I have begun to feel like a burden.

Since my return, I have slipped easily back into my role in the household, even taking on new chores to alleviate Pierre. He is sixty-eight, and though his body continues to be fit and healthy, but he is still an aging man, and it doesn't feel right to have him outside chopping wood or climbing ladders to fix the leaking roof if I am right there.

"Let me, Pierre," I say now, taking the axe from him. He nods, patting my stubbly cheek in thanks, and I watch him head inside. I smile. The last time he'd done that, my skin had been smooth, the face of a boy. Now I was as bristly-cheeked as he, though his stubble had turned completely white, while mine grew thick and dark like my father's.

I get to work, and before long, I am sweating despite the cold.

I've stripped my jacket and accumulated a significant pile of firewood by the time I hear the back door creak open.

"Five more minutes and I should be done," I call over my shoulder, then slam the axe into another log, cleaving it in two.

"Abel, come quick!" I hear Marie shout, ignoring my remark.

I wipe my forehead with the back of my wrist and turn to her. She's waving me inside, her old face beaming with an excitement I haven't seen since the day I made a miraculous appearance.

"What is it?" I ask, dropping the axe as I hurry to her. She does not reply, only rushing forward through the house and pushing open the front door. I follow her, frowning. What could possibly have happened?

Outside the front of the house, I look up and down the road, immediately spotting Pastor Trocmé's little car. He has stopped at the end of the street, outside the Basson's house.

I narrow my eyes, trying to focus on the scene in the distance.

"What's wrong?" I ask Marie and Pierre standing beside me, all of us staring ahead.

"It is another survivor come home," Marie says, "It must be. I saw someone in the passenger seat as the pastor drove past."

"They are getting out," Pierre mumbles.

A skeleton steps out of the passenger side. Dressed in a woollen dress and tights that are too baggy on her. I watch as the figure takes the pastor's hand and gingerly walks to the Basson house.

A lump forms in my throat as understanding dawns on me.

"Alma?" I gasp, "It is – isn't it? – it's Alma?"

Marie and Pierre gawk at me, incredulous. And then, unable to hold back, I am running towards the Basson house, desperate for it to be true.

Alma

I take the pastor's hand and step out of his car, suddenly nervous.
Will they recognise me? Will *Maman* even be inside? Will I survive any more heartbreak if she is not?

"Be strong," the pastor says, like it's that easy, "The worst is behind you."
He knocks on the door, and I can hear footsteps inside, the radio being turned down. My heart is like a hummingbird, its wings beating wildly against my protruding ribcage.
And then the door opens, and I can no longer hold in my despair.
I fall into my mother's arms, and she stumbles backwards, stunned by what she sees – her daughter, back from the dead.

"Alma?" I hear behind us, my father's voice catching with confusion and hope.
I look up and meet his incredulous stare. He has aged ten years in the time I have been gone. And I am sure he is thinking the same about me.

"It's me, *Papa*," I mutter through my tears, "I came back."
It is all I can say, all that I need to say. For now.
And without hesitation, he is on the floor with us, his protective arms wrapped around me and *Maman* as she kisses my bony face and cries into my short hair.
We are all crying, even Pastor Trocmé.
And though my heart hurts with the too-big emotions of love and loss and everything in between, I know that I am safe. I know that I have my life ahead of me. And whatever happens next, it cannot break me, because I am home.

Epilogue

One year later

Alma

Though the war has ended with Germany's surrender, the nightmares continue; and I'm quite sure I will never shake them.

When they rouse me from sleep, as they often do, I reach across the bed and take his hand. More often than not, he is awake too, and he pulls me to him and holds me close, all too aware of the anguish I may never overcome. Because he has lived it, too.

Not in the same way I have, for no two journeys are ever the same, but he understands my grief and suffering better than anyone.

We have healed, a little, through our shared pain. First as friends and quickly as lovers. Maybe our shared trauma brought us closer? Maybe it was always meant to be? I don't know, and it doesn't matter.

In the beginning, we shared our experiences with one another. I know all about Frida and the murderer that was her sick father. He knows about Wolfgang, and the sacrifice he made to save me. We listened, and still do, to what the other had to say. But we were also acutely aware of what was left unsaid, perhaps better than most.

I cherish him for the comfort he provides, the warm embrace, the knowledge that I will always be damaged and his acceptance of it. I offer him the same, and, between the two of us, we are almost a fully functional person.

In time, it will get easier. Or so they say. I will have to wait and see if that's true.

But until then, I am thankful and happy to have found him.

"Bad dream?" he whispers into my hair now, which has grown to my shoulders since my escape from Auschwitz. I don't think I'll ever cut it again.

I nod my head and grip his arm tighter.

"The same as last night?"

I don't tell him that this dream had not been of dead bodies, or of the constant smoke billowing out of the crematorium. This dream had been of something else, the small sliver of goodness that had come out of that Hell.

Wolfgang has been coming to me more often lately, though I cannot think as to why. In my recurring dream of him, he is standing on a grassy hill overlooking a river below, when he turns to me and extends a hand. His scarred lips curve into a smile as I stand beside him.

Go on, he says in my subconscious, his voice echoing, reminding me this isn't real, *Take a look.*

And I do, I look down at the valley and the glittering river below. A bird flies over us, and just ahead, two deer are grazing.

It is beautiful, I whisper, *All that life.*

Wolfgang nods, *It is*, he says, his voice growing suddenly faint. I look at him, fearful that he will leave me. Though he already has.

Go and live it, Alma, he says, looking at me so intently I think that maybe I am not dreaming after all.

Will you stay? I ask, my voice breaking.

He shakes his head, *You no longer need me*, he says with a cheerful grin, *It is time you let me go.*

And that is where I wake, with my protestation on my lips and Abel's comfort just inches away.

He tightens his arm around me now and exhales, nestling into my neck, "It's okay, Alma," he says quietly, "I'm here. Nothing will ever hurt you again."

And I believe him. I wholeheartedly do.

There is love here, one I know can grow into something beautiful. Even now, at the start of our journey, there is enough here that I want to build a life with him, and raise children who will hopefully never know the horrors their parents have faced.

I want to start off by saying thank you to my readers! Your love and support never fail to astonish me! It is because of *you* that I am able to continue doing what I love.
If you enjoyed this book, please remember to leave a review on Amazon or Goodreads, or share it with a friend.

This book is a work of fiction, and while the main characters within them are fictional, I drew inspiration from several real accounts to shape the characters' experiences during WWII.

- <u>Wolfgang</u> – his story is based on several I found while researching for this book. While unfortunately few and far between, there are some incredible accounts of German officers trying to help those they were taught to hate. This ranged from as little as smuggling prisoners' food or blankets, to aiding some of them avoid capture and even to escape concentration camps.
If only more had been like Wolfgang.

- <u>Annika</u> – While she and most of the characters in her POV are fictional, their activities in the Dutch Resistance were based on very real occurrences. The Netherlands, as well as the rest of Europe, fought back against the enemy. Annika and Helga luring out Nazi officers and disposing of them, as well as cycling through their small village and shooting them in broad daylight were based on real accounts of the Dutch Resistance, specifically the actions of sisters Freddie and Truus Oversteegen.

Mr and Mrs van der Meer, who they met on their travels, were fictional characters but I wanted to include them to emphasise that the Dutch Resistance consisted greatly of ordinary people. Checkpoints were often simply citizens' homes, as they wanted to help however they could.

The Hidden Village of Vierhouten – this mostly underground secret village was, incredibly, real. The founders and leaders known as Tante Cor, De Boem, and Opa Bakker, were all real people, who, through their efforts, helped to save not only Jews but also Allied pilots and even German deserters. It's discovery, as depicted in this book, is also true, including the assassination of those captured. Opa Bakker was arrested in February 1945 and executed on the 2nd March, together with other resistance fighters. Tante Cor survived the war and died in 1989 and was buried in the presence of many.

The medical student – who, in this book I named Dr Stern, though we don't know his name – was also real. He was a young Jewish student who was unable to finish his education to become a doctor due to the war.

Little Herman was also real. His full name was Herman Löwenberg, and he was just five years old when he arrived alone at the Hidden Village. Nobody knew how he got there.

- <u>Abel</u> – His time at the Hitler Youth, where he hid his own identity and struggled with who he was, was based somewhat on a very real account of a young Jewish boy who managed to convince the Nazis upon his capture that he was an 'ethnic' German. This young man survived the holocaust by hiding in plain sight. His name was Solomon Perel.

Professor Weis (The Yeti) and his daughter, Frida, were completely fictitious. Their storyline is entirely made-up for the purpose of entertainment. There was no mysterious murderer going after innocent children during that time.

None that we know of, anyway.

- <u>Alma</u> – While she is also fictional, the village she grew up in and returned to is very real.

Le Chambon-Sur-Lignon and its people's efforts to help those who were being targeted by the Nazis is all true. Pastor Trocmé, as well as his wife Magda, and also his cousin Daniel, really did exist, and all their efforts mentioned in this book are accurate. Their non-violent resistance helped to save thousands of lives.

Daniel Trocmé sadly died, as mentioned in this book. But Pastor Trocmé survived, being released despite refusing to sign the oath of fealty to the Vichy Government.
Alma's escape from Auschwitz in this book, while perhaps appearing almost too easy, is based on real escapes from Auschwitz.

9 781738 577873